mapping Utah

mapping Utah
love and war in the wilderness

DENNY WILKINS

.

Printed by CreateSpace, an Amazon.com company.
Available from Amazon.com and other retail outlets.

ISBN: 0-615-94285-7
ISBN-13: 978-0-615-94285-8

Cover design by Holly McIntyre Hartigan
Cover photo by Lunamarina

for

Carrie Andrews

and

Madelyn Fitzpatrick

acknowledgments

For many years, this novel gathered digital dust on an external hard drive in my office. It emerged every few years, only because I felt compelled to update the technology used by the characters. Then it would be consigned back to the hard drive.

You're reading this largely because one person wrote these words to me: "I believe in this book." That was Kelly Zientek-Baker, a former student of mine, who decided to take it upon herself to publish this novel. How ironic that Kelly, who once took an editing course from me, taught me how to properly edit a work of fiction. Kelly also designed this book. She has earned thanks I'll spend a lifetime providing.

I owe thanks as well to Dr. Richard Simpson of the Department of English at St. Bonaventure University. He read a draft and encouraged me to "press on" with the work.

Thanks go as well to another former student, Holly McIntyre Hartigan, for the compelling cover she designed.

I hope, when you're done reading, you conclude you got your money's worth.

d.w.
St. Bonaventure, N.Y.
November 2013

Chapter 1:

April 3, after dark, near La Pine, Oregon

Kara shivered in not quite sleep. The fatigue of many miles driven had conspired against her. The rain drummed incessantly in her ears while the cool air of the lakebed country nagged at her body. Her muscles were cramped from too little room in the back of the brown Subaru. *Why the hell am I doing this?* If time had passed since she had driven off Route 97 south of Lava Butte to rest, she could not tell. She opened her eyes. Water undulated darkly down the windshield, disfiguring the world outside her all-wheel-drive hatchback. Sitting up, she pressed her forehead against the back of the driver's seat. She shivered. The day had been warm when she'd left Portland.

Hunched in the cramped space, she pulled on a faded white sweater she'd been using as a pillow. She fumbled through a cargo bag for her black cotton tights and put them on. He had given the tights to her, back when she'd been so attracted to him. *Am I now? Still?* She sighed. Feelings fade. Love lives, then dies. *Has it?* Her hands rested on her thighs, drinking in the softness of the tights against the hardness of her quadriceps. She had worn the tights around their apartment because he had told her once that they were sexy. His hands would caress them before he'd ease them down around her knees and kiss her tummy, his tongue licking over her groin. Kara shook her head. *Not now.* She reached for the odd, mesmerizing, frustrating, maddening map. *The damn map.* She clutched it against her chest, lay back, and closed her eyes.

She longed to stretch. *My legs are too long. Why aren't they retractable?* Comfort eluded her. Kara was tall and, depending on whose truth prevailed, either skinny or slender. He'd called her "scrawny" and "too thin" once. *No. I'm lean. I'm slender. I'm not "scrawny." I'm ... I'm ... god damn it, I'm supple and graceful and slender. I'm fucking hot, damn it.* She sat up, pissed. At him. At the map. At the rain. At the cold. At everything.

She piled some of the stuff beside her onto the front seats to make more room — the cargo bag; the big blue beach towel; a small leather case with an old iPod she used as a backup hard drive and accessories; a canvas bag filled with biking clothes; her "healthy back" one-strap leather go-bag crammed with digital cameras and iPad and MacBook and phones; and more assorted clutter that called the back of the hatchback home. She had a MiFi, a solar panel that enhanced the battery, and a cigarette lighter adapter for the power cord. The laptop, tablet and, cameras were her only extravagant possessions besides the mountain bike on the roof rack. She'd built it herself.

Dad the Engineer and her brothers had taught her tools before she could ride a bike. She had a photograph in a black plastic frame from Walmart. It showed her at four years old, her face wrinkled with distaste, her hands covered with grease, holding a bicycle chain with outstretched arms as it were a nasty snake. *A mechanical family.* She fixed things — a doorbell once, a toaster once, her bicycle — before her first kiss at a pre-teen party at Johnny Blevins' house. Afterward, she fixed the derailleur on his bike. She got no kiss for that. He never kissed her again. But a few times in high school, he had stopped by Dad the Engineer's garage. He'd asked her if she could figure out why his carburetor was coughing. And if she'd adjust the timing on his pickup another time. He'd looked at her in a funny kind of way. She never figured out what that look meant. *What was it?*

She got out of the Subaru. The rain struck her face softly and wet her short, dirty blonde hair. She closed her eyes, licked her upper lip, and tasted the rain. *Why did I do that?* The rain soon chilled her, so she climbed back inside. She rearranged her gear. She lay down on her back, diagonally across her shelter, head bumping the hatchback door, her legs between the seats. *Better. I can stretch my legs.* She slipped a cargo bag under her knees as a bolster. *Much better. Much, much better.* She closed her eyes, hoping for comfort.

She slept fitfully. She dreamed she could hear each rain drop die in a tiny explosion against the metal canopy over her. She dreamed of symphonies as the squall swept over the car and sang throatily against the roof. She dreamed of the petite, dancing notes of a lone piccolo as the rain diminished to a few staccato drops. She dreamed of long, bright days and longer, loving nights. She did not dream of answers. Only of questions forming.

Kara woke just after midnight. Lightning married the sky to the ground in sharp, hot flashes. Thunder returned. Rain fell steadily but not heavily. She sat up, turned on the interior light, and looked in the rearview mirror. Her hair was tousled. Hazel eyes flecked with green stared at her. The dusty tracks of dried tears trailed down her cheeks. *Did I cry? I don't remember crying.* She liked her face. Mom's pretty face. She snapped off the light. *I miss Mom.* Her mother had taught her to play the piano. But she had died when Kara was nine years old. It had been the only time she'd seen Dad the Engineer cry.

She leaned against the side door and took hold of her toes, legs out straight, to stretch her calves. She enjoyed that, the feeling of kinked muscles unkinking. She liked her legs and took care of them. Her first coach had preached stretching as much as weight training. Kara liked the hardness of her body, the result of subtle sculpting with weights and rigid adherence to a low-fat diet. She liked wearing tight clothing that hinted at the latent muscularity of her arms and shoulders and thighs.

She'd always worked out in front of mirrors, watching her muscles contract and release. She never considered it to be narcissism; rather, she appreciated watching her muscles perform their functions. *My body works well. It lets me ride hard.*

Sometimes he offered to massage her legs, but that kindness usually revealed itself as mere prelude to sex, an artificial foreplay. She wished he'd do it just as decent muscle therapy after she'd had a long, hard ride. *That would really be caring.* She imagined someone — him, *hell, anyone* — massaging her legs. Renewing her legs, refreshing them, getting them ready for the next day's multi-K workout. *They deserve better.* Her hands kneaded her calves. She lowered her forehead to her knees to stretch her back. *What the hell am I doing here? I should be back in Seattle.* She looked out the window into the dark, sugar pine forest that surrounded the Subaru, hiding a half mile off the highway. She shivered again.

Kara had driven to Portland Friday night and stayed in a small motel off Burnside Avenue. She made the six-hour drive at least once a month. Dad the Engineer had preached that change is as good as a rest — when needed and appropriate. So she escaped Seattle — *let's be honest, I got away from him, too* — for the freedom of solitude in Portland. She loved her Saturdays in the stacks at Powell's. She had money — she worked long hours and invested much of her income with great care — to flee Seattle and buy books. Lots of books. She'd wandered through the bookstore and added several books for the growing stack on her night stand. Having books unread meant tasks to be completed. Always have a project, Dad the Engineer had cautioned, so Kara read voraciously.

Walking through the little room with the travel books, she had found a folded Rand McNally highway map on the floor. Something about the map kept her from returning it to the display. The title read "West Central United States." *Odd.* She'd seen Rand McNallys that covered several states but never a region carved out of the middle of the far West like that. The map rested warmly in her hand. It was silent but oddly communicative and irresistible, so she bought it. Nothing had been irresistible for a long time. In Seattle, the relationship had lost its fervor, its energy, its compelling newness. *Hasn't it?*

Kara had left Powell's and walked down East Burnside and up 9th Avenue to the welcoming red façade of Fuller's, a diner where she'd parked. She'd sat in front of a cheese omelet that had grown cold as she examined the map. It covered a region south and east of Portland, east and north of Los Angeles, north and west of Four Corners in Utah, and south and west of Billings, Montana. She'd dwelled on Oregon, looking at the blue, red, and light brown highways and the gray "unimproved or dirt roads" and the green forests and the bright blue sea and lakes and the thin blue rivers and the pink borders around national forests and the cities in a big bold font and the *nowheres* in a tiny lightface font. She needed a holiday. *From him. From everything.* All those colors ought to be explored. She asked herself, *Where would you like to go today?*

Sitting in the car, Kara had thought of work, of living together, of being apart, of being together again for the sake of a needed togetherness in her life. *Was this love? Is this what love became when it fell silent, when it became only rituals and routines?* Options had been reviewed. Dad the Engineer had always insisted on having Plan B, Plan C, and Plan D if Plan A, the preferred option, hadn't worked. It was early Saturday afternoon. She had time. Tuesday's deadline could wait. *I can do that work anywhere.* Her wireless MiFi and her iPhone and satellite phone could send her productivity anywhere from anywhere. Kara hated radio shadows, the tunnels and valleys and repeaterless landscapes of so much of the West that left a cell phone addict inventing profanities. *Always the Girl Scout. Semper paratis.* Kara had booted her Mac, guessed at the URL for Rand McNally's home page, and typed:

http://www.randmcnally.com/

It'd worked. She'd searched the catalogue but could find no listing for a "West Central United States" map. That had mystified her. The map did not exist. *But it did!* It sat in her lap. She'd fingered the paper. The map was tangible.

When she climbed into her Subaru, she hadn't really

decided anything. It just kind of happened. She'd driven up Burnside, and without thinking about it, turned south on 405. She'd refused to consider consequences as she followed I-5 south. At a rest area south of Portland, she'd opened the map and looked at Oregon, then Nevada, then Utah. She'd pursed her lips, grabbed her iPad, and quickly touch-typed an e-mail, which she preferred over texting. Typing with thumbs never made sense to her.

To: TopDog@WebWideWorks.com
From: kara@WebWideWorks.com
Subject: holiday
Cc:
Bcc:
Attachments:

_____

hi, hon ...

i'm not coming home tonight ... i'm really tired and i need some rest ... i think i'll take a little drive and find a motel tonight ... maybe cruise around the deschutes sunday or just drive somewhere ... i should be back monday night ... well, maybe tuesday night ...

i've got the mac so i'll work a little at the motel ... i can get most of it done ... i've done all the formatting for the site, all the video's in place, just need to finish the links and touch up the grafix ...

i know the deadline's wed., but i'll make it ... you know i always do ... yep, that's my specialty ... making deadlines .. haven't missed yet ... so don't worry ...

don't forget to feed petey ... and we ought

to start giving him his heartworm pills
again ... it's that time of the year again,
you know ... and you forgot my chocolate
bunny this year ... shame! ... i need to do
some thinking too ... you know that ... i
figure just getting out on the road for a
while will clear my head a little ... i really
need that right now ... i'll be okay ... and
don't forget to water my plants, will you,
please ...

luv ya :-)

k.

Kara's finger had poised over the send button, not moving. *Am I lying? Maybe a little.* She tapped the button and sent the e-mail. *Maybe a lot.*

She had turned east on Route 58 at Eugene. She'd driven comfortably into the darkening of day's end. Hours later, driving had become a chore. She'd turned off the highway and driven through darkness on a dirt road. She found a turnout in the trees out of sight from curious or malevolent strangers. A touch of fear accompanied roadside solitude at night, but she'd never admit it. *Never.*

Now here she was in the middle of nowhere and she didn't like being alone *so what the hell is going on? I'm tired and I just want to go to sleep and drive back in the morning.* Her monthly enchantment at Powell's had vanished. *I was raised in Iowa. I should be used to nowhere.* But she had never really adjusted to rural isolation and left to go to college in Seattle. *Or did I never adjust to such a dysfunctional family?* She hunted for her old plastic camping mug insulated with blue ensolite and gray duct tape. Dad the Engineer would have applauded her ingenuity if he'd lived — *apply available resources* rang truest in her memory of her father's dicta. Like her brothers, she'd sought her father's approval in acts of mechanical creation and adaptation. Build it well, and he would grudgingly bestow approval. When she'd fallen in love with the written word while smitten with her ninth-grade English teacher, Dad the Engineer had pored over her writing, horrified by her seedling desire to create fiction. He'd counseled her into a world of hard facts, objectively displayed, neatly arranged. Thus half of her dual degree — the half in journalism. Write tight, write bright, she'd been taught. She had discovered the effectiveness of the Web as a profitable means of instruction earlier than most and became a creator of Web pages for a consultant — *him*. He specialized in intranet sites for corporations that wanted online training materials. *Him*. Working with him by day, screwing him by night. *Three years now. Day after day. Night after night.* His company had expanded into websites for schools that wanted in on the bandwagon of online courses. Lately they had begun to produce software shells for MOOCs — massive open online courses. She had become an innovation engine for distance learning. Kara had grown with the company, making a helluva lot of money.

She frowned at the brown, muddied streaks inside the mug. *I should hose this thing out some day.* She drank the rest of the lukewarm herbal tea she'd brewed earlier and listlessly tossed the mug onto the front seat. She tried to get comfortable again. *No such luck.* She took a small black MagLite from her bag, turned it on, and opened the map. The light stabbed at the silent map. La Pine, not far from where she had parked, earned only barely readable small print — a little nowhere lost in a big nowhere.

Kara cracked open the side window and inhaled cooler, fresher air. She had decided to take her bike at the last minute before departing for Portland. She didn't know why, and that puzzled her. She never had taken it along before. Now it just sat on its rack on top of the hatchback, getting soaked despite its expensive cover. *I bet it's pissed, too. That new chain lube had better work.* She took good care of her bike. Maintenance, saith Dad the Engineer, prevents breakdown of available resources. *Why'd I bring it?* Some tiny and irritating tension in her throat and chest would not let go. The map lay beside her.

Condensation on the windows blurred what was real and what was not. The hatchback shook slightly. The wind had risen. *Where is reality when I really need it?*

Kara wanted to sleep. She wanted to crawl beneath her down coverlet in her own bed in her own home where she could stretch and toss and turn and let tense muscles release. She wanted this, this *whatever the hell it is*, to go away. Sleep had been her habitual escape from melancholy. But the busy fingers of something knifing at her confidence would wake her, only to find him snoring or inattentive.

She closed the window against the rain and piled all her unused clothing and her canvas and cargo bags at one end of her mobile metal tent. She braced her feet against the rear hatchback door and wriggled to get comfortable. She put the MacBook in her lap, booted it, and opened a new file. She pulled down "Save as ..." from the menu, stopped to think, then named the file "Specifications, map." Analysis calmed her. She methodically typed in everything she'd thought about the map since leaving Portland.

Chapter 2:

April 4, after midnight, near La Pine, Oregon

Kara stopped typing. The wind buffeted the car, causing her to hit the wrong keys. Typos in her professional work disgusted her. She closed the file and packed her MacBook away. The car was parked under trees off Lava Cast Forest Road, hidden from passing traffic. The rain had stopped. The condensation on the windows had evaporated. She could see outside. But cold had seeped into the car again, slipping under the defenses of sweater and tights. She slipped into her Tyvek. She had earned the paperlike, colorful jacket. While in college, Kara had ridden in the STP, the 200-mile Seattle-To-Portland bicycle race. She'd been in terrific shape then, training five hours a day despite the rigors of school. She'd ridden the STP in one day, leaving Husky Stadium at five in the morning and finishing thirteen hours later. *What a ride, what an incredible ride.* But she'd had no money after that. She'd graduated. She'd needed a job. That's when she'd met him and begun to freelance for him. Then she'd become his first employee, the sex had begun, and she eventually moved in with him. She'd stopped training so relentlessly. He hadn't liked her taking so many of their evenings to train, riding more than 200 miles a week. *I don't have time to ride hard anymore.* Her hand drifted to her thigh and squeezed it tentatively. *Too soft. I want to be in shape again. I want to be hard again.*

She was glad the rain had stopped. Seattle's rain often infuriated Kara. More than 40 inches had fallen since New Year's. Portland had always been an escape from Seattle's dreariness that seeped into her by Christmas, slowly eroding her sense of well-being. He'd told her once he didn't like being around her during the winter. He made PMS jokes about it. They offended her because the taunts said he didn't want to understand her. *Seasonal affective disorder,* she'd claimed as she fled to the tanning salon for light, and, she'd admitted to herself this year, escape. *He never wanted to work on us when it was tough going. Winters are hard for everyone.* She pressed her lips together. *Maybe I don't want to work on us, either.*

She got out of the car. *I need a new mood.* A healthy wind tugged at her, so she leaned against the door, hugging herself against the chill. *No, it's not really cold. It's cool and clean and fresh and the air is alive and snapping and leaping at me. Is it trying to dance with me?* She skipped around the car, her arms spread wide. The wind whipped lustily at her Tyvek and rippled through her hair. It curled around her legs like the light touch of his cunning fingers, intent on foreplay. Then the windy devil scurried away through the trees.

She sat on the hood. *What time is it? It's so dark.* To the southeast, the lightning flashes of the squall line winked at her from many miles distant. The flashes were somewhere over Christmas Lake Valley east of Route 31, the map would have told her. She missed the rain now. *Why did it leave me?* The hot, fierce thrusts of crackling bluish-white light outlined the serrated edges of the forested hills of the Deschutes National Forest. Her throat ached. *God, where is the magic?* She remembered walking on a ridge in the Cascades. She had lingered there, trying to extract everything about the feeling of being above timberline — *especially the magic, the fleeting, dangerous, electric magic.* A terrible storm had caught her. The lightning had been so close, so tangible. She'd heard the buzzing, inhaled the ozone, and seen the cold, blue shimmering glow around her ice ax. She had felt so exposed, so helpless, so trapped. *So ready to be taken.* She had stripped off her pack and her rope and had sat on them and waited for — *for what?* Everything had flowed in slow motion. Thick, columnar lightning had kissed her and toyed with her but deserted her. Afterward she had been wet, cold, tired, and unexpectedly frustrated — afraid of being taken but wanting it all the same.

Kara inhaled, longing to flood herself with the fresh, biting scent that lingers after mountain storms. *It's only ozone, but I want more. Much more.* She got back into her car. She zipped up her Tyvek and draped clothes across her legs. Kara lay awake, listening to the wind tease her, telling her cruelly that the lightning had deserted her for something — *someone?* — else.

Chapter 3

April 4, dawn, northwest of Paisley, Oregon

The Subaru glided along Route 31 through the Deschutes National Forest. The early-morning sun rose behind the young trees. They were all the same, small in size and alike in age, the consequences of timber baron monoculture. They cast long shadows that fell like flickering prison bars across the highway. It tired her eyes. *Too much blinking.* Roadside brush and trees flashed by. Stands of mailboxes marked the turns onto wide, dirt side roads. Rutted furrows in the forest near the road led to idle skidders. Chainsaws howled in the distance. Pickups of all sizes, rust-tinged colors, and ages ferried cordwood to hungry wood stoves beyond the horizon. She didn't like this forest. It didn't feel pretty. It didn't look pretty. *Death row for trees.* A jeep carrying two men cloaked in hunter's orange turned onto a side road. She wondered what they sought in the forest. *Wood? A deer?* She didn't like the killing of animals. Near Fort Rock Junction a side road led to several piles of crushed rock as tall as houses. She parked amid the piles and got out. Squatting near one of the piles to relieve herself, she thought of Seattle. *I should check my e-mail.* But no cell service here —

that would mean getting out the MacBook and hooking it up to her pricey BGAN terminal … *a pain in the ass.* She shuffled toward the car, facing the sun and appreciating its warmth on her legs. She shrugged off her Tyvek and the sweater, tossed them into the car, and got in. She examined the map. No lodestone, no direction, no sign, *no heartbeat.* Kara put it on her lap. She felt uneasy. Putting on her sunglasses, she started the Subaru and returned to the highway. Occasionally she glanced to the side and saw her bike's shadow, keeping pace with the car. *I wish I could ride this fast.*

Route 31 traced a delicate line between Christmas Lake Valley and the rising hills of the Fremont National Forest. The myriad greens of the forest met the light browns of the dry lakebed in an unlikely marriage along the road's path. She liked both. To the east were the lakebed and its distant gathered waters of snowmelt, the cattle of isolated ranches, and small, black faraway dots she guessed to be birds. To the west were tree-lined slopes and high meadows under small, puffy morning clouds destined to be afternoon cumulus. The Subaru hummed along, passing Paulina Marsh, Silver Lake, and Picture Rock Pass. *Elevation 4830.* Kara liked numerical details. *Latitude, longitude, altitude. They place you. They give you a sense of where you are.*

Near Paisley a roadside sign announced its population — fewer than 300. She passed the Assembly of God Church, crossed the Chewaucan River and pulled into the Sunoco station. An elderly man in faded blue overalls filled her tank and washed her windshield. He asked if he should check her oil. She said no. He smiled at her, and she smiled back. She handed him her Amex. *Eleven point seven gallons, at three fifty-three a gallon, that's forty-one thirty.* She recorded it in her expense app on her iPhone and figured the mileage. *Twenty-six point seven miles per gallon.* That matched past data, she reflected.

Her stomach rumbled with hunger. "Sir, there a diner in town?" she asked.

He pointed. "Over there," he said. "The Homestead Cafe."

She lingered, hoping he would say more. *Anything.* But he just handed her a little red plastic clipboard with her receipt to sign. He walked away with his copy. She stood there, holding her receipt. She called after him. "Hey."

"Yes, 'm?"

"Have a good day, sir."

The old man smiled, touched his cap, and vanished into the shadow of his office. She looked up at the sun and wished it a good day, too.

She parked in front of Paisley Mercantile. Inside the Homestead next door she ordered scrambled eggs with toast and tea. She didn't have anything to read. She didn't like the idleness of waiting alone for food to be served. She drank her tea slowly, leaving the last few sips when it grew lukewarm. She smirked. *Am I here because he's lukewarm now?*

After breakfast, in the car, she looked at the map again, plotting, pondering, choosing. *Seattle's too hard a drive to get back by Monday night.* Something scolded her, telling her she'd let events choose her, not her choosing events. Dad the Engineer would frown. *Failure to plan leads to failure to achieve.*

She walked to the Mercantile, passing an alley closed off by three sheets of plywood. Someone had painted a western scene on it, depicting an Old West town with a dirt main street, a shopkeeper in front of the OK Grocery Store with wife and children standing docilely behind him, the Gotcha Bank, the Jail, the Red Dog Saloon, the Hilarity Roost Hotel, a stable called Hotel D'Horse, and cattle being herded down the street by a cowboy. *Oh God, that cowboy. I must've watched too many Westerns as a kid with the brothers.* The lanky man in the painting, his upper lip festooned with a thick, black handlebar mustache, sat astride a dark chocolate horse with a blonde mane. He wore a black vest, a long-sleeved white shirt, black hat, gloves, leather chaps, and boots. *All that leather. How mythically heroic.* The cowboy's eyes were hooded. Kara felt they were staring at her private places and private thoughts. *Why is he looking at me like that? Does he know something I don't know?* She walked on, then looked back. *Get a grip, girl. It's just a painting.*

In the Mercantile, she picked several large, tie-dyed bandanas from a display. She bought a sleeping bag and closed-cell foam pad. *I'm tired of shivering instead of sleeping.*

She got back in her car but was reluctant to be on her way. She looked around. The village had a K&L Market, a laundromat, and a real estate agency. A signpost across the street near a fenced-off basketball court proclaimed distances to Coffee Pot Flat (13 miles), Dairy Creek (22 miles), Silver Lake (50 miles), and Valley Flats (22 miles). Kara liked signs with the names of roads, canyons, mountains, towns, villages. Several pickups were corralled in front of the hardware store. Men in flannel shirts, boots, and faded John Deere caps leaned against a pickup, talking. No one moved quickly. She sensed a pace slower but more purposeful than she knew in Seattle, a gentler pace she never experienced in the furious work of cranking out intranet pages and MOOC software. She produced, but the pace was never gentle. *He's such a workaholic. Just like Dad.* Had she finally pleased him before he died? *He never told me.*

The hard disk of her laptop held an unfinished project. Its deadline loomed. *I'm so far from Seattle. I bet he's pissed.* She could file using her sat phone setup, but still ...

Minutes passed. She didn't move. A sigh. A shrug of the shoulders. She retrieved her iPad and MiFi, and booted. Her finger danced across the screen. She had mail.

> To: kara@WebWideWorks.com
> From: TopDog@WebWideWorks.com
> Subject: Re: holiday
> Cc:
> Bcc:
> Attachments:
>
> _____
>
> Okay. Enjoy your little drive.
>
> Here are the last links to add (besides the ones you're already responsible for):
>
> https://www.OnCourse.org/~tutorial7/

https://www.OnCourse.org/~tutorial8/
https://www.OnCourse.org/~tutorial/exam
review7/
https://www.OnCourse.org/~tutorial/exam
review8/

Need the finished site late Tuesday,
remember. We do the presentation at 4
Wed.

Kara fumed. *My "little" drive? He doesn't even say he misses me. That prick.* She hit "reply." Her hands shook as her fingers struck the keys.

To: TopDog@WebWideWorks.com
From: kara@WebWideWorks.com
Subject: Re: holiday
Cc:
Bcc:
Attachments:

_____

sometimes you'r so fucking dense ... i'll
have the damn site to you by wed a.m. ...
and since when do *we* have to be
toegther to make a presesntation? ... you
uslally do alla that ... you and your damn
political shmoozing ... i'll try to be back ...
maybe ... i need down time and after you
get the site i may just take it

No sig. Typos. Misspellings. She didn't care. She hit "send." *He can be such an asshole.* Shaking, she stowed the iPad. She stomped on the accelerator and fled south. The jitters in her arms and legs wouldn't go away. She flexed her forearms. *I probably shouldn't have done that.* She sagged against the seat. *Am I just looking for a reason — any reason — to not go back?*

She looked up at the hills to the west. Could she rent a

cabin for the summer in a mountain meadow above Paisley, deep in the Fremont National Forest, surrounded by the pines? *That would be so nice.* They were just pines to her; she always called them simply "needle trees." She didn't yet know the names of these proud species — ponderosa, lodgepole, and sugar — but someday she would. It would be nice to live up there, away from the rush. Her life, as chaotic as it seemed to be, was in Seattle. *At least it has been.* Besides, she thought, *I'd go nuts in the hills after a while. What would I do up there?*

An hour later, she slowed the car. The afternoon sun flooded through the windshield and felt hot on her thighs. She reached behind the seat for a towel and draped it across her lap. She had no light pants. *I need more to wear.* She made a mental note to add "get summery clothes" to the to-do file in her iPhone's notes app.

She saw a family in a nearby field, Mom and Dad on horseback wearing Marlboro uniforms — jeans, denim jackets, bandanas at the neck, and tan-colored Stetsons. *Are all cowboy hats Stetsons?* A daughter, maybe twelve years old, rode energetically while the horses of Mom and Dad loped easily along a dirt path that paralleled an irrigation ditch. A small, long-haired dog that looked like Lassie dipped in ink yapped at the heels of the girl's horse. Kara watched the girl for a while. *She's not so little.* She remembered her thirteenth year and a boy's eager hands. She had liked it. *Why does lovemaking seem so matter-of-fact these days? When did it become just fucking?* She pushed her foot against the gas pedal.

To the east a plateau rose a thousand feet above the lakebed. She turned the Subaru onto the wide dirt shoulder. She got out and opened the map on the hood. It told her she had stopped halfway between Paisley and Valley Falls, where Route 31 meets Route 395. It told her the high plateau was called Abert Rim. She surmised the Abert to be volcanic. She remembered her basic undergraduate geology course — "rocks for jocks" — at the University of Washington. She'd escaped the math requirement with it and an eye-fluttering plea to her adviser. *Volcanics.* The Northwest was one huge series of lava flows. *A fault scarp. A big one. It's three degrees cooler up there.* Details, technical details. How-to's. Her world revolved around technological minutiae, around explaining how to program computers that shut things off and turned things on without a human's touch. Like the computerized hydro dam controls for which she'd once designed an intranet training site. *He'll be hurt — no, pissed as hell; he never gets hurt — if I don't get the new site to him on time.* She folded the map. *Guilt, guilt, guilt. Damn it.* She sat on the hood, her heels hooked on the bumper. Sparsely vegetated lakebed flats reached east, the cliff of hundreds of feet of darkly colored Miocene basalt rose ahead, and the eroded, green Oligocene foothills lay to the west. *I like it here.* She named it *the Land of No Urgency.* She smiled. *They never heard of deadlines here.* A barbed wire fence ran next to the road. She gingerly stepped over it into the field, unzipping her Tyvek. The cloistered moisture on her bare chest evaporated, cooling her.

The tufts of green bushes grew fewer. She liked walking. She waved her arms by her sides, over her head, behind her. She took off her bright red Converse sneakers. The flat, warm brown ground was firm under her feet. She looked behind. Footprints followed her. She skipped, then ran lightly for a few hundred yards, but had to stop to catch her breath. *Damn. I've got to find time to ride more. I'm so out of shape.* The highway was distant, so she slipped off the Tyvek and dropped it. She liked the valley floor, this ancient lakebed devoid of trees, of shrubs, of flowers, seemingly of life itself. *And it's dry.* She imagined herself dancing on an enormous ballroom floor. Sitting down, she stretched for a while. *At least I'm still flexible.* She placed her forehead on the ground between her legs and nuzzled the earth with her nose. She liked the salty smell. She sat back, her hands pressed into the earth. She looked up at the hills, enjoying the warmth of the sun on her bare chest. *Yes, a cabin, a small cabin, a wood stove, a bed, something for music, and a desk to work at. But doing what?* She sighed, retrieved her Tyvek, and slipped into it. She picked up her Converses and walked back.

She stopped at the Valley Falls general store, a small, low

building whose paint had faded to a dirty yellowish brown. *This place belongs in the Grapes of Wrath. Old, so old, and so lonely.* She bought a Diet Dr Pepper — noting it cost an ungodly ten quarters. She bought a postcard from the wizened, silent man behind the counter. She wrote an I'm-sorry-let's-make-up message and addressed it to her home. She got back in the car and continued south on 395. She knew she'd never mail the card. She lowered the window and held it out. It fluttered noisily and slipped from her hand. In the rear view mirror, she saw it drift to the roadside, one more piece of roadside trash.

Landforms fought as Abert Rim to the east and the highlands to the west closed in and squeezed out the lakebed. The road curled through a little valley cut by a small stream. The highway crossed a bridge. A sign said Loveless Creek. *How appropriate.* Within a mile a small rest area invited her. She parked and walked through a grove of alders to the creek. Shedding her clothes, she waded in. She daubed at the water with her bandana and bathed herself, wiping away the gritty dust of the road and the cold sweat of not knowing. She lay in the sunlight on the far side of the creek behind a tree and spread the bandana to dry. She fell sleep. The tree's shadow moved across her an hour later, and she awoke, feeling slightly chilled. She dressed, waded across the creek, and returned to the car. She didn't feel so tired now.

The junction of Route 140 and Route 395 came quickly. She knew she would head east on 140. She didn't even bother to ask the map. Anticipation, a feeling of *at last, something's finally happening,* grew as the car covered the quarter mile from the crest of a hill to the intersection. The highway led into the Fremont National Forest, then climbed into the foothills. Patches of snow hid from the sun under trees. *Nothing likes to die.*

Chapter 4:

April 4, morning, Mexican Mountain wilderness, Utah

The tall, gaunt man with an austere, unshaven face marred by a nose broken in some dim barroom past stood impatiently beside a hellishly expensive high-definition Sony videocam. It stood ready, mounted on a robust carbon-fiber tripod planted near the edge of a steep-walled arroyo. Next to the man stood a camera operator, looking through the viewfinder toward a dark blue Chevy Blazer parked atop the opposite wall edge of the arroyo a hundred yards away. Its supercharged, 572-cubic-inch crate engine rumbled impatiently at idle, 750 horses waiting to stampede. This was no normal Blazer; its 24 forward gears made highway travel cumbersome. It had been trailered over a rough access road to this once-quiet place and now sat mounted on adjustable shocks with 17 inches of travel. The 46-inch Mickey Thompson Baja Claw tires cost nearly three thousand dollars a set. The tires sat squat, inflated to only five pounds of air pressure. This Blazer could crawl over virtually any obstacle.

Dressed in black despite the growing heat of emerging

spring, the thin man pulled a radio from his belt. Sunlight reflected from the large, oval, silver buckle stamped with the letters "XOX." He nodded to the cameraman, then spoke into the radio. "Now."

The Blazer roared. The rapacious treads of its tires clawed into the earth, throwing cryptogamic soil into the air. The rutting beast tore into a complex of microscopic vegetation, killing a web of miniature rootlets that bound the loose, sandy soil together, allowing it to resist erosion. The Blazer cleared the edge of the arroyo, briefly airborne before it crunched down onto the dry wash. The left front tire landed on a night snake sunning itself on a small boulder of quartzite, killing it. The tires ripped into sands and gravels. The cameraman panned the Sony expertly as the Blazer roared up the wash. The driver, the owner of a Phoenix real estate and development company, yanked the steering wheel, slewing the Blazer into a spinning slide.

"Damn, this is fun," he shouted, a small man in a big machine wearing a bright red, visored helmet fitted with radio. The roar of his bored-out engine drowned out his voice.

"Cut," radioed the thin man. The Blazer halted, its engine slowing from a malicious howl to a disgruntled idle. The cameraman picked up the Sony and hiked a hundred yards down the bank to set up the next shot. The thin man walked to a dark green Jeep Cherokee with an official-looking emblem on the side. He spoke to a squat, sweating, heavyset man leaning against it, smoking a cigarette. Eyes hidden behind mirrored sunglasses, the fat man rested his hand casually on the pistol in his holster. As they spoke, oil from a tiny leak in the oil pan of the Blazer soaked into the gravel, waiting for rain drive it down into the water table. The fumes of the Blazer's exhaust hung over the wash. A canyon wren, fed up with the odor, abandoned its nest to search for peace and quiet elsewhere to try to have children with its mate. Individuals of a dozen different species of insects, two species of reptiles, and three species of arachnid had been crushed under the knobby tires.

The cameraman set the Sony about 40 yards from the edge

of the arroyo and waved. The real-estate developer had backed
up the Blazer against the far wall of the wash, pointed toward
the steep bank and the Sony beyond.

The thin man spoke into the radio. "Again."

The Blazer's tires churned deeply into the wash bottom.
The Sony caught the undercarriage as the Blazer roared up the
bank. It flew free for a moment, then smashed down, ripping
into more cryptogamic soil, and braked a few yards from the
camera.

The thin man spoke into the radio again. Three other rock
crawlers waited their turns on the far bank. The owner of a Salt
Lake City bank holding company, perspiring under the hot sun,
sat strapped into his tricked-out, bright orange Jeep with fat
tires, light bar, and heavy steel roll cage. In a rebuilt
International Scout, given new, evil life by a big-block Chevy
V-8, sat a middle-aged lawyer from Price. His pudgy waistline
quivered as he goosed the engine impatiently. The CEO of a
Denver financial services company hunched over the steering
wheel of his powder-blue Bronco, its 427-cubic-inch engine
purring throatily. All wore headset radios. Each had paid
$10,000 to star in their private videos, showing them at their
heroic best, wrestling their mechanical beasts through one of
the most fragile ecosystems on the planet. The videos, they
presumed, would impress their wives, girlfriends, and
mistresses. Only four copies would be made — one for each
client. The thin man shot these private videos in roadless
wilderness areas where ORV use was hotly contested by
environmentalists. But his customers demanded the picture-
postcard scenery such wilderness areas contained to provide
dramatic backdrops for their egos. *I whacked the wilderness*, they
could tell their women and their presumed male inferiors. The
thin man would pocket $40,000 — in cash — for a day's work,
selling Conquest of Nature as theater.

At the thin man's signal, the ORVs roared three abreast up
the dry wash, their tracks decimating more diminutive life. The
three maneuvered their vehicles, backing up, going forward,
then backing up again, until they were lined up side by side,

facing the already wounded stream bank.

"Now," said the voice crackling in their headsets.

The three ORVs, packing nearly 2,200 combined horsepower, attacked the bank. Tires ripped apart sand, gravel, soil, and two burrows containing just-born pocket mice. The Sony caught the three ORVs as they roared up the bank and slewed to a stop. A second Sony, high on the rim of the canyon walls above the wash, caught the powerful vehicles from above.

"Cut." The thin man nodded in satisfaction to the fat man. They examined a map laid on the hood of the Jeep, planning the next sequence.

None noticed the roiled tire tracks in the bank of the wash. When rain fell, the stream bank would erode severely. None noticed the ancient soils, torn by sixteen tires that cost more than the annual salary of a seasonal Forest Service or Bureau of Land Management ranger. The fractured, broken, and crumpled soils would take a hundred years to recover. None cared. But rangers would not see this. The fat man in the Cherokee had seen to that. He kept track of rangers' comings and goings and sold that information to the thin man. He earned his silver, too — in cash.

High in the blue Utah sky, a dark speck, circling above the video crew and their eager actors, dove toward the earth beyond the canyon rim. It was the job of one man with a rifle on the rim to watch for it. But the action, the loud roar of the engines, the dust drifting like thin smoke in the air, had distracted him.

Moments later, an engine's high-pitched wail echoed off the canyon walls. The video makers did not hear it over the snarling of so much horsepower. A yellow, high-winged ultralight aircraft, kept aloft by barely 100 horsepower, dropped in a shallow dive at almost a hundred knots and screamed over the dry wash. A broad, stocky man in a dark jumpsuit sat in the front seat, a gloved hand on the stick, his other hand holding two round objects. The left wingtip of the small aircraft carried a small GoPro videocam, switched on and rolling. The man on the rim with the gun swore and blew a whistle. He fired the rifle but missed. He was hurried and nervous — nervous because the thin man would be pissed. And he was dangerous when irritated.

The yellow plane flew ten feet over the ORVs as the pilot slung two balloons. The first burst on the Blazer. Black acrylic paint splattered over the hood and onto the windshield. The second struck the helmet of the Salt Lake banker, cascading paint over him and his expensive leather bucket seats. The ultralight screamed up canyon, over a ridge, and out of sight. The thin man, anger pulsing in the veins on his temples, turned to the fat man.

"Keep that fucker off my ass, goddamn it."

"You don't pay me to take care of him," said the fat man, the bright speck of metal on his chest shining in the sun.

"I won't pay you a fucking cent if you don't," said the thin man. "This isn't making my clients happy."

The fat man nodded. "I'll have him watched," he said. "But it'll cost you another thou. He's a smart fucker, and I'll have to be careful."

"Just do it," said the thin man. "Just fucking do it."

Chapter 5:

April 4, mid-afternoon, near Adel, Oregon

Kara's car climbed over Warner Pass (she noted the elevation, 5,846 feet) as the highway snaked through high mountain country. She crossed minor summit passes separating small, flat, newly green meadows. Small streams — Rosa Creek, Straw Butte Creek, Walker Creek, and others — rushed past the lingering snow clinging to their banks. The car descended through narrow, winding valleys. In the wakening meadows lay ponded water, banked and waiting to either percolate into the earth or depart as runoff to enter bigger creeks and then even bigger streams and then rivers and then ... *to be controlled by the computers operated by men trained by the intranet site I did for the dams downstream.* The thought startled her. Sure, she recycled — *didn't everyone in Seattle?* — but green had never been her motivating politics. She had never seen these birthplaces of water so clearly before. She had never wondered where the water came from when she sat at her desk at home, writing the script that would tell the engineers which buttons to push, which on-screen commands to select, which gates to open, which turbines to turn on or off. Water was just water; always

there, behind the dam, waiting to become water for drinking
and bathing and watering the lawn and washing the car and
producing electricity for coffeemakers and big-screen LCD and
3-D TVs and DVRs and recharging cellphones and laptops
and running air conditioners and the technological toys in the
apartment they shared.

She felt warm, like being overdressed on a hot day. Her
cheeks were flushed. Sweat slickened the hollow of her neck.
She had to finish that damn website. He needed it. The client
had been clamoring for it for weeks.

The fresh, aromatic landscape drifted past. Spring carried a
unique scent, and it masked guilt. Brown-branched bushes with
reddish, almost flame-colored tips lined the stream banks. She
wondered what they were. She imagined them afire, warming
the meadows of early spring. A bird flew across the road in
front of her, too quickly for her to imprint more than its blue
color and some ... *was there some brown there, too?* Birds with very
long tails sat on the barbed wire fences next to the road.
Iridescence in their tails delighted her. She analyzed the
landscape as a three-part stack. At the bottom were water,
snow, stream banks lined with bushes and needle trees, and
meadows with yellow and brown birds pecking in the young
grass. Above floated a canopy of puffy, postcard-perfect
clouds in the azure afternoon sky. In between was an
enormous volume of air in which some birds flew near the
road and others she guessed were hawks soared unconcernedly
among the clouds. Later she deduced another component —
the surface of the water. Black-and-white ducks, big ones and
little ones, poked and probed in the shallow water near the
stream banks. Should she add water as a volume, too? And
what about fish in the streams? *Silly question.* But she liked how
she saw two-dimensional planes and three-dimensional
volumes and how they fit neatly together. Dad the Engineer
would have liked how she compartmentalized input for
productive analysis. Smiling, she drove on. Rigorous analysis
begets vindication and victory.

The road wound downhill through a narrow, steep-walled

valley cut by Drake Creek. The stream ran over bedrock, carving waterfalls. Kara stopped near the larger ones and listened to the water roar. It thudded against her chest. She remembered the incredible shuddering noise of water rushing through and over the dams she had visited. *Does water make that same rushing sound whether captive or free? Is there a sense of restlessness in the sound of water cascading to freedom over the crest of a dam? Was it really freedom? Or just escape from the enslavement of hydraulic head?* She had never considered the notion of ponded water as captive water.

The clouds had congealed into bulwarks of gray ahead. *It will rain again.* She didn't know if she welcomed it. *I don't want to be rejected again.* She shook her head. *I'm losing my mind. I know it. This is really all a dream. I'm not here. I'll wake up in the morning and we'll make enough love to get through another day and he'll take me to work and I'll upload the damn website and we'll both be satisfied. Or whatever it is that we fake as satisfaction.* She heard Peggy Lee singing: *Is that all there is?* She thought about satisfaction as she drove. *Life in Seattle wasn't really that bad, was it?*

The narrow, stream-chiseled valley became a broad, flat floodplain in Adel. She topped off the gas tank out of habit at the Adel General Store. Her mileage was down a few mpg, and she wondered why. She checked the map. All it would do was welcome her to Greaser Reservoir. She drove on. The highway paralleled Thief Creek. Broad expanses of water mingled with mudflats alongside the road. There reposed birds, big birds, maybe a few thousand of them. She recognized the ubiquitous Canada geese. Had she a bird book, she would have known the others, too — some canvasbacks and cinnamon teal, dozens of sandhill cranes, and hundreds of great blue heron and snow geese. She had never seen so many birds at once. At most, she had seen a few hundred Canadas feeding at Gas Works Park. He had taken her there for after-work walks that began as disagreements that became make-up sessions that became make-out sessions as they sat on the stone walls with their feet dangling in Lake Union. *Why do we fight so much? And why do we fight over such insignificant things? Why do we bury the significant things?*

She thought about significance. *Should I e-mail him and apologize?*

As the Subaru sped along a dike across Greaser Reservoir, anxious, milling cattle trapped between the fences lining the road blocked her way. Kara pulled over. Brown cattle, black cattle, and calves moved like a skittish mob toward the car. Two men on horseback darted from one side of the road to the other, waving their hats, trying keep the cattle away from the fences. Their large, teary eyes were filled with the fright of unexpected change. Tags hung from their ears, pinned by large metal staples. She fingered the silver loops penetrating her own earlobes. She got the first prick in her left ear when she was thirteen. It had hurt. Eight years and nine pricks on two ears later, she had been suitably adorned for the young-adult nightlife of Seattle.

The herd reached the car, and the cattle separated into two streams, ignoring her. They were taller than the car. Kara could not see beyond them. A brand — kind of an N and a C linked by a dipping loop — was burned into their right flanks. A cowboy emerged from the mooing sea. He had a drooping mustache, a pink undershirt, and chaps and spurs. He wore a suede jacket and a sheepskin hat and rode a buckskin through the wailing cattle. He leaned on the pommel of his saddle. He was handsome in a craggy sort of way. *Like the ones in the movies.*

Kara rolled down the window. "What happened?" she asked.

"A wreck," he said, his eyes flicking restlessly over the herd. The sun was behind him. His bearded face was indistinct in shadow.

"God, was anyone hurt?" she asked.

He chuckled, the curt laugh tourists get. "It's not that kind of wreck," he said. "A wreck's when the cattle get out of control. Can't do a damn thing with them. Mind backing up beyond the bridge? It'd help."

"No problem," Kara said. She backed up past where another rider was herding the cattle through a gate. They ran into a field alongside an irrigation canal and slowed to a walk as they scattered throughout the field. She got out to watch. The

lights of cars hundreds of yards away winked as their drivers
tried to weave through the mob of cattle. *Impatient bastards.* A
semi drove down the road, acting as an impromptu cowboy,
herding them along. Sheepskin Hat rode back to her. "Sorry
about this," he said.

"I don't mind," she said. "I'm in no hurry." She couldn't
think of anything else to say. Neither, apparently, could
Sheepskin Hat. He watched the cattle. She watched him. She
sensed he was uncomfortable about that but didn't want to
ride away. *Or is that what I want him to be feeling?*

"Does this happen often?" Kara asked.

"No," he said. Kara waited. *Does he want me to talk?*

A car honked its way through the cattle, spooking them. A
rack on its roof held several snowboards and bright neon
clothes hung in the back seat. BMW, California plates. *Wouldn't
you know it. A skier. What a fuckhead.* Several cattle, fleeing from
the car, bulled against the fence. Sheepskin Hat bolted for the
spot, slapping at cattle with his hat and driving them onto the
road. He jumped down and yanked the fence upright.

He rode back to her. She liked that. *We're connected.* She felt
protected, standing next to his horse. She liked that, too. *I'll
never make it as a feminist.*

Sheepskin Hat pulled out a pack of cigarettes, flicked one
out, and lit it. He only used one hand. *Just like in the movies.* He
offered the pack to her. She hadn't smoked since abortive
junior-high attempts but took one. *Keep the connection.* Sheepskin
Hat bent over and lit hers, shielding the flame with his hands.
She tingled. *I'm gonna wet myself.* She felt a touch of shame for
acting like such a hussy. *Why the hell should I feel bad about getting
turned on like this? I'm not going to do anything, damn it.* She looked
at him again. *Am I?*

She took a hit and exhaled. "You look familiar," she said.

He grinned. "Hey, all cowboys look the same."

She waggled the cigarette at him. "No, I think I've seen you
before."

He pushed his hat higher on his forehead with a forefinger
and smiled.

"I'll bet you came through Paisley," he said.

"Yeah," Kara said. "And?"

"Stop at the Merc?"

"What?"

"The Mercantile," he said. He grinned broadly now.

"Oh. Yes."

"Well, then you probably have seen me before."

"Wait a minute," she said. "That mural in the alley?"

"Yep," he said. "My sister painted that. Took a picture of me on my horse. Painted that rider from it."

"It's the eyes," she said. "They're very striking."

He flushed a bit. *Jesus, a cowboy blushing?*

"Yeah, I've been told that," he said. "Never thought they were special."

"Well, they are," she said. *I think I want to climb onto your horse and fuck your brains out right here in the saddle.* She waited.

Sheepskin Hat's grin softened into a sad smile. He wasn't blushing now. He looked intently at Kara, standing beside his horse, hands on her hips, head back and gazing up at him. *C'mon, cowboy. Your move.*

Other riders appeared as the last of the cattle neared the open gate. They bunched around the Subaru, and the interruption irritated her as they traded cowboy talk about moving the herd. A brown pony edged between her and Sheepskin Hat. Braids tied with faded yellow ribbons framed the face of its rider. Kara grew angry — *Jealous? Envious?* — as the cowgirl edged Sheepskin Hat away, cutting her stray away from the temptation of the open range and back into the herd.

Sheepskin Hat rode away, back into Western mythology. He didn't look back. Kara dropped the cigarette to the road and ground it out with her heel. She got back in the car and headed east on Route 140, driving down a highway covered with cow shit.

Chapter 6:

April 7, morning, Green River, Utah, west of Greasewood Draw off Route 24

Noah no longer lifted weights to become stronger. Although he did not lift as a religion, he lifted religiously. As he neared forty years old, maintaining rather than gaining strength and increasing endurance had become his mantra. His friends called him obsessive. He'd reply, "I simply like to argue with gravity." That's how he defended his daily hour of squats, presses, pulls, crunches — and his daily run, which he hated. But he ran. If he couldn't become stronger, he could always endure.

Noah was five feet, nine inches tall. A modest height, but Noah impressed people by being as wide as most doorways. He had stopped growing upward in the tenth grade. Like so many gangling, awkward teens, he turned to the levitation of iron to produce, through sweat and the discipline of thousands of repetitions, what nature would not. He left high school for Colorado State as a squat, 240-pound fullback who had no need for outside speed in setting WAC rushing records. Now he weighed 210. He had let go the thirty pounds that had made the difference between being tackled by a cornerback and scoring a touchdown. While doing his master's at Colorado School of Mines, he chose to carry thirty pounds of field gear rather than those same thirty around his midsection.

He yawned. He put down the two dumbbells he'd been using for curls. He was tired. He hadn't slept well. He had dreamed, and he rarely dreamed. He thought about it, sitting on a cottonwood stump next to his outdoor gym. It sat outside a decade-old, thirty-two-foot travel trailer that had only traveled from a used car lot to his land west of state Route 24. The gym sat behind a post-and-beam hangar covered with corrugated aluminum. He built it for his stable of ultralight aircraft and the parts of several more. He made a modest living, though he didn't need to, as the owner-operator of a charter air service housed at Green River Municipal Airport. He preferred his ultralights to his Cessnas, a Skylane and a twin-engine Skymaster, when flying in the backcountry. Low and slow. That's how he liked it. The big birds just ferried people and things from Point A to Point B. Where's the fun in that?

This morning, he'd flown back from Moab in his Skymaster after ferrying two lawyers from Price to a court date there. He'd followed Route 191 north. He had plenty of altitude. The rare calm air made the flight uneventful. He'd banked west where 191 ended at I-70 at Thompson Springs. On a whim — he'd thought it was a whim until he began having that damned dream — he had flown west past Green River. At 5,000 feet above ground level, he'd seen a line of thunderstorms looming well beyond the Swell but headed for the Fishlake National Forest. Lightning stitched the earth in the distance as if targeting its strikes. He'd turned, landed, and trundled home in his decades-old Land Cruiser, an FJ55, the long-bodied wagon. He had a premonition that something was wrong somewhere for someone. He'd gone to his gym. There he could think.

He hoisted the dumbbells for another set with his eyes closed. That kept the sweat out of his eyes. As he lifted the dumbbells, the slow, rhythmic extension and contraction of his muscles produced the meditative experience that had counseled and consoled him for more than 25 years. But as he curled the 55 pounds in each hand, lightning lashed through the darkness behind his closed eyes. He'd seen lightning many times in the field work of his previous life. Once it had struck mere yards from him. Such strikes were the random acts of a higher power he respected but did not fear. Yet the flashes he saw earlier had seemed thrown with malevolence, as if a hunter had been toying with a wounded prey. And for the third night, he had the dream again. A shadowy, weeping figure ran through darkness, illuminated by the strobe-like flashes. He couldn't make out the frightened, frantic face. That's what woke him. That anonymous face. An open mouth, filled with silent screams.

He walked to his trailer, disgusted that a chance thought born of an odd dream had disrupted his ritual. Inside, he showered and donned khaki cargo shorts and a black sleeveless T-shirt. He'd never admit that a remnant of collegiate ego about rippling biceps remained tethered to his self-image. His mirror reflected an ordinary face, skin leathery from the sun, with a nose more pedestrian than patrician thanks to an elbow-first hit by a Utah State linebacker. But he considered the architecture of his body as fair compensation. Women had found him physically acceptable. But they never stayed. Nothing endured. He shook his head, recalling breakups, partings, doubts. He'd accepted his fair share of fault. Dark brown eyes looked back at him over a dark brown beard tinged with gray. He focused on work. He had a lesson later. An accountant from Moab had called, wanting to learn to fly an ultralight.

His ultralights sat like awkward, grounded insects in the hangar. He had four, not counting his Buckeye-powered parachute. It had been his first, back in an earlier life when he needed access to tight spots in the backcountry. It could land and take off within twenty feet. He smiled. How beautifully these aircraft could fly. He hated selling them, but that's what he did. He bought semi-wrecked ultralight and sport aircraft that had fallen out of favor, rebuilt or refurbished them, kept the ones he liked, sold the others. He'd flown two dozen different ultralights. But he'd never sell his Buckeye — or his Drifter. Especially the Drifter. He thought about the accountant. He'd want to buy an ultralight with serious balls. His kind always did. He'd have to tell him that he'd need a sport pilot's license. That would cost time and money. Anything with a Rotax 503, even the single-carb version, or larger engine would probably be over the 254-pound limit for unlicensed operation.

The accountant would be irritated. He'd change his mind and consider other options than the Hartshorn Flight School and Air Charter Service. Noah considered calling the accountant and explaining it. The hell with it, he thought.

He'd bought the Drifter because he'd needed the power of its Rotax 912 to carry his field gear in the second seat. That had saved enormous time, hopping from field site to field site. It had proved to be financially productive. It was his tool of choice for the ultralight lessons with accountants from Moab, bankers from Salt Lake City, and lawyers from Price. But few appreciated the true joy of ultralight flight — low and slow, barely a wingspan above the slickrock. He reveled in that. But that sermon usually fell on agnostic ears.

As he preflighted the Drifter, he glanced at the sky. The deep clear blue was bereft of wind or cloud. That meant an easy lesson. But something skritched at him. Damned if he knew what it was. It wasn't the dream, but it was connected somehow. In his past life, he'd always solved real mysteries, created by man or nature — and profited. He'd been a scientist, a creature of deductive reasoning. Now a mystery concocted in a dream nagged at him. He pulled out his cell phone. He called the accountant and proffered advice, explanations, and apologies. The accountant thanked him and promised to get back to Noah. He would, perhaps, buy one of Noah's ultralights after taking lessons. Shaking his head, he pocketed the phone. Misjudged another human being. Shame.

Chapter 7:

April 4, late afternoon, east of Guano Valley, Oregon

The car, a wedge of dark brown metal dissecting the landscape, cast a long, slender shadow as it sped east along Route 140. It ran on autopilot, because Kara had a headache. She rifled the glove compartment for ibuprofen. She felt cool, so she rolled up the window. Her legs, though, were hot and tingly. *Too much sun.* She glanced down. Her thighs seemed redder. *Funny, I usually tan easily.* She remembered the anti-depressants. The doctor said the drug would leave her photo-sensitive. Stay out of the sun, she'd told Kara. They'd both laughed. Who worries about too much sun in a Seattle winter? She'd hated the pills and chucked them.

The low sun bronzed the underside of the thickening dark clouds that hung over the Oregon plateau. Earlier the car had climbed a steep grade (7 percent, the sign said) to Blizzard Gap (elevation 6,100 feet). No more trees. No more soft, calming green. Just a featureless, undulating plain dotted with tufts of stuff that looked like sagebrush — *Isn't that what it always is in the cowboy movies?* Unkempt fences isolated dense slabs of dirty snow from the highway — bad-ass snow reluctant to step aside for spring. It'd been hours since she'd seen a house or even another car. Near Hawk Valley a rusted, burnt-out frame of a trailer lay broken-hearted next to the highway. Just west of Guano Valley, she passed a half-eaten roadside carcass of a deer or an antelope. Wolves? Buzzards? *Monsters?* Maybe one of the coyotes she'd seen loping in the brush near the road had eaten it. *They're scavengers, aren't they?* She thought of Sheepskin Hat. *If he'd asked, would I have gone through with it?*

As twilight dimmed into deepening gray, flashes of lightning danced over the distant horizon. A dark cliff, several hundred feet high, waited silently ahead. The car climbed the winding road slashed in its face. No guardrails. The strobe-like flashes in the sky illuminated the potential consequences of not minding the road. The shoulder of the highway was neighbor to nothingness, a nearly vertical drop to the plateau below. She parked at the top of the cliff to stretch. She walked toward the cliff's edge past a sign that said Doherty Rim (elevation 6,420 feet). Another sign beside the opposite lane gave her a warning she didn't need now — "8 Percent Grade, Three Miles, Last Warning, Trucks Use Low Gear." *Last warning. Advice? Or prophesy?* She walked to the edge of the rim. The great emptiness below held only a deserted, ancient shack she had passed earlier. A spidery network of rutted dirt roads crisscrossed the plateau on journeys to nowhere *or everywhere, if you're an optimist.* The faint light electrified the dark colors in the layers of lava in the cliff. Blacks grew iridescent *like that bird's tail,* browns swelled with lustrous yellow, reds deepened so darkly that they looked like freshly shed blood. Hearing the first, distant rumble of thunder, she drove on.

She felt uneasy, and she did not know when that happened. She tried to laugh it off. *If I'm uneasy now, does that mean I was easy earlier? They thought so in high school.* She shook her head. *What a sick joke.* She wondered about parameters ignored, about shifting conditions, about when something transitioned into something else. Earlier she had parked to watch the last light fade, to see day become evening become night become deep, dark, dangerous night. Words, she thought, but not actualities. She couldn't find the dividing lines between day and twilight and night and deeper night. Even television, she thought, is only a series of increments, flickering images rescanned every thirtieth of a second. She gathered and recorded the data: It's dark. It's after sunset, after twilight, but the night isn't completely black. Dark grays lurked among the blacks, an impression of uneven thickness of clouds, of uneven depth of darkness. Maybe the moon and the stars were lighting the clouds from above, or the clouds were uneven in thickness. *Or maybe the night has just not fully defeated day yet.* No boundaries, no limits, no lines drawn in the sand as a dare to the next step. Kara could find no distinctions with which to organize gradations between day and night. *Shouldn't I be able to?*

She stood on the cooling Oregon plateau, shivering as she yawned. The sun had left her, and here, high on the plateau, she seemed too close to the thick, gray clouds that had been tinged with sunlight and had been quite beautiful. Now they hovered over her, around her. They were bulky and big, rumbling with thunder and alive with lighting. Firecracker bursts crackled inside the black clouds. That's how the cattle must have felt — hemmed in, closed off, shut out. She knew kinship — *I'm glad I'm a vegetarian.* But that politically correct dietary habit had waned. The occasional bacon at breakfast. The quick trip through the Golden Arches for a Big Mac because she never had time for lunch. *Riiiiight. Solidarity with cattle. Now I know I'm losing it. I'm over the edge. I'm a wreck. I should be stampeding, too.*

She got out her sweats and a lacy white camisole. She'd always thought it was sexy and assumed he did, too, because *he gave me the damned thing.* Kara disparaged it in his presence but in fact she loved it more than any other clothing she owned. She stripped off her Tyvek and shorts and stood shivering under the dark sky. She walked around the car, rubbing away goose bumps. *This feels dangerous. But I like it. I like it a little dangerous now and then. Don't I?* She looked up and down the road. *It's okay.* She'd see the lights of cars miles away. Plenty of time to hide behind clothing. Nevertheless, she slithered into her lacy thing, pulled on sweats, and slipped into her Tyvek.

She drove on, using Driving Position No. 4, favored by the brothers who'd taught her to drive, laughing at her most of time. They'd taught her several. No. 4 was left foot planted on the dash next to the door, left hand at the bottom of the wheel, right hand tucked part way into the top of her sweatpants. *Sixteen and oh, so cool.* But she still drove like they taught her, yawning occasionally, weary from the miles driven and the pasts revisited.

The lightning no longer hid above the clouds. An occasional bolt struck the plateau. Silhouettes appeared in bright, brief flashes. Some looked like horses. *Mustangs?* Once, the car's headlights framed deer, nibbling on grass. *Am I a deer?* She imprinted the colors of the beautiful, slender animals — white, dark honey brown, a bit of black on the horns. A sign corrected her, saying that she had entered the Charles Sheldon National Antelope Refuge. Later, in a hollow protected from the rising wind, she drove through a silver heaven come to ground — motionless, interleaved sheets of mist hovering about three feet thick on the highway; probably, she assumed, condensation fog formed where the warmer, moist air sat undisturbed on the cold road. Meteorological analysis dispelled the grasp of melancholy. But the luminous magic of the miniature landscape clutched at her for many miles.

Near the Nevada border, hunger stopped her. She got out of the car and munched on a PowerBar while leaning against the hood. Lightning outlined the contours of distant hills. Upthrust tendrils of rock formed triangles of land shaped like a lady's fan illuminated at its edges. She slipped her hand under her lacy thing and touched her breast. *I have this world to myself.* Big, pulsing shocks lit sixty or seventy degrees of the horizon, underscoring the texture of the clouds. *Like seeing God's balls. Strange. Does anyone think of lightning as feminine? I don't want to. I want it to be a man. I want it to hit me and get me off, like I know sex ought to be sometimes.* Kara sighed. *Why am I here?* A gust of wind snatched the PowerBar wrapper from her hand.

Kara longed for the lightning prancing like a centaur in the distant peaks. She slammed her hand on the hood. *Damn.* She pulled the zipper of the Tyvek all the way up so the collar rimmed her neck and chin. She got in the car and opened the windows and sunroof. She put on her faded Campagnolo cap. She pulled on her leather gloves and started the car. She dialed up a playlist of violin concertos by Prokofiev on her iPhone. She yawned. She adjusted the earbuds. Kara grasped the gear shift and pulled it out of park into first. Her foot flattened the gas pedal, and the tires threw gravel into the face of the wind. She spun the wheel, and the hatchback slewed toward the road, accelerating rapidly. She shifted into second and let the engine whine and scream until the speedometer shouted 50. She pushed the shift lever into drive. Her car had an automatic transmission; she didn't have to shift, but she liked to. It made her feel good. It made her feel like her brothers must have. *It makes me feel competent.*

The cool air roared through the interior of the car, blowing loose papers about. The map fluttered noisily in the passenger seat. Kara snatched it and tucked it under her lacy thing. The edges of the map poked insistently at her breasts. Sitting with her hands on the wheel, she breathed heavily. *Why has this fucking map become so damn important?* The cold touched her again. She pushed the heat control to full. The distant lightning laughed at her. *Damn you.* She rubbed her eyes. She was tired and jittery.

After a few miles, the jangling in her forearms eased. Her thighs stopped quivering. The tense muscles in her groin unkinked a bit. Kara and the Subaru ran hot, straight, and true astride the centerline, hell-bent for Nevada. The car knew what Kara wanted. It watched the road. It looked for obstacles. It kept Kara out of harm's way while a distracted, sleepy Kara watched the lightning. They chased the lightning together. *We both know the stakes.*

They swept through occasional rain. The rising wind cracked the clouds open, and they saw the full, fat, laughing moon. Moonlight and starlight sparkled on the raindrops captured by sagebrush at road's edge. The air smelled of sage and the freshness of the wind-driven night. Kara and the car had never run better or faster. They fused themselves to the road.

They dashed downhill from the Oregon plateau toward the Black Rock Desert through a narrow canyon near Thousand Creek Ranch. The car carved a fast, delicate line. Torn remnants of clouds hugged arroyos and gulches and little side canyons, hiding from the reaping wind. The moon and the stars transformed patches of fog and cloud into silver ghosts. *I wish I had a pendant of clouds.* Her breasts felt as if they had been caressed with a warm, damp washcloth. She slipped her hand under the Tyvek and the lacy thing and touched the map. It reassured her. *I wish I knew why.*

They raced onto the desert floor. They had closed on the lightning. The ragged summits of the mountains and the boiling interiors of the squalls shone in every stroke. Her mind tried to catalogue every fragment of atmospheric violence. Each time the lightning struck, she wanted to possess it. She wanted to contain, control, and capture the ferocity of the squalls. But she couldn't. *I'm not competent.* She badly wanted to sleep.

They gained on the storms. The squall line became a circle, surrounding Kara and the Subaru in an eye of momentary calm. Kara asked the car to coast to a stop and wiped her eyes with the back of her glove. She got out and walked around it slowly, watching the lightning taunt her as it, too, circled the car. Something inside hurt, something secret, something unfathomable. *I love you,* she screamed at the lightning. *Why do you keep me away?* Attracted to the dangerous, rejected by the dangerous. *Why, god damn it, why?*

To hell with you. Kara decided to dance alone and got back in the car and turned off the headlights. Her eyes adjusted to the monochromatic light of the hiding-and-seeking moon. She drove onto the barren surface of a broad playa in Bog Hot Valley. The car carried Kara onto her empty ballroom floor. *Should I curtsy before I begin to dance?* The end of the playa lay miles distant. With all-wheel-drive, she could dance here without worry.

Kara guided the hatchback through long, exploratory curves, getting a feel for the playa's hard but slick surface. Tightening the turns, she found the instant when the tires lost traction and the car danced on the edge of adhesion, pitting speed against radius of turn. She pushed the Subaru faster until the turns became pirouettes and the car would spin around and around and drift to a stop. Kara would press the accelerator and do it again, spinning the car. The tires tracked an intricate passion as Kara flaunted herself before the circling lightning that flashed angrily beyond the windshield. She drove to the end of the playa, turning and spinning the car with the freedom of a child who knew not an adult's inhibitions. She raced the car in long dashes along the edge of the playa, turned, and let the hatchback spin at its own will across the desert pavement. She taunted the lightning. *You should have taken me when you could.*

The lightning marshaled an army to punish the infidel for her insolence. It sent forth its heavy armor — the dense, soaking squalls lashing out of hidden canyons preceded by its plodding foot soldiers, the low, swirling, scud clouds. Above, the towering, night-cloaked cumulonimbus rumbled with salvos of thunder. Small but furious masses of rain raced onto the playa, cutting off her path to the highway. *Fuck you.* She studied the advancing army of rain. *You won't get me.* Kara knew how to deal with rain. She liked rain; she walked in Seattle's rain often just for the sheer pleasure of feeling it fall on her. Kara drove straight at the nearest line of squalls. Just before the onrushing rain swallowed them, Kara darted into a narrow gap between squalls. The wind drove rain through the window and sunroof, wetting her face and hair. A tiny rill trickled down her cheek. She licked the moisture at the corner of her mouth. *Lightning's blood.*

The car broke through the line of squalls and rushed toward the highway. It bucked over hummocky ground as it fought through the wind rushing down from Oregon's high plateau. They reached the highway and fled east past rutted side roads leading to forgotten box canyons like Bottle Creek Canyon. She ignored them. In the movies, posses trapped the bad guys in them. They offered no sanctuary. The squalls raced across the Black Rock Desert to intercept her. Kara aimed the car at the heart of the first squall and burst through it. She looked in the rearview mirror. The squalls nipped at her. The lightning danced in the peaks with other lovers — *how fickle*. It hurled thunder from the mountains, passing sentence on Kara. The car could go no faster. Her pursuers closed. *I'm scared.* The harsh wind screamed through the window and sunroof. It gripped the back of Kara's neck. She was so tired and she didn't know how to get away, so she closed her eyes and dreamed, and in the darkness of her fraying consciousness she saw an enormous white spinnaker, full, lush, and pregnant, blossoming in front of the car. Its Dacron handmaidens reached out to Kara and the little car and pulled them swiftly away from the frustrated squalls.

Kara never saw the sharp curve west of Denio Junction. The Subaru flew off the cliff into space but she feared nothing now and dreamed that the spinnaker would become a parachute and gently lower her through soft, warm rain and find her shelter from the storm. And it did.

Chapter 8:

April 5, late morning, north of Escalante, Utah

The ultralight, despite Noah's many attempts at muffling the big Rotax engine's whine, usually announced itself a few seconds before it would rise from its furtive, belly-to-the-ground approach. It was his favorite tactic. The rock crawlers liked plateaus and ridges for thematic scenery. They thought the high ground would allow them to see him first. But he found arroyos and gullies and fins to hide in as he approached.

The yellow Drifter, his favorite, sped through a narrow canyon in the Box-Death Hollow Wilderness Area, west of Capitol Reef. Noah knew this old river channel intimately, so, despite the apparent danger of wingtips striking sedimentary walls, it seemed just another routine, quick in-and-out. He knew that on the plateau above the western wall, six powerful off-road vehicles were racing, one at a time, up a slickrock slope. Where the slope broke, cameras were set up — one to catch the undercarriage as it rose into view, huge wheels off the ground, and two on either side. The thin man's clients favored this place. The middle camera would catch the snow-capped Henry Mountains to the east; then, suddenly, their big rock crawlers would rise up from seemingly nowhere, blotting out the Henrys. Rich men conquering nature, captured on

DVD, sold well here, he thought.

But the wives, mistresses, business associates, and others who watched the videos in private screenings did not see how the rock crawlers, in their miles-long approach to this fragile place, cut across the migration corridors of elk and mule deer. The mammoth tires crushed the riparian habit of several species of reptiles and amphibians. Oil pans brushed stream bottoms, soiling the food bank of bottom-feeding fish.

Noah would only get one pass. That was his ironclad rule. Only one pass. This time would be difficult. He had four balloons, three for whichever rock crawlers hove into view. He knew the thin man's routine here, so he'd find them clustered at the bottom of the rise, waiting their turns to roar up the slope. Easy targets, ducks in a row. The fourth balloon was for the fat man's Jeep. He really wanted to hit that. Badly. He had bright red paint today. That'd look good on the green of the Jeep.

He reviewed his plan as he guided the Drifter up the canyon. Firewall the throttle. Pick up as much airspeed as possible. Pop up quickly above the rim, sun behind him, and dive on the crawlers, dropping the balloons. Bank right to ascend the slope and skim over the Jeep. Make the last drop. He grinned. That would put the plane right in the middle camera's view. Ruin the shoot. Bank right again and dive back into the shelter of the narrow canyon. He'd be over them for perhaps forty seconds. He checked his ammo in a little box tethered to the floor under his legs. He was ready. He eased the throttle forward. He watched for a large sandstone boulder at the base of the western wall, his marker for popping the plane out of the canyon and over the plateau. He yanked the stick back and the Drifter rose swiftly from the canyon floor.

Four men, separated by about 20 yards each, stood just back from the edge of the canyon wall. All had assault rifles. They fired as he flew overhead. Noah could hear bullets whistling past over the roar of the engine. He glanced left at the wing. He saw sky through several little, ragged, round holes. He banked sharply away and looked for the crawlers.

The thin man had fooled him; four of them sat idling on the slickrock, but each a few hundred feet from the others. Two more men with rifles fired at him. Noah pulled back on the stick and banked again, but he had lost airspeed. He had to get back to the canyon. He looked down. The four men on the rim were running for the edge of the canyon, anticipating his move. He pushed the nose of the Drifter sharply down and leveled off a few feet from the slickrock. He flew directly at the four men. They froze, then dropped to the bedrock. But one stood, aiming. That shot chipped the prop, and the imbalance left the Drifter vibrating as Noah dove it into the canyon. He leveled off and flew downstream, throttling back.

The Drifter yawed left. The wing fabric had torn, diminishing lift. He fought vibration and yaw as he made his way to Blue Spruce Creek, then south, following Forest Road 153. If he could only make it to Escalante, he thought — but twelve miles later, the rent fabric of the wing fluttered uselessly, and the Drifter had lost too much lift. He set it down while he still had control on the road near Black Hills, just north of Escalante Petrified Forest State Park. He shut down the engine and unhooked his seat belt.

Noah stepped from the plane, bent over, and vomited. He took a few uneasy steps, then fell to the ground, breathing heavily. After a few minutes, he took off his helmet, set it in the cockpit, and pushed the Drifter onto the side of the road.

He pulled out his cell phone and spoke one word to dial: "Annie." It rang, then: "Noah?"

"Yes, Annie. I need help."

"Oh, crap. What happened?"

"They knew I was coming."

"How?"

"I don't know. But the Drifter got shot up."

"Noah, it isn't working. Those guys will kill you."

"Well, they missed me. But they chipped the prop and ripped up the left wing."

"Jesus, Noah."

"Would you go to the hangar and get another prop and

some fabric? I'll meet you at Escalante Muni. I can fix the Drifter and fly it back."

"Okay, but—"

"Please, Annie. No buts. Not now."

Annie did not answer. He only heard her disconnect. But he knew she'd do what he asked. Annie was, among other qualities, reliable and discreet. That's why he'd hired her.

He knew she was right. It wasn't working. He'd have to be more careful, or he'd have to stop

Chapter 9:

April 5, midmorning, off Route 95, north of Winnemucca, Nevada

Heat and light coaxed Kara from a dream. Glare forced her to squint when she opened her eyes. Dusty brown surrounded her. No rain. No lightning. No floating through the sky. Nothing. She rolled onto her side. Rivulets of sweat ran down the hollow of her throat. She felt gritty everywhere. A fine, tan-colored sand had partially buried her. She was in a sleeping bag. She unzipped it and flung it open. She lay still, enjoying the sun penetrating and easing her pains. A breeze dried her, and she brushed off the sand with her hands. A lump under the bag poked at her side. She must have rolled her sweats and shorts and panties and Tyvek into a pillow. *Damn. I suppose they're all wrinkled now.* She sat up, briefly alarmed. *Where's the map?* She thrust her hand into the rolled-up clothes. The map scratched her hand. The relief irritated her, because she didn't know why she felt comforted by the map.

She lay on her back. The sun felt wonderful. She remembered a sci-fi story about spacecraft with huge silver sails powered by the pressure of the sun's rays. *Solar wind. How big would the sails have to be?* Kara loved the imagination possible in science.

Sculpted mounds of sand rose to each side. Dunes. *What the ...?* She stood, arched her back, and craned her head back and forth. She walked haltingly around the tiny dry world occupied only by the blue of the sky, the brown of the sand, and the purple of the sleeping bag. *I need life. I need green.*

Kara stuffed her clothes into her sleeping bag and rolled it up. She slogged through the sand to the top of the nearest dune. *How did I get here?* The little Sahara in which she had slumbered ended three or four dunes away, all downhill. She could not see her car. The dunes hid part of the highway, and she assumed that the hatchback was parked out of sight. *It damn well better be there.* Beyond the road a river curled through a broad, flat, nearly treeless plain dotted with big green circles of irrigated land. Dust rose in the breeze as several large green tractors — John Deere's biggest — rent the earth. To the west a small city held fast to the riverside. *Winnemucca?* Behind her lay more dunes. The tracks of dirt bikes threaded over them. They wouldn't last. Already drifting sand obscured the tire marks. North of the dunes alluvial fans rose on the flanks of the blackest mountains she had ever seen. The ragged peaks looked angry and ugly. *Did they try to trap me, too?* She flipped the finger at the Bloody Run Hills.

She took her clothes from the sleeping bag. They were still damp. *Why are they wet?* She spread her sweats atop the sleeping bag to dry. Though the wind was light, sand grains tumbled along ripples on the dunes, climbing the windward faces and rolling down the lee side. She stretched her arms over her head and lifted her face to the sun, willing the remnants of sleep away. Her arms fell to her sides as she walked aimlessly along the dune.

Scattered blades of grass, never a colonial clump, grew in the sand. The lonely green fronds waved in the wind. *Why do I assume they're lonely? Just because they're single?* Sand grains struck the blades, shaking them. Solitary bugs left crooked trails that disappeared in the drifting sand. *If they get lost, how do they find their way home?* The sand on the windward faces of the dunes was firm, the slip faces only slightly less so. She liked noticing that. *I'm a good noticer. That's why I'm good at my job.* Guilt stirred — *that goddamned unfinished site* — before being pushed away.

The breeze ruffled her hair. The air was devoid of scent. Pausing, she examined her footprints, fascinated that her trail was becoming less distinct with each tick of some natural clock. *I can't find my way back, either.* She glissaded down the face of a large dune, enjoying the freedom of the sand erupting behind her bare feet. *It's like skiing. Wouldn't it be great to ski naked in the spring?* Laughing, she tried a few parallel turns. *It's like heavy corn snow.* Being nude in such surroundings was exhilarating.

The sun was warm, almost hot, but the soft breeze kept her from sweating heavily. She loved these dunes. This was a simple place; just sand, sky, sun, and self. *Barren's not the right word. It's ... stark. That's it. Stark. No. Uncomplicated. That's the word. Shit, that's not it, either.* Lifting her arms, she tried one of her jazzercise pirouettes. But she literally drilled herself into the dune, lost her balance, and fell, laughing.

She got up, regretting her spontaneous, rambunctious play. *I'm supposed to be working. Or did I never learn to play?* Sand grains between the cheeks of her ass chafed. Her inner thighs felt gritty. She stopped, legs apart, and the wind teased away the moisture adhering sand to skin. The wind played with her pubic hair. *It's kind of long. I should trim it. He likes it short.* She dusted her thighs with her fingers and then her buttcheeks, keeping her fingers away from *that place*, even though *that place* seemed grittiest of all.

Analysis provided avoidance. Kara noticed the sporadic placements of a leafless bush half as tall as she. She touched a thorn, and it penetrated her finger with ease. She drew back reflexively and licked the drop of blood sitting fat and swollen on her finger. The salty taste left her mouth dry. She tugged at the nettle. It did not surrender gracefully. *Like men*, she decided. She yanked it out.

Kara walked through a hollow between dunes. The top of

the dunes seemed indistinct. *Is it a mirage?* The sand-laden wind curling over their crests blurred the horizon, a miniature, low-level windstorm coating the dunes like frosting. What she had seen in individual ripples she saw over entire dunes. *So this is how dunes move.* She marched up a slip face, singing gaily, *Oh when the dunes, go marching in ...* She grimaced. *That's really bad.*

Kara walked toward the road, shuffling her feet in the drifting sand, feeling it swirl about her toes. She wasn't sure where she'd left her sleeping bag and clothes. She'd stumble across them sooner or later. Discarded debris was scattered here and there, lone warts on softly wrinkled skin. Bottles, cans, pieces of cardboard, short hanks of rope and a rifle with a broken stock. People had littered this place. Kara found an empty six-pack carton. Inside were two used condoms. *I guess once wasn't enough.*

She found an old chaise lounge, the cheap kind with the ugly yellow and green plastic webbing, and lay down to rest. The sun bore down on her. She felt relaxed. She thought of Seattle. The dunes relaxed her. Seattle didn't. *Why?* It wasn't that Seattle didn't relax her, she decided. It was just hectic. The relationship had been kind of hard-driving. *I never get a rest. It's a helluva ride, but it's exhausting.* The deadline depressed her. *I should work. I really should.*

She got up and jogged to the edge of the dunes. Below her was the Subaru, windows and sunroof open. *Christ! My Mac!* She half-slid, half glissaded down the dune and darted to the car. *I should have put on my clothes.* She grabbed a T-shirt and a pair of shorts and her laptop. She hurried back to the imagined security of the dunes and climbed out of sight from the road, breathing heavily. *I'm so out of shape.*

She dropped the extra clothes next to the chaise lounge and sat. Opening her Mac, she turned the screen away from the sun so she could see it, connected her MiFi, and booted. She ignored her e-mail. She worked for a while, adding links, checking links, occasionally reorganizing the links, placing video where it ought to be. Beneath her, a column of ants trudged tirelessly along, toting food. Overhead, a prairie hawk soared, looking for field mice at the edge of the dunes. Kara did not see nature now. She saw only hypertext.

An hour later, she had nearly finished, only needing to add the latest links he'd sent. She opened her mail program and saw a message from him. She did not read it. She did not want to open his old message and read the links, either. *Not now. Later.* She opened a new mail message window.

To: TopDog@WebWideWorks.com
From: kara@WebWideWorks.com
Subject: OnCourse project
Cc:
Bcc:
Attachments:

_____

almost done ... only have to add the links you sent ... will finish tonight and upload the site to the server ... won't be able to make it back in time to present with you.

I should tell him where I am. But she didn't and sent the message. After putting away her laptop, she lay in the chaise lounge, arm flung over her eyes. The sun drew perspiration from her that outlasted the late-morning breeze, so she got up. She saw scattered, brilliant red dots, bright, beautiful flowers growing on the northern edge of the dunes. *Why didn't I notice these before?* They covered the slip face of a dune that met the sagebrush plain. The plants reminded her of rhubarb; at least the stalks and leaves did. Each plant seemed to have several flowers, bunched tightly on a central stalk. *Safety in numbers? They're beautiful. Then again, maybe they look so good because there's nothing here to compare them to.* She slid her hands over her body, her small breasts, her slender waist, her narrow hips, her long legs. *Willowy. That's me. Or am I willowy because there are no willows to compare myself to?* The bright red blooms seemed out of place, incongruent among the dunes. *I wonder what they are.* She thought about getting her camera to photograph them. She dug her toes into the sand until her foot disappeared among millions and millions of sand grains, end products of erosion. The sand below was cooler, moister. She looked at the flowers at the dunes' edge. The thorny bushes lived only in the hollows of the dunes. Understanding bloomed. But the flicker of insight fled. *It'll come back. It has to.*

An old hourglass Coke bottle stuck out of the sand, the ribbed kind that knew only the days of Classic Coke. The top had been broken off. She picked it up carefully, but the edges had been sandblasted smooth. She liked the frosted look and carried it with her, a token of the dunes, a hard-copy reminder of an evanescent place she had come to love.

A decrepit Volkswagen van stopped next to the dunes. Teenagers emerged with Frisbees, iPods in their ears, and dark glasses with garish, fluorescent frames and several packs of Keystone Light. They saw her. The boys pointed. One raised his cell phone and pointed it at her, taking a picture. Kara could see the tanned, blonde, giggling girls wearing very short cutoffs and the skimpiest of halter tops. *Like me when I was fifteen and flirting.* The boys huddled, pointing at Kara. They edged toward the first dune, moving toward her, the girls obediently following. She waited until she saw one boy raise his cell phone again. She stood with legs apart, pussy hair fluttering in the wind, arms crossed under her breasts. Guessing when he was about to trip the camera, she unfurled her arms, raised one hand and gave him the finger that the Bloody Run Hills had earned. The boy lowered the phone and looked away. He got the message: *Don't fuck with me.* The boy called out to the others and pointed at Kara. Her finger rode high in the air. They looked at their girlfriends, then to Kara, then at the girlfriends. The boys veered away, not walking away from Kara, but not toward her, either. They were saving face, pretending that making a bluff at her had been their intention. The teenagers moved south along the road, ducked under the fence, and disappeared. She fumed. She'd had a good time here. But she felt ripped off to have it end like this. Grabbing her belongings, she hugged them against her chest and strode past the brilliant red flowers to the road.

She didn't give a damn whether anyone driving by saw her nude, but nonetheless she slipped into shorts and a T-shirt. She threw the rest of her gear into the back seat. She drove until she found a dirt road that led past a cap-rocked butte to the river.

She got out of the hot car, still sweating — *I should fix that damn air conditioner* — shed her clothes, and walked into the stream. It was early spring cold, but she kept moving until the water touched her chin. She swam into the gentle current with strong strokes. The river wasn't wide, so she had to lift her head to see the meanders and avoid cut banks. When exercise had eased anger, she swam to the bank away from the road and climbed into the sunlight, wet and flushed. Kara lay on her back, eyes closed, in soft, tall grass in the shadow of a lone cottonwood. She listened to the squabbling of crows above her. Later, she swam back, and the map told her that she had endured her melancholy next to the Little Humboldt River.

Chapter 10:

April 5, afternoon, next to the Little Humboldt River, near Winnemucca, Nevada

Kara lay nude in the sun after her swim. She methodically sunned her front, then her back, then her sides, for five minutes each, followed by an extra ten minutes for her front. She felt oddly diabolical about her rotisserie method of tanning. He liked tan lines. He'd told her once that they turned him on, and here she was, intent on obliterating them. She put on her hot-weather uniform, a black Speedo swimsuit and a pair of dark green running shorts. She liked the way the colors looked against her tan, how the Lycra suit and nylon shorts washed easily and how they dried quickly. *Good road clothes.* She put on the Bollé mountain sunglasses she'd bought at REI a long time ago. She supposed she ought to get newer shades, cool ones, like those wraparound kinds. But she loved her old shades. They had been places with her. On ridges in the Cascades. In rafts on the Willamette. In kayaks out on the Sound. They had a history with her. They'd been companions. *I like history. I like wearing pieces of the past.*

Looking at herself in the side view mirror, she thought of

the nymphets in the dunes. *Now this, girls, is buff.* She got in her car proudly and drove to Winnemucca, retreating first to the dunes to photograph the red flowers *those damn teenagers cheated me out of.*

She knew she ought to call. She'd been gone, *what, three days now.* He'd be worried, despite her e-mails. *Wouldn't he?* She drove on, and soon Winnemucca surrounded her with its assaulting signage and neon proclamations of restaurants, casinos, motels, gas stations, pawn shops, and supermarkets. She stopped at a modestly priced motel near the center of the little city. Spending a night in a motel was against the code for road trips, *but damn, I need a break.* She strode into the office, Bollés coolly in place, insisted on a corner room — *I want that quiet you advertise outside* — and, on getting one, acquiesced to sign the register. She carried her bike into the room along with an armload of clothing. She remembered the map and realized she had thought of it only once all day. She got the map from the car and spread it over one of the bureaus. She stared at Utah for a long time. She didn't know why, and that angered her. She showered with a dinky bar of Dial soap, dried herself with an undersized bath towel, flopped onto one of beds, and fell asleep.

She awoke in late afternoon. As she rubbed her eyes, a clunking noise came from the air conditioner. *A broken compressor, I'll bet.* She called the desk and complained. We're sorry, they said, we'll try to get it fixed tomorrow. No, today, she insisted. We can't, they said. Give me another room, she demanded. They compromised. If they couldn't get it fixed by eight o'clock, she could move to another room. She hung up, dissatisfied. *Why am I so bitchy?*

Kara put on her Speedo to retrieve an old blue Kelty cargo bag from the hatchback. She dumped the contents on one of the beds. The bag had become a clothes bin; she spent so much time in proper adult business clothes that she kept stuff in the car to slop around in or bike after work. She looked over her stash — his sweatshirt and sweatpants, a fisherman's sweater, two pairs of underwear, a pair of black cotton tights, two pairs of ragg socks, a pair of Levis with torn knees, her lacy thing, and two pair of white tanks. Not much of a stash. No bras. She cupped her breasts in her hands. They fit easily into her palms. *Not much need for one, either.* She put on the Levis and white tank top and laced up her red Converses.

She went outside. *I should walk.* She needed the rhythmic motion of perambulation. Within two blocks, she'd made up her mind about Winnemucca — she hated it. It was a city, a town really, of big, pricey SUVs contrasted with loud, older, big-tired, four-wheel-drive pickups that carried their dents as proud scars of unknown battles. Men wore variants of the same costume — cowboy boots; Stetsons of various whites, tans, and browns; a blue or brown denim shirt with western trim and accents and snap buttons; and solid indigo Wranglers — no stonewashed freaks here. No artfully torn knees, either. She saw few young people. Winnemucca wasn't a dirty town, but she felt hot, dusty, and grimy within those first two blocks.

A man, old but not elderly, leaned against his pickup, watching her. He had a native American look — dark, reddish-brown skin; a long black pony tail streaked with silver; a bright yellow Levi shirt with the fake rhinestone studs on the pockets; a black string bolo with a silver-and-turquoise choker; and worn jeans and dusty boots that had seen a life of work. He smiled, not with a leer but with admiration, it seemed, for what he was seeing. Kara had always been a sucker for open adoration. The leathery creases on his sun-darkened face all led to his eyes. They gave him warmth; they gave him life. She liked him but didn't know why. She crossed the street and walked up to him.

"There a drug store here?" she asked.

He removed his Stetson and waved it toward downtown. *They remove their hats when talking to a woman.* Courtesy. Civility. She liked that.

"How far?" she asked.

"Just keep walkin', pretty lady," he said, gravel rattling around in his throat. "A few blocks, on the right."

"Thank you," she said. She stood motionless for moment,

then touched his arm. "Thank you," she repeated. She crossed the street. *I bet he's watching my ass.* She glanced back. He was, still smiling. She put her hand on her cheeks ostensibly to smooth the tight denim — *that center seam rides up, you know.* She looked back and grinned as she walked away. He waved. *That wasn't mean, was it? I should be more decent to decent men.*

In the drug store, she walked through the aisles, filling a basket with the sundries a decent bathroom should have. Perfume, eye shadow, and eyeliner did not make the cut. *Who am I going to impress here? Got to keep things simple.* On a counter stood a display of condoms. She didn't have her birth-control pills. They were back in Seattle. *Am I going to get laid out here? Do I want to?* She decided to get some Trojans, just in case. *I'm such an optimist. Or am I just faithless?* She paid the cashier and got directions to a bookstore.

She walked to a small, white frame house. Inside was a bookstore that sold only used paperbacks. A little white poodle dogged her heels as she pulled several novels from the shelves, some mysteries, some spy thrillers, a romance or two. *What the hell. Mindless reading. Road books. That's what I need.* At the last moment, she plucked a feminist writer off the shelves. *Token homage to the sisterhood.* On another shelf, one book a little thicker than the rest, a little taller than the rest, stuck out a bit farther on the shelf, too. It was somehow different. That made her think of the map — *that oddball Rand McNally.* Just like all the rest, but not quite the same. She pulled it out. It had a picture of a large dam on the cover below the title, "Cadillac Desert." It seemed to be about the issues surrounding Western water. She was curious. She took another book with a quirky title — "The Monkey Wrench Gang." She paid and headed back to the motel.

A sign pointing to the Winnemucca Convention Center told her a baroque string quartet was appearing that night at eight o'clock. The notion of a culture of classical music in Winnemucca surprised her. She decided to go.

Kara showered again and considered her clothing choices. The Kelty held nothing suitable, at least by Seattle standards, for a night of serious chamber music. She pondered her black tights, then decided to go with the Levis. *When in Rome.* She shrugged on the lacy thing, slipped into her Tyvek, and tied a blue bandana around her head. She put money and her license in a wrist wallet and walked to the convention center. She arrived early, as planned. Only a few people stood in line at the box office, but cars and pickups were pulling into nearby parking spaces. She asked for a seat as close to the stage as possible and found her way to an aisle seat a few rows from the front. She loved string music and enjoyed watching it as well as listening to it. They'd gone to see a friend, a young woman dressed in a long, black, low-cut evening gown, play the cello at her master's recital in a small concert hall. The woman had played a few of Bach's suites for unaccompanied cello, which were among Kara's favorites. She'd loved the dimly lit closeness of the hall, the delicacy of the young woman's fingering, the brightly varnished golden color of the cello nestled among the long folds of her black gown, and the glorious vibrations that had resonated in her chest. That night had redefined intimacy. *He was with me, but he was not.* As Kara sat in the convention hall in Winnemucca, she wondered why the cello affected her so. *It makes me want.* Want had always been sexual to her. *But I don't know anymore what "want" really is.*

Others entered the hall, walking down the aisle, greeting friends, making their way to their seats. Kara sensed that everybody knew everybody. Most wore wedding rings. About half were men, half were women. No children. *Couples. Lots of couples.* These people did not bring into the hall the roughness of the streets of hot, dusty, late-afternoon Winnemucca. Civility, Western-style, glided quietly around her. Husbands walked with wives. The man carried his Stetson in one hand and held his woman's hands in the other. When a couple reached their aisle, the man stepped back, bowed slightly, and held a hand out low toward the row to guide the woman to her seat. The woman nodded politely, sat down, and reached for her husband's hand after he had adjusted his butt a few times in the leather seat and settled against the backrest. Kara smiled, delighted, as Stetsons mushroomed on men's laps all around the hall. *No place else to put 'em.*

Kara liked their clothing. Some wore Wranglers, but only new, sharply creased, deep indigo denim. Fresh polish glistened on the boots. Their jackets marked them as Westerners by the cut of the lapel, the shaping of the pockets, the turquoise buttons on the cuffs, the suede accents on the shoulders. The women wore dresses that weren't quite formal evening gowns but would be overdressing for a cowgirl's Saturday night out at the saloon. The younger women dared a hint of décolletage; the older ones dressed sensibly. Couples spoke closely, men leaning toward their wives as whispered somethings were exchanged. The women seemed low key, attentive to the men, even demure. She tried to read their eyes, to search for the dullness, the lack of sparkle, in the eyes of a cowed spouse. She found none. She sensed strength in them as well as furtive playfulness, of letting the men feel like men as much as they wanted. *This isn't what she expected here. This isn't it at all.*

Kara felt chagrined when she realized she had been slumping lower into her seat, an unconscious defense against perceived conspicuousness, a single amid couples. She felt out of place, but *damn it, my money's as good as theirs.* She glanced around, sure that people were staring at her. A few people looked at her, but she could not tell if the cause was idle curiosity, the bright bandana, or a well-disguised interest in the breasts riding free under the lacy thing. Kara looked at her breasts, then at those of the women around her. Hers were slightly concave on top; theirs were convex, fuller, rounder. *It's their bras.* But she felt diminished nonetheless, as if these women had a secret that she had yet to discover. *There must be magic in mating.*

Suddenly she felt they must all be thinking, *Why is this girl alone?* Kara felt tears tiptoeing into her eyes as the house lights dimmed. *I'll be damned if I'll wipe them off. They made their choices. I made mine.* But she listened to the first two pieces listlessly and left near the end of the last movement of the last sonata, slipping down the aisle before the rising house lights could catch her.

She walked through the warm, desert air of the downtown night, thinking of *the fucking map*, of Seattle, of the unfinished website, of thunder and lightning and fear. She thought of hot days, sleepless nights, and inept lovers. She shoved her hands in her pockets and swore. She had data. She grunted, thinking of Dad the Engineer. She had available resources. She could find an answer. *But what the hell was the question?*

Kara bought a bottle of Chardonnay. Inside her motel room, she set up the laptop, opened the bottle, and filled one of the two cellophane-wrapped plastic glasses she found in the bathroom and changed into her writing uniform — the black tights and a sweatshirt. She wrinkled her nose as she pulled it on. *Shit, this really stinks.* She yanked it over her head and threw it to the floor. She sat in front of the Mac, noted the time — 9:52 p.m. — and entered it in a memo file in her iPhone. She loved the phone. She kept music, photos, contacts, to-do lists, her billable hours, *her life* on it.

The concert faded away, Seattle faded away, uncertainty faded away. Everything faded away save the keyboard and the screen of the MacBook Pro. Kara re-entered her familiar world of XTML, of JavaScript, of InDesign, of attributes turned on and attributes turned off, of browsers, of methodically organized links, of tables and frames, of digital images, of linked PDF files. Lots of coding. She just needed to add the last few video links. She sighed, reopened the irritating e-mail he'd sent, and retrieved them. She ignored his new e-mail. Kara was focused. The wine, untouched, lost its liquor-store chill. The new links, to her dismay, did not fit logically into her original design. *Damn.* A sip of warm wine fortified her. A few links changed here; a few more changed there. The pages still did not flow logically in a proper sequence. She reconsidered the design. Too many graphic elements. A grandiose banner floating on the home page consumed too much screen real estate. *That had been his idea.* He wanted more video; she advised more text. Video and graphics summarized, but words taught best, she believed. Video got attention, he'd said; she countered that the site was an online educational course, that people had to follow a text-based sequence. The need for organized, useable information, not the whim of graphic or video eye candy, kept their attention, she'd argued. She removed several videos that slowed the load time for some links. She cleaned up a few redundant links and inserted return-to-home links at the end of each tutorial. She checked coding tags. A few missed end tags were fixed. Colors were altered slightly to make the text easier to read. She added self-help and feedback blog features. She worked. She analyzed. She had learned print page design in journalism school. But she'd long ago realized that designing Web pages differed from designing newspaper pages. She also considered that students might print out these pages to read at leisure later. She adjusted the site for that. She designed and programmed steadily, occasionally stopping to drink more wine.

Hours later, Kara logged her time in her iPhone: 5:08 a.m. *Tuesday already.* She stretched. She sensed a lengthening, darkening distance between her and Seattle but pushed the thought away. Drinking the last of the wine, now warm and flat, she made a face, went into the bathroom, and urinated. She could sleep now. *Damn thing's done.* But he'd want rewrites of this or that. He'd want the links arranged differently. She grabbed the motel's wireless signal and watched, bone-weary, as the project uploaded itself out of her life. Kara slept into late afternoon. She dreamed of a large, empty ballroom with no ceiling, just darkness from which a misting rain fell softly on her.

Kara awoke, sat up, and rubbed her eyes. She stretched for a while. Soft light from the Mac's screen seeped into the room. She showered and put on her tights and the lacy thing. Sitting on the bed, she stared at the laptop as it stared at her. She got up and opened Outlook. Two new messages from him waited, not one. She opened the latest.

To: kara@WebWideWorks.com
From: TopDog@WebWideWorks.com
Subject: Re: OnCourse project
Cc:
Bcc:
Attachments:

It's midnight. Where is it?

And please, please *call* me. We need to talk.

TD

Kara stabbed the delete key. Her hand trembled as her finger traced across the track pad to select his earlier message. She wouldn't like it. She hated confrontations. She could argue technical points on anything. Yet the heat of angered and hurt hearts fighting left her shaking. Even over e-mail. She thanked God they'd never developed a "texting" relationship.

To: kara@WebWideWorks.com
From: TopDog@WebWideWorks.com
Subject: Re: holiday
Cc:
Bcc:
Attachments:

>sometimes you'r so fucking dense ... i'll have the damn site to you by wed a.m. ... and since when
>do *we* have to toegther to make a presesntation? ... you uslally do alla that ... you and your
>damn polite shmoozing ... i'll try to be back ... maybe ... i need down time and after you get the

>site i may just take it

What'd I do? What'd I do? Sheesh, Kara.
What the hell has gotten into you? You've
been gone for two days and something's
turned you into a raving monster. I know
you've got a temper, but you seemed okay
when you left. Is it Petey? He's okay. Just
kind of low on energy, I think. You know,
the heartworm pills kicking in.

I don't know what to say to you. We never
really talk anymore. What's troubling you?
What have I done? I know I've put a lot of
pressure on you over the past month with
this OnCourse thing, but you know how big
a contract it is for us. It could lead us to
really expand what we're doing. It's our
first educational site and the market's huge
for it.

I wish I was there so I could talk to you. I
wish I was there so I could tell you I need
you back here. It's just not the same
without you, and somehow, you're not the
same right now wherever you are. And
where are you? What's come over you?
Sure, I'm *dense*, as you said. But what
the hell am I dense about?

And what are you *doing* wherever you
are? You're no loner. You've always had to
be the center of attention. This is so unlike
you.

Your note really hurt. I don't know what I
did to deserve such tripe. I'm just trying to
make things work out for us. When you
moved back in again at Christmas, it made
me so happy to have you here again. Yeah,
we fight a lot, but all couples fight, don't
they? We *are* a couple, aren't we?

I need to hear your voice. I need to hear
you.

TD

Kara winced. He was hurting; so was she. *But it's just not working.* She dressed in biking gear and got her bike off the roof rack. *Screw the helmet.* She rode out of the parking lot onto Winnemucca's broad streets.

Her legs loosened as the rhythm of riding returned. She rode up Water Canyon, standing on the pedals, rocking the bike from side to side. She stopped at an isolated picnic table in a recreation area. For an hour, she sat motionless. Tired, dismayed, disillusioned, she rode back to the motel room. Setting the laptop on the bed, she knelt, selected "reply," and began to type.

To: TopDog@WebWideWorks.com
From: kara@WebWideWorks.com
Subject: Re: holiday
Cc:
Bcc:
Attachments:

---

i hurt so much ... i know you do, too ... but
i've hurt so much and so hard for so long and
i just don't want to hurt any more ... when i
moved back in, i thought it was because i
was *supposed* to .. and no, i don't know
what "supposed to" means ...

so much of the hurt is because we never
speak of love ... we never talk about feelings
... no, no ... i don't mean that we never say
"i love you" or never talk about emotions ...
but even when you do, it's almost as if it's an

obligation ... you do it because you're
supposed to do it ... if you can understand
that, then you'll know why i felt i was
supposed to move back in ...

all this pressure that we're both under ... it's
rotten ... it's confining ... part of it, i guess,
is that your soul is in building your -- it's not
our -- company ... admit it -- it is yours.
it's your *life* ... it's not that i feel like i'm in
second place ... and i don't want to fall back
on saying that i need to go find myself ... i
know myself, i think ...

i like the work we do ... i want to keep on
doing that ... you know i'm good at it ... but
right now i need to be away ... i wish i could
tell you why ... i really don't know myself ...
something's changing in me .. i don't know
what it is ... it's affecting me, and because
it's affecting me, it's affecting you ... and i'm
truly sorry for that ...

i don't know when i'll be back ... in ten
minutes i could drive back or i could drive to
some far away place ... i just *don't know*
... i don't know what i want ... it's just that
i'm here now and need to be here now and
there's nothing i can say or do to explain it
...

i don't know what else to tell you right now
... i think of you ... i think about us ... but i
think more about what *hasn't been* than
what *could* be ... i need to think about
something else for a while ... i need to find
out *what it is* that i'm supposed to be
thinking about ... oh god, i wish i could
explain it ... something's calling to me and i
have to go find it ... it's so frustrating ... and
you're right ... i don't like being by myself ...
maybe that's really why i moved back in ...

but i've got to do this ... i don't know why ...
i'm so, so, so, so, so sorry ...

please take care of petey ...

k

    She hit "send." A black bar crawled across the transfer dialogue box. Her sorrow left, whisked away at several hundred *kbps*. She opened a new window, addressed it to him, and typed "bill" in the subject line. She entered her hours and computed her fee. She typed, "Total: $11,473." She was financially sound — *he pays well, I'll say that* — but she had little cash with her. She'd rather have some cash on the road instead of using her plastic all the time. *I'm going to keep heading east. I don't know how I know, but I know that.*

    She opened the map and traced a route into Utah. *Let the damn map tell me where.* Her finger stopped at Green River. Far enough for the check to have time to get there. *At least the sonuvabitch pays fast.* Close enough to change her mind and go back. She typed, "Mail a cashier's check to me c/o General Delivery, Green River, Utah, 84525." She didn't type "k." *This is business.* She used her professional sig file — full name, snail mail address, cell and sat numbers, her own LinkedIn, Facebook, and blog addies and her Twitter handle. She sent it.

    Kara filled the other plastic glass with water. She closed the blinds, then took off her black tights and her T-shirt. She sat on the floor, her back against a bed. She sipped at the dank, bitter water. She wanted to cry, but couldn't. She fell asleep on the floor.

Chapter 11:

April 6, late morning, in the motel, Winnemucca, Nevada

Kara awoke to the glow of the screensaver on her laptop charting a fractal fantasia. She hadn't shut it down. *Again. Bad habit.* She'd slept late; noon would arrive soon. *Damn. So much for an early start.* She felt lethargic. She thought of her e-mail message and sighed.

Breakfast beckoned; caffeine called. Kara showered and dressed — Levis and Tyvek. Tucking the map into a pocket, she walked downtown to the Winners Inn Casino. Inside, she found Pete's Kitchen and ordered a cheese omelet, home fries, the Texas toast, orange juice, and tea. She wondered if that would be enough. She opened the map on the table to look at Nevada. *Okay, damn you, where are you taking me today?* She stared at Nevada as she sipped at the tea. Staring offered no insights. The inscrutable map never gave a discernible inkling of where to turn until the turn was there. *Maybe the map just makes me think about direction, and some other instinct makes me choose which direction. And maybe I'm going nuts.*

Breakfast was real. Everything else, Kara decided, was not. She ate quickly and got the hiccups. That always irritated her. The results of hurrying usually did. Kara knew she lived in haste because of deadlines and prayed that preparation and research would ward off errors inherent in rushed execution. Everything had been in its proper place in Dad the Engineer's workshop. He had always sketched out his projects, drawn the right tools and materials, and arranged them in the order he would need them. *Preparation. Preparation. Preparation.* Kara sighed. He had only been unprepared once in his life, and it had emotionally numbed him for the rest of his life.

Kara passed through the sportsmen's store as she walked back to the motel. It was empty save for a young woman wearing a denim skirt and a white blouse buttoned to the neck behind the counter. She smiled and asked if she could help. Kara muttered no, she'd know what she needed when she saw it. She picked out some clothing — a white wide-brimmed canvas hat, two pairs of loose-fitting khaki cotton pants, a few pairs of white painter's pants, a few each of white and blue denim long-sleeved shirts, a dark green fatigue sweater, and black and red pairs of Sierra Designs Quick-Dry nylon shorts. She picked up a bottle of Dr. Bronner's, some sunscreen and a large athletic squeeze bottle, the kind with a hooked spout used by football players. She was tired of sleeping in the car, so she got an inexpensive free-standing tent made mostly of mosquito netting. A parabolic fly would be nice to read under, providing shade at midday. She picked up tent poles to pitch it with. The young woman politely accepted her MasterCard. Kara roamed the aisles again. She passed through the makeup goods aisle, then retraced her steps. She picked up a few essentials, foundation, eye shadow, a few tubes of lipstick, and such. *Who knows? I might want to get lucky some night.* She cut off a yard of Cordura nylon pack cloth off one of the rolls of cloth along a wall and picked up some thread and a package of needles. Kara looked at the collection. *I guess I'm really not going back soon.*

The young woman asked, "What will you do with the cloth?"

"I'm not sure," Kara said. "Maybe make some extra pockets for my pack."

"That's a good idea," the woman replied. "Tell me, are you

traveling? Are you spending much time in your car?"

"Yes," said Kara. "Why?"

The woman smiled and reached under the counter. "You may need this," she said, bringing out a toothpaste-like tube.

"What is it?"

"Velcro cement," she replied. "And some Velcro." She cut three feet of Velcro from a holder on the wall. "I'll throw it in, on the house," she said.

"Thanks. But what'll I do with it?" Kara asked.

"When you leave, pass by the red pickup outside. It's my boyfriend's. Look inside. You'll see what I did."

"Okay, thanks," Kara said. The woman pushed two bags full of purchases across the counter. Kara took them and walked to the door. She opened it with her elbow, then stopped. She looked back at the woman, standing behind the counter.

Kara said, "You've been nice. I appreciate it."

The young woman smiled and said, "You're welcome."

Outside, Kara looked in the pickup truck. The dashboard sported pockets the young woman had sewn from the Cordura and attached with Velcro and glue. The pockets had a strip of appliqué tape that matched the color of the interior. She nodded in appreciation. *I wonder if he asked her to do it, or if she surprised him.* She smiled as walked back to the motel.

Kara took everything out of the car and toted it into the motel room. Then, after donning a Speedo and her new black Quick-Dry shorts, she borrowed a hose from the desk clerk and washed her bike, carefully lubricating the chain and the derailleurs. She washed the car, too. Back in the motel room she organized, packing her clothes into the Kelty bag. They didn't all fit, so she put some in a duffle bag. She opened the road tools box and eyed the socket wrenches and screwdrivers and the spark plug gapper and the WD40 and the odds and ends she'd collected over the years of caring for the car, things like a spare rotor and distributor cap and an oil filter wrench, a line tester, spare plug wires and the very, very large screw driver she usually kept on the floor under the driver's seat. She was often downtown in Seattle at night and liked having it handy. She didn't touch anything; she just needed to see it, to see tangible evidence of preparedness. An act of renewal. *I can fix anything. That's good, isn't it?* Examining the bike tools box, she sorted and arranged the Allen wrenches, the small screwdrivers, the chain tool, the third hand, the spare chain links, the extra sprockets, the spare tubes, the spare spokes, the tire patch kit, the spoke wrenches, the 15mm wrench for removing the rear wheel, the coiled wire waiting for a broken shifter or brake cable, the wire cutters and other doodads collected through building and caring for her bike.

Be prepared. Kara needed to know, to the very last item, what she had. Census of available inventory was ingrained in her. It brought comforting order to her life when chaos otherwise reigned. *Everything has a purpose. I have every tool I need and none that I don't need.* All her other road gear, piece by piece, she piled on a bed — a small field pack with first-aid gear and binoculars, the sleeping bag, the foam pad, the new tent, the jug of water for the radiator, the Lemon Fresh Joy and the Turtle Wax and chamois cloth, Windex and paper towels and other, scattered necessities. She dug into the Kelty cargo bag. Inside were a few of his clothes, a T-shirt, a pair of sweats, some socks. She threw them into a wastebasket.

She was ready to get back on the road. *On the road.* She liked the ring of that. She liked to drive. She liked to watch the landscape pass by, an endlessly changing face *of a what? A friend? A lover? A stranger?* She didn't know. She'd never been on the road day after day by herself. Her past trips with him had destinations, the Wenatchee to go rafting, the North Cascades to hike to the snowfields, the Peninsula to walk the beaches in isolation, British Columbia to canoe in the high mountain lakes and swim shivering in the small, cold tarns above timberline. No drive lingered more than a day. Each began the same way. She'd organize the gear, he'd load, she'd drive, he'd set up the big Sears holiday tent at the campground, she'd cook when they had to. Those trips had cadence. *Now I have none. I have to make a new rhythm.*

She deleted her purchases from the iPhone's to-do list. "Finish website," read another entry. She vaporized it with the delete key. She loved her toys. She could do virtually anything with her phone and iPad and their dozens of apps. Her Mac could handle images from her digital cameras, video and still. She photographed everything at clients' sites. Gauges. Dials. Machinery. Room layouts. Photographs and short videos were her notes. And in a wireless-less wilderness, she could transmit virtually anything via her sat phone and BGAN terminal. Efficiency, Dad the Engineer had preached. Photographs became website graphics. Clients liked the touch, they'd told her. But she liked the photos and vids mostly as notes, from which she wrote the necessary instructional text.

Kara packed everything into the Subaru and returned her room key. *Past two o'clock. Ready to go.* She opened the map for reassurance. It said nothing. But something surging in her said, "East." The tires squeaked against the parking lot pavement as she pushed hard on the accelerator.

Kara drove east along Interstate 80, eager to leave Winnemucca but anxious about the absence of an understood destination. To the north the dunes were small and featureless against the backdrop of the serrated Black Rock Mountains that loomed behind the Bloody Run Hills. She thought of the lightning snapping and burning in the air above the peaks and remembered the ferocity of coyly dueling with the lightning, wanting it so badly and being frightened by the intensity. *But it was just a dream, wasn't it?* The solitude of the dunes had been comforting. *That was no dream.* Their simplicity had been peaceful counterpoint to warring and whoring with the lightning. *Maybe I liked them because they roamed, too. They're not worried about getting from A to Z. Why am I?*

Rolling now. Cruise control on, over 75 but under 80. The car liked this pace. Windows down, air rushing in and rustling light, loose things in the hatchback. Ronnie Earl and the

Broadcasters on the iPhone, Derek Trucks next, Norah Jones off stage and waiting. The Bollé glacier glasses defending against the glare. Sunscreen on the nose. Running hard and fast due east, the westbound sun behind. She scanned left to right, right to left, left to right, and out to the horizon, warily watching cumulus clouds humping up imperiously. The occasional small brownish bird darted from the grasses along the edge of the highway. Long-tailed birds flew across the highway to land on fence posts. She spurted water from the squeeze bottle onto her face, shoulders, and upper chest and swished it around with a face cloth. She drank often and had to stop along the side of the road to refill the water bottle from a five-gallon jug of water. *I need more water.* At her next stop, she punched up the to-do list and entered "more water containers."

Kara drove in the left-hand lane as much as possible. The relentless assault of big trucks had heavily rutted the right-hand lane. She checked her rear-view mirror often for traffic overtaking her. But the big semis would catch her lost in thought and roar past on the right with air horns blaring, their slipstreams buffeting the car. The number of eighteen-wheelers surprised her. Far more of them populated I-80 than the four-wheelers. She read their names and wondered where they came from, where they were headed, what they were carrying. Pacific Intermountain Express, YRC Freight, UPS, Seward Motor Freight, FedEx, Schneider National, J.B. Hunt, Old Dominion, and Allied ("The Careful Movers") Van Lines. Tandems and triples. She'd catch them on the hills and slip into the right lane on the downhills. Soon, they'd roar by, their powerful diesels augmented by gravity. Stetsons and sunglasses obscured the faces of the men — *Where are the women?* — at the helm of the Kenworths, Peterbilts, Whites, Macks, Volvos, and Navistars. *Should I get a CB radio? Maybe they're all on cells or sats these days.* Kara wondered about the choices that placed them in a cab high above the road, running relentlessly mile after mile. *Running from what? Or running to what? Or did they just like the running?*

After a few hours she tired. *So soon?* She blamed the heat.
Nothing vitalized her. The barren landscape no longer
impressed her. *Nevada's kind of dull.* Her reality narrowed to a
badly maintained interstate running through wave after wave of
dusty shades of brown, tan, and faded yellow. *There's no green.*
It's so lifeless. So utterly lifeless. Hills rose devoid of trees, looking
like legs with varicose veins. Every wrinkle, every indentation
showed. Roads ran like thin scars around and over the hills.
They looked like an elderly woman undressing for the doctor.
No beauty. Just dry, scaly folds of skin dotted with liver spots.
Nothing resembled Seattle, where vegetation rioted under the
endless rain that drizzled down seven months of the year. She
urged the Subaru to go faster. *I want outta here.*

Kara turned off Interstate 80 at Battle Mountain. She didn't
care what the map thought about the choice. She just wanted
off this road. The car carried her down the main drag, a wide
road that paralleled the railroad tracks. She just shook her
head. *Worse than Winnemucca.* She stopped to buy gas, another
water container, more Diet Dr Pepper, a cooler, and some ice.

Lining the street in front of the dingy storefronts were old,
mud- and dust-covered pickups, the kind that always seemed
to hold a half dozen or more Indians, men and women with
long, blackest-of-black hair tied behind their heads and silent,
round-faced children nestled in the jump seats. *I know I ought to*
call them Native Americans but I really don't like doing things I ought to
do. She was hungry. After slipping a loose-fitting T-shirt over
her Speedo, she slipped into one of the bars and sat at the
counter. An elderly waitress, her white hair in a disheveled bun,
took her order for an egg salad sandwich. Video screens lined
the countertop. A tall man, dark and burnished but yellow of
teeth, played video poker under his coffee mug. Several
quarters were scattered around his plate. She absorbed the
faces in the room. Old, lined, weathered, tired faces. *God, a*
whole town of Dorian Grays. Battle Mountain stank of decay. It
was a mining town, and mining was hard, tiring, and
dangerous. She'd seen pictures of mines. *They kill the earth.*

She ate quickly, paid her bill, and walked down the street to a hardware store. She put on her best smile and asked the teenaged boy behind the counter it she could fill her water containers. He told her it'd cost a buck and a half for each gallon container. Her smile vanished. "Water's not cheap here, ma'am," he said. *That's absurd.* But she paid and lugged them to the car.

At the entrance to the main street, she looked left to Interstate 80, conscious of the map resting on her lap. Whim turned her right, back to Battle Mountain, and south on Highway 305. Near an overpass over I-80, she turned into a side road near the post office.

She bought a postcard at a convenience store. She scribbled his address on it and a simple message, *I'm sorry,* and walked to the post office. She paused in front of the mailbox outside and wondered *Should I really send this?* She dropped it in the slot.

Chapter 12:

April 6, late afternoon, Route 305 south of Battle Mountain, Nevada

The highway climbed the flank of a barren hillside. Some overzealous high-school kids had painted the letters "BM" on its slope. She regarded the house-sized letters not as civic pride for Battle Mountain, but rather as a symbol of her disdain. *"Bowel Movement" fits that burg better.*

The Shoshone and Fish Creek ranges bordered the broad Reese River valley that embraced Route 305. The rough, saw-tooth Shoshone summits to the southeast did not seem as angry as the Black Rock Mountains had. Perhaps color made the difference. These mountains wore a supple sheath of soft brown, sometimes tan, sometimes buff yellow. They sat silent under the blue sky, minding their own business without guile or pretensions. Indifferent. *Yes, that's the word.* The only green lay in a narrow stripe down the center of the valley where a small stream meandered.

Kara saw the old Battle Mountain Gold Co. mine near Copper Basin soon after leaving town. There were other mines, Copper King, Copper Queen, the Lucky Strike, and the Irish Rose, but the Battle Mountain mine seemed so *big*. Giant earth-movers had chewed two teeth of Antler Peak to the gum line. Terraces of talus ringed its flanks. The browns, tans, and yellows of the mountain's guts spilled from one terrace to the next. Fingers of dark, reddish, dried-blood brown ran down the talus slopes. *Why do I associate things like this with "manmade" rather than "womanmade"?*

Another mine loomed. She drove nearly 30 miles before she got to it. Western distances seemed small to the eye but were long to drive. Other old, faded signs sprouted by the road: Alta Gold Co., NERCO Minerals Co., Elder Creek Mine, Echo Bay Minerals Co. Kara stopped. She shaded her eyes and looked at the chopped-off, heavily terraced mountains. *What kind of people would do this?*

She fingered the thin gold choker around her neck that'd he given her after the night they'd first made love, that night in the office when they were struggling to beat a deadline and they'd been tired but close and they'd just grabbed each other next to the copier and he only bothered to unzip his pants and drop them and raise her skirt before they fucked each other silly on the carpeted floor. She saw the bleeding abrasions on his knees afterward and kissed them and said she hoped they didn't hurt and he said that it'd been worth it but maybe they'd better find a bed next time and let's get back to work. *Back to work. Always back to work.*

Kara got in the car, engine and thoughts idling. She touched the gold choker again, wondering about the true cost of things both material and spiritual. She drove on, keeping her eyes on the road and avoiding the mountains to the west for a long time.

Kara didn't know where she was going. It bothered her that she didn't feel a rhythm yet. In Seattle he had disrupted her routines. She didn't like him using her corner-of-the-bedroom office because he moved things. She'd insisted that they keep their things separate in the bathroom. He said she was finicky. She replied that she was meticulous. He said that living with her was like living with a boarder, that she wasn't a partner, that she wasn't meshing into his life. *Why do I have to do the meshing?* She wanted things in their place. Order allowed her to function. She'd said that if she couldn't function well, then meshing was impossible.

Kara decided to create mini-destinations, to forget about the ambiguous A to Z and travel from A to B, from B to C, from C to D. She considered the possibilities. *Geographical locations?* She ruled that out. The map might turn her before she reached the place she picked. *Time?* No, she thought that would be too artificial, too regulated. *I'm not a damn stopwatch, for chrissake.* Music. That's it. Playlists on her iPhone. They differed in duration. Each time a playlist ended, she'd stop. Hers weren't endlessly long. It'd be about an hour and a half, maybe two hours, between mini-destinations. She stopped to scroll up a new playlist. She got out of the car, walked around to stretch her legs, eyeballed the scenery, squirted herself with the squeeze bottle, and popped a Diet Dr Pepper from her cooler for the next stretch. She watched for streams to bathe in, but the few she saw were either very small and shallow or still and coated with greenish muck.

The new regimen pleased Kara. Rhythm born of invention. She sat back and absorbed her surroundings, focusing on the outer world and ignoring the inner. Names of places and roads on lonely signs delighted her. Buffalo Valley, Daisy Creek, Antelope Valley, Carico Lake Valley, Iowa Canyon, Hall Creek, Boone Canyon, Ravenswood, Vaughan Ranch. As the mountains moved closer, narrowing the valley, she sensed greater intimacy. Side roads quickly disappeared into little canyons and she wondered where they went to, who lived out there, and what their lives must be like. The Shoshones to the east squeezed the small stream close to the highway. Cattle were scattered among the tall meadow grasses. But they avoided the barren, white ground next to the stream. *Salt. It looks so much like snow.* A playlist ended. She parked near some flowers.

Several clumps of shrubs dressed in spring clothing of long, yellow-green leaves overshadowed small but lovely rose-

colored flowers. Then memory filtered out the beauty to leave
only the gray, rigid branches covered with spines. She touched
one and it drew blood from her thumb. It was the spiny plant
from the dunes. She had discovered greasewood. She would
come to know its name, that it sent roots as deep as 50 feet to
find life-sustaining water. Later, farther east and at higher
elevations, she'd wonder why she didn't see it anymore.

Evening arrived. She hadn't really driven very far, having
started late. Stops had been long. Kara enjoyed wandering
along the side of the road among the flowers. At one stop, she
found bluish-purple flowers that she especially liked. She got
her Canon and photographed them. Later, she photographed
some yellow flowers as well. The images would lay in digital
limbo until she could buy a guide and give names to the
flowers. She fastened the broken Coke bottle rescued from the
dunes to the dashboard with duct tape and dribbled water into
it. She picked some yellow flowers and put them in the bottle.
She drove along with the flowers waving in the moving air.
Their scent was pleasing. She liked carrying a talisman of the
landscape.

Later, she parked next to a deserted farm. She walked for
an hour along a rutted dirt road that she guessed hadn't been
used for decades. It still seemed fresh, though. Probably the
dry climate kept vegetation from reclaiming the road. In the
wet Northwest, such roads vanished overnight.

Stops cost time and expended daylight. She needed a haven
for the night, a real destination, a sleep sanctuary, and she
didn't know where or how to find it. The car sped through the
mountains' lengthening shadows for another hour. She parked
below a stone cabin that sat on a flat-topped hillside beside the
road. She walked up to it. The cabin, roughly the size of her
small living room in Seattle, had no roof, but she didn't think it
would rain. She inspected the cabin's dirt floor in the
deepening twilight. There were no signs of creepy-crawly
things, the bugs that somehow grew to nightmarish size in a
child's dreams. If she placed her sleeping bag in the doorway,

she could see the car. Satisfied, she returned to the hatchback for sleeping bag, foam pad, her go-bag, water bottle, flashlight, and *the damn map*. Deciding to read for a while, she chose the odd book with "monkey wrench" in its title.

She settled into the cabin, laying out the foam pad and sleeping bag. She folded the Speedo and the Quick-Drys and put them where she could quickly find them. She sat in the doorway for a while, holding the map. The desert cooled quickly, and she shivered. Slipping nude into the bag, she wriggled about, trying to get comfortable. She picked up the book. Reading required effort. She had to hold the book up to catch the dimming light coming through the doorway. Her arms tired. When the light faded, she turned on the flashlight but found no place to rest it. She tried balancing it on her shoulder, near the curve of her neck, but it rolled off whenever she turned a page. *I need a decent lantern.* She closed her eyes. The book rested on her chest, covering a breast like a little pup tent. The silence grew deep and insistent. She was accustomed to noise, the clattering of printers while she wrote, the cacophony of engine and road noise as she drove, the rumbling of traffic outside their bedroom window as he snored. He fell asleep after making love. Kara never could. The rumblings in her groin took time to subside. It always irritated her that he left her so quickly. *Men just don't get it.*

In the distance, an engine whined. The sound closed, rising in pitch. A few minutes later something, she couldn't tell what, car or pickup, rushed by. Its headlights fell briefly on the car. *Should I move it out of sight?* The sound vanished. She tried to sleep, but her ears remained too alert for other cars. She heard another rush by. She tried to divert herself by watching the stars. *This isn't working. It isn't like this in the movies.* Sleeping under the stars should be idyllic, poetic, communing with some *better-than-me* being.

She dozed. Another car approached like the others. It slowed; then the sound of downshifting. She scrambled to her hands and knees. Headlights moved into the pullout where the Subaru was parked. Kara rushed into her Speedo and stood in the doorway. The headlights clicked off. A door squeaked. In the starlight she could see a pickup and a dark form moving around her car. Kara knelt and felt the ground for a rock, a stick, anything club like. She heard a zipper, then liquid sloshing onto the ground. The zipper closed, followed by the squeak of a door opening and closing. The pickup's headlights clicked on, and it left, crunching gravel. The sound quickly faded. Kara's breath came in gasps. *This isn't right. This just isn't right.*

The headlights cut through the darkness as the car sped through the night. Kara had been unable to sleep. She'd listened obsessively for stray mechanical sounds in the night. Each time a car passed she watched through the doorway until its lights had disappeared. Kara had given up. Gathering her things, she'd trudged to the car. As she got in, a phone had beeped, buried in a cargo bag. *Damn, it's him.* Her cell phone had been out of range; he'd called the sat phone. Opening the beeping bag, she had touched the phone. The beeping stopped. She'd sat motionless. *It's him. I just know it's him.*

She'd driven away from the stone cabin, searching for seclusion. A few times she saw something perhaps suitable in the roadside darkness. But nothing seemed *right*. She kept going. A sign warned, "Road Under Construction." The road widened to hard-packed gravel. Fluorescent orange surveyor's tape hung from wooden stakes. Workers had left construction vehicles, big ones, big yellow Caterpillar bulldozers and multi-tired Bucyrus -Erie earthmovers and graders, parked in formation in staging areas.

House-sized piles of gravel sat by the road. She slowed the car, switched off her headlights, and crept into the construction yard. It held a few trailers, pickups, big watering trucks, a concrete mixing plant, a line of Porta-Potties, more big bulldozers and earthmovers. She threaded the car through the piles of gravel to a spot that couldn't be seen from the road and parked. The sat phone beeped again, insistently. She did not punch the talk button. It stopped beeping. A moment later, it beeped again five times. She did not answer.

Kara felt jittery. She wished she knew those biofeedback tricks people used to relax. She rubbed her face. *God, I'm so tired.* She rested her forehead against the wheel. Tears welled in her eyes. Conspiracy was arrayed against her and she didn't know why and she wished she were back in Seattle and that this would all go away. The beams from a pickup's headlights moved into the yard. A spotlight swept the grounds. She froze. The truck stopped, and a door opened. After 10 minutes, someone got back into the truck. It rumbled back to the highway. She counted the gear shifts — one, two, three — as the truck accelerated. Kara eased the car through the gravel piles to the road. She fled south, her foot pressed hard on the gas. *Even Joseph and Mary didn't have this much damn trouble finding a room at the inn.*

She came to an intersection. The sat phone beeped. *Make it stop*, she prayed. She turned left into the darkened town of Austin, lit dimly by a few, scattered streetlights. *This is so dismal.* Starlight shone on doublewide trailers, set into excavations hacked into a narrow chisel-cut canyon. The highway climbed through a series of switchbacks. A sign said, "Six Percent Grade." She did not know what highway she was on and *I don't give a shit right now, either.* Keeping her eyes open on the tight curves was hard. She was so tired. The phone beeped again. She gritted her teeth until it stopped.

The car passed through a shallow saddle and reached Scott Summit. She drove into the entrance to Bob Scott Campground. Cars, trucks with campers, and RVs were parked in a few campsites. She chose a site with no neighbors. Parking close to the picnic table, she opened the door. She unfolded the map, and by the dim glow of the interior light it told her she had covered only 88 miles since Battle Mountain. *So few miles and I'm so tired.*

She turned off the light and got out, leaving the car door open. She crawled into the sleeping bag on the table without undressing. The phone beeped and she silently screamed *stop stop please stop let me go let me go.* She got out of the sleeping bag, reached inside the car and flicked the phone off standby. Back in her down cocoon, she fell asleep quickly, lying on her side facing the car, embraced by its open door.

Chapter 13:

April 7, after midnight, Greasewood Draw, west of Green River, Utah

Noah couldn't sleep. He guessed it was because of the wine. He was a beer guy, and not much of that, either. But Annie and Doc had shown up unannounced at his trailer and shanghaied him to dinner, ostensibly for an easy-going friends' night out — but it had quickly turned into a loving intervention. He hadn't liked the philosophical inquisition regarding means, ends, and morality Doc had put him through — after Doc had slipped him plenty of Chardonnay. Annie had, good-naturedly he hoped, chided Noah about the amount of time he was spending in an empty bed these days. Later, Doc had driven Noah back to his trailer with Annie trailing to retrieve Doc — but only after they had extracted a promise from Noah that he'd watch his back more carefully.

He loved Doc and Annie, but he still chafed at their unwanted counsel. He could handle what he was doing. He just had to figure out how those assholes knew he was coming. He had an idea, but he needed more evidence. Maybe that's why he couldn't sleep. Noah rolled off the bed and slipped into his canvas shorts. He flicked on the light in his small kitchen and sat in the breakfast nook. He reached for a notebook and pen on a shelf.

He divided several pages into two columns and wrote "Pros" in one and "Cons" in the other. He wrote steadily for an hour, then put down the pen. He got up, opened the door, and walked outside in the moonlight. Utah was quiet. His mind wasn't. Something kept itching at him and had for days. Maybe it was just Annie and Doc, getting on his case. He went back to bed and eventually slept, albeit fitfully.

Chapter 14:

April 7, midmorning, Bob Scott Campground, east of Austin, Nevada

Kara woke to a clear, indigo sky. Sitting up, she greeted the sun. Cold air surprised her, and she burrowed deeper into her sleeping bag. The open door of the brown hatchback mouthed good morning. Small trees circled the gravelly campsite. *More needle trees.* Some had odd-looking, leathery, green branches. She guessed they were cedars. *Or are they junipers?* These looked like trees from home, only shorter, sparser, far less opulent than the evergreens on the Peninsula. The campsite boasted nothing but scattered trees — no grass, no endless ground cover of salal, no huckleberry, no Oregon grape, no lichens or mosses or fungi. *And no banana slugs, either. Home, but not home.* She deserted the sleeping bag, donned her new sweater and Levis, and sat in the car. She punched up her iPhone's to-do list and jotted "take pix of needle trees" and "buy a decent macro lens."

She listened. Just nature sounds, not human ones. Wind rustled through nearby trees. Large, black birds called raucously as they skittered among the trees. She wondered if they were crows. They weren't; they were ravens. Much later, she would figure that out when she saw crow-like birds soaring and realize she had never seen crows soar in Seattle. By then, she would have studied a bird book, and she would notice in the ornithological write-ups that ravens soar and crows don't. That would delight her. Observe, record, know. *Input begets analysis begets identification.* There would be order in this, and it would bring her satisfaction. But not today.

She brewed tea and munched on a PowerBar. After tossing her bedroom into the hatchback, Kara sat in the car, eyes closed, head against the seat rest, hands folded in her lap. She listened again, recording, hearing everything and nothing. The wind had picked up, gusting through the trees, and she could hear pinpoints of sound as the needles clattered against each other. She heard more bird noises, too. Different from the crows, though. She heard the Dopplerian cries of cars and trucks approaching, passing, and receding on the highway. There seemed to be many more big trucks. *Why?* She didn't yet know about the rest of the massive mines peeling Nevada's skin for subcutaneous copper and other minerals. She heard voices, warped by the wind, and she couldn't make out the words. Other campsites, other people, other lives. Tears welled in her eyes. She refused to blame loneliness.

Kara remembered people she had seen since Portland. Sheepskin Hat. The old Indian in Winnemucca. The smiling young woman who'd given her the Velcro. She wondered why they had been chosen. *What made them memorable? What touched me?* She peeked into her memories. More people lived there than she realized. A heavyset man, not fat, wearing dirty jeans, boots and a faded cowboy hat. A big gray beard. He had climbed into a bright yellow Ford pickup parked by the side of the road south of Paisley. A rusted hulk of a horse trailer had been hitched to the Ford. *Had he looked at me?* She didn't think so. A waitress in Winnemucca. She looked Spanish, dark hair, dark eyes. Kara had covertly looked at her figure, envying its fullness. Kara had liked the huskiness of the woman's voice, the ease of her smile, the second cup of tea brought without bidding. In Battle Mountain, Kara had seen a woman, tall, wearing a narrowly cut denim jacket and Stetson, getting out of her car and walking toward a nearby house. Kara liked that woman's resolute, purposeful walk. And then the Subaru had carried Kara away.

What had made them fragments of the landscape her wide-angle eyes had recorded? *Are they lessons?* Was it color? The yellow of the truck? Was it sound? The woman's voice? Was it a sense of elegance? The tall woman's appearance and walk? Kara succumbed to a feeling of having yet not having. *Is it desire? No, but there's a sense of fulfillment about them that I don't understand.* She hated not knowing more than anything else. *People are puzzles I rarely solve.* She had never solved Dad the Engineer. She ground the thoughts away. She did not want to deal with who she was and who she wasn't. Not today. Not tomorrow. *Maybe next week.*

She walked around the campground. Eclectic elements of humanity occupied campsites, a camper here, a van there, an old VW bug parked next to a Day-Glo orange tent. The van had been gently rocking. *Getting laid in the middle of nowhere. Love? Lust? Just another booty call?* The walk calmed her, and she went back to her car. The wind carried fragments of other lives in other campsites to her as she rummaged about the car, sorting for order's sake the minutiae of her life piled haphazardly behind the front seats.

She sat on the picnic table, wishing for isolation so she could peel off her clothes. She liked baking in the sun. She pulled the straps of the Speedo off her shoulders and raised her face to the fully risen sun. She was thirsty and hungry. She ate another PowerBar and made more tea. Sipping it while walking around the car, she traced a finger through the Nevadan grime coating it. *I should wash it.* But that would cost water. She retrieved her Mac, set it on the picnic table, attached her sat phone, then booted it up. She waited, trying not to think about what she was doing. She checked her e-mail. Several messages. One from him. She sighed. *Consequences.*

There's always consequences. She clicked on the message, noticing it had no subject line.

> To: kara@WebWideWorks.com
> From: TopDog@WebWideWorks.com
> Subject:
> Cc:
> Bcc:
> Attachments:
> _____
>
> Decide.

That goddamned son of a bitch. The lone word burned. *Decide.* She shut down the laptop and closed it, resting her hands atop the Mac for several minutes. With eyes closed, she listened again to the commingling of natural and unnatural noises around her. The world of lonely people, the world of nature alone. The sounds of their intersection clattered around the campsite. She put the Mac back into the car. *Decide?*

She sat on the picnic table, head cradled in her hands. *I guess I have, haven't I?* So much to say, so little to say. Estrangement had become escape. She put the sat phone on standby, but she knew it would not beep again. She got into the car and drove slowly down the rutted gravel road to Highway 50. The car rattled over a cattle guard and stopped.

Time for a map check, she decided. To the right, west, lay Austin, minutes away. There would be a diner. But Austin had been depressingly gray. To the left, east. Kara added the black numbers along the bright red line that depicted Highway 50. Seventy miles to Eureka. Kara smiled. *Numbers never lied.* They sat there, smug in their certainty, resplendent in their precise representation of reality. An hour and a half. She'd eat there. But she didn't move. Had she decided? No advice came from the map. *I will not cry.* The sadness she knew had always been there in Seattle coursed through her. *It could have worked. It should have worked. I could have handled it.* New Age relationship repair gimmicks raced through her mind. *I could go back. I could cut back on days with him. I could work somewhere else. We could talk.*

A horn honked, startling her. The formerly rocking van filled her rearview mirror. An arm extended out the window, waving impertinently. She turned left — east — and drove the car hastily onto Highway 50, passing a weathered wooden sign that said, "Leaving Toiyabe National Forest — Land of Many Uses."

Kara drove prudently, not too fast, not too slow. The slipstream whipping her hair against her neck felt good. The sun eased the morning chill. She worried about where she'd stay that night, wanting guarantees of privacy, silence, and security.   She thought like an animal, expecting threat, assessing threat. Landscapes came and went. The car climbed through a succession of tiny meadows. A small stream played tag with Highway 50, moving away, then coming closer. Beside a small, rundown log home stood a ramshackle corral. Horses bent low to browse on tender early spring grasses. *Is this where people came first a hundred years ago? To high ground? To where there's water? Did they bring cattle? Were the winters harsh?* She imagined the loneliness of a life filled with work, with no contraception, trapped in a tiny house in a bleak, cold, white landscape and choked by the claustrophobia created by crying children. Was the pain of living on 160 God-battered acres worth the supposed independence homesteading grants provided? These people must have been tough. *Were they loving? Or were they always too tired, trying to gather life's makings by winter's deadline?* The stream cut into a hard land. *Water*, she decided. Water is the magnet, the lure. *Water rules.*

In her little cocoon, she digested the 70 miles to Eureka. She passed Round Mountain, Hickison Summit (elevation 6,564), Stoneberger Creek, then cruised onto the broad expanse of Bean Flat. Lone Mountain beckoned to her. Many miles separated the notations of geographers. The dry, barren landscape mesmerized her. The vastness, the emptiness, touched her. No, it wasn't the emptiness; rather, it was a longing she had never known before. *Where there is nothing do you long for something?*

Half way across Bean Flat, Kara needed a break. Her foot lifted from the accelerator, and the car drifted to a stop on a hard-packed dirt shoulder tinged with white. The highway sliced through a dusty white oval seemingly devoid of life. Kara turned off the engine and felt the wind-whispering silence of the Basin and Range. She stepped out and walked along the roadside. Katabatic winds flowed down from the Simpson Park Mountains, sweeping across the playa and rustling the branches of a succession of sagebrush, then greasewood, then saltbush, each lusting more for salt than the previous. To the north, guarding Grubbs Canyon and Flat Canyon, a small dune field crouched at the edge of this horizontal world where it gently turned up an alluvial fan to the mountains. She had not yet refined her senses as she would be taught later. She could not hear the diminutive kangaroo mice, no longer than her forefinger, burrowing in small hummocks, darting across the open from one clump of rabbitbrush to another. The rattlesnake would never be heard until it struck. Even the squeal of the mouse as the snake coiled and squeezed the life out of it would be lost in the wind. She could not hear the seeds of grasses and sagebrush, borne by wind miles from their birthing place, striking the ground, some to take root, others to wither. Lost in the wind were the sounds of scarlet gilias, globemallows, paintbrush, golden asters, blanket flowers, and lupines unfurling under the spring sun. Nor would she easily see them without a lush green backdrop of grasses the arid desert forbade.

She kicked a stone, unmindful of life where human senses suggested life was not possible. She kicked it again into a small shadscale. She could not hear the cattle, far from the road and away from the playa, scattered here and there, foraging on native grasses as well as exotic ones like cheatgrass scattered for their presumed benefit. She could not hear them, each grazing over a long workday, destroying 100 acres of native grassland in a month. Month after month after month.

A few strides away, a longnose leopard lizard, startled by the noise Kara made, scampered for shelter. In a saltbush stand a wolf spider spun webs to snare flies buzzing unnoticed around her. Miles away, a pronghorn, feeding on forbs and sage, lifted her head. It fled north, leaping 20 feet in each bound, running to safety as fast as Kara drove her car. A bird, its wings held in a V, glided over the road near a stand of sage. Kara caught sight of it, recording detail. Sharp, hooked beak. Larger than the birds around her Seattle feeder. A white rump. Slim but long-bodied. Gray above, white underneath with reddish spots. The bird never reached more than a few dozen feet above the ground. It flapped its wings intermittently; it tilted sharply as it glided, its head cocked to one side. The northern harrier could hear what she could not — the cacophony of life in the desert. It *listened* for its prey; it did not look for it.

She remembered a sky laden with bald eagles as she stood on the bow of a ferry plying the Inland Passage off Calvert Island in British Columbia. Her arm was around his waist. The eagles careened through the air, *kree, kree, kree-ing*. She envied them. *Eagles mate for life*.

He had turned to her and said, "Eagles are scavengers, you know."

She'd yanked her arm away and walked to the other side of the bow. She'd wondered if eagles did it in the air. *I wish I could make love in the air*, she had thought then — and wished now.

The harrier moved down the line of sage until it vanished. She picked up the stone she'd been kicking. She looked at it, gray, vesicular, and bland, as many volcanics are, and threw it hard away from the road. It startled the leopard lizard in its new-found sanctuary, a flat slab of Silurian shale lithified from grains of sand that water had carried away from Lone Mountain millions of years ago. The lizard scampered away. Kara never saw it die when the talons of an unseen hawk swooped from the sky and struck it.

She drove east. Near Three Bars Road, at the rim of a playa, sat an old, boarded-up house with no glass in the windows. The roof sagged. Nearby, a six-inch pipe stuck out of the ground. Water spewed from its spigot over the hard, brown dirt. Evaporation kept the small puddle from becoming a pond. She thought of lives busted, water wasted.

In the 70 miles, only two vehicles shared the highway. Halfway, a westbound school bus passed. Only four, maybe five children were scattered among its seats. Later, a brown Jeep with several dents on the driver's side passed her. It appeared in the rear view mirror long before it sped past her. The woman behind the wheel lifted her hand slightly from the steering wheel. Kara waved too late. The Jeep had passed. She'd seen creases around the woman's eyes, a glimpse of a hard life but a good life. Had the woman descended from the generations past who built the cabins deteriorating in the small meadows near the passes?

She wished someone were with her, his arm resting on the seat back, his hand massaging her neck as she drove. He used to do that, in the beginning, when they'd take long drives through the Cascades to hike or camp or ski. She missed the gentle, idle kindness. Then they'd gotten busy, and he'd brought his laptop on trips. He'd work as she drove, asking questions, requiring answers. She liked to drive and hated to be distracted from that pleasure. She missed the beginning, when romance was a focus and not a chore.

The car alternately climbed gentle grades up alluvial fans to minor passes and down similar grades to flat playas. Scruffy, nondescript vegetation covered most of each playa save for a small, bare mudflat at the center. They looked like misshapen bulls-eyes, brown and anonymous in the center and encircled with bathtub-like rings. *More salt*, she thought. *Evaporites.*

Large, fenced plots of lands bordered the highway. Each had a picnic area with corrugated roofs over tables scoured by a relentless wind. Tall, brown signs proclaimed their function:

"US Department of Agriculture, Bureau of Land Management, Woods Crested Wheatgrass Seeding, 1300 acres, seeded 1955." Then another similar sign with similar wording: "Lincoln Crested Wheatgrass Seeding, 3400 acres, seeded 1955." Later, she saw "Pony Express Wheatgrass Seeding" and "Stoneberger Crested Wheatgrass Seeding."

Much later she would think of the seedings as biological deserts. She would learn about overgrazing and the political skirmishes fought in Congress over the ranchers' "rights" to graze cattle on federal land. She would learn the seedings displaced natural habitat and sustained only cattle. The pronghorns — she adored those ungulates she'd seen in the high plains of Oregon — roamed elsewhere, seeking a natural mix of grasses, forbs, and shrubs on which to survive. When she would come to learn about monoculture, she would remember this place, understanding why she'd seen sage sparrows, Brewer's sparrows, and sage thrashers flit through plains of sagebrush, but not here. She'd know why the bottoms of these Nevadan playas knew few sage grouse.

A dirt side road curled past a playa onto higher ground. A crude sign — "alfalfa for sale" — was nailed to a post topped by an aluminum mailbox. *A long drive for hay.* Neighbors must cling together out here. Drives to church, to school, to the market for milk were commitments, not idle choices. Large chunks of a hot working day spent in a pickup pursued that which made life possible. A convenience store was a block from their apartment. He complained when he had to go to the store. He didn't have the time, he'd say. She went instead.

The car growled up another long grade to another unnamed summit. She stopped in a pullout next to a lone picnic table. She got the Mac, stepped out of the car, and set the laptop down on the table. Opening a new file, she keyboarded the first of many notes about her journey and what she had seen. Later, she would make the first of many notes about what she had felt. But that would come much later.

In Eureka, she stopped at the Nevada State Bank. She used

her Amex to get a cash advance and went next door to Raine's Market to roam the aisles. She needed the proximity of human beings, if not actual human contact. She found a straw cowboy hat with a floral headband. *I like it.* The hat sat well on her head. A mirror told her that pushing the hat slightly forward, its brim hung low and shading her eyes, made her look ... *hardened. Like Sheepskin Hat's girlfriend.* She put it back. No room in the hatchback. Choices had to be made. She bought a few tank tops and a pair of gray sweatpants. At the last minute, she bought topographic maps, all of land through which Highway 50 passed. A teenager strode to the register carrying silver nylon biking shorts and a neon-colored tank top. Kara's notions of cowboys and cowgirls changed a little.

She bought cheese and bagels and more ice for the cooler and more Diet Dr Pepper. No one paid any undue attention to her. People went about their lives, either respectful of or oblivious to her presence. She wondered which.

The car carried her away from Eureka, back into the rhythm of basin and range and the continual recording of detail. The long grade up Pinto Summit (elevation 7,376 feet) was followed by the curving descent down the alluvial fans on the northern end of Little Smoky Valley. Then a straight shot across the valley, past the intersection of Highway 892 and its grubby huddle of mobile homes, and up a gentle rise to Pancake Summit (elevation 6,157 feet). The hatchback rolled effortlessly downhill, down more alluvial fans, onto the flat of Newark Valley, broad and featureless save for the occasional rusty tank where dust devils whipped at cattle gathered for water and eroded the broken sod. She realized the fodder for the dust devils was linked to the erosion. The car snaked up to Little Antelope Summit (elevation 7,433 feet). Life returned. The higher the car carried her, the more green she could see. Trees appeared, short and scrubby, near the tops of the alluvial fans, then, higher on the mountainside, they gained stature. The air smelled fresher. Sweeping down to the next playa, the car carried her across Jakey Valley, a dull brown flat spotted with the leathery green of greasewood and saltbush. A tattered orange windsock fluttered near a dirt airstrip. Next to it rested bales of hay, piled as high as a house. Cattle milled nearby. The immenseness of western distances touched her again. *They have to fly in the hay.* Images of flight, of her in the air, floating, drifting, soaring, danced in her mind. *Love must be flying. Love must be weightlessness, a floating shoal of selfless souls.*

The car sped over Robinson Summit and down onto Copper Flat. The setting sun behind cast the shadow of the car on the highway ahead. *All I do is chase my shadow. No, all I did was chase his shadow.* She would never brand her inner monologue as introspection. Dad the Engineer had not taught that. Situational analysis, he had counseled, bested all problems.

The car carried Kara past Keystone Junction, and through the rare curves on Highway 50 between Garnet Hill and Saxton Mountain. She did not wish to *feel* any more today. No thoughts of the past or fears of the present. No emotional contention. *Don't fuck with me. No damn map today, either.* She wanted to drive and enjoy it. Let conflict confront her tomorrow.

The car flashed past a sign: "Ely Grazing District." Sheep, freshly shorn of winter's coat, grazed in a field. *They look like poodles.* Nearby the long, black arm and counterweight of a pump toiled ceaselessly, drawing water from hundreds of feet below where it hid in fault-shattered Permian shales and sandstones and filling a black metal tank. *Everyone uses the water. They waste none out here. Or least they try not to.* She thought of the Columbia River, water as prisoner, held until it runs through turbines and creates electricity. *We use the land. We use the water. We all just use, use, use.*

The road shed the last of its curves, leaving a straight shot to Ely. Ahead, something large loomed. Even miles away, the brownish wart on the landscape, a tailings mound, looked hundreds of feet high and a mile wide. She stopped on the shoulder. Beside the road towered several huge, yellow Bucyrus-Erie ore trucks with tires taller than she was. The mine dwarfed both the trucks and a small hill in the foreground. The scale of everything in the West amazed her.

Such open spaces. Such large things. Such great distances. Such people, like Sheepskin Hat, so mythically larger than their real lives.

She could not see the bottom of the pit. A bluff of talus piles rested against its walls. She fished through the topo maps and unfolded the quad for Ely. The mine was clearly marked by the tightly packed 50-foot contours. The roughly circular contours told her the mine was several hundred feet deep.

A sign pointed to Ruth. She turned onto the road, curious. The car rounded a turn and fell behind a shiny, black pickup with big, knobby tires and the faint outline of a gun rack in the tinted rear window. They neared the talus bluff, heavily eroded into ragged scars and gulches. Some older scars sprouted vegetation. She wondered what kind of bushes and trees could find life in such an ugly place. The pickup headed toward a tall, red building shaped like a silo and topped by a gantry. The car closed on the pickup. Despite the dust raised by its big tires, its black paint gleamed. She couldn't see the driver. An arm lounged out the window, a hand resting on the side mirror. The heavily muscled forearm was darkly tanned with a black, indecipherable tattoo. She chuckled. *Popeye the Sailor Man.*

A large sign warned: "No Unauthorized Personnel Allowed on Mine Property Without Written Permission from Security Director. Report To Mill Office, Open 6 a.m.-3 p.m. Monday To Friday." The black pickup drove to the silo. *Must be the mill office.* When she parked in front of the office, the driver of the pickup was gone, its interior a mystery shrouded behind smoked glass windows. Leaving the car, she found a man in a security uniform standing near the office door. Security Man approached her. His eyes hid behind mirrored sunglasses. She looked back at him through her Bollés.

"Can I help you, lady?" Security Man said, his clipboard held at his side.

"I'm lost."

"Where you tryin' to get to?"

She thought fast. "Ruth."

"You passed it. Go back down, head west. You'll see a road

on the left." His gruff, curt voice grated on her.

Kara nodded. "Thanks. Say, what is this place?"

"Robinson Mine, lady."

His eyes flicked down briefly. *He's checking me out. What a prick.*

"You mine gold here?"

"Copper."

"No gold?" She smiled.

"We mine mostly copper here, lady. It's a metals company. There's probably a little gold."

Kara nodded, looking at the silo building. "Could I look around?"

Security Man took off his glasses and squinted at her. "Why?"

"Just curious."

He brushed dust from his creased chino trousers. "It's a dangerous place, lady. Lots of trucks movin' on the roads. Really big trucks. Ore movers. Don't want any accidents here. You don't want to fuck with those trucks."

"Oh."

He smiled, a thin, flat grin that wasn't really a smile.

"I suppose you could drive around the mine. That road goes up to Route 6. Take a right at the summit to get to Ruth. Just drive really close to the right side of the road when you go around blind curves."

He put his mirrored shades on again.

"Um, thanks. Appreciate it."

"Be careful, lady."

As she got back into the car, she glanced at him. He'd taken a radio from his holster and was talking into it, looking at her. He watched her while she backed up and turned around. She could see him in the rearview mirror, still watching her, talking into his radio, as she drove back out onto the dirt road.

The car chugged higher up the road toward Murry Summit. She passed a mill complex. Chain link fences guarded a parking lot containing what looked like a significant percentage of the state's pickups. Men gathered at turned-down tailgates.

Coleman coolers of all sizes and descriptions lay open. There were big men. Little men. Some with T-shirts, some shirtless. All wore dirty, dusty jeans and scuffed work boots. A few pointed as she drove by. A faint hoot slipped through her open window. *Men. Jesus.*

The road approached a summit close to the edge of the mine. She stopped, heeding the warning to keep the car on the far right of the shoulder. She walked across the road and looked down into the mine. At the bottom were hundreds of piles of rent earth dumped from trucks. She saw a pattern. *They make up a quilt.* The mounds of blasted rock were red, tan, brown, yellow, and all their combinations. *No green. No green anywhere.* She looked to the horizon. Winter snow clung to the peaks of the Egan Range to the north. *Two different worlds.* Her eyes roamed the many terraces that descended to the bottom of the pit. The mine resembled an upside-down wedding cake, stair casing down instead of up. Deep in the pit's heart was rock stained red, dusky, purplish. *Like so much dried blood after a kill.*

She glanced down the road. A few hundred yards away the shiny black pickup with the big knobby tires was parked. Popeye's arm rested out of the window, dangling listlessly against the side of the door. *Is he watching me? What for?* She looked back at the mine. Words darted through her mind unbidden. *Raw. Jagged. Bleeding. Wounded. Scarred.* She supposed her reaction to a large mine was typical. *Mines aren't pretty.*

The pickup crept closer. She could not see Popeye's arm. The smoky window was up. The pickup's engine idled low, gruff, and ominous. *Must be a 460. Big engine.* She got her camera and snapped pictures of the mine.

The black pickup growled into raucous life. The big, fat tires clawed the dirt, throwing gravel as the truck slewed toward her. She ran to the car and slid behind the wheel. She'd left her engine running. She floored the accelerator, the all-wheel-drive firmly grasping the road. The car darted in front of the pickup. Its shiny chrome grille filled the rearview mirror. The pickup bumped the car. *What the fuck?* The Subaru skidded. The pickup bumped it again. *Whywhywhywhy?* She drifted the car through turns, glad her brothers had taught her how to control her car. She looked in the rearview mirror again. The pickup had fallen back, but its big knobby tires clawed relentlessly after the Subaru.

Ahead was a stop sign and the pavement of Route 6 beyond it. She glanced in her mirror. No pickup. A guttural roar flooded through her window. *It's beside me!* The outside mirror reflected the truck swinging out to overtake her. She braked hard. The truck shot forward past the car. She stuck the Subaru on its bumper. *Let's see how you like it, asshole.* Popeye, riding on those tall off-road tires and a high-rise suspension, would be unable to see her in his rearview mirror. She slammed the gear lever into second and floored it, flashing by the driver's side of the truck as it slowed for the stop sign. She held her breath, praying that Route 6 contained as little traffic as the Loneliest Road in America. The Subaru shot across the road, tires squealing as she turned left. She looked back. The pickup had stopped. She pulled onto the shoulder and watched the truck in her rearview mirror. The smoked window descended. Popeye's forearm appeared, then rose straight up. All the fingers but the middle one curled into a fist.

Kara stepped out and stood next to the car, hands on her hips. Popeye's arm disappeared, and the smoky window rose. She raised her arm and gave him the finger. *You bastard.*

She darted into the car and drove downhill in the shadow of Ward Mountain into Ely. Twenty minutes passed before she stopped shaking.

She parked beside a police car at a Pizza Hut. An officer in the car was removing that flat-brimmed hat state troopers everywhere seemed to wear. She waved to get his attention. He rolled down his window.

She approached the police car. "Officer?"

"Sheriff. Sheriff Lamson."

"Sheriff, I want to report a hit-and-run. Some jerk just tried to run me off the road and hit my car trying to do it."

He nodded, his expression unchanging. He stepped out, reaching back in his car to retrieve his hat. He spent more time than necessary, she thought, putting it on. He stepped past her to the rear of the Subaru. He raised a boot-shod foot and rested it on the bumper. He was taller than she.

"So what happened, miss?"

She told him. His face hardened at the mention of a camera.

"You a reporter, lady?"

The change from "miss" to "lady" did not escape her.

"What's that got to do with it? That jerk tried to hurt me."

"They don't like reporters up at the mine. Now, you a reporter?"

Kara snapped at him. "No, for chrissakes. I'm not a reporter."

The sheriff sighed heavily and took his foot off the bumper.

"Then what were you doing taking pictures?"

"Why the hell do you need to know that? You going to do anything about this or not?"

"Lady, there's been problems at the mine. People sabotaging stuff."

"Look, all I know is that this jerk tried to run me off the road."

"You give him reason?"

"No, god damn it, I didn't."

The sheriff pointed at her license plate. "You're not from around here."

"So what?"

"So, people could be suspicious about what you might be doing."

"Sheriff, a guy tried to run me off a public road with his truck. A public road. What I was doing on it is no one's business but my own."

The sheriff walked back to his police car, slipped into the driver's seat, and picked up the mike on his radio. He spoke softly. Kara could not hear what he said. A static-filled voice replied. Kara leaned toward the open door. He stopped talking and looked at her. "Step back, lady."

Kara leaned against her car as the sheriff spoke into the radio for a while.

He hung up the mike and turned to her. "Anyone else see this, lady?"

"How would I know? I was trying to stay the hell out of that asshole's way."

"Profanity doesn't help your case, lady. Now, security at the mine has no record of anyone working up there with that truck's description, they said."

Kara fumed. "How big is Ely?"

"'Scuse me?"

"How many people live here?" she asked again.

"About 4,000. Why?"

"'Cause I can't believe the sheriff of a place this small doesn't know every damn pickup in town."

The sheriff glared at her. "Lady, I suggest you forget this little incident. Your car's undamaged. If you want to file a complaint, I'll investigate. 'Course, you'll have to come down to the station and make a statement. If there's a trial, you'll have to return to testify. And it'll just be your word against his. Whoever he is," the sheriff added hastily.

Kara glared at him. "Forget it. Just forget it."

She stomped into Pizza Hut, bought a small cheese pizza, and carried it back to her car. The sheriff was still there, talking on the radio. She drove away, the Subaru's tires squealing briefly, and headed south on Highway 50.

The sheriff's car followed at a discreet distance. Several miles out of town, near Gallagher's Canyon, it turned around and headed back toward Ely. *That son of a bitch knew who it was. I know he did.*

Kara fled east out of Ely into deepening twilight, her peace of mind lost — *hell, it was stolen.* She was tired, nervous, and dirty. After several miles at hectic speed, she saw a sign near a dirt road curving around Comins Lake: "Private Property

Open to the Public." She silently thanked the El Tejon Land and Livestock Company and drove in warily past a few pickups. Two men in waders fished in the western end of the pond. She drove farther until she heard a low-pitched, thumping sound. A diesel engine. A pump. It was transferring water from the pond into an irrigation ditch. She parked in an out-of-sight spot. She ached everywhere. The pizza atop the cooler smelled warm and inviting. It disappeared quickly.

She got out of the car, taking her toilet kit and a towel. She walked to the irrigation pipe and looked around. No people, no vehicles were in sight. She undressed and stepped into the water, gasping at its initial cold kiss. She washed her hair. She even took time to shave her legs and armpits. Dry, clean, and smooth, she fished her black Lycra tights out of the clothes bag and slipped into them. She tossed her new sweatshirt onto the hood.

A deer appeared, maybe 50 yards away. She sat on a boulder and watched it browse through the grasses, occasionally lifting its head and looking at her. Overhead, twilight deepened, shadowing the land. Cirrus, streaked with red and pink, drifted in a violet sky. A ghostly silver tinged the cirrus. She liked the softness of sunset. *I don't see many sunsets in Seattle.* Her hair was finally dry. She blew a kiss to the deer when it bounded away.

She stood beside the car, holding the sweatshirt, watching the sky. The subtle colors granted the cirrus by the setting sun were soon overwhelmed by the melancholic silver from the fully risen moon. What had been so softly brilliant dripped with drab sadness. Indigo night had begun swallowing the sleek, satin cirrus. *Even the sky has a food chain.*

The car's headlights sliced into the deepening night that cloaked the dry bones of Willow Creek flats. Kara slipped into a zone, somewhere between fatigue and sleep, in which she felt she could drive forever. She scrolled to Brahms's German Requiem on her iPhone, and its soul-touching initial notes swept over her, quieting yet complicating her melancholy. The warm night seeped through the open windows. She felt sticky under the sweatshirt. But she didn't want to stop and change into a T-shirt. Slowing the car, she took her hands off the wheel and quickly yanked the sweatshirt over her head, then resumed speed. The night air curled over her chest. There was something about driving a long ways, something about the softness of the not-yet darkness, something about the absence of constant recording and observing, something about lyrical and lonely but life-affirming music that affected her. The faded yellow passing lane flickered past in the car's headlights. She tucked the map into her waistband. *I'm drifting. I'm drifting to nothing. I'm sinking into something. I don't want to go there. Not now.*

She stopped the car on the shoulder. Booting the Mac, she opened the file named "specifications, map." She keyboarded what had happened. Analysis to the rescue. Again.

At Taylor Canyon, Highway 50 rose into the Schell Creek Range. She stopped at Connor Pass and walked to the middle of the road, feet and chest bare. Moon glow fell on a dirt road on the south side of the highway. She drove up it to an isolated clearing. To the west, the lights of Ely glowed in the sky. Her anger had dulled to irritation. To the east, darker spires rose into the less-dark night. Windy Peak, Bald Mountain, Baker Peak, Pyramid Mountain, and Mount Washington, the tops of the last great range hurled up by orogeny from surrounding basins, hovered over her, dark outposts on the horizon.

The night was cool, so she slept in her sweats in her sleeping bag, insulated from the rough ground by her foam pad. Around two o'clock, a distant mourning woke her. Half asleep, dreaming, she listened. The wind carried the cry of a coyote searching for something. Its solo rose amid a chorus of crickets, and lulled her back to sleep.

Chapter 15:

April 8, 5,000 feet AGL, en route to Green River Municipal Airport from Kanab, Utah

Noah was pissed. He firewalled the throttles of his Cessna Skymaster down Runway 19 at Kanab Municipal Airport, wing lights stabbing into the darkness. He eased the stick back, lifted the plane just off the tarmac, and let the airspeed build. Then he yanked back *hard* on the stick, and the Skymaster shot into the black night at max climb. He held it there until he reached his IFR altitude and turned to a heading that would take him home to Green River Muni.

Two lawyers had hired him to fly them to Kanab for meetings. They said they'd be done by 5. He'd been looking forward to the flight back. The low sun would have electrified the Grand Staircase and Kodachrome Basin. The late-afternoon sun would lend a golden glow to the spring snow atop Boulder Mountain. He lived for such rare moments of clarity and beauty.

But the assholes had said the meetings were running long, maybe 5:30, then 6, then 7. He'd sat waiting in the airport lounge, fuming. Then they called him and said they were staying the night and could he pick them up the next afternoon and he grudgingly said he would and he'd stalked out to his plane and invented new profanities as he preflighted the Skymaster. He'd bill the bastards for two flights and then some.

But the evening air above Utah was uncommonly calm, and the lack of customary turbulence soothed him. He watched the lights of Canyonville, Henrieville, Escalante, then Boulder slowly pass beneath him. To the northeast, Hanksville glowed slightly. To the northwest, lightning winked. Probably a storm over the Wah Wah Mountains, maybe the Confusion Range, he guessed. Too far away to trouble his flight tonight.

But ... that lightning. It bothered him. He kept having that dream. A storm, a face he could not make out, screaming. He'd asked Doc about it, and all Doc said was "Just listen to it. It doesn't have to make sense." That, of course, forced Noah to accuse his longtime friend of being "more irritatingly vague than usual."

After another half hour, Green River hove into view. He knew the airport intimately, southwest of town, not far from his home. He broadcast on Unicom to alert any traffic of his presence, then keyed the mike quickly three times on the frequency that would turn on the pilot-controlled runway lights.

Nothing happened. He keyed the mike again. He shook his head. Damn. Still, it was a clear night. As he circled the airport, he could see a sheen of reflected starlight that delineated the runway from the surrounding earth. That'd be good enough. He began his approach, turning downwind, then base, then final, turning on his wing lights. He pulled full flaps, slowly throttling back to reduce airspeed. With runway lights out, it was important to keep that landing speed slow and runway roll minimal. The Skymaster, barely above stall speed, cleared the runway's threshold. Noah prepared to flare for touchdown.

"Holy shit!" he yelled, cramming the throttles forward, pulling back on the stick and bleeding off the flaps. The twin Continental engines pulled the Skymaster to safety, clearing by only a few feet something long and dark lying across the runway. He climbed and banked into a left-hand pattern around the airport.

He keyed the mike. His radio was still tuned to Unicom.

"Cessna Whiskey Tango Hotel Niner Niner Six, calling in the clear. All traffic, avoid Green River Muni. Obstruction on runway. Repeat, obstruction on runway. No runway lights, repeat, no runway lights. All traffic, avoid Green River Muni. Obstruction on runway. Out." He repeated the warning on the universal emergency frequency, 121.5.

That done, he pondered where to land. As he sorted through his options, the radio crackled.

"Cessna Whiskey Tango Hotel Niner Niner Six, this is Green River FBO. State your intentions. Over."

"Annie?"

"Yes." She kept a small apartment just off the airport grounds. He knew she monitored Green River Unicom, the local traffic radio frequency, when home.

"I want to land on the dirt on the west side of Runway 31. Take my Land Cruiser and park it next to the threshold, lights on, pointed down the runway. I'll come over the top. Over."

"On my way. Over."

"Call the FAA first. Tell 'em to get a NOTAM out." NOTAM was pilot slang for "Notice to Airmen."

"Okay. You all right on fuel?"

"Yes. Out."

As he circled, he could see Annie's car leave her apartment and race to the airport. She got into his Cruiser and positioned it as he'd asked. He carefully flew the landing pattern and put the Skymaster on the ground. He taxied to the hangar and parked the Cessna. Annie picked him up and they drove onto the darkened runway. Slowly, Annie edged the Cruiser down the centerline.

The headlights caught something low, laid across the runway. She parked. They walked to it.

"Christ," Noah said, nudging his foot against it. "A steel I beam."

"It would have ripped out your landing gear," Annie said

quietly.

"Yeah."

"Bet there's a reason the lights are out, too," she said.

"Yep. Somebody screwed with the lights. Probably cut a cable."

She put her hand on his arm and turned him toward her.

"Noah ..."

"I know what you're going to say."

"Then why keep doing this?"

"You know why."

She kissed his cheek. "If I had married you, this would be grounds for divorce."

He hugged her. "You made the wise choice."

They walked back to the Cruiser.

"The FAA said they'd have someone here in the morning to investigate," Annie said.

"Good luck with that," Noah said.

She grabbed his arm again.

"Noah, he'll kill you."

"Good luck with that, too."

Chapter 16:

April 8, morning, near the Nevada-Utah border

Kara's oldest brother had described driving a muscle car at high speed as a dream world of incomparable highs beyond the wildest hallucinations of illicit narcotics. *He oughta know. He tried every mushroom in sight.* Her brother and Dad the Engineer had dropped a bored-out, big-block V-8 into a '34 Ford coupe. He had lost his license for speeding. He drove anyhow, sans license and relentlessly fast. He died at age 22 in that coupe, pulverized against a utility pole. *Do I miss him?* She had feared his lust, his thirst for the reckless. She wondered if after he died, she had become a coward. *No, I learned to minimize risks.* Physical risks. Intellectual risks. *Emotional risks.*

Kara needed to feel risky today. She needed to take some improbable chance, however large or small, that said *I'm alive, god damn it!* She pushed harder on the accelerator. The hatchback sped along the arrow-straight highway onto the western edge of Snake Valley at nearly 90 miles an hour. "Hot, straight, and fast." That's what her brother had said once. His death had not visibly saddened Dad the Engineer. He had not wept over her brother's casket. Her father had admonished the surviving siblings to avoid speed, calling it "an inappropriate lack of caution in response to unknown risk."

But for weeks afterward, her father had been listless. He'd avoided the machine shop in the garage where the aged roadster had been reborn as a streak of Chevy-powered lightning. He'd sat in his reading chair, that vinyl Barcalounger with the matching ottoman, pretending to read. Then he'd disappeared into his workshop in the basement, day after day, night after night, emerging only to eat and sleep. That had marked his desertion of the family. True, he spoke to the siblings when necessary, but mostly to deprecate for failure to attain perfection. An A-minus didn't cut it in the world of Dad the Engineer. Lesser achievements were met with subtle derision. He trained them no more. She missed the earlier Dad the Engineer. He had at least smiled at her a bit. When her brother died — *Oh, god, did he just not turn the wheel? Did he just want out?* — the man who was her father had died, too, his lifework scrambled against that utility pole. Kara pushed her family out of her mind. *Focus on the external.* Seek patterns around her, not patterns within her.

For mile after mile, no cars or 18-wheelers appeared, either westbound or eastbound. There was just the Subaru, a lone gnat of a car on the thin black chalk line snapped across Nevada's bleak, brown and dirty-white landscape. The slipstream whipped at the side of her head. The air was just right, not too hot, not too cold. She checked the gauges. Water, okay. Oil pressure, a touch high. She backed off the accelerator. The car eased its rush *to where?* Epithets were hurled at the map. It had lost its luster, its allure. She didn't want to look at the goddamned thing anymore. Because she could not fathom discernible patterns in the map, it dissembled instead of assembled her sense of worth and cracked her self-esteem like a pebble hurled maliciously through a pane of glass. Its mysteries had become too obtuse, too tiresome, too consuming, too corrosive of long-held illusions.

She thought of Seattle, of work, of her dead brother, of vast distances, of her mother, of dozens of painful fragments of her life. *A string of goddamned A-minuses and B-pluses. Not all A's.* Too much. Too much to analyze. *Too much to cope with.* In her senior year in high school, her father had scolded her for not being able to solve a homework problem. "Problems are only solved," he'd said, "with methodical, unemotional concentration." In her room, after he'd left, she tried to focus on the problem. Frustrated, she'd pushed the paper and calculator away and opened the door to leave. Her father stood outside, his arms folded across his chest. He'd said nothing. He didn't have to. His eyes, flat, stern, distant but compelling, had sent her back. She solved the problem — but only after a furtive call to a classmate. She'd hated asking for help with schoolwork. Even then, her father's code of self-reliance had marked her.

Screw this. She slumped into the seat and settled her eyes on the dot Highway 50 made ahead on the horizon. That's better. Cruise control. *Good ol' highway hypnosis.* Ahead lay mountains, the Confusion and House ranges.

The Subaru darted hour after tiring hour through a landscape dotted with brownish clumps of vegetation. The highway climbed an alluvial fan, descended, then climbed another alluvial ghost of melted glaciers past. She passed a sign. *I'm not in Nevada anymore.* The House Range had two notches that left curious blocky summits. She could see rock layers in the Confusion Range but did not know that hundreds of millions years ago, inland seas in the Devonian and Permian eras teemed with life. Later, she would learn to look for evidence of death in the lithified remains of the sea, trilobites, graptolites, brachiopods, conodonts, corals, sponges, gastropods, and others. These limestone and dolomite highlands reigned over land that had been less resistant to the ceaseless assault of ice, wind, water, and gravity.

Rhythm. That's what she needed. That's what she felt. The drone of the tires. The rush of the slipstream, caressing her neck. The subtle, high-pitched whine of the Subaru's six-cylinder engine. She floated along in the metronomical passage of time and distance, slumped in the seat. The sun, hot and insistent, shone through the window and warmed her thighs. The car tended to business, slicing nimbly into the turns of

King Canyon.

The car sped up and down gentle grades. Around sweeping curves. Across the Tule Valley graben. Across a black macadam sea. The Subaru thought for the distracted Kara, guiding itself through a broad turn at Skull Rock Pass. Thermals ahead blurred Lake Sevier, an immense, flat, gleaming, dry lakebed of white precipitates. The Cricket Mountains to the southeast rose on the far side of the lakebed, surreal and mystic through the haze. She smiled. *I could vanish there. I could float through the sky and dis—*

The car slammed into a seething, frothing, thick, flame-orange swarm of locusts. A living, breathing, opaque communal mass, tall as a house and hundreds of yards long, snaked its way across Highway 50. The windshield smeared into a reddish darkness. She slammed on the brakes. The Subaru skidded and spun out of control. She wrestled with the wheel. The blanket of dead locusts on the windshield blinded her. In a nanosecond of insight she saw through her dead brother's eyes the onrushing utility pole and felt *what he must have felt* as he fought to turn the steering wheel of the skidding coupe and with sudden clarity realized the futility of his existence and then his hands let go of the wheel and his arms folded across his chest and he felt free at last and she understood and she envied him and lifted her hands from the wheel feeling only sadness and defeat and regret and *I never really had a chance.*

The spinning Subaru burst from the Stygian morass into sunlight. Automatic responses kicked in. She turned the wheel against the skid. She braked, head out the window. Locusts struck her face, stinging like thrown pebbles. She recoiled, terrified. The car stopped on the shoulder. She sat in the car, heart racing. *Did I really do that? Would I have done that? Oh, God, dear Donny. I didn't know. I'm so sorry.* Genocide glazed the windshield. It sickened her in memory as much as in reality. An insensitive state trooper had told her the condition of Donny's body in the wreckage.

A rough side road led to the shore of Lake Sevier, a large dry lakebed. She had to get off the goddamned highway. *Now.* Looking out the driver's side window, she slowly drove down the road, fearing for the car's undercarriage as it bounced over potholes and large rocks. She stopped on a patch of level ground overlooking the dirty-white shoreline a few hundred yards away.

She opened the door, crying. Dead locusts fell on her head and shoulders. Yanking the seatbelt free, she ran for a few dozen yards before falling. She looked back at the Subaru. A reddish-yellow, furry, matted mass of dead and dying locusts encrusted the chrome grille and the hood. Atop the car, thousands of locust corpses soiled the front of her bike. *Thank God for the cover.* She walked closer, hesitantly, until she could see individual insects. Some fluttered in lingering life. Bile rose in her throat. She choked it down and walked away from the car.

Shaking uncontrollably, she sat on a rock, arms across her chest, hands clutching her shoulders, her back to the Subaru, breathing heavily and rapidly, almost hyperventilating for a half hour. A startled pocket mouse scurried into its hidey-hole as she stoically walked back to the car. She wanted to puke. She steeled herself, pretending that the organic mass was only dirt, just road grit and grime. After removing her bike from the rack, she removed the cover and tossed it several feet. She got out a bottle of Windex and a long-handled ice scraper. She tied a bandana over her face, covering her mouth and nose. She plowed through the locusts with the scraper, pushing them into a clump on the far side of the windshield until only an organic sheen coated the windshield. She flipped away the snowbank-like mass of insects. After soaking the windshield with Windex, she rubbed it clean with paper towels. She cleared the headlights. The Subaru reappeared. A thick mat of insects clogged the grille. Using a stick and scraper, she poked at the mass, knocking clumps of squished insects away. One spot resisted. She poked at it several times. Then she saw what the lump was — a small brown bird, embedded in the grille, dead. She turned away and vomited.

An hour later, she had restored the Subaru to minimal
roadworthiness. She'd poked the bird out of the grille and
immediately moved the car twenty or thirty yards away. She sat
on another rock for a while. *Too much death.* Her brother. Her
mother. Her father's body, eventually, had followed his heart,
giving out slowly until he just stopped living and needed burial.
She needed to *do* something, to feel something *physical.* She
stripped and put on her riding shorts, cap, and a black halter
top. She rode her bike over the rough ground onto the dry
lakebed. This was what she wanted. Elemental nothingness.
Endlessly horizontal. Hard. Unyielding. She stood on the
cranks, attuning herself to the cadence of pedaling. The bike
crunched over the desiccation cracks. She pushed toward the
distant Cricket Range. But hours of riding would not bring the
Crickets to their knees.

She rode hard for a half hour, her eyes squinted nearly shut
from the reflected brilliance of the lakebed, even through her
dark Bollé glasses. Perspiration vanished as it was produced;
she marveled at that. Her lungs burned from effort, from the
week of lethargy. *Has it been that long?* She stopped pedaling,
hands off the handlebars, and coasted. She swiveled on the seat
and stepped onto the playa. She lay the bike on the hard
surface and walked. She took off her right shoe and touched
her foot to the white, salty surface. Warm, but not
uncomfortably so. She removed the left, too. The playa
crunched under her feet, and she liked it.

Blinding whiteness surrounded her. A thin arrow of tire
tracks led back to the shore. The Subaru was a small speck. She
looked at the Crickets. Then the House Range. Then the
Confusion. She was sweating. No motion, so no evaporation.
High in the peaks, sheets of orographic rain fell into oblivion,
evaporating before they reached the ground. *So cool. I wish I was
up there.* But she liked where she was. *Warmth.* She lay on her
back, placing her cap over her face to fend off the ferocious
sun. The lakebed did not feel gritty, just dusty, like talcum

powder. The hard surface was a bit uncomfortable. *Like a bad futon.* She wondered what it would be like to make love out here. *He sure as hell wouldn't like it.* She remembered lying in the sun next to the Little Humboldt. Her hand drifted over her tummy and onto her groin.

She yelped and scrambled to her feet. A reddish welt rose on the back of her right thigh. Something had bitten her. This most barren of landscapes teemed with life intolerant of thoughtless intruders.

Kara dressed and woodenly rode back to the shoreline. Moving with purpose, she half shoveled, half swept piles of dead locusts into the filthy bike cover and dumped them in a large mound. She picked up the paper towels strewn on the ground and threw them onto the pile. Wet, gooey fragments of insects stuck to her hands. She didn't give a damn. She found the dead bird, picked it up in her bare hands, carried it to the knee-high pile, and laid it to rest. She got her iPhone, selected a particular artist, and hit "play." She poured gasoline from a Sigg bottle onto the orange mound. She tossed a burning match onto the dome of dead insects. Flames quickly erupted, consuming them. Acrid, black, evil smoke roiled upward in the still air. From the speakers in the car, the Crazy World of Arthur Brown screamed — *I'll teach you to burn.* She sat next to the pyre and watched until the fire died, leaving a black, sticky goo. She wept for her brother. She had not cried at his funeral. Dad the Engineer taught stoicism. His progeny had practiced it under duress.

The sun neared the House Range, deepening the shadow cast by the car. It looked like shit. But its windows and radiator grille were clear. Those were her triage priorities: She could see, and the car could breathe. *I'm so damned tired.* She drove the car behind a hummock, out of sight of passersby. She camped by the lakebed. Trucks rolled by on the highway. Phobias born in adolescence lingered.

She felt dirty and sticky. Opening the hatchback to get her

sleeping bag and pad, she smelled remaining locust goo. *Oh, crap.* But something else wrinkled her nostrils. A rank aroma floated out of the car, the odor of days and nights on the road, of unwashed clothes, of a beer she'd spilled two nights before. *This sucks. This just sucks.* She spread a large nylon tarp on the ground. She removed every box, bag, and unhoused object from the back of the car. For nearly an hour she sorted and repacked her belongings. A small dust broom evicted any remaining debris. She placed everything back into the car, reserving her usual diagonal sleeping space.

The sun settled behind the summits of the House Range. She stripped and sponged herself, removing that awful feeling of stickiness. She stood motionless, feeling the cool air on her shadowed back side and the last rays of the sun warming her chest and stomach. Pinpricks of distant headlights descended from Skull Rock Pass. She put on clean underwear and a tank top before slithering into her sleeping bag next to the car. She lay on her back, watching the evening deepen into twilight. To the west of Sawtooth Mountain, the house in the House Range, dark clouds hovered. Venus rose, a pinpoint of light hovering over the gloom of the night-dark cumulus. A rising moon silvered the tops of the clouds. She shivered. *It's coming for me again.*

The desert awoke. Pocket mice scampered out of their burrows to forage among the sagebrush and saltbush. A loggerhead shrike roosted atop a shadscale, seeking prey. Scorpions prowled; lizards hid. Amid that welter of life, she dreamed of bright flashes of light, dancing around her, taunting her. Inside the car, the map was silent as she slept.

Chapter 17:

April 9, late morning, next to Lake Sevier, Utah

Dawn crept over the dry lakebed. North of Lake Sevier, low, gray clouds, indeterminate of mood, drifted under thin, high cirrus stalled over the desert. The rising sun turned the heat from spring to summery. Kara woke, feeling as sweaty and sticky as she had the night before. Her watch told her she'd missed breakfast time by a long shot. She was hungry. But she didn't want to move. She didn't want to do anything. *I just want an end to this.*

She rose and repeated her sponge-and-water-bottle bath. In Speedo and Quick-Drys, she settled into the driver's seat and started the car. It bounced over the rough ground, then onto Route 50. She never considered turning west. She drove slowly, barely 55 miles an hour. Big trucks and small cars whipped past the Subaru. The twenty-five miles to Hinckley crept by. She saw nothing that enticed her to stop, not even a diner, so she continued east toward Delta.

The stark, dirt-dry brown of northern Nevada receded, becoming Utah. Lush, circular fields of newly planted crops sat thick and green on either side of the road, separated by thin spears of sand and an occasional dune. She thought of Winnemucca. *Have I come so far yet gone nowhere?* Trees that looked like birches — *aspen?* — lined the highway in places. Metal millipedes spouted water onto the fields. Irrigation beget arable soil beget people beget growth beget more people.

First things first. *Food.* In Delta, she ate breakfast at a small cafe. At a Chevron station, ten dollars and her promising-nothing smile, both given to an eager teenager, produced a hose and pail. The last of the locusts surrendered to water, a sponge, liquid Joy, and an hour of elbow grease. She breathed through her mouth the entire time, fighting the gag reflex. Just the memory of the yellow and red smears of dissembled locusts disgusted her.

The Subaru shone, free of locusts. But Kara stank. Just the thirty-five miles into Delta in the Subaru — *Who needs a functional air conditioner in Seattle, for chrissake?* — had left her feeling sticky. She would have turned the hose on herself at the Chevron station, but that damned acne-scarred, pimple-faced teen-ager had kept gawking at her. She didn't want to give him some locker room talk about this broad in a wet Speedo. She drove slowly through the eastern fringe of Delta, fighting off the heat with the car's underpowered fan. Ahead, a sign pointed to Route 6. She turned north. *Screw the map.*

The highway ferried the car alongside the meandering Sevier River to the east and Union Pacific railroad tracks to the west. A freight train rumbled north with the car, keeping pace. *Damn, am I driving that slow?* But she didn't have the energy to drive any faster. She glanced at the train. Hundreds of empty ore cars, one bleak, gray car after another, lined up in mute testimony to the harvest of the land. All were headed somewhere to engorge themselves on more coal to power the air conditioners and electric lights and toasters and microwaves and computers and stereos and TVs and water heaters in some 1950s all-electric land over the horizon. To the west was the Intermountain Power Project. Tall transmission towers marched from it two abreast, ferrying the bulk of the 13 million megawatts produced each year by its coal-fired plants to California.

South of Lynndyl she pulled off the road onto Taylors Flat until she could find a place to squat and pee. Digging out her camera, she photographed a bush with tiny white flowers, then others, some with pink, others with purple flowers. Nearby, unnoticed, a large mill processed beryllium, a mineral mined in western Utah where Tertiary volcanics intruded and reacted with Paleozoic limestones and dolomites. She didn't know that. She wouldn't have cared. Not today. Only pretty flowers mattered today.

She drove north toward Jericho Junction, passing the Gilson Mountains to the east. Dunes proliferated and rose higher and higher to the northwest. As the car closed, black spots on the dunes resolved into people. She stopped, and binoculars drew her close to a family — mother, father, little boy, little girl. Behind them the rows of dunes marched into the Little Sahara, home to windblown sand from the Pleistocene delta deposits of the Sevier River. Mommy and Daddy sat next to picnic fixings atop two Coleman coolers. Brother and Sister jumped off the lee face of the dune, sliding and tumbling down it. She sensed their laughter. Tears trickled down aside her nose, over her lip and into her mouth. The brine cloaked her tongue. *Dad, where did you go?* She reached for the Mac, booted it, and wrote in haste.

To: TopDob@WebWideWorks.com
From: kara@WebWideWorks.com
Subject:
Cc:
Bcc:
Attachments:

_____

i killed millions of beings yesterday and burned them and i'll probably burn too some day ... i saw mom and dad and the kids living life and i've seen nothing but

death and i'm lost and i'm tired and i don't
understand at all

no one knows me ... no one ever knew me
... i know you never knew me because you
never wanted to and i never wanted to let
you know me because you weren't the one
i wanted to know me ... so i have no idea
why i should ever come back ... there's no
sense in pretending anymore that we were
ever in love in the first place

i have to go i have to run i have to do
something that lets me undo for what i've
done and do what i haven't done

    The next time she checked her e-mail, she'd see the subject
line "Undeliverable Mail." She'd be confused. Then she'd see
she had somehow, despite Outlook's automation, gotten his
address wrong and discover he'd never received her ravings.
She'd shrug her shoulders and marvel at her electronically
transmitted insanity. The parting had come and gone and only
she would know exactly when. She'd wonder if fate had
corrupted the address. She wouldn't care. *Seattle didn't matter any
more.*

    She turned east at Jericho Junction. The road carried her
into a small, nondescript valley, irregularly shaped by
coalescing alluvial fans on either side. Shot-up road signs
appeared, their lettering and numbers obliterated by teens with
guns and little else to do. The road climbed as the car puttered
through gentle curves. Dark green trees appeared. The road
meandered and the vegetation came closer. She liked it and
stopped. She saw more flowers and spent an hour taking
pictures, walking, stretching, yawning, looking at the tall green
trees and the short, light-green shrubs. She decided, when she
became Queen of All That Is, she would close this road and
keep it for herself. Gentle wind, cool air. *I need more of this.* But
today, she couldn't stay, so she drove on.

She came to an intersection. One last sign, but with fewer bullet holes. 1812, read a sign. *How appropriate. Why not just fire Tchaikovsky's cannon at it?* She followed Route 132 through Nephi to Interstate 15. She pulled onto the shoulder by the southbound on-ramp. *Damn.* She sat undecided. *I don't need the damn map to tell me where to go.* She thought of turning back. But that meant facing issues. *I don't want to face any goddamned "issues" right now.* She decided to take I-15 south. *Yeah. Vegas. Get the hell away from this. Nice hotel room. Sauna. Massage. Gamble. Make some dough.* And she could. She knew probability theory, and she could count cards as well as professional gamblers. *See? I don't need you, map. I don't need you at all.*

The car dawdled along the western edge of Juab Valley. Faster interstate traffic flashed past. Late afternoon had arrived when she saw the green, white-lettered exit sign: "Scipio. Highway 50." Las Vegas lay south on I-15. *I don't really want to go to Vegas. Too many people.* She pulled onto the breakdown lane of the off-ramp. She closed her eyes. A headache drummed at her temples. Too much squinting in the sun, too much staring at the road. *I'm so damn tired. If I could just rest for a while.* A Maverik gasoline double tanker rumbled by, and the car lurched in its slipstream. Kara drove to the end of the ramp. Shaking her head, she motioned the Subaru east on 50. The detour had been no detour. *Fucking map. It always wins.*

As she drove past Scipio, her body screamed *Clean me. Soothe me.* Her arms ached from dealing with the locusts. Her thighs ached from riding. *How did I get in such bad shape?* She stopped at an irrigation ditch near the road, intent on sneaking a dip. But cars passed frequently, and she feared slighting some local taboo. *Probably too cold, anyhow.* She drove on, bathing a fantasy.

Miles later, sunlight reflected off Scipio Lake next to the highway. She got out of the car, a bottle of Dr. Bronner's in hand, and strode to a line of sagebrush paralleling the road. An old barbed wire fence, hidden in the shrubs, stabbed her on the

thigh. *Shit. What next?* The puncture wound did not seem
serious, so she climbed over the fence and walked quickly to
the edge of the lake. She undressed behind a young tamarisk
and stepped into the spring-cold water. Nearby fluttering
sounds startled her. Waterfowl scampered away. She lathered
herself with the peppermint-scented liquid and washed her
hair. Then another noise, behind her. She lifted her head, as
deer do, alert for danger. She was not alone. A Townsend's
solitaire flew out of a juniper. She sat down in the water and
quietly watched the life around her. The suds floated away.
American widgeon swam idly by. Beyond them, Canada geese
sailed in a slight wind. American coots, small, duck-like birds,
kept their distance, upturning themselves to feed on the
shallow bottom. Keeping to themselves, as lovers do, pairs of
horned grebes romanced, entwining their long necks. *Such a
simple, uncomplicated life they have.* She returned to the car and
ministered to tired muscles with a sports creme. She drove on,
body silent, mind numb, soul screaming.

Shadows lengthened as the Subaru droned along Route 50,
paralleling Round Valley Creek south of Scipio. The sun
bronzed the puffy white cumulus towers east of her,
somewhere over the Fishlake National Forest, high in the
Sevier Plateau. Below them, junipers and the occasional
Ponderosa pine proliferated. *A forest. On a mountain. This isn't
Nevada anymore.* She pressed on the accelerator. *It'll be cooler up
there.*

In Salina, someone fed her. She didn't notice the name of
the diner or her waitress or what she ate. Lingering over tea,
she dozed until someone nudged her politely awake. She
finished her tea quickly and left a nice tip.

The cumulus over the Fishlake darkened. She didn't notice.
The food left her even sleepier. A motel? *No.* Kara's tiny
universe contained only her, the car, and the road. To be
separated from the Subaru she could not bear, even if it rested
just outside a motel door. She could only drive on. That's all
she knew. *So tired.* She just shrugged when Route 50 merged

into I-70.

The Subaru labored up the long rise west of the Sevier Plateau, its engine pinging from the oxygen starvation of altitude. Hours of dulling fatigue were spiked by seconds of frantic fear of mechanical failure and rejection. But the car droned on, and Kara's heaving chest subsided. The sky darkened more.

Kara fought to keep her eyes open. Rumble strips in the breakdown lane saved her twice. *Have to stop. Just have to stop.* She turned off at Exit 61 and drove along Gooseberry Creek, seeking sanctuary. But after a few miles, she gave up. The road had no shoulder. Dirt roads led into the mountains, but each entrance was gated with a fence. Nothing felt *right*. Nothing felt *safe*. Yawning, she drove back to the interstate. Rain splattered on the windshield.

She turned off at Exit 71 and crossed an overpass. A dirt road went left. She crept onto Taylor Flat and parked behind a stand of tamarisk. A stream gushed nearby. In the twilight, deer browsed. This would do. No highway sounds. Nothing but silence, save for the stream and cooling-down sounds from under the hood. Rain fell heavily, then, suddenly, lightning cracked nearby, loud and burning bright. She hurriedly drove back toward the interstate, frightened. The headlights arrested something bright and yellow. Two large Caterpillar road graders sat on a parking area of hard gravel. She parked the car between them. Lightning crackled, but farther away. It recognized her sentinels. Kara stepped into the rain with a towel. She undressed, let the rain wet her, and dried herself. She climbed into the car and struggled into her sleeping bag. She felt so confined.

Twilight passed quickly. She lay in her bag, whipped. She tried to sleep. When she closed her eyes, she felt nauseated, as if spinning out of control. It pissed her off that she had to keep her eyes open. At least, she thought they were open — the night outside was black. No stars, no moon. No light at all. *A sensory-deprivation tank. That's what I'm in. I'm reduced to nothing.* She wanted to cry. *I am unnoticed. I don't exist. I'm not here anymore.*

I'm not anywhere. I'm not anything. As her eyes closed and the car did not spin, she cradled a breast with one hand, her pubis with the other. *I am me, aren't I? I can feel, can't I?* She felt ugly and folded her hands across her stomach. She waited for sleep, for oblivion, *for the end of this*, whatever *this* was.

Chapter 18:

April 9, early evening, Greasewood Draw

Noah drove slowly back to Greasewood Draw from Green River Muni in his Land Cruiser. It had been a long day. A flight to Moab, ferrying a lawyer to a deposition. Another flight to St. George for a woman visiting her grandchildren. Pleasant talk during the flights with decent folks, ceiling and visibility unlimited, mild turbulence, but still, a long day. He was tired. He'd slept fitfully for the past week, getting up in the wee hours and floundering around his hangar, doing busy work on his fleet of little planes, work unneeded by the planes themselves.

Sunset crowded in on remaining daylight as he turned off State Route 24 onto the dirt road that led to his trailer, a quarter mile inside Greasewood Draw. He looked at the darkening western sky, mindful of heavy cumulus building over the Swell. He cooked supper lethargically and sat on the steps of the trailer to eat without any sense of pleasure or fulfillment. He took a beer from his fridge, drank it without enthusiasm, then walked down his dirt driveway for a while, listening. He heard nary a bird or insect, or wind stirring cottonwood leaves.

A faraway crack of lightning caught his eye, followed by the distant bass of thunder that resonated more in his chest than his ear. He turned and jogged back to his hangar. He topped off the fuel tank of his Drifter. He preflighted it carefully as if he intended to fly. He checked his search-and-rescue kit bag to ensure it was fully stocked, then stowed it in the Drifter.

He returned to his trailer, stripped, showered, and lay on his bed. Hours later, he was still awake.

Chapter 19:

April 10, dawn, off I-70 near Exit 71, east of Salina, Utah

The thunderstorm struck again before first light. She bolted awake at the first crack of lightning, sentinel Caterpillars be damned. *It's here. It wants me. Oh, God, not now. Not now!* Wind rocked the car. Rain pelted the roof, then hail. She cupped her hands over her ears against the shrill din. Kara cowered under the sleeping bag until past dawn. *I have to escape. I have to get away.*

Desperation flung back the sleeping bag. She fumbled around in the gray dawn and pulled a sweatshirt over her tank top. She slid awkwardly into black Lycra shorts, hitting her head on the door handle and yowling. She climbed over the seat and started the car. The Caterpillars did not say good-bye. Hunched up tight to the wheel, peering into the rain, she drove hurriedly back to the interstate. Lightning flashed above her. Maybe it was a dream. Too little sleep. Too much turmoil. Too much thinking. Too much feeling. Too much change too fast. Too many nights parked not far enough from the road to feel safe and too far to feel connected to — *to what? God damn it, to what?*

She drove fast. The car didn't want to go that fast. It knew better. The wipers barely swept the windshield before the rain smeared the glass again. Ahead, she sensed light, or at least lighter grays. She urged the car to go faster. *Get me away.* The Subaru screamed east onto the San Rafael Swell. The sky lightened. A sliver of blue pushed between the clouds and the ground. The car dashed through the rain, through the threats, real or imagined, to the sunlight. Her temples throbbed. Her eyes hurt from staring through the rain-slickened windshield. Her breath came in ragged gasps. *Almost there. Hurry.*

South of Window Blind Peak the car broke into sunlight. Kara slowed to a stop in the breakdown lane. Draping her arms over the wheel, she rested her forehead against them. Crying never brought relief, so she rarely did. But now, she wept. Minutes passed. Tears eased. She lifted her head and looked up at the highway. Her foot touched the accelerator.

The car crept along in the breakdown lane. She didn't use her flashers. Big trucks and small cars honked in anger when the car drifted into the travel lane. The car coasted into a rest area and stopped, straddling parking places.

Kara stepped out and walked to the end of the rest area. The sun illuminated the northern reaches of Arches National Park, where narrow fins of reddish Entrada sandstone rose like tall slivers at Devils Garden and the Fiery Furnace.

She walked back to the car, yanking the sweatshirt over her head and throwing it to the ground. She wriggled hurriedly into her Tyvek and slipped on her riding gloves. She took out her helmet and set it on the pavement beside her sweatshirt. Unlocking the roof rack, she lifted the bike down. Her Bollés. She couldn't remember where she'd put them. *Fuck.* She opened the driver's door and looked for them. There they were, tucked into a visor pocket.

She put them on and walked her bike to the edge of the pavement. She rode south, away from the rest area toward Rattlesnake Bench. On her bike, she sought her last chance for escape.

Chapter 20:

April 10, early afternoon, Greasewood Draw, west of Green River, Utah

Noah could no longer resist the compulsion. His instincts were screaming. Something was wrong somewhere. He had to find it and fix it. He'd heard the distant rumbling of thunder beyond the Swell to the west. For two more nights, he had dreamed. And he didn't like it.

He climbed into his high-wing Drifter and fastened the four-point harness. He pulled the safety pin of the BSR safety chute and started the big Rotax 912. He checked his instruments. He firewalled the throttle, and the Drifter accelerated down the dirt runway behind his hangar. Going hunting, he thought. But for what, he had no idea.

Two miles north, a man sat in an old camp chair, shaded by the awning hung from a camper perched in the bed of an old Ford pickup. He heard Noah's Drifter before he saw it and set down the paperback he'd been reading. Lifting powerful Zeiss binoculars, he watched the Drifter rise from Greasewood Draw. He noted time and direction on a pad next to his beer, sitting on a wooden box he used as a footrest. Picking up a radio, he clicked on the "talk" button and spoke.

"He's up. Headed due west over the Swell."

He put down the radio, retrieved the paperback, and resumed reading.

Noah flew west through the notch carved in a hogback of Wingate sandstone by Caterpillar and Bucyrus-Erie to allow safe passage for Interstate 70. Engineers had simplified the landscape merely to get the family Volvo with Mom and Dad and the 2.2 kids and 1.7 dogs to the Grand Canyon, or some such overvisited altar of natural wonder, three minutes sooner. He marveled at the cliffs towering a quarter mile over the highway. He still loved road cuts as windows looking back in time. But life as a geologist for the mining industry was ancient Hartshorn history. Now he confronted county commissions and, occasionally, various Utah state legislature committees. He argued against the creation of roads in wilderness and for the closing of those that existed. His credo — "roadless wilderness" — had irritated plenty of ORVers, public officials, and oil, ranching, and mining executives. Noah knew the right words. He knew the economic doublespeak because he used to be "one of them goddamned profiteering land rapists," as a few of his environmentalist friends would say.

He nudged the stick back to gain altitude. He needed to see farther. I-70 lay below, leading him west. Why was he following this? He did not know. He relied on instinct and intuition born in a dream. Several eighteen-wheelers rumbled east, a few more west. Very few four-wheelers. All was as it should be. A slow day on the double ribbon in west-central Utah.

The Drifter neared an eastbound rest area. From here tourists could see into the heart of central Utah, a grand view of the red rock country. But the rest area was empty. No rubber-necking, digital-point-and-shoot-toting visitors today. The Drifter droned on westerly. A thought skritched in the back of his mind as he flew over the next rest area. He circled over it. A small, brown car sat alone. That wasn't unusual. These rest areas were often empty. But the thought nagged. He growled to himself, banked the Drifter, and overflew the rest area again. He circled twice, looking for a pattern — or a break in a pattern — that presented a problem. Someone had parked that car askew, across the diagonal spaces. Tourists are regimented. They park however the lines tell them to. He lowered the nose, losing altitude, and flew less than a hundred feet over the rest area. The door of the car was slightly ajar. The hatchback was open. A sweatshirt lay on the ground, half hidden under the car.

The skritching intensified. He circled the rest area, checking wind direction. Young junipers leaned away from westerly winds. He landed, just clearing a small hill at the east end of the truck parking area. Noah braked hard. He killed the engine, yanked off his harness, and jogged to the car, a Subaru hatchback. Picking up the sweatshirt, he looked into the car. He opened the door. The interior smelled awful, like the odor of several days without a decent shower. Nothing seemed amiss. Just a lot of gear carefully packed in canvas carryalls and duffle bags in the rear, contrasting with other things strewn carelessly. A bicycle tire pump lay on the passenger seat. Water bottles were scattered in the back. A tool kit. A spare wheel. He sniffed. That scent. Then he had it — chain oil. He rode a mountain bike in the backcountry frequently. Keys had been tossed onto the floor mat on the driver's side. Who would leave a car unattended? He walked to the southern end of the rest area. Ridges of Navajo sandstone descended southeast to a flat saddle two miles away. He walked back, tugging at his beard.

He leaned against the car, the skritching now in full alarm. He slapped his forehead. All this bike gear — but no bike. After locking the car and pocketing the keys, he ran back to the Drifter. For the first time in his memory, he did not preflight an aircraft.

Chapter 21:

April 10, early afternoon, off I-70 near Justensen Flat

Kara flew over the handlebars. Her head struck a rock as she landed awkwardly on the slickrock. She moaned before drifting into unconsciousness. No more lightning. Just blackness. Just nothingness.

Two hours later, what sounded like a loud, irritated fly buzzed overhead. Soon, a man with purposeful brown eyes jogged easily over a small sandstone rise. He was a few inches shorter than she but broad through his chest and shoulders. He slipped off an aged but supple leather pack, setting it down next to the woman he'd seen from the air. A mountain bike lay wounded a few yards away, its front rim bent. She hit something, he thought, as he knelt.

Squeezing her hand, he spoke softly to her.

"Hi, I'm Noah. I'll take good care of you, so don't worry. Just relax."

He didn't think she'd hear it, but he always spoke reassuringly to those whose injuries he tended. Part of his rhythm. Part of his training. *Follow the routine. Follow the drill.*

Consistency bred safety and sound decisions. He told her quietly what he was doing.

Her skin was pasty white. Placing his fingers on her neck, he checked her carotid pulse. Fluttering and rapid. Damn, he thought. He unzipped the silver windbreaker and lifted her tank top. No wounds there. Hemodynamically stable. No arterial bleeding. A jagged cut on her left forehead accompanied by a quarter-sized, half-inch-high contusion. Bleeding from broken skin over her left ear. He passed his hands along each arm, then each leg, squeezing gently. No broken extremities. He pressed his palms against her rib cage, feeling carefully down her sides. When he touched her left side a few inches above her waist, the woman moaned and rocked her head. Good. Enough residual consciousness to reflect pain. Probably a cracked rib, maybe two. No neck fracture either. Take no chances. Brace it anyway. Pinching the skin on her forearm, he noticed it was inelastic. Dehydration? Blood pressure? He removed his cuff from his pack and quickly checked her BP. He unclipped her day pack, carefully pulling its straps from under the small of her back, and fastened it to the frame of her smashed bike.

He cleaned and dressed her wounds with gauze pads and butterfly bandages. He held her hands. Cool and a little clammy. He placed his palm on her chest and looked at his watch, counting her respirations. He brushed her thigh, reaching for his pack. She winced. He rolled up the leg of her shorts and found a puncture wound. He quickly cleaned and dressed it.

He retrieved a small transceiver from his pack. He took her hand, holding the radio with his other hand and flicking the "on" switch with his thumb. In the silence of backcountry Utah, his low, bass voice rumbled softly as he spoke into the radio.

"Whiskey Hotel Tango two niner two to base."

The radio crackled. "Go, Noah."

"Annie, I'm two miles southeast of the rest area eastbound at mile 120, in that hollow east of the main rise. East of

Justensen Flat. Got an accident with PI." Annie was FBO —
the fixed base operator or manager — of Green River Muni.
Had been for years. She worked for Noah part time,
coordinating his charter business. A competent woman. He
liked competent women.

"Woman. Unconscious. Head wound. Two, actually," he
said.

"I'll patch you through to the clinic."

"Thanks."

That would take a few minutes. He waited, holding the
young woman's hand.

"Noah?" the radio spat.

"Jane? That you?"

"Yes. I'm ER today. What have you got?"

"Unconscious woman. Late twenties, possibly a bit older.
Laceration on her forehead, inch-high swelling just above the
eye. Possible skull fracture left side, probable concussion.
Possible rib fracture, left side. BP, 90 over 55. Pulse weak and
thready. She's getting shocky. Skin's a little clammy.
Respirations steady and regular. There's also a puncture
wound, left thigh. Infected. Looks a day or two old. Pallid skin,
almost gray. No bracelet."

Noah was thorough. He noticed the presence — or
absence — of medical clues such as med-alert bracelets
warning of drug allergies or other conditions that could
precipitate unconsciousness.

"Doc's here. Let me put him on," the radio said.

He waited. The radio crackled again. He knew it was more
Doc Andersen's voice that crackled, not the radio. The doc, an
old-school rural GP who hated his insurance-mandated
linguistic conversion to a PCP, was the lone local physician in
Green River for two generations of central Utahns.

"Sounds like a concussion, Noah. Handle her for skull
fracture, too. What happened?"

He looked around. Wasn't hard to figure out. "There's a
mountain bike here. Looks like she fell off. Probably
something spooked her."

"Neck issue?"

"No, I've seen her head move a few times."

"Put a collar on it anyhow."

He clicked the "talk" button twice in assent as he reached into his pack for a cervical collar.

"Noah, can you get her out?"

"Think so."

"Which toy you in?"

"My Drifter."

"Good. You land near?"

"About a quarter mile. I can get her to it pretty easily."

Doc didn't ask whether he could carry her to the Drifter. But the carry meant a chance of aggravating her injuries. Add the risk of an ultralight aircraft bouncing through turbulent air. But Noah had done it before. Many times. Doc knew Noah understood the issues and would act accordingly, as he always did. The local S&R guys were lucky to have him around. More than once, Doc knew, Noah had acted swiftly and decisively. His experience had saved lives.

"Watch that rib cage. ETA?"

"About thirty, thirty-five minutes, including flight time."

"Noah, I could call down to County for the chopper."

"Too long. She's shocky. That pulse worries me. Call Air Life. They'll get there about the time I will. You'll probably decide she'll have to go to Grand Junction or Moab."

"Okay. We'll be waiting."

"I'll report on rolling. Out."

Noah put the radio away. The Drifter was a yellow spot against the small, sunbaked brown swale. He briefly reviewed the issues of takeoff roll, best angle of climb, density altitude, and — he glanced at the woman — about 120 pounds of added weight. He knelt down beside her.

"Sweetie, here's what we're going to do. I'm going to carry you for a bit, and then we're going for a commuter flight. No in-flight movie, though."

He thought she smiled. He fastened the cervical collar around her neck. After slipping on his pack, he squatted beside her. Sliding his left arm under her shoulders and his right arm under her thighs, he carefully lifted her, her head tilting back despite the collar. He talked as he carried her, telling her about the rock they walked over, the plants they passed, the animals that scurried out of their way. The woman was dead weight in his arms, but an easy carry for a man used to lifting eighty-pound two-stroke engines in his hangar. Halfway across the reddish sandstone, her arm moved around his neck.

"Don't worry. I've got you," he whispered. He thought he felt her grip tighten. The intimacy always astonished him, that instant bond between the helpless and the helper, no matter what the level of unconsciousness.

He fastened the woman into the rear seat of the Drifter with the four-point harness. He reconsidered the problems of weight, lift, drag, and center of gravity. Although he had room for a safe takeoff, he took no chances. Damn density altitude. He'd have to lighten the load. He removed the ultralight's full auxiliary five-gallon gas tank. Forty-five pounds gone. That'd be enough.

Noah had only one helmet, and it had a mike that plugged into the Drifter's radio. So he needed it. He wrapped gauze carefully around her head, covering her eyes to protect them from the insults of wind and insect collisions. He fastened her arms to her sides with duct tape to keep them from flopping around. He taped her knees together to keep her legs from splaying.

Noah put on his helmet, slipped into the front seat, and fastened his harness. He ran his checklist, then punched the starter. The 110-horsepower Rotax whined into life, its four-bladed pusher prop clawing into the desert air.

He spoke into the mike. "Whiskey Hotel Tango two niner two to clinic. Rolling."

Two clicks of acknowledgment in his earphones answered him. He released the brakes and advanced the throttle. The Drifter accelerated and rose sluggishly, skimming over the top of a ridge, its left tire grazing the top of a particularly tall juniper. Thank God for serious horsepower, he thought.

He pushed the stick forward and to the right, diving and turning into the canyon on the far side of the ridge, trading hard-won altitude for precious airspeed. He knew the canyons. He knew the land and its topography intimately, having flown through the Swell — *his* Swell — hundreds of times, often in desperately poor conditions. Near the end of the canyon, he'd coaxed enough airspeed out of the Drifter to climb above the terrain.

He flew the Drifter to I-70 and banked east. If he had to land, he wanted the highway near so an ambulance could reach them. He could see Green River Muni. East of it lay the golf course near the medical clinic.

Noah could feel the woman shifting in her seat. If she spoke — or screamed or yelled or sang — he would not hear her over the roar of the Rotax. He wondered what motives in her life had left her injured and concussed miles from the rest area. Evidence suggested her bike ride was more than an impulse. The unlocked car. The sweatshirt dropped to the pavement. The keys left carelessly in plain sight. He focused on flying the laden Drifter. It's a mission, he told himself. Pay attention. Minutes later, the Drifter landed on the fourth fairway. Noah taxied to the white Air Life Bell 412 chopper, its blades slowing. It had just landed, too.

The doc and two paramedics waited until he had cut the engine. The doc, a tall, lanky man, elderly but agile, nodded to the medics. After cutting through the tape, they eased Kara onto a litter. Doc checked her vitals. He looked at Noah, who was hurriedly removing his helmet and harness.

"Problems?" Doc asked.

"None. How is she?" Noah swung his feet onto the ground and stood.

"Shocky. BP's a little low. Looks real dehydrated, too."

"Prognosis?"

"She'll be out for a while. How long, I can't say. Got an ID?"

Noah nodded, rubbing his chin. He'd never admit that he did it when he couldn't figure out something. A thinking gesture. A stalling gesture.

"Noah?"

Noah rummaged through the small day pack but found no wallet.

"Nothing. I'll get the car. We can get a name from the registration."

"That'll help," Doc said.

The doc and the medics lifted the litter into the waiting helicopter and locked it in place. Standing to one side of the door, Noah stared at Kara.

"Start an IV of D5W," the doc told one of the medics. She nodded and slipped nimbly into the aerial ambulance.

The doc turned to Noah. "You going back out now?"

Noah didn't answer.

"Noah?" Doc said.

"What?"

"I said, you going back out now?"

"Yes. I'll call when I know something."

Doc put his hand on Noah's arm. "You okay?" he asked.

"Yeah. Why?"

"Just a feeling, Noah. Talk to me soon."

Doc got into the chopper, and it lifted off, pirouetted, and rose, tail high, on a south-southeast heading for Moab. Noah watched the chopper vanish. Still rubbing his chin, he found a phone in the clinic, and called Annie. She used to do odd jobs in exchange for free flying lessons from local instructors, including Noah. She just never left, and eventually became the FBO. She knew him well, including his warts, which included a total lack of business sense. So he'd hired her to watch over him and his brood of aircraft.

"Annie, care to help with a ferry?"

"Just say when."

"Now. ETA, six minutes."

Noah preflighted the ultralight again, and flew to Green River Muni. He landed long enough for Annie to climb into the rear seat and fasten her harness before taking off again.

Many days later, when Noah brought Kara to her rescued car, she'd find it clean. He wouldn't tell her the where and why of its pristine condition. Many weeks later, Annie, influenced by a few beers, would tell Kara that Noah had flown back to the rest area. He had hiked the four miles to her bike and straightened seven mangled spokes and its bent front rim by hand. He'd ridden it back to her car, put the bike on its rack, drove the car to his trailer.

Annie flew the Drifter back to Green River. Noah drove the Subaru to his trailer and searched it. After searching his patient's belongings, he found the car's registration and license in her wallet in a briefcase containing a computer. The license and registration gave only a P.O. box in Seattle for an address, but he had a name at last — Kara McAllister. He called the Seattle police, identified himself as a member of Green River's Search & Rescue Unit, and told a sergeant what he needed. A computer search turned up nothing. Law-abiding, he thought. Or smart. Calling the post office, he was shuffled to a supervisor who would tell him nothing. He called information. "That number is unlisted," he was told. He called the *Seattle Times*. A sympathetic reporter could provide no help.

He sat at his kitchen table with her license. The bureaucratic photo had been kind to her, and she smiled from it. He smiled back. The text told him, "DOB: March 12, 1983. Height: 5-8. Weight: 120 lbs. Organ donor." He nodded. Right on the money. He found a picture in the briefcase. It showed her and a smiling, bushy-haired, smooth-shaven man in dark glasses, arm in arm, a mountain in the background. Rainier, he noticed.

He dug deeper into the briefcase. He pulled out a Magellan GPS unit. He was no technophobe, but he hated the substitution of backcountry experience and commonsense with techno-gadgets. He'd done S&R too many times to yank out hikers failed by technology. He tsk-tsk'd at the picture of Kara.

"Sweetie, you should know better."

Deeper in the pack were a Leatherman tool, a set of spoke wrenches, a spare cable, and a wad of duct tape wound around a 16-penny nail. He revised his opinion upward. He picked up the GPS again and idly passed it from one hand to the other. On the back was a piece of tape with some writing on it. Her name. And "If found, call 206-555-1402." Gotcha, he thought.

He dialed the number. Inside Kara's briefcase, something beeped. He opened it. A sat phone? Noah was curious. He took it out, wondering why she had one — and why she'd left it on standby.

The switchboard operator at Allen Memorial Hospital in Moab needed several minutes to track down Doc. Noah relayed what he'd found.

"Well, at least we can put a name on her chart. We'll get her insurance info and everything else when she wakes up."

"She okay, Doc?"

Doc was silent for a moment. "Noah, she's comatose. GCS seven."

"Oh, shit."

"The surgeon's drilling her head now to relieve cranial swelling."

"Prognosis?" Noah asked quietly.

"Well, look at it this way. If you hadn't found her, she'd be dead by now."

"I'm coming down."

"Okay, but there's nothing you can do here."

"She's got no one around here, Doc. I can at least sit in her room and keep her company."

"Okay, then. See you when I see you."

Noah went home and changed, then flew his Skymaster to Moab and took a cab to the hospital. He went straight to the ICU. Doc met him at the door and told him to wait.

"What gives, Doc?"

"Just wait. They're still working on her." Doc stepped into the ICU.

Noah shrugged his shoulders and walked down to the waiting room. The coffee machine ate one more quarter than it should have and gave him sugar when he didn't want it. He took the tiny, eight-ounce Styrofoam cup and its steaming black caffeine to a chair. He didn't like such cups and preached a Mr. Coffee and mugs to the staff of the Moab clinic to cut down on waste.

He sipped at the coffee. Mostly he waited, sometimes walking around the waiting room, sometimes sitting, sometimes staring at the clock and watching the snail's pace of the minute hand. Down the hall, Doc stepped out of the ICU and motioned to him. He got another cup of coffee for the doc, who had his own caffeine addiction. In the ICU, Kara lay face up on a tilt bed, used to keep her blood from pooling. An oxygen tube hung from her nostrils. Restraints and padding kept her from moving. An IV ran from a stand into her left forearm. The cut on her forehead had been bandaged. Gauze covered her head. Her skin looked transparent. Blue veins threaded her cheeks, not the rosy blush of conscious life. She looked like hell, and although he had seen worse, it unnerved him.

The doc motioned him to a corner, away from Kara. Noah handed him the cup. Doc nodded and sipped at it.

"You did a good job on the cut. Won't be a scar," the doc said.

"How is she?"

"She's out. On dexamethasone. The surgeons decided to keep her under until the swelling in her brain goes down. Two cracked ribs, left side. You called that. Lots of abrasions and contusions, mostly on the left side. Almost missed a hairline fracture above the occipital orbit, left side, in the CAT scan. Another fracture over her left ear. All will heal nicely, I think. But she's pretty sick. Electrolytes were way down. Somehow, she got herself dehydrated. Might have caused her fall. She could have simply passed out on that bike."

Noah nodded. The doc sipped at his coffee again.

"Doc, what aren't you telling me?"

"She'll be okay. Good thing you found her when you did. I don't know why you went looking for her, but if you hadn't ..."

"And?"

The doc looked at him over the rim of the cup.

"They're keeping her under for a few days. Just to be on the safe side."

Noah glowered. "Jesus, Doc, get to the point."

"She'll heal. But not quickly. And she's going to be plenty sick when she wakes up. Pain. Nausea, probably. They'll probably keep her a week or ten days or so 'til those fractures are healing well. But she's not from 'round here, you know. ID says Seattle. Probably just passin' through."

"Yeah?"

"Noah, she can't travel. You couldn't track down anyone up there to notify. We'll keep trying. But she'll need a good month, probably more, after she's discharged to recuperate. Instinct tells me she won't like nursing very much. She'll need a place to stay, and someone to keep a medical eye on her. And I doubt she'd tolerate well our local nursing home."

Noah stared at him, wide-eyed. "You mean you want me to—"

"Well, Noah, you're the Good Samaritan of record in this case. You're nominated." He raised a hand to fend off a Noah retort. "Yes, I know she's a consenting adult and can veto all these decisions. But she's not going to be a fully functioning consenting adult immediately after discharge. I can't have her check into a motel for those first few days. Someone's gotta look after her and make sure she takes her meds until we can find some kin to come for her. Or she tells us what kin to call. Or she tells us to ... well, you know."

"Crap."

"Stick her in your trailer," Doc said. "It's habitable."

"But Doc, I don't want to do—"

"But nothing. Do it."

Noah looked across the ICU at Kara, unconscious, badly hurt, alone.

"Okay, damn it."

Doc clapped him on the shoulders. "That's the spirit."

"You're a goddamn dictator, you know that, Doc?"

He grinned. "Just doin' what's best for the patient."

Doc picked up Kara's wrist. He looked at his watch for a minute.

"Pulse has recovered nicely. You were right not to wait for the chopper."

Noah mouthed a profanity at the doc and moved toward the door. Doc smiled in his kindly, I-got-you-now way.

"And Noah?"

"Yeah?"

"Try to be personable for a change when she wakes up."

"Hell, ain't I always the epitome of charm?"

Chapter 22:

Pinpoints of light dotted the darkness. Like starry skies, but without the winking. Rising from blackness, she caught a thermal and soared, arms outstretched, over brown buttes and tan mesas that blurred and shifted. She flew over deep, chaotic canyons, their edges rimmed with a dusky red dimming to darkness below. She heard muted voices and soft music. But she tired and sank into the darkness of a deep canyon. She rested. She would try to fly again later.

Kara lay unconscious in her second full day in the ICU. That day became another and another. Drugs kept her comatose. Doctors monitored her. Vital signs improved. Electrolytes climbed. Broken bones began fusing. But slowly.

Noah stayed longer on each visit, sitting in a dull orange hospital chair. He canceled lessons and charters. He found Kara's phones and computer. He packed them and some of her clothes and left them in a duffle bag next to Kara's bed. An investment in hope for recovery, he thought. He had brought in his old boombox and older mix tapes acquired in one of his earlier lives. Doctors had no objections. She could use the stimuli, they told Noah. Just a matter of reducing the swelling in her brain. Then they'd halt the dexamethasone. She needed rest, they said. When they stopped the drug, she would drift in and out of a semi-waking state, they said. And she would not remember doing so.

Noah would play New Age music. He'd sit on the floor, eyes closed and legs crossed. Noah was not a religious man. But he did believe atmospheres of calm brought spiritual peace. Doc joked about it, dismissing it as so much biofeedback. Just a slowing of respiration, he'd said. The hospital staff was used to Noah. They did what was medically necessary for Kara, ignoring Noah.

On the fourth day, the doctors stopped the drug. Late that evening, after checking her pulse, Noah sat on in a chair next to the bed, watching. Enya serenaded them. He daubed her forehead with a moist towel. Kara stirred. Her eyelids fluttered. Then her face softened, and she slipped back to wherever she was hiding. But he'd felt it. He had felt her squeeze his hand. He leaned over and whispered.

"Come back. Please. Come back."

On the evening of the fifth day, Noah read in the chair. The boombox offered Windham Hill. Kara shifted slightly on the bed. Her mouth frowned, and her face grimaced. He stopped the tape. Her mouth relaxed, and he watched her chest, rising and falling under the hospital blanket, slow in its respiration.

"You know, sweetie, I don't think I liked that all that much, either."

He swore to Doc later that she grinned. He replaced the tape with Hans Zimmer's "Millennium," one of his favorites. Calm settled on her face. The nurses had noticed, but he would never admit, that he watched her face more and more. Hour after hour, he tried to read her face, to understand its subtleties of expression. He heard a cough at the door. A nurse stood there.

"Noah, everything okay?"

"Vital signs stable."

"I'm not talking about hers, Noah."

Noah glared at her as she chuckled and left the room.

At 1:37 p.m. on the sixth day Noah sat. He did not read. He did not think. At least, he tried not to think, not to expect, not to anticipate. The boombox oozed Hearts of Space. He closed his eyes, centering himself.

A voice startled him.

"If I have to listen to any more of that New Age crap, I'm going to puke."

Kara's hazel eyes bore into him, clear, evanescent, penetrating.

"You're awake." He couldn't think of anything else to say.

"I've been awake for an hour."

Noah moved to the bed and reached for her hand. She pulled it away.

"Who the hell are you?"

He backed away. "Um, I'm Noah."

"Well, Noah, where the hell am I?"

"Allen Memorial Hospital. In Moab."

Noah pushed the nurse's call button. "You had an accident," he said.

Furrows deepened on her brow. "An accident?"

"Fell off your bike."

She closed her eyes. "On my head, I suppose."

"Yep. On your head. And a few other places."

Kara's surgeon strode into the room. "Leave us, Noah," he said bluntly.

Noah turned toward the door wordlessly.

Kara called after him. "And don't call me sweetie."

Chapter 23:

April 18, late morning, Allen Memorial Hospital, Moab, Utah

Kara had been moved to a semi-private room in which she was the sole occupant. As Noah passed the nurses' station, an RN smiled at him. "Visiting Ms. McAllister?" she asked.

"Yep. How is she?"

She shrugged. "Okay. Still sleeps a lot. We have to wake her every hour. That, well, that annoys her."

"I can understand that."

"I mean, it really annoys her."

Noah cocked his head slightly. "What else?"

"Those cracked ribs hurt. That annoys her, too."

"Sounds like everything annoys her," he said, chuckling.

"That's putting it mildly."

"Bad patient?"

"Remember back when you broke your leg and we had to pin it?"

"Yeah. Don't remind me."

"Remember how well you behaved?"

"Um, I was annoying?"

"Damn, you were impossible. But she makes you look like an angel."

"That so?" he asked.

She put down the chart she was holding. "Noah, she's polite. We like her. There's, well, there's a sense I have that she's really a sweet person inside."

"And on the outside?"

"She's a bitch."

Noah went to Kara's room, curious. The door was open. He walked in. A fresh bandage was wrapped around her head. She'd have a nasty headache. Having a hole drilled in one's skull never improved anyone's disposition.

Her eyes opened. "Thank you," she said, her voice whispery and hoarse.

"For what?"

"They said you found me."

He pulled a chair next to her bed and sat. "You're welcome."

"And next time, knock," she said sharply.

He looked at her askance. "'Scuse me?"

"Don't walk into my bedroom without knocking, please."

"This is a hospital room, Kara."

"At the moment, it's also my bedroom."

Kara was polite, but she was damn well going to stake out her turf. Noah would respect her privacy — or else.

"How are you feeling?"

"Like shit," she said.

"Could you be more specific?"

"Why? Are you a doctor?" She turned her face away from him.

"No, I just wanted to—"

"Look. I don't like being in hospitals. I don't like being hurt. And I don't like every goddamned stranger around here asking me how I feel. I'm tired of being poked and probed and pissing through a tube. Okay?"

"Sorry. But I do mean well."

Kara yawned and turned toward him. "I'm sure you do."

"They'll take the catheter away today, anyhow."

She glanced at him. "Yeah?"

"Yes. One of the docs told me."

Her face reddened. "What business does my doctor have discussing me with Joe Blow off the street?"

"Well, he—"

"Look," she said. "They told me you probably saved my life. Did save my life, as far as I'm concerned. And there's no way I can ever repay you for—"

"I don't need 'repayment.'"

"Well, you—"

"Listen, I answered a call," he said. "I'd have done it for anyone. I've hauled more than two dozen badly injured people out of the middle of nowhere. If I have offended you somehow, I apologize. You can be as pissed at me as you want, for whatever reason you want. But I don't need to be repaid, and I don't need to be thanked. I hope you heal quickly with little pain. Have a nice life."

He felt suddenly embarrassed at his sharp words, so out of place and uncalled for. They surprised him, let alone her. *Why did I say that?* he wondered. He knew she was right; he had no business discussing her medical condition without her permission. But he turned on his heels and walked toward the door.

"Wait," she called.

Noah stopped at the door and turned. "In case you haven't noticed," he said, "you're in a hospital, and you've just come out of a coma. Any EMT worth his salt would let you rest."

Noah left, closing the door. Kara lay back in her bed, sullen.

When had she become such a bitch? she asked herself. *And why did he turn into a bastard?*

Chapter 24:

April 19, early afternoon, Allen Memorial Hospital, Moab, Utah

A soft knock-knock sounded on the door. Kara fumbled for the bed control. She pressed it, and the bed whined until she was sitting up. Her ribs hurt like hell. Wincing, she said, "Come in."

The door opened. "Is it safe for the bearer of more apologies to enter?" he asked warily. The patient did not smile.

She checked him out. Looked him over. Considered his essence. Noah was no idiot; he knew he was being assessed. It made him feel uneasy, as if he might fail this subjective test. She reached across the bed with her right hand. "Hi. I'm Kara McAllister."

He took her hand, firmly but cautiously. "Hi. I'm Noah Hartshorn."

"Please to meet you, Noah."

"Likewise."

She withdrew her hand and said nothing more.

Noah sat, hands in his lap, his fingers investigating each

other. He inspected her. Beneath the bruises and the short, cow-licked, blonde hair that had not seen a decent shampoo for days, her face was regaining some pink.

She covered a yawn. "Why do you wear your beard so bushy?" she asked.

One hand fled to his face, brushing through his beard.

"No reason. Just the way it grows," he said.

"Oh."

"Why do you ask?" he asked.

"Forget it. I pissed you off enough yesterday."

"Ms. McAllister," Noah said, "you had every right to bark at me. I should not have been talking with your doctor without your knowledge and consent. I should have stuck to reporting your condition from the field. I'm sorry."

Kara's eyebrows raised slightly. She had not expected such formality."

"Thank you. And that's now ancient history, okay?"

Silence seeped into the room. Noah found a chair and sat.

"So what don't you like about it?" he asked.

"About what?"

"My beard."

Kara winced. Breathing would bring discomfort for some time to come.

"It hides you," she said.

"What do you mean?" he asked.

"Oh, don't make a federal case out of it."

"I'm not."

"Are too."

"So, we're retreating to kindergarten?" he said, grinning.

A stabbing pain in her side cut short her laugh. "Pax?" she ventured.

"Sure. Pax. Now what don't you like about my damned beard?"

She grinned at him, and he absorbed small things about Kara without realizing it — the little crinkles around her eyes that danced with mischievous merriment and the thin but graceful lips that illuminated her smile beyond mere expression of delight.

"Trim it," she said. "You'll look, um, more dignified."

He raised his chin archly, mocking her. "I'm not dignified?"

"I don't know if you are or not. I'm just talking about your appearance."

"So I look undignified?" he asked, a sly smile creasing his face.

She turned away. He guessed she was thinking. He didn't know and wondered if she wanted him to leave. But, in truth, talking tired her.

"Noah, who are you?"

"I don't know how to answer that."

"Tell me about yourself, please."

"Wow. I got a 'please.'"

She shot him a nasty look, a glare in which her eyelids narrowed to slits.

"When someone saves my life, I want to know more about that person. That's reasonable, isn't it?"

"Yeah, I guess so."

"So who are you?"

"Well," he said, "would you prefer the history or the advertising?"

She chuckled, her quick smile flashing like neon, then grimaced.

"Please, don't make me laugh."

"Laughter is the best medicine, you know," he said.

"Not for these goddamned ribs."

"Right. Sorry." He paused. "What are they giving you for the pain?"

"Vicodin."

"It working?"

"Not really."

"Why don't you ask for Demerol?"

She frowned. "No thanks. Allergic to it. Sends me into deep depression."

"You've had it before?" After he spoke, he realized he was unsure what he referred to — the drug or the depression. She nodded.

"When?"

She shrugged her shoulders. "I've cracked ribs before."

"How?" he asked.

"Racing mountain bikes. I seem to have this habit of falling off."

He chuckled. "Staying on is the point, isn't it?"

She looked at him sharply. "You're really good at changing the subject."

"What subject?"

"You," she said. "And I don't want history or advertising."

He leaned back in the chair. "What do you want?" he asked.

"Verbs."

"Verbs?" He was curious.

"History and advertising are nothing but adjectives. They tell me nothing. Adjectives are cheap. Verbs tell me what people do. So tell me what you do." She paused, then added, "Please."

He grinned. "Well, let's see. I fly. I teach people to fly. I shuttle. I—"

"Shuttle?"

"Shuttle. When people raft down river, somebody's gotta move their cars to where they'll pull off the river. I'm the somebody who does that."

"Oh," she said. "What else?"

"I read. I read a lot."

"What kind of stuff?"

"Just stuff. Books about nature. Some philosophy. Some politics."

"You an environmentalist?" she asked.

"I've been called worse."

"Such as?"

"Well, the worst I've heard is 'goddamn tree-hugging motherfucker.'"

She laughed. And winced. But kept laughing.

"I said don't make me laugh."

"Sorry. Really."

"Who called you a motherfucker?"

"Hmmm. There are so many. County commissioners. A guy who runs a four-wheeler backcountry expedition outfit and seems to have declared war on me. Oh, a few state legislators. Some staffers from the BLM, too."

"BLM?" she asked.

"Feds. From the Bureau of Land Management. Lots of federal land out of here, and they set resource-extraction policy. I annoy them, too."

"So you're a popular guy," Kara said.

"Yeah. Real popular, I'd say."

"What'd you do to piss them off?" she asked, yawning again.

"Reminded them of their responsibilities."

"Sounds serious," she said. "What responsibilities?"

"To nature. To wilderness. To their children."

"Their children?"

"Yes," he said. "To their children. To leave enough wilderness intact for them to enjoy. And to let them decide how it should be used. Or not used."

"Nice soapbox you have."

"I suppose so," he said.

Her head tilted in that way people do when they study someone closely.

"So, Ms. McAllister, what—"

"Don't call me that."

"Call you what?"

"Ms. McAllister. Please, just call me Kara. Okay?"

"So tell me your verbs, Kara."

"Me?"

"Yes, you." He paused for effect. "Please."

"Well, I guess they would—"

A knock at the door interrupted her. A nurse stood there.

"Kara," the nurse said, "time for vitals and pills."

She frowned and looked at Noah. "See why I hate hospitals?"

Noah moved toward the door as the nurse entered, a little

paper cup with a single Vicodin pill in it, the route to release of some of her pain.

"Noah, would you excuse us?" the nurse said.

When he reached the door, Kara called to him. "Will you come back?"

He turned. "Do you want me to?"

Kara pursed her lips. "Yes," she said. "I suppose I could tolerate it."

He grinned. He'd lost Round One. Round Two? Probably a draw.

After Noah left, Kara called for the nurse.

"Yes, Kara?"

"Would you please ask someone to bring me the form on which I designate who doctors can tell about my medical condition?"

"Sure," said the nurse. She returned in a few minutes and left the form.

Kara picked up her cell phone. She rolled through her contacts for TD's number. She stared at it for several minutes. She sighed.

Seattle is so over.

She deleted TD's contact listing and set down the phone.

Kara picked up the form. She wrote two names on it — Hannah Butler, listed as "friend," and Noah Hartshorn, listed as "TBD" — and signed the form.

Chapter 25:

**April 23, mid-morning, Allen Memorial
Hospital, Moab, Utah**

As Noah walked toward Kara's room, her surgeon approached
him.

"Hey, Noah, how's things?"

"Fine, Greg. You?"

"Okay," the doctor said.

The doctor led him away from Kara's room. "I need to talk
to you," he said. "There's no medical reason to keep Kara here
any longer. So I've told her I'm going to release her today. Doc
told me she'd be staying with you."

Noah nodded.

"You know the routine," the doctor began.

Noah held up his hand. "Stop, Greg. Kara's pissed that
docs and nurses have been talking with me about her medical
condition, so I —

The doctor grinned. "You don't know?"

"Know what?"

"She appended her medical disclosure form," the doctor
said, suppressing a laugh. "You're on it."

"Say what?" Noah said, blinking.

"So," said the doctor, "listen up. She's been groggy off and on. Getting better, but she still faces lengthy recuperation. She may have spells of disorientation from time to time, so she can't drive. I'm going to tell her that her recuperative routine should be rest. And I mean bed rest for at least a few weeks. She isn't going to like that."

The doctor grinned. "I think you've seen her independent streak."

Noah nodded. "I don't envy the nurses."

"She still sleeps quite a bit, though she's out of danger from coma relapse," the doctor said. "She should start walking around after a week or so, getting some exercise. She'll be a little unsteady for a while. Those ribs? She shouldn't be alone, especially while she's taking the meds. And she's still a little dizzy."

"I'll say," Noah said.

The doctor chuckled. "That's not what I meant, Noah."

"I know, I know."

"Look, I'm going into her room and tell her she can leave. And I'm going to tell her what I just told you. No driving. No exertion. Lots of rest."

"And who's going to tell her about this, um, temporary nursing home?"

"Well, you've built such a rapport with her over the past week," the doctor said, chuckling softly. "Doc said to let you do it."

"Oh, Christ, Greg. She probably thinks I'm an ax murderer or worse."

The doctor smiled and turned back toward Kara's room. "Just turn on the charm, Noah. I know at least one nurse who will swear to your charm."

"Why, you sonuva—"

The doctor grinned. "My headache is now your headache."

Noah called after him. "Can she fly?"

The doctor thought for a minute. "Find smooth air and avoid altitude."

Noah nodded.

"And bring a barf bag. Fifty-fifty she uses it."

Noah waited outside Kara's room for ten minutes after the doctor left, holding a large duffle bag and stalling. Finally, he knocked. An exasperated "Yes?" rewarded him. Kara sat on the far side of the bed, facing away from him, still in her hospital gown. It lay open, exposing her back. Her shoulders were shaking.

"Hello," he said softly.

Kara sighed and straightened up. "Hi." He could barely hear her.

"You okay?"

She turned slightly and snapped at him. "Oh, I'm just peachy. They're tossing me out of this place. I've got no clothes, I've got no car, I don't even have my go-bag or my keys or my ID. What the hell do they—"

"Kara, you never wanted to get out of a place as badly as you do this hospital. So stop whining."

She glared at him. Noah tossed the gym bag on the bed. It bounced once and came to rest against her. "This might help," he said.

She turned and put the bag on her lap. "What's this?"

"Open it."

Tugging at the zipper, she opened it. Inside were sandals, a pair of painter's pants, a white camisole, underwear, bra, her go-bag, and a fistful of PowerBars.

"Food!" she exclaimed. "No more goddamned Jell-O. God, this hospital food absolutely bites." She tore open one of the bars and bit off a chunk.

Noah half-sat, half-leaned on the bed. He watched her devour the PowerBar. She even eats with passion, he thought.

"Thank you," she said.

"You're welcome."

She dumped the bag's contents onto the bed. She buried her face into the camisole. Opening her go-bag, she emptied some of its contents onto the bed, too. Her keys. Her wallet. Her Leatherman. "How did you get these?" she asked.

"Hey, when I do a rescue, I rescue everything."

She smiled. "Hartshorn, you might just turn out to be okay."

Noah turned away, blushing.

"So where's my car? Is it okay?"

"It's in Green River. Full tank of gas. Cleaned and waxed, too."

She stared at him. "You washed it?"

He shrugged his shoulders. "I made arrangements."

She nodded, raising her eyebrows.

"Would you please give me a lift to my car? I want to—"

"You planning to go somewhere when you get to it?"

Her eyes moistened.

"Kara, I'm sorry if I—"

His hand instinctively reached for her shoulder before consideration stopped it. He reached around her, pulled a Kleenex from the box on the bed stand, and handed it to her. Picking it up, she dabbed at her eyes.

"Back to Seattle, I guess," she whispered. She slid her legs off the bed onto the floor and began to stand.

"Kara, don't do—"

Noah caught her as she toppled. He held her against his side.

"Dizziness," he said. "You've been horizontal for a long time."

She nodded dumbly. He lowered her onto the bed, her feet on the floor.

"I've got to get dressed," she said quietly. Noah just stood there.

"Noah."

"What?"

"I've got to dress."

"Oh? Oh. Sorry. I'll get the nurse. Wheelchair time."

Her face reddened. "I'm not leaving in a goddamned wheelchair."

Noah walked to the door, turned around, and crossed his arms.

"Then you're not leaving here. Hospital policy, lady."

Kara fumed, eyes still wet, but said nothing.

"Dress. But please don't stand." He walked to the door.

"Noah, are you always such a prick?" she called after him.

He chuckled. "No. I just like abusing invalids."

She stuck her tongue out at him. "I'm not a goddamned invalid."

During the short drive from the hospital to a small, private airfield, Kara said nothing. Much of the time, her eyes were closed. When he stopped next to his Cessna Skymaster parked on the grass, they opened wide.

"We're going to *fly* to Green River?"

"You'd rather walk?"

Kara stared at Noah as he stowed their bags in the Cessna.

As he helped her from the pickup, she said, "You're just giving me a ride to my car. Understood?"

Noah nodded. "Absolutely."

"Long's we understand each other."

He helped her into the Skymaster. As he closed the door, she said, "I can drive long enough to get to a motel. Don't worry about me."

"Sure."

Noah ran up the Cessna's engines, checking the magnetos. He filed a VFR flight plan for the fifty-mile hop to Green River Muni in his deepest airline captain voice. Kara was slumped in the seat, her face ashen, her posture listless. He wondered if the docs should have kept her longer.

Ten minutes later, the Skymaster was at two thousand feet AGL, above ground level, on a west-northwest heading. Kara's curiosity overcame dizziness, fatigue, headache, and rib pain. She looked out the window. Noah skirted the western edge of Arches National Park. He called out the sights as they slipped under the starboard wing. He pointed out the Courthouse Towers, Salt Wash, the Windows arches, the Devils Garden. In the distance, Delicate Arch shone surreal in the late morning Utah sun. Kara stared at it.

"That's Delicate Arch?"

"You know it?"

"It's on the cover of my Rand McNally," she said quietly.

She sank back into her seat. She said no more. He banked to port.

"That's the Canyonlands, Kara. Closest to us is Dead Horse Point. You can drive down Shafer Trail onto the White Rim Sandstone and—"

Kara snored softly. He returned the Cessna to a northwesterly heading. He shrugged. So much for impressing a woman. The Cessna bucked once in a patch of turbulence. Kara awoke, eyes wide, momentarily fearful. She saw Noah and remembered where she was. She fell sleep again but did not dream.

Noah landed the Skymaster at Green River Muni. Kara never stirred as he shut down the engines, got out, and tied down the Cessna. He retrieved their gear and toted it to his Land Cruiser. He returned and shook Kara on the shoulder, rousing her into the half-awake, half-asleep netherworld of the truly tired.

"We're here, Kara."

"... where ... why did you ... my car ... is it—"

He unfastened her seatbelt and lifted her easily from the plane before she could protest and set her down, holding her around her waist.

"Walk, Kara."

"... don't want to ..."

"Just lean on me. Over here. That's it. Just a little more."

He eased her into the Land Cruiser, and her head rolled back against the headrest, eyes closed. She mumbled, but he couldn't make out what she said. After buckling her in and bracing her neck with a pillow, he started the Land Cruiser and drove out Old State Route 24. The Land Cruiser jostled Kara as it trundled over the quarter-mile-long dirt road to his hangar and trailer in Greasewood Draw. She stirred but did not waken. He parked close to the trailer. Kara's Subaru sat nearby.

Noah unbuckled her seat belt, carried Kara into the trailer, and lay her on his bed. He checked her vitals. Her pulse was steady, but a little fast. He placed his hand on her chest and counted her respirations. Seventeen. Good. He rested his palm on her forehead. Cool. Not clammy. His hand lingered there, on her forehead. He pondered whether to undress her and put her to bed.

He turned on a window fan. The trailer had no air conditioning. He filled a Nalgene bottle with water and set it and a mug on the nightstand. He slipped off her Converses and covered her with a blanket. Even in the warmth of afternoon, he knew she would chill and wake. He didn't want her to vanish.

Noah sat at his kitchen table and sipped at a Lone Star beer, thinking about the past, which he hated doing. He disliked reminders of mistakes made, paths not taken, women left behind. Or doing the leaving, he thought. Melancholy seeped out of the cubbyhole he'd locked tight by attention closely paid to flying, lobbying, shuttling, hangar puttering, reading, anything he could do to keep his mind rooted in the present. Now her. Now this unexpected apparition. Now this nascent but strengthening feeling, born of instinct and nurtured by a flight guided by a dream to a broken mountain bike and a stranger who spoke in a defiant, coarse language of barely repressed anger and avoidance. He walked into the bedroom. She had not moved. Sleep had relaxed the hard set to her face. He went to the hangar. He'd been able to ride Kara's bike from Justensen Flat, but it needed work. He straightened the rim on Kara's bike, removed the chain and cleaned and oiled it, and replaced a broken brake cable. He hung the broken cable from a nail over his workbench. A talisman.

Life is happenstance. No broken brake cable, no Kara.

Sunset passed. He ate a fried egg sandwich, but found it bland and tasteless. He read for a while, then studied some briefing papers. He would testify at a legislative hearing on a Wilderness Study Area designation for part of the Swell in a few weeks. He pushed the papers away, got up, and leaned against the doorframe of his bedroom. He couldn't see her in the darkness but heard her restless sleep. Every few minutes she rolled from one side to the other. A few times she moaned. He plugged in a nightlight. Its soft glow illuminated her. He returned to the kitchen and lay on the couch. He listened to her breathing until he was satisfied she had fallen asleep. Then he, too, drifted into sleep.

Noah woke when Kara cried out shortly after midnight. She sat up, eyes blinking wide open in fright. Her head craned back and forth as she looked hurriedly through her unknown surroundings.

"Who ... Oh, god ..."

He moved to the bed. "It's me, Kara. It's Noah. You're okay. You're safe."

"Noah?" She rubbed her eyes with the other hand.

"Yes, Kara. It's all right. You're in my home. You're safe."

Kara was shaking and breathing in deep, shuddering gasps. "But how—"

"I'll tell you in the morning, Kara. Everything's okay."

He moved closer to her. Recognition dawned on her face. "Noah ..."

He touched her forehead. It was hot. She leaned against his hand.

"Dream ... all that noise ..."

"Just a dream, Kara. You're okay now."

He slipped his arm behind her shoulders. "Lay back, Kara. It's okay."

"My side hurts."

"I know, Kara. But you're healing. You'll feel better soon."

Her eyes closed, but she was grimacing with pain. He poured water into the mug. He held her with one arm and put a Vicodin on her tongue.

"That's it. Open wide. This will help you, Kara."

She sipped at the water. She made a face. "Tastes bad ..."

"Iron, Kara. I'll buy you a Brita filter tomorrow."

He got a washcloth and soaked it with warm water. He swabbed her forehead, her face, her neck, the swell of her upper chest. "That feels good ..."

"Sleep, Kara. I'll keep the bogeyman away."

"I feel ... sweaty ... dirty ..."

"Then let's get some clean clothes on you." She did not resist. "... 'kay."

He pulled the camisole over her head, averting his eyes from her breasts. He held a clean T-shirt. She lifted her arms and winced.

"No, Kara. Hold your arms out, not up." He pulled the T-shirt onto her arms, then threaded her head through the neck. He patted her hand. She reached for it and held it tightly. "Lay back, Kara."

He thought better of removing her painter pants. They could wait. He pulled the covers over her and stood.

"Don't go ..."

"I won't, Kara. I'll be right here."

Kara's grip loosened. She had fallen asleep. But he didn't want to move his hand. So he sat awake in his bedroom, with this stranger, for a long time.

Chapter 26:

April 24, dawn, Noah's trailer, Greasewood Draw

Noah woke up, still in the chair. Kara breathed quietly, her eyes open but vacant. She had that thousand-yard stare, looking into the future and not seeing it. He waved his hand in front of her face. Her eyes followed his hand.

"Good morning, Kara," he said softly.

"Hi," she said weakly. "Where am I?"

"Green River. In my trailer. Do you remember leaving the hospital?"

She shook her head. "Thirsty ..."

Noah fetched water and a Vicodin. "Here. Swallow it, please. Good girl."

He helped her hold the mug as she drank. Her eyes closed and within moments she was asleep again. He wrinkled his nose. Kara's BO had reached the danger stage. He went to the kitchen and made breakfast for himself.

He called Annie, who was also a paramedic, and asked her to come out and help clean up Kara. Annie said she would come by later in the afternoon. Noah spent the morning sitting at his kitchen table, trying to convince himself that circumstances were normal, that the book he was reading he comprehended, that the letters to legislators he penned were coherent. Occasionally, Kara would moan, and he would hustle to the bedroom to check on her. But she seemed okay. Her skin did not seem as pallid as the day before, and she was not flushed or sweaty. When Annie arrived, they woke Kara. Introductions were made, but Kara spoke little and made no protest as Annie helped her into the shower. They put her in bed, clad in fresh underwear and T-shirt. Noah hated seeing her this way, in a condition not her choice. Annie told him Kara needed care, and that hygiene was part of that care. Until she could do it for herself, someone would have to help her.

In the morning a noise from the bedroom woke Noah. He had slept on the couch in the main room of the trailer. He rushed to the bedroom and found Kara sitting on the floor. "Goddamn it," she said.

Noah sat in the chair and watched. "What are you trying to do?"

"Pack. What the hell does it look like?"

"Oh." Noah nodded, arms across his chest. Each time Kara tried to stand, she grew dizzy and fell back on the bed. She crawled to the other side of the bed where Noah had placed her bag. He'd stacked some of her clothes he'd washed the day before atop it. Each movement left her gasping. Opening the bag. Stuffing clothes into it. Crawling back to the bed stand for her wallet and go-bag. She stood, bracing herself against the wall.

"Going somewhere?" he asked.

"Motel."

"Okay." He leaned back again.

"You're enjoying this, aren't you?"

"No, I'm not."

"Why aren't you helping?"

"No one asked."

She shot him a dirty look. "Prick."

"Probably. But how do you intend to get to the motel?"

"Drive." She shook her keys at him.

He picked up the vial of Vicodin. He read the label. "Lessee, says right here, 'Medication may cause dizziness or drowsiness.' Hmmm. There's more. Says, 'Medication may impair your ability to drive or operate machinery.'"

"God damn it, I know what it says."

"So you're going to drive, eh?"

"Yes, damn it."

"Probably hit a tree. That'd be okay, assuming it's just you. But suppose you hit another car? Hurt someone else?"

She glared at him. "You really are a prick, you know?" she said.

He stood and picked up the bag. "I'll carry this out to the car for you."

He walked out of the room. "Coming, Kara?"

He heard her shuffling, hands on the wall for balance. She reached the bedroom doorway, a hand on each side, face flushed, body shaking. When she fell, Noah moved cat-quick to catch her. He lay her on the bed. She dry-heaved harshly. He sat in the chair and waited.

"Don't want to stay here," she said, slurring her words.

"What do you want?" he asked.

"Be ... by myself."

"You can't be by yourself for a while, Kara."

"Can't ... stay here."

"Can if you want to."

"Don't want to ..."

"Want to what?"

She turned her head away from him. He could barely hear her.

"Don't want ... don't need anyone."

"Well, right now, you do. Circumstances suggest it's me."

Kara cried. Noah felt helpless and could only wait until the tears passed.

"So I'm ... a prisoner."

"I could take you back to the hospital. Or to a motel. We could get a nurse to look after you until you can travel. Or you

could stay here. I have room and I'll leave you alone, save for
what you can't do for yourself."

Biting her upper lip, Kara reddened. She fell silent for a
while, then: "Noah?"

"Yes?"

"Can I stay here ... for a while?" Her voice was almost
inaudible.

"Yes."

"Thank you," she said.

He wondered how much it cost her to ask. And why. She
slept for most of the day and into the next, waking only for
Vicodin and tepid soup.

Chapter 27:

April 27, late morning, Noah's trailer, Greasewood Draw

On the seventeenth morning since Utah had struck down Kara and the fifth of her internment in Greasewood Draw, Noah sat in the small dining nook of his trailer, flailing with his bookkeeping. He didn't need the modest income from his charter service, but he fancied himself a businessman and tried to do the things a businessman should do. He sipped coffee while entering figures into the accounting software Annie had pestered him into buying. He had few debts other than occasional credit-card bills and other household expenditures. He owned his trailer, paid cash for the well he'd sunk for water, and last year had paid off the short-term note for the 22 acres he had corralled from two owners. He'd rebuilt his ultralights for very little money. He still owed some money on his twin-engine Skymaster, his only truly expensive toy. The leasebacks on his Cessna 206 covered its payments. Money didn't worry him. He had other resources beyond his flying enterprises, which were hobbies designed to merely break even every three years out of five to keep the IRS off his back. He owned little else, save his Land Cruiser, which he'd salvaged.

Noah believed in salvation through reclamation. He rebuilt things. He made them well. He renewed their utility.

He glanced into the bedroom. Kara was asleep, covered only by a sheet. He'd have to figure out how to cool the trailer. Summer would broach soon. He shuddered to think what she'd be like when Utah warmed up. He abandoned bookkeeping and stepped quietly into the bedroom. The sheet draped over her chest rose, then settled as she inhaled and exhaled. He touched her forehead. It was cool. She stirred and her hand cradled itself under her cheek.

Noah walked the four steps to the kitchen. The trailer was tight quarters — one room with kitchen, breakfast nook, a couch, a small desk; a small shower/bathroom; and his bedroom. People had to get along in confining places. He boiled water for tea. She'd be up soon. He'd seen how she slept, how she turned from one side to the other, kicking the sheet down, just before waking. He guessed she did not like confinement. He rummaged through a tin for some Darjeeling. He covered the pan — he had no teapot — with a crudely cut circle of closed-cell foam from a camping pad. He set out a mug and spooned in sugar.

"Hey." Her voice was thick as slurry as it drifted into the kitchen.

"Good morning," he said, in a warm but neutral tone. His behaviors were changing. Solitary life had allowed him to kiss off social graces. Kara rolled onto her back and stretched. The sheet slipped down to her waist.

Kara blushed and pulled the sheet up. "I don't remember wearing these clothes," she said.

"You were redressed."

"You've got some nerve."

"You stunk. And I didn't do it. Annie did. So your virtue was safe."

"Oh."

"I'll make a fortune selling photos, though."

That earned him a dirty look. He was getting used to it.

He pointed to a stack of neatly folded clothes — bras,

underwear, Quick-Drys, tank tops, sweatshirts — on a stool next to the bed.

"I washed them last night."

She looked where he pointed. "Oh. Thank you. Again. That was kind."

He stood, not moving. The clothes were farther than she could reach.

"Turn around, for chrissake," she said.

Noah chuckled. He got a mug for her. She slunk across the bed, grabbed clothes, and hurried into underwear, Quick-Drys, and a T-shirt. She began to stand but lurched, off balance, as Noah returned. He caught her upper arm to steady her and felt its supple strength. Not a bicep of power; rather, a bicep of lean, purposeful, long-haul muscle.

"Easy, Kara. Don't rush things."

He steadied her as she sat down. She winced, a consequence of a deep breath expanding cracked ribs that didn't want to be expanded yet.

"I'm tired of being dizzy."

"It will pass."

"Not soon enough."

He handed her a mug. She sipped at the tea, nodding to him.

"I don't mean to be an ungrateful guest, but this tea sucks."

Noah chuckled. "It's a decade old or so. I'll get some new stuff later."

"Herbal, please," she said.

"Herbal?"

"Caffeine can make you weird, you know."

"I've been drinking a dozen cups of coffee a day for twenty years, lady."

"And you're not weird?"

Noah sat on the floor. "Well, maybe a little. What do you call weird?"

She rested the mug on one knee, cradling it in her hands. Her eyes roamed around the trailer.

"Well, living in a trailer — how long, did you say? — isn't

exactly sane."

"No, but it's paid for. And I don't need any more room than this. "

"For now, maybe."

He looked at her quizzically. "What do you mean by that?"

She smiled. "Oh, nothing. Just being a wiseass."

Noah sensed Kara retreating. She was in unknown terrain, a long way from home. Discretion told him to tread lightly. He went back to the kitchen nook to pour tea for himself. Kara sat up gingerly, then tried to stand. She wobbled a bit, but caught her balance. Noah noticed. Experienced paramedics notice everything. She had lots of recovery time and predictable setbacks ahead. The surgeon had told him to consult with Doc daily, more if warranted. He returned to the bedroom and knelt in front of her. A tiny cowlick, a legacy of sleep, rose from her head and, without thinking, he patted it down. Her head leaned toward his hand.

"I'm a mess," she whispered.

"You're no more a mess than anyone else getting up in the morning."

"Is that supposed to be a compliment?"

"Just the facts, ma'am."

She smiled. "You're a doofus."

"Am not."

"Are too."

He touched his forefingers to the skin just below her eyes. "Look up, please."

"Why?"

"Med check, girl."

She looked up as he pulled down on the soft skin under her eyes.

"Now to the sides. And down." She did as he asked. "And?"

"Your eyes are clear, pupils equally dilated and reactive."

"Oh, you say the sweetest things," she said, mocking him.

He took her wrist and looked at his watch, timing her pulse. "Apparently, your heart exists and is still beating. All indications to the contrary."

She yanked her hand way from him. "Wiseass."

"Yep."

He sat and sipped at his tea. She was right. It tasted like crap. He'd never noticed.

"You've been pretty gonzo for the past few days," he said.

"My head still hurts."

"It won't much longer, Kara."

"Noah?"

"Yes?"

"Why am I here?" she asked.

"No room at the inn," he said.

"Don't be a smartass," she replied.

He looked up at her. "Doc's orders."

"The doctor?"

"He's just Doc. You'll meet him. He's been tending you. In fact, he flew down in the chopper with you to Moab. Kinda rare for him, taking such an interest in a case. Technically, you've been discharged in his care."

"So why am I here, stuck with you?"

"I have better manners," he said, suppressing a grin.

"Like hell you do."

He explained that he, Doc, and the staff at Moab had not been able to reach anyone to notify about her accident. And Kara had never volunteered a friend or a relative to notify.

"So Doc said bring you here. I'm a paramedic, and you need — needed — looking after."

She said nothing for a while. "Thank you," she said.

"For what?"

"Taking care of me." She hid a soft smile behind a sip from her tea.

Noah got to his feet. "Breakfast coming up. And you need a shower."

She steadied herself against the wall of the trailer until she was sure the dizziness remained at bay. She walked to the tiny bathroom, found a clean towel hanging neatly from a rack nearby, and stepped part way inside. Stopping there, she looked at him, his back to her, minding breakfast fixings on the stove. In the quiet trailer, the sound of bacon spattering was loud and harsh. She closed the door and showered.

Chapter 28:

May 3, late morning, Noah's trailer, Greasewood Draw

"My head hurts."

Doc had predicted Kara would relapse. She'd try to do too much. On the ninth and tenth days of her Greasewood Draw internment, she had fiddled with her computer for several hours. Then she'd done some light housekeeping after Noah had gone into Green River for groceries. So, on the eleventh day, Kara lay in bed fidgeting and complaining, the thin sheet pushed down to her waist. Bed rest left her white cotton tank top wrinkled. She felt like shit, she thought, so she must look like shit.

Noah, making a cup of herbal tea, turned from the kitchen to look at her.

"Do you feel anything else?" he asked.

She glared. "Isn't a headache enough?"

"I'm sorry. I didn't mean to make light of it," he said. "I mean, do you feel any pain, anything, anywhere else?"

"My stomach hurts, too."

"Nauseated?"

"Yeah, a little."

"You feel dizzy at all?" he asked.

She shook her head. "My side still hurts. Every fucking breath hurts."

Her chronic pain eroded any feeling that healing was occurring. She had not slept well, either. For the past few days, despite Noah's urging, Kara's fluid intake had been low. Told she wouldn't drink, Doc had predicted her headaches would return, linked to dehydration rather than her head injury.

"Make her drink some damn water," he'd instructed Noah.

He took a bottle of spring water from the fridge and carried it to the bedroom. Drink, he motioned. She did, making a face. He sipped at his tea, then set the mug down on a shelf. He rested his palm on her forehead.

"You're not hot. No fever."

She looked up at him. "It's eating me up."

"What do you mean?" he asked.

"I can't think. I can't think of anything else but this damn headache."

He stood. "Get up, please."

"What?"

"I said, get up."

"I don't want to get—"

He pulled her gently but firmly until she sat upright. He sat on the bed beside her and put his hand between her shoulder blades to brace her.

"Feel dizzy now?"

"No."

"Stand up, please."

"I don't want to."

"Stand up."

"No," Kara said stubbornly.

She was a temperamental patient. But he'd been doing his job. He did not tell her that, each night, he had taken her vital signs while she slept. He did not tell her that he had taken her temperature under her armpit. He did not tell her that he had rested his hand on her chest, counting her respirations. He did not tell her that he had taken her pulse at the wrist. He did not tell her that he sat in the chair next to the bed for hours, in the middle of the night, thinking. He did not tell her that he'd called the doc to report that she was spending too much time in bed. Beyond more fluids, Kara needed to walk around, Doc had said, to get the blood moving through her system, to revive her, to stimulate the desire to be well as well as get well.

"Stand up. Please."

Reluctantly, she swung her feet to the side and onto the floor.

"Dizzy now?"

"No," she said. He set clean shorts and T-shirt on the bed beside her and turned away.

"Can you change okay?" he asked.

"Well, now, that's pretty insulting," Kara said. But she removed the not-so-clean underwear and T-shirt and slipped into the clean clothes while sitting.

"You can turn around now." She sighed. "I'm already tired again."

"Stop whining."

She reached out and poked him. "I'm not whining."

"Yes, you are."

"My head hurts. I can whine if I want to."

He led her to the door of the trailer. "Take the water bottle."

"Where are we going?"

"You need exercise," he said.

"I don't want to."

"You want to get better?"

"Yeah, yeah."

He stepped onto the ground. "Then come on."

He helped her down, then slipped his arm around her waist. They walked slowly. She shuffling along, protesting, small clouds of dust bursting from the dry earth with each step. "I hate this," she said. "You're a bastard."

"Yes, I'm a bastard. Keep walking."

Every few dozen steps, he stopped and insisted she drink some water.

"You want me to drown?" she said.

"No. I want you to drink."

They walked on. On the far side of his runway stood a small grove of tamarisk fringed with pinkish spring growth. One tree, near the center of the grove, stood a little taller than the rest. Noah often sat there to read. The curve of the trunk snugly fit the curve of his back. After leaning against its trunk, he motioned to her to sit.

"Don't want to," she said.

"Okay. Just stand there. But please drink more water."

Kara took the water bottle from him, pulled the nipple out with her teeth, and squirted a little into her mouth.

"Who are you?" she asked.

"Beg pardon?"

"I asked, who are you?"

"At the moment, your nurse."

"I don't want a nurse," she said.

"What do you want?" he asked.

"I don't know. I just don't want to hurt anymore."

She drank more water. After handing the bottle back, she pressed the heels of her hands against her temples. "God, I hate this."

"The headache?"

"No. Needing this ... this damn baby-sitting."

Noah tensed. She saw it and her face softened.

"I'm sorry. I didn't mean it like that. I'm so grateful to you. It's just that, well, I ... Oh, shit. Forget I said anything. I'm, I'm ... Fuck. Just ignore me."

Noah nodded. "So, your headache gone?" he asked.

"No, it's not."

"Then please sit."

She gave him the look women give men who tell them what to do — and are right. She wriggled against the tree, trying to find a sweet spot. Neither spoke. He moved closer and glanced at her. Kara's eyes were closed.

"Kara?"

"Um?"

"Just checking."

"On what?"

"You know what."

She sighed. "My head hurts."

He put his hand on her shoulder. She stirred. He turned toward her ear.

"Breathe slowly, Kara. Slow breaths. Exhale. Enjoy your lungs."

Her eyes flicked toward him. She took a deep breath and exhaled slowly. She winced. But she endured. Her ribs were healing. She relaxed.

"That's it," he whispered, delicate fractions of an inch from her ear.

Barely audible, she spoke. "What are you doing to me?"

"Sending your headache away, Kara, that's all."

She leaned against his shoulder. "Okay," she whispered.

"Find your lightness, Kara. Don't ignore your headache. Just tell it to go away, to leave you, to find its own home. And breathe, Kara, breathe it away."

She murmured, shifting against him, sliding into the crook of his arm.

"Some damn New Age crap, isn't it ..."

He nodded and his nose grazed against her cheek.

"Tickles ..."

She fell asleep. He folded his hands in his lap. He paid attention to the rhythm of her breathing as he tried to ward off the Minions of Headaches Everywhere. As her breathing slowed, he eased her down until her head rested on his thigh. Noah stroked her forehead with his fingertips, from the center to the right temple, from the center to the left temple. Over and over. The wrinkles on her forehead eased.

He chuckled as she snored. He looked up to the San Rafael Swell to the west. He imagined himself aloft in his Drifter, adrift at the whim of thermals and unpredictable currents. That kind of unpredictability he could handle.

But Kara was unmapped terrain. He thought about how men are measured, how men had measured him, how women had measured him. He stroked her forehead. He'd known her only for twenty-three days — and she'd been out cold for much of that time. Noah sighed. *Once more unto the breach, dear friends, once more.*

Chapter 29:

May 8, early morning, Noah's trailer,
Greasewood Draw

Noah sat hunched on the edge of the couch, trying to wake up. With Kara now ensconced in his trailer, he'd slept in his cargo shorts instead of his normal naked state. He glanced at the open bedroom door. He'd closed it the night before.

"Kara?"

He peeked in. The blanket had been thrown aside as if the occupant had left in haste. He looked in the bathroom. No Kara. He ran outside. "Kara!"

No answer. He cupped his hands about his ears, closed his eyes, and listened. A canyon wren warbled from somewhere high on the cliff behind the trailer. A light wind rustled the leaves of the cottonwoods and the tamarisks next to the stream. Then ... *clink*, *clink*. Metal on metal. He looked inside the hangar. No Kara. From outside, *clink*, *clink*, again. He jogged to the rear. Kara was trying to lift a fifteen-pound York plate onto an end of the bar resting in its holder on his pressing bench. It slipped from her hand and fell against another plate. *Clink*. She sank to her knees and lowered her head onto the bench. Her chest heaved. She winced from the pain of her cracked ribs. She sat back and covered her face. He walked to the bench and sat.

"What are you doing?" he asked softly.

She didn't answer. Weakness would prevent her from injuring herself. Intuition told him that no one stayed in Kara's life for long by telling her what she should or should not be doing. He reached for her shoulder, but she slapped his hand away. She squatted and tried to lift the plate again, but clutched at her side as the ribs protested. She dropped the weight. *Clink.*

"Lessee," he said. "Two fifteen-pound plates. Thirty pounds for the bar. That's about sixty pounds. And what do you plan on doing with this?"

"Curls," she panted.

"I see," he said. "Trying to set some kind of post-op record?"

She glared at him. "It's what I'm used to lifting."

"When's the last time you lifted that?"

She shrugged.

"Do you want help?" he asked.

Pain and frustration etched her face. "No, god damn it, I don't need help."

"I didn't ask if you *needed* help. I only asked if you *wanted* it."

She leaned against the bar, breathing heavily, every breath inciting her ribs to riot. She's tough, he thought, but an idiot. Or ... or driven. By what?

"I'm weak," she whispered.

"So you say."

"Don't make fun of me."

"I'm not. What do you want to do?"

"I need to get stronger. I'm out of shape."

He nodded. "Touch your head," he said.

She did, patting the sides and top of her head with her right hand, her left side compromised by the reluctant ribs. "What do you feel there?" he said.

"Just the stubble where they shaved my head."

"Exactly."

"So what?"

"You've got two cracked ribs and a slight fracture in your skull just above your left ear. There's also a tiny orbital fracture as well. Near's I can recall, you had surgery just four weeks ago because your brain swelled and damn near killed you. They filled you with anesthesia. A doctor drilled a half-inch hole in your head to relieve the pressure. They used a really powerful steroid to knock you out for several days. You spent more than a week in a coma."

"So?" she gasped.

"So are you out of shape? Or are you just temporarily wiped out by a serious accident and some serious doctoring?"

He flinched at her angry look. "Don't patronize me," she said.

"I'm sorry. I don't mean to seem as if I am. But if you feel you have to lift, just use the bar. Just to warm up. Forget the plates for a bit."

She said nothing. Taking a deep breath, she grasped the thirty-pound bar. Noah could tell she had trained with weights. The good posture. The feet, shoulder width apart for balance. The slightly flexed knees. He straddled the bench facing her, the bar between them. She tried to curl the bar, but she could only manage one curl before she winced from the pain in her rib cage. She tried again, her lips quivering. The bar didn't move as high as the first curl. It fell back with a clank. Tears seeped down her cheek before she turned away to hide them.

"Try negative resistance," he said.

She glanced over her shoulder at him.

"If you can't lift, then lower. Got to start somewhere."

Kara folded her arms across her chest and looked at him in a way that men never understood. He'd learned that times came when women measured men against some emotional baseline, some heartfelt standard, some memory of men past and others imagined. Her blue eyes brightened, focusing on his.

She nodded. A slight dip of the chin. He raised the bar to her chest.

"Lower," he said. "I'll spot."

He took most of the weight as the bar sank to its holder.

"Again."

He let her take a little more of the weight, then lowered the bar.

"Again."

Her forearms trembled. When the bar clinked into its holder, she gasped and buckled at the knees. He stepped quickly behind her and wrapped his arm around her waist, avoiding her ribs and holding her up, her back against his bare chest.

"I'm so weak." She sighed.

"It will pass," he said.

"Damn well better."

"We can rebuild you. We can make you better than you were. The six-million-dollar Kara."

She chuckled, then winced. "Don't make me laugh."

"This little escapade sure won't make Doc laugh."

"No, I guess it won't."

She looked at him anxiously, realizing what he'd said.

"You're not going to tell him, are you?"

He grinned. "Hey. I'm no snitch."

He motioned her to the bench and sat behind her. He kneaded her shoulders. Kara stiffened. "Relax, Kara. Just relax." But she did not.

"Raise your right arm beside your head," he asked. Reluctantly, she did. He placed his left hand on her shoulder and grasped her hand with his right, carefully pulling her arm back toward him.

"Shoulder's tight," he said. "You need stretching. Now the other one."

He stretched each shoulder socket gently, easily, but firmly. He took her head in both hands, rocking it back and forth. He kneaded her shoulder blades and lats. She remained stiff, rigid, unyielding.

"On your back, please," he said. She lay back. Standing in front of her, he raised each leg, leaning it on slightly, stretching the hamstrings. He massaged her calves and quads. She lay rigid on the bench, her teeth clenched.

"Don't fight me, Kara," he whispered. "Don't fight relaxing. Stretching and massage are part of the med plan. You'd do it for me, wouldn't you?"

His lopsided grin prompted a tiny smile. He straddled the bench, over her hips, and lifted them, stretching her back. He raised her legs again, stretching the hamstrings. She relaxed. But moisture gathered at the corners of her closed eyes. He didn't understand, so he looked away. Her issue. She'd make it public when she chose. He rubbed a sports creme into her biceps, triceps, and forearms. They'd done the work today. They needed the most care.

He fetched a towel. He draped the towel over her, from under her chin down to her knees. Then he left. Hugged by the silence in the hangar, Kara cried. From revelation, not sadness. She had discovered a patient, caring man who bore no expectations of *quid pro quo*.

Ten minutes later, hearing his footsteps, she sat up and dried her eyes. He carried a wooden box containing two three-pound dumbbells, two five-pounders, and two ten-pounders. If the weight was a strain, it did not show.

"Begin with these," he said. "In the trailer. Curls, presses, and shoulder work. Two sets only, ten reps as target. When the ribs quiet down, some abs. Only when I'm around. Just for caution's sake. Stretching and muscle massage afterward. After you get used to these, we'll come back. Deal?"

She sighed, masking her gratitude. "Okay, okay. Deal."

He walked her toward the trailer, but she lifted his hand from her arm.

"Don't do everything for me, Noah."

"I won't."

"I don't like being weak."

"No one does, Kara. No one does."

The next morning, after breakfast, Kara, resplendent in her black Speedo and red Quick-Drys, announced her intention to take a walk.

"Want company?" he asked.

"Do I have a choice?" she said.

"No," he answered, filling two water bottles from the new Brita pitcher he kept in the fridge. She was carrying a two-pound weight in each hand. He took the weights from her hands and replaced them with the water bottles.

"Just think of them as adjustable weights," he said. "Give me a minute to change." He stepped into the bedroom and slipped into his cargo shorts and a tank top. When he emerged, Kara was gone. She was walking past the hangar toward the dirt road that led to Route 24. He caught up to her quickly, but walked behind so he could check her sense of balance. She tottered a bit, but never enough to stumble and fall.

Her face was strained after fifteen minutes. Still, she did not stop, pumping her water-weighted hands as urban powerwalkers do, high in front, high in back. She sweated profusely.

"Easy, Kara. That's enough for day one. Let's head back."

She ignored him. He quickened his pace and caught her elbow.

"Hey. Please. Enough."

"I'm not tired," she protested. "Let go."

"You don't have to get it all back in one day. You know about training. Start slow. Add a little each day."

"But I've got so much to—"

"But nothing," he said. "Christ, Kara, you're so stubborn. Why do you insist on trying to get everything back at once? Are you always this impatient, so hard on yourself? Can't you take a break? Be a little easy on yourself?"

She whirled on him and threw the water bottles down on the ground.

"God damn it, I hate it when people tell me that. I hate it. So knock it off!"

"Kara, I didn't mean to—"

"Like hell you didn't." Her face reddened. "You're like all the others."

"What others?" he asked quietly.

Kara cried softly, covering her face with her hands. Noah knew that it embarrassed her, and that she tried to hide it. She probably didn't understand why she wept so easily and often. The constant discomfort from her ribs, the meds, the fitful sleep, had eroded control of her emotions. She'd flare: It was normal; it was natural. He'd wait it out. He'd help her wait it out, too.

He embraced her tentatively, wrapping his arms loosely around her back. Her face pressed into the crook of his neck. Her fists rapped against his chest as she wept convulsively. He moved one hand to the back of her head and stroked her hair. Were she stronger, he knew, these mood swings would lessen. But she needed these breaches of her own taut protocol to deal with her own devils.

"It's all right, Kara. Whatever it is, it will pass."

"You don't understand," she gasped.

"I don't need to."

Kara lifted her head. "You don't?"

"No. *You* do. When you do, you can decide whether you want to tell me. If you don't, that's okay, too. I don't need to pry."

She rested her forehead against his chest again. The fists relented and after a while she lowered her hands until they rested on his hips. They slipped around his waist. Her breasts pressed against him, her hips warm against his, her thighs brushing against his. It didn't feel sexual. Not now. In other circumstances, yes. But this? Perhaps gratitude, perhaps emotional release, perhaps a need for solace. Affection? Maybe. Just maybe.

She turned and was gone, walking back toward the trailer, breaking the connection. He lagged behind, still watching his patient for signs of progress — or relapse.

Kara walked every morning, sometimes with Noah, sometimes without. They would talk. She learned about his flying, about running a business in the middle of nowhere, about his minor fame as a cog in the local search and rescue community. He preened one day when she told him she was impressed by that and thanked him again for finding her. He learned about her Web business, about her uncompromising belief in researching a client's project needs before writing a single line of code. He learned about her minor fame as a mountain-bike racer in the Northwest. But neither really learned much about what made the other tick. Just long walks with guarded, factual conversations masquerading as human communion.

One morning, half way down the dirt road, she stopped and faced him.

"How'd you find me?"

"'Scuse me?"

"When I fell. You told me in the hospital you were out on a call. How'd you find me?

"Just luck. Out for a joy ride."

"C'mon, Noah," she said. "I don't buy needle in a haystack. How'd you find me?"

"A dream," he said presently.

"A dream?"

"Yes. A dream told me something was wrong."

"How?" she asked intently.

"I dreamed I heard someone crying. I kept seeing a face."

"Was it mine?"

"I don't know. It was dark, except for the flashes of light."

Her face paled. "Lightning?" she asked.

"Could've been, I guess. Why?

So she told him. About the lightning. About being chased. About her dreams of dancing on a huge ballroom floor with her electrical lover.

"I know you think I'm crazy," she said. "I know *I* think I'm crazy."

He smiled.

"What do you think?" she asked.

"I don't. I just accept."

They walked for a while. "Noah," she said, "you're inscrutable."

"Ah, so," he said. She punched his shoulder.

After their walks, he would spot her while she lifted. First with the dumbbells inside the trailer, then, after a week or so, outside in the gym. She progressed rapidly. But she tired easily. After lunch, she would nap, and he would go the Green River Muni to give lessons or fly a charter. In a few weeks, her pallor gave way to richer, healthier color, the soft bronze granted by the bright Utah sun. One day, arriving home early because of a canceled lesson, the trailer was empty. Standing by the door, he looked out toward the rim of Morrison sandstone behind the hangar. A few hundred yards away, Kara lay motionless on the ground face down at the base of the cliff. He ran toward her, alarmed. He stopped when he saw the towel under her. She was nude, asleep, and sunbathing. Returning to the trailer, he sat at the kitchen nook, thinking. He looked out the window at her, her nudity indistinct at this distance.

Opening the fridge, he took out a Lone Star. Try as he might, he could not get the image of an unclothed Kara out of his mind. Naked and wounded in his bed was one thing, but nude and healthy under the sun was quite another.

Chapter 30:

**May 19, mid-morning, Noah's trailer,
Greasewood Draw**

Kara walked out of the trailer with her tea. Noah sat under his tree, reading. She realized it was *the map* in his hands. She froze, not knowing how to react. The map had been her friend, her enemy, her confidant, her nemesis. But it was *her* map.

"Interesting map," Noah said, looking up at her approach. "Where'd you get it?" he asked.

"Portland. At Powell's."

"What's Powell's?"

"A bookstore."

His eyes roamed over the map. "Never saw a map like this."

"Oh?"

"Yeah," he said. "I've seen Rand McNallys of the Northwest, Southwest, you know, states and regions. But this, this is really strange."

Kara said nothing. Wind rustled the leaves of the tree. Noah leaned against its trunk, the map on his lap. "There's a story here, isn't there?" he said.

"I suppose," she said.

He nudged her with his elbow. "So tell me."

"I can't."

"Why not?" he asked.

"I just can't."

The teasing transformed itself to concern. "What's wrong, Kara?"

"Noah, I just can't tell you about that goddamned map. I don't know how to."

Noah folded the map. "Kara, we don't know each other well, do we?"

"Well, no," she said, her eyes downcast.

"Do you want us to know each other better?"

She scuffed at the hard earth with her heels. "I guess so."

"Well, isn't this a good place to start?"

"I don't know."

"Well, why not?"

"You'll think I'm crazy. Nuts. A whack job."

Noah chuckled. Kara shot him a dirty look.

"Kara, please don't take this wrong, because I don't mean it to be like it sounds, but I already think you're nuts."

That earned another dirty look.

"Kara, haven't you noticed that I'm a bit of a whack job myself?"

"Well, yeah, I guess. But I'd never say that."

"What would you say?"

Kara tilted her head back, thinking. "I'd say you were, um, eccentric."

"Gosh. You're tactful. I didn't expect that," Noah said.

"You're obnoxious."

"I'm a guy. We're proud of that quality, you know."

"Then you're quite a guy."

Noah chuckled.

"Hey," Kara said after being quiet for a while.

"What?"

"How did you get hold of the map? Why'd you go into my car?"

"I didn't. I found it here."

"Here?"

Noah propped the map it against the trunk. "Like this. It was here when I came out this morning."

"How could ... I mean, I always lock my car. Habit."

Noah got up, walked to her car, and pulled on the door handle. "It's locked."

He returned to the tree and sat. "Kara?"

She drew up her knees and pressed her face against them, her arms circling her lower legs. Noah slipped his arm around her shoulders.

"Talk to me. Please."

She rested her head against his shoulder, sighing. "That fucking map."

He said nothing.

"That goddamned, motherfucking map."

She turned in his arms, picked up the map, and threw it as hard as she could. It fluttered through the air and landed not three feet away.

"You throw like a girl."

"I'm not a girl."

"True, true. You're a paragon of feminine virtue, a Helen among mere mortals, a woman of—"

Kara was crying. She buried her face against his shoulder.

"That map is driving me crazy. It's, it's ... I swear it's evil. I mean, I look at it and I don't see anything but I kept driving and turning from one road to another and I didn't know why and the lightning at night tried to kill me and I got scared and I got lost and I wanted to go back but I couldn't go back and—"

He touched a finger to her lips. "And now you're here."

"Oh, c'mon. That's just co—"

"Coincidence?" he said.

"Yeah. That's all it is."

He reached for the map. Opening it, he pointed to Green River. "Us."

"Us?"

"I don't believe in coincidence, Kara. Things happen.

Things we don't expect. Things we can't predict. But they happen, and they happen for a reason. I ended up here. You ended up here. Neither of us planned that."

"I don't believe that. I mean, I believe that, but ... Oh, crap. I don't know."

"I'm not saying fate has preordained my life. But I learned long ago to, well, you know, go with the flow. Be flexible. Adapt to what happens."

"If you use another cliché, I swear I'll kill you."

That threatened fate he believed. "So tell me the story," he said.

"About the map?"

"Yes, you nitwit, about the map."

"Don't call me a nitwit."

"What should I call you?"

"I don't know yet."

"Yet?"

"When I know, I'll tell you what you should call me."

He studied the map, tracing a line with his finger.

"What are you looking at?" she asked.

"There's something here. Somewhere. I want to find it. This map brought you here. I want to figure out where it's taking you."

"Why?"

He fell silent, looking up at the bright Utah sun. "I don't believe in coincidence. But I believe in preparing for, um, eventualities."

"What eventualities?"

He folded the map and put it down on the ground.

"I'm just mumbling. Forget it. Tell me about the map."

Kara sat up, arms around her lower legs again, rocking forward, backward, forward. In the bland tone of a documentary narrator, she told him everything about the map. In the sharing she chanted a prayer for security and serenity.

Chapter 31:

May 21, early evening, Ray's Tavern, Green River, Utah

"I want to go out." Kara had awakened from an afternoon nap.

"Take me to dinner," she commanded.

"Kara?"

"What?"

"Would you like to go into town for dinner?"

Kara threw back the covers and sat up quickly, smiling brightly.

"I thought you'd never ask."

She had showered and dressed in a pair of white painter pants and black cotton tank top. Noah liked her minimalist approach. Simple silver earrings, a touch of lipstick, and a hint of eye shadow. They left the trailer and walked to the Land Cruiser. He strolled behind, still watching for signs of dizziness. Doc had said those spells would come and go, slowly decreasing in frequency. They got into the Cruiser. She tapped him on the shoulder.

"Gee," she said. "Our first date."

His eyes rolled upward.

"I'm kidding, I'm kidding," she said.

When he started the Cruiser, she said, "Buick V-8?"

He nodded, surprised. "How'd you know?"

She grinned. "I know engines," she said. "You should have used a small block Chevy."

"The hell you say."

He let out the clutch and the Wrangler ATs dug into the dirt, throwing clumps of earth behind as they headed to Green River. The Cruiser bounced over the rough road, and Kara complained. "Why don't you get a decent car?"

"Nothing wrong with this one," he said.

"Sucks."

"Why?"

"Needs shocks, for one thing."

"Land Cruisers aren't built for comfort."

"It needs a fuel pump, too."

"The hell you say," he exclaimed.

"Pull over and stop."

Noah did so. The Land Cruiser rumbled quietly. "Hear that?" she said.

"Hear what?"

"A slight clicking from the rear. That's the fuel pump. It's going sour."

Noah grunted and popped the clutch. The Cruiser lurched forward.

After a while, Kara asked, "Where'd you get this, anyhow?"

"A salvage job."

"Excuse me?"

"Guy abandoned it in the Book Cliffs. Blown engine. No one could tow it out. So the jerk left it. I bought it for a buck from the insurance company."

"So how'd you get it out?"

"I have friends in high places," he said.

"Gee. I'm impressed."

"I mean it. A pal in the Air Force Reserve lifted it out with a chopper. Wrote it off as a training exercise. Then I rebuilt it."

Kara nodded. "Seems old."

"Only on the outside, girl."

"I'm not a *girl*," she scolded.

"I suppose not," he said archly.

"Just so you know, you sexist pig."

"You mean ageist pig."

"Huh?"

"Calling you a girl has nothing to do with gender. Only age."

"Noah, you're irritating."

"Indeed," he said. "Years of experience of being right."

"Good grief. You're ... you're ..."

"Right? That the word you're looking for?"

"You'll pay for this, boy."

"Why, you ageist pig, you."

She smacked him a hard one on his shoulder, and he chuckled.

"What year?" she asked.

"What year what?"

"The Cruiser, stupid."

"Oh. It's an '83."

"Hey," she said. "I was born in '83."

"Well, don't worry."

"Worry? What do you mean?"

"We can salvage you, too."

She punched him in the shoulder again. "You insufferable wiseass."

Two dark vehicles trailed about two miles back, just right for keeping the Cruiser in sight but not close enough to be noticed. After Noah parked across from the Melon-Vine market, a dark green Cherokee and a black Hummer — a big H1 — parked a block away. A tall thin man and a short fat man walked toward Ray's Tavern and lingered outside, arguing. Then the thin man slipped inside.

Noah and Kara walked into Ray's Tavern. Her arm rested easily in the crook of his elbow. "Table or booth?" he asked.

"Booth," she said, walking to a corner under pictures and posters on the wall near the back pool room. She waited so he could choose where to sit. He appreciated that. Like Wyatt Earp did once too often, he sat with his back to the door. Kara, a semi-committed vegetarian in a cheeseburger bar, ordered a cheese omelet with bean sprouts. The waitress, a woman in her 40s with leathery skin and a slight stoop, stared at Kara blankly. No bean sprouts, Kara was told. "Really?" she said.

"Kara," whispered Noah, "this isn't Seattle."

"Whoa. I'll say," she muttered.

Noah asked for a cheeseburger. Kara complained her plain cheese omelet was too well done; Noah just ate without comment. Apple pie followed for both.

"Do you bitch about everything?" Noah asked.

"I only bitch when things aren't right."

"What makes things right?"

Kara put her fork down and rested her arms beside the plate.

"Attention to detail does. Disciplined effort does. Commitment does."

Noah nodded. "I agree."

"You do?"

"Yep. You ought to be committed."

Kara threw a french fry at him. It bounced off his forehead onto his plate. He speared it and ostentatiously placed it into his mouth.

"Thus do I refute you."

Shaking her head, she resumed eating. "Noah, you're really weird," she said, slipping her fork into another bite of omelet. Noah started to reply, reaching for his mug of coffee. "It takes one—"

A large, hairy hand reached over Noah's shoulder, picked up his mug, and poured the steaming coffee onto his plate, turning his supper into a dark brown sea with a large bun island and little french fry canoes.

"You prick," said someone behind him.

Noah turned slowly, his face expressionless. A tall, ugly man, burly, head topped with unkempt dark hair, his body thicker around the middle than the chest, stood beside the booth. Behind the man stood others. One had hooded eyes that darted furtively around the diner. The other wore a Stetson too big for his thin, short body. Furtive Eyes and Little Man were good soldiers, standing behind their man — but safely behind. They knew Noah. Most folks 'round these parts did.

The big man held Noah's mug in his hand and glowered at him. Noah knew the type well. The high school graduate who never left town. Working at odd jobs. Getting fired when the boss couldn't put up with the buried anger over life's real or imagined insults. The guy in his thirties who used to be a defensive tackle on his high-school football team because he was too bloody slow to play anywhere else. The guy who'd let his 220 pounds of hard muscle run to seed as a decade of too many nights at the tavern bloated him, leaving him far too heavy but with the lingering illusion of his past fitness.

On one side of the man's stained denim shirt was a patch that read "Xperience Offroad Xtreme." On the other side, a matching patch offered identity, but a grease stain muddled the lettering: "B-t-h." Around his fat waist was a belt adorned with a silver buckle bearing the logo of a local off-road vehicle club.

"And your problem is?" Noah said softly.

"You dumped black paint on me last week in the Book Cliffs, asshole."

Noah glanced at his soiled supper and looked at Kara.

"I think he owes me $8.95, don't you?"

Shock owned Kara. She just nodded, staring at the threesome.

"You owe me a paint job, you fucking bastard."

Behind him, the two sycophants nodded vigorously. Noah said nothing. He picked at his fries, ignoring B-t-h. "And why is that?"

B-t-h put both hands on the table. Thick, black hair coated his forearms.

"Because you're the dumb fuck who dropped it from your goddamned pissant airplane."

"So. You drive a blue Blazer? With that cute pyrotechnic detailing?"

"It's ain't cute, asswipe. It was fucking expensive and you ruined it."

"And you drive your cute little Chevy into roadless wilderness areas where it's against the law to do so?"

"I drive any fucking where I want, asshole."

"How unfortunate. Got proof that will stand up in court?"

The other two guys, as if rehearsed, said, in unison, "We saw you do it."

Noah nodded slowly. "So the three of you will testify that while driving illegally in a roadless wilderness area, some apparition pisses black paint all over this Blazer? Damn. I'll have to invite the BLM guys to hear you say that. Lessee, what's the fine for that? Kara, remind me to check—"

B-t-h's right hand left the table and flashed through the air, striking Noah on the left temple. A ring on B-t-h's hand sliced a deep, two-inch gash on Noah's cheekbone. He did not flinch. He sat immobile, looking at Kara.

The smack of fist against flesh froze the other patrons and servers. Noah's silence eroded the confidence of the sycophants. They backed up, a baby step at a time. Without looking away from Kara, Noah spoke. Kara couldn't reconcile the softness of his voice with the fury in his eyes.

"You have two choices. The first is simple. Be gone before I count to ten and turn so I can see you. The second is—"

B-t-h telegraphed his punch. "Why you fucking sonuva—"

He pulled his arm back too far; his fist took too long to arrive. Noah's hand met his fist and closed around it. His eyes never left Kara's. B-t-h moaned as Noah's fingers dug deeply and painfully into the back of the bully's fleshy hand as Noah twisted his wrist. B-t-h sank to his knees and desperately tried to tear his fist away. Furtive Eyes and Little Man retreated again. Noah looked toward a tall, thin man, dressed in black slacks and a black shirt with pearl-white snaps, foot on the bar rail, a beer in his hand. The man's face boiled with hate. Noah squeezed harder as he matched the man's glare. He dropped B-t-h's hand, but not his stare.

B-t-h clamored to his feet. "This ain't over, asshole," he screamed.

Noah looked at him, almost sympathetically. "You guys always say that," he said quietly. "The only part of you that's in shape is your mouth."

B-t-h glared and motioned to his cronies. The three strode to the door past people who until now had feared them. Noah had wounded them. He should have known better, he thought. Beckoning to Kara, he slid out of the booth and put a twenty on the table. She hurried to the door, then stopped. Noah had walked to the bar to face the thin man, whose lips moved malevolently as he uttered words she could not hear. Noah shook his head, adamant about something, and turned away. As Noah walked back toward her, Kara saw the tall man raise his hand, point his index finger at Noah's back and mouth, "Bang."

Kara stood next to the Cruiser, eyes intent on Noah.

"What happened?" she asked.

"Just a difference over how life ought to be lived."

"Don't be so obtuse. What pissed him off?"

Noah explained. He followed the comings and goings of local ORV groups, particularly professional tour operators, and especially Xperience Offroad Xtreme, because they often ventured into wilderness areas illegally — and immorally.

"So I discourage them," he said.

"With paint?"

"Yep. I dive bomb 'em with the Drifter and drop balloons filled with acrylic paint on them. Tough to clean off."

"I can see why he's pissed."

"And I get pissed when they drive over vegetation that will take a century to recover because an asshole wants to play with his fucking Blazer."

He walked around the Cruiser and got into the driver's seat.

She hurriedly climbed in. He drove toward Old State Route 24, out past the airport.

They rode in silence until she asked, "Who was the guy at the bar?"

Noah looked at her, then back at the road. "He's a goddamned industry."

"Noah, do you always talk in riddles?"

He grunted. "Sorry."

"So tell me."

He sighed. "Jack Nash is the Warren Miller of the ORV crowd."

"Warren Miller? The guy who does all those ski movies?"

Noah nodded. "Yeah. Nash does videos, guidebooks, writes columns for ORV mags. The works. He owns XOX. Those three morons work for him."

"Obviously he doesn't care much for you. How come?"

"Those videos sell because he makes them in places of spectacular scenery. He used to make them near Kanab, around Bryce and Zion, until places inside national parks began to appear in them. The park service more or less ran him out of southwest Utah, and he moved up here. Now, he's very careful. His videos may show scenes in out-of-bounds areas — those are what sell his videos — but never with ORVs in them. When people complain about it, he says he hiked in to take those videos.

"And he writes guidebooks and how-to books that encourage people to drive off road in wilderness areas. Plus he's a shithead.

"He makes private videos, too. He makes a shitload of money by offering trips that trespass on wilderness areas for rich clients with huge rock crawlers. And he films 'em. Sells 'em to the clients for a boatload of bucks. When I find out he's doing a private shoot, I get in the air. I know where he likes to go. He's not hard to find, even though he thinks he is."

"How do you how when he's going to do that?" she asked.

"A friend at a Salt Lake bank. When Nash goes in with big cash deposits, much bigger than he gets from a usual trip, she calls me. And I go hunting."

Kara nodded, encouraging him to continue.

"He's also a player in a few anti-wilderness groups. Every time some of the local greens, here and in Moab, hold events to highlight environmental damage, he shows up, handing out leaflets. Last time I went up to Salt Lake to testify at a hearing on a wilderness bill, he showed up with a caravan of more than two hundred ORVs, and they all parked in front of the Capitol building. Helluva photo op for the news crews. Yes, you could say we don't get along."

"So you harass him," she said.

"I'm not the bad guy here, Kara," he snapped.

"Why not? Dropping paint on people's property isn't exactly kosher."

He chuckled. "Yeah, I suppose not. But to charge me with something, they'd have to admit to an illegal activity of their own. I'm careful, Kara."

"I hope so," she said softly. "'Cause I'll bet they're getting careful, too."

The Cruiser approached the entrance to Greasewood Draw, passing a tamarisk grove. Noah didn't notice the dark green Jeep Cherokee hidden in the foliage. Inside it, a cigarette glowed.

"Noah?"

He sighed. Kara's concussion symptoms had waned considerably. Her brain was now fully engaged in investigative mode.

"Why didn't you hit him?"

"Who? Nash?"

"No. The fat guy."

A cunning smile etched itself onto Noah's weathered face.

"Oh, I'm going to," he said as he turned into Greasewood Draw.

"Yep. I'm going to hit him," he said. "With the district attorney. Assault and battery. He goofed. Usually he avoids witnesses. But not this time."

Kara chuckled. "Noah?"

"Yes, Kara?"

"Is your middle name Machiavelli, by any chance?"

They drove along Noah's private streamside road toward the trailer.

"Noah, stop."

She turned on the overhead light.

"You being Mr. Boy Scout, there's no doubt a first-aid kit in here somewhere."

"Under your seat," he said.

She reached down and retrieved the first-aid kit.

"Turn your head to me," she said. She cleaned the gash with a gauze pad and put a butterfly bandage on it.

"You should get stitches."

"Don't need 'em."

"I say you do."

"You're not a doctor."

"Fine. Be scarred for life. See if I care." She snapped the first-aid kit shut and shoved it under the seat.

"I'm not a pacifist, Kara."

"Then why didn't you defend yourself? God, he blindsided you."

"Did you want me to?"

"No, but—"

"Did you expect me to?"

Kara looked away. "Yes," she said quietly.

"Why?"

"Because that's what guys do. That's what my brothers did."

"I'm not your brother."

"I know, but—"

Noah pushed up his sleeve. "Kara, feel my bicep."

He flexed his upper arm. Gingerly, she put her hand on it.

"Squeeze. Hard," he said. She did. Her eyes widened. "Oh my god."

"I've been lifting weights for more than twenty years. I

know how to do it. I do it because I like it and because it makes me feel good. It makes me able to endure more than most people can. I'm as strong as an NFL lineman. I can lift all the weight that the scouts put players through at the NFL combine."

Kara nodded. "You would have killed him."

"Oh, probably not. But one blow in anger would have left that asshole in a very bad way. I hope I'm old enough to defend myself in other ways."

"Like calling the DA?"

"Like calling the DA. And the occasional balloon filled with black paint."

He shifted into first and the Cruiser rumbled back onto the road.

"Noah?"

"Yes, Kara."

"Turn around."

"Um, and why should I do that?"

"Because we're going to the clinic. You're not a doctor. And I'm betting the doc on duty will tell you, you're getting stitches. So turn around. *Now.*"

Kara's personality had begun to reappear — her occasional abrasiveness, her straightforward approach to problems, her sensitivity when appropriate, and her ever-present but often disguised caring for others had returned intact. And persuasively.

So Noah did as he was told.

Chapter 32:

May 24, early morning, Noah's trailer, Greasewood Draw

Noah walked into the trailer after working out. He wore running shorts and a towel draped around his neck. Kara, as furtive as Noah, stole a glance. He was 46 inches around everywhere. Nature had constructed Noah's body as a cylinder, broad across the shoulders, broader across the chest, and thick and muscular around his abdomen. She was growing used to his body, to his unexpectedly catlike walk. He seemed too chunky to be stealthy. But he was. He smiled and stepped into the shower. She was working on her computer. Her headaches were diminishing. She was healing.

"What are you doing?" he asked after drying off and pulling on his cargo shorts.

She looked up from the screen. "Just organizing my pictures."

"Excuse me?"

"Jpegs. Pictures. Images. You know."

"No, I don't. May I look?

"Sure."

She slid across the seat against the trailer's thin aluminum wall. He sat beside her. The seat wasn't very big, so the side of his chest, his hips, and his thigh pressed against her. She didn't mind. Small trailer, small spaces, designed for one. Two people made for close quarters and occasional body brushes. She liked that. Kara had come to believe she drew from his strength when he touched her. And she liked it when he touched her. His awkward chivalry had its own special grace.

Pushing the computer in front of him, she pointed to the screen, filled with thumbnails of digital photographs and other files.

"What are all these?" he asked.

"Image files."

"What are they for?"

"The Web pages I've built. I organize them using this software called Photo Mechanic. When you've got this many, you need to be able to sort through them quickly."

"How many do you have?"

She chuckled.

"Thousands, organized by different projects I've worked on."

"Sheesh. You must have a huge hard drive."

She elbowed him. "Oh, I do. And two external drives for backup."

"Oh. What kind of photos?"

"I take digital photographs as notes when I go to a client to plan a website and research its content."

For several minutes she explained what she did for a living. Calling up several stored projects she'd done over the past three years, she showed him several of the institutional and educational websites she'd constructed.

He nodded in appreciation. "I'm impressed."

"You should be. I'm good at what I do. I made a lot of money doing it."

"Made? Not make?"

She stopped talking, flustered.

"Sorry," he said. "Didn't mean to touch any sore spots."

"It's ... It's just that ... shit."

He touched her hand briefly.

"Kara, let it be. I didn't mean to snoop. Show me some of those pictures."

Noah pointed to some thumbnails that looked like flowers. She clicked on one, and it spurted into a full-screen image.

"Hey," he said. "That's a milk vetch." He moved his face closer to the screen. "Hmmm. It's crescent, not painted. Got egg-shaped leaves, not the threadlike ones on a painted milk vetch."

"Really? Didn't know what it was," she said. "In fact, I don't know what most are. I've been meaning to get a flower guide to try to ID them all."

He pointed to his library, resting on two shelves above the kitchen nook.

"There's several up there. Use any you wish, any time."

She clicked on the image, and it shrank to a thumbnail.

"If you'd like," he said, "I'll look at them and try to help."

She clicked on another flower thumbnail. "I would like that. Thanks."

They huddled cheek-to-cheek over the screen. Noah knew most of them. Another milk vetch, this time rimrock; serviceberry; wedgeleaf; spectacle-pod; Datil and Harriman's yuccas; rabbitbrush; Mormon tea; a few sagebrushes; Fremont's cottonwood; a tamarisk; saltbush; blackbrush; greasewood; and others that drew a furrowed brow as he guessed. Noah stood. Kara wanted to pull him back. She enjoyed this. She liked this common talk, common work, common interest. She'd had that in Seattle, hadn't she? But this seemed new somehow.

"Want some tea?" he asked.

"Yes, please." She keyboarded some of the IDs into the notes section of several images as Noah busied himself with tea things.

He hadn't put on a shirt. She watched the muscles of his shoulder blades articulate as he lifted this and put down that and moved this and set out that.

"God, Noah. Where'd you get all those muscles? Not just from lifting," she blurted.

He glanced over his shoulder. "What?"

"Never mind."

"Never mind what?"

"It was nothing."

He turned back to the stove. He'd heard what she said. It pleased but embarrassed him. He'd been dressed like this with other women. Annie had been a guest. So had that nurse from Moab. But with Kara, this was different.

"I'll give you a B. Pending verification, of course."

"What?" he asked without turning around.

"You identified 85.7 percent of the pictures we've looked at."

Noah turned around slowly. "God, you're anal."

She glanced at him sharply. "Excuse me?"

"Sorry. It's just that you're so precise in everything you do. I'm not knocking it. Hell, I'm a pilot. A lack of precision would kill me."

She looked at him, in a mock haughty way. She winked.

"Boy, you danced your way out of that one. And, yes, I'm anal. So there."

He ferried tea to the table. "Show me more. I want an A," he said.

She chuckled and clicked on a thumbnail. Common paintbrush, he said.

"Kara, what are the numbers below the photo? The others had 'em, too."

"They're GPS coordinates."

"You use GPS?" He didn't tell her he already knew she did.

"Yep. Hand me my go-bag."

"Your what?"

She pointed to her leather shoulder bag in the bedroom. "My bag. Over there."

He went into the bedroom to retrieve it. She watched his shoulders again. He handed her the bag, and she pulled out her Magellan GPS receiver. She turned it on and pushed a button.

"We're sitting, plus or minus three feet, at four thousand, four hundred and seventy-eight feet. And the kitchen table is at thirty-eight degrees, forty-nine minutes, sixteen seconds north and a hundred ten, twenty-seven minutes, and 37 seconds west. Give or take a second or two, I suppose."

"God, you're such a techno weenie," he muttered.

She poked him again. "And you're really a damned Luddite."

"Geek."

"Tree hugger."

He poked her. She poked him. He chuckled. She blushed and clicked on another thumbnail. He sipped at his tea, cupping the mug with both hands, watching her face as her finger danced on the track pad. He looked at the screen.

"Holy shit!"

Kara was startled. He jabbed at the screen, his face glowing. "Where the hell did you take that picture?"

"West of Nephi somewhere. Why? What's wrong?"

"Nothing's wrong. In fact, if that's what I think it is, you're about to become famous in the botanical world."

"Huh?"

He stood. "How's your head? Any headache?"

"Okay, I guess. Just a little washed out."

"Up to a road trip?"

"Um, sure, I guess."

He grabbed a T-shirt. "Pack up your toys and get ready to roll."

Chapter 33:

May 24, afternoon, west of Nephi, Utah

They arrived at an obscure side road near Furner Creek off the highway with the shot-up road signs in barely four hours. Noah parked the Cruiser next to a large juniper. Kara, reading coordinates on her GPS, pointed the way. Noah, looking at a map, said he knew the place. They stopped several times to check their bearings, her with the GPS, him with the map. Part way into the valley, she remembered where she'd taken the picture.

"Up there, about 20 yards."

Noah nodded and walked on. Then he stopped. He bent over a brown-stemmed bush with narrow-cut leaves and small pink flowers. He sighed.

"Yes. That's it. To think I've walked through here a half dozen times."

"That's what?"

"Clay phacelia."

"And?"

He straightened up. "You bring your phone?"

"Just my cell. Hope there's a repeater somewhere around here."

"Mind if I make a call?"

She dug her iPhone out of her go-bag. He dialed and waited.

"Bill? Noah. I think I've got something you ought to see. ... Yes. ... I'm standing next to a small stand of clay phacelia. ... No, I'm not sure. That's why I'm calling. Don't want to start anything without a positive ID. ... Yeah, I can give you directions and meet you back here if you want."

Kara listened. Then, excusing herself, she took the phone from Noah.

"Hi, Bill. I'm Kara. You got a computer?" Noah frowned, annoyed.

"You do? Oh, you're in your office? Where? Salt Lake? Good."

Kara explained her plan. "Give me 20 minutes. Then I'll e-mail some photos to you. Then you can call us back. Got it? Okay. Noah says 'bye.'"

Kara gave Bill her cell number and punched off the phone. She put her hand on Noah's hip and edged him aside. "Stand back, boy. Momma's got work to do."

Noah held up his hands, bowing and scraping as he stepped away.

Kara got out her Canon and took several photographs of the flowers, the stalk, the leaves, and then an overall shot of the plant. She transferred the images to her Mac via USB. Noah edged closer to watch. She hooked up her MiFi, attached the photos to an e-mail, and clicked "send." From start to finish, she needed only twelve minutes.

She sat down and smiled at Noah. "Now we wait."

He sat down next to her. "Kara, that was sharp. Quick thinking."

She was pleased. "It's nothing. It's what I do on a project. No biggie."

He shook his head. "You're going to have to technify me."

"Technify?"

"End my Ludditeness. I should know more about this stuff."

"Well, sure, if you want. Damn, I wish he'd call."

He clapped her on the shoulder. "Give him time. He's thorough and methodical. If anyone can ID that sucker, Bill McCorrigan can. Best botanist in Utah. I've used him on a few projects."

"What kind of projects?"

"Long story. I do things for an environmental group."

"Things? Sounds mysterious."

"Not really. We investigate roadless claims. Inventory proposed wilderness areas."

"Inventories?"

"We locate and ID plants, animals, and so on. And look for endangered species. I do mostly the roadless claims."

Kara nodded. He chuckled. "Flying's just my day job."

She smiled. "Tell me more about—"

The phone beeped. She handed it to Noah.

"Bill? What have we got? ... Positive? ... Good. ... Yeah, we're in that proposed WSA we worked on last fall. Don't want to give the name over the phone." Noah listened for a few minutes.

"I agree," he said finally. "We ought to get the word out on this. How you want to handle it? ... Through university PR? ... No ... Let's do it through the project. ... Yeah, I can do that. I'll write it back at the airport and e-mail it."

Kara held out her hand for the phone, the look on her face suggesting faint tolerance for incompetent children. Noah handed it to her quickly.

"Bill? A suggestion? ... I can do that right now, from here. ... Yes. ... Yes. ... Yeah, I have a good friend with the Associated Press in Seattle. Does green stuff. I can send it to her. ... I'll need some info from you. ... Sure. .... You as the source of the ID? ... Sure, we can slip in the word tentative, just to cover you. ... Good idea. We'll leave the actual location vague. How about simply 'west central Utah'? ... Okay, now tell me about the plant. ..." As she listened, Kara keyboarded notes into a new e-mail window.

Kara listened for a while, then asked a few more terse

questions.

"Okay. Got it. I'll get it off in the next half hour. ... Yes, I'll cc a copy to you. ... Really? That's sweet. ... Sure. I'd like that. ... No, a good Chardonnay will do. Thanks. Bye, Bill."

She punched the phone off and set it down. "He's nice."

"Sheesh, you sounded like you were making a date," he said.

"I did. He offered to buy me dinner if I'm ever in Salt Lake."

Noah grinned. "His wife would love that."

"He's married?"

"Yep. Sorry."

"Damn. Sounded so cute over the phone."

"Well, stop being so smug. We've got work to do. You write. I'll survey."

Kara composed the press release faster than most people could type. Noah counted plants, identified associational vegetation, and verified the location on a topographic map. Each worked at his or her share of intuitively divided labor. Neither saw the other steal a glance every now and then.

Thirty-seven minutes later, Kara clicked the send button in Outlook. An hour later, a reporter at the AP bureau in Seattle checked her e-mail and recognized Kara's e-mail address. She opened the file and read it. Then she printed it and showed it to her editor. He told her to post it on the "A" wire after she called McCorrigan at the University of Utah to verify the source.

Kara sat at the kitchen nook early that evening, her Mac on the table. Noah was in the hangar, doing something or other with his aircraft. Must be a substitute for sex. She grinned. She wondered what sex would be like with him. She walked to a window where she could see into the hangar. Noah futzed with an engine lit by a work lamp hung off a wing strut. He saved my life, she thought. Was she just grateful? She wrapped her arms around herself and swayed, watching his bare back, its muscles tightening, releasing, tightening, easing, as he wrestled with a prop.

The laptop beeped. She had e-mail from a Seattle AP address. She darted to the door.

"Noah!"

He raised his face from the engine.

"It's here."

She was reading the e-mail as he walked in, wiping grease from his hands. Sweat and oil slickened his forearms, matting down the sun-bleached hair. He sat next to her and looked at the screen.

> To: kara@WebWideWorks.com
> From: butlerha@ap.org
> Subject: the weird plant
> Cc:
> Bcc:
> Attachments:
>
> _____
>
> Kara,
>
> Great to hear from you. And nice scoop. Thanks for sending it my way. We're running it as you wrote it. I called McCorrigan and added a few grafs and a quote re the WSA angle, that's all. It went out under my byline, miscommunication between me and my editor. He thought I'd written it. Sorry I'm stealing your thunder.
>
> And how did you find yourself in the middle of nowhere? Call me and tell all.
>
> Oh. Forgot. If you're reading this tonight before 9, could you e-mail me some photos? The god types here want permission to send out one as a Laserphoto. And I *will* make sure you get the photo credit.

Copy of the story's below.

----

a1402
ar
AM-Rareplant Bjt 0324
Rare Plant Found in Controversial Proposed
Wilderness Area

By HANNAH A. BUTLER
Associated Press Writer

SALT LAKE CITY (AP) A specialist in rare
plants at the University of Utah said today
that one of the rarest plants in the United
States, thought to be limited to one small
canyon in Utah, has been found in another
canyon in west central Utah.

Professor William McCorrigan, a nationally
recognized expert in rare botanicals, said
that while identification of the plant, the
rare clay phacelia, remains tentative, he is
convinced that photographs of the plant
taken by two field botanists and reviewed
by him can be no other plant. He plans to
survey the site himself in the coming week.

The plant, previously thought to exist only
in Spanish Fork Canyon, was discovered
earlier today by the two botanists, and
digital photographs were transmitted to
him from the site. The cluster of
approximately 20 plants sits in a
controversial wilderness area proposed by
a citizens' wilderness group and opposed
by the Bureau of Land Management.

"These plants will need the full protection
of federal law," McCorrigan said. "Their

discovery lends credence to the argument
that this proposed WSA (Wilderness Study
Area) is desperately needed to protect an
obviously delicate ecosystem."

McCorrigan said that discovery of the plant
needs immediate investigation. The
Spanish Fork Canyon colony, he explained,
is pollinated by an equally rare species of
bee called hylaeus granulatus.

"Finding that bee at this new site would
also virtually mandate full protection of this
wilderness area," he said.

The Spanish Fork Canyon colony,
discovered in 1978 with approximately 200
plants, had dwindled to fewer than 20
plants by the beginning of this decade, he
said.

McCorrigan refused to give the precise
location of the new find, citing the need to
protect the site from collectors and curious
tourists.

McCorrigan said he plans to contact
experts from the State Arboretum of Utah
and the Center for Plant Conservation at
Harvard University to consult on
recommending measures to insure the
plant's survival.

Oh. P.S. and all that. TD told me you're not
coming back, that you'd split up. Sorry.
But to me, no real surprise. He's a jerk.
What happened? Tell Hannah all. Love, H.

Noah chuckled, pretending he did not see the P.S.

"We're field botanists now?" he said. "Sounds downright professional."

Kara reddened. "I didn't do that," she said.

He nudged her with his elbow.

"Well, I guess it's half right. You're a botanist," she said.

"Amateur class. Still, I've found two new species in the past four years with Bill. Even got to name one after myself."

"You're making this up."

"Nope. Solanum hartshornoria. A kind of nettle."

Kara made a face. "That figures."

"Wiseass."

"Name dropper."

"Geek."

"Luddite."

Noah leaned back, his palms flat on the table. He said nothing for a while. He just looked at her intently, his head cocked slightly to one side.

"You done good today, Kara. We found those plants at three o'clock. Now it's almost eight, and the world knows about them. That's a good thing. You may have saved them. You and your toys."

"Eight? God, I've got to e-mail Hannah. 'Scuse me."

Kara busied herself with composing an e-mail. Noah stood, and for the first time in years he didn't know what to do with himself in his own home.

Chapter 34:

May 25, morning, Noah's trailer, Greasewood Draw

Noah remembered when he fell in love with Utah. He had been a transport driver — a C-130 pilot for MATS, the Military Air Transport Command — in the Air Force. After mustering out, he'd driven slowly south to the Lower 48 from his last posting at Elmendorf outside Anchorage, savoring landscapes. He'd seen Utah from 30,000 feet in the driver's seat of his Herc. He'd fallen for her dusky dark reds, her soft, subtle browns, her muted yellows and tans and occasional greens six miles below, a land carved into canyons and spiked with volcanics. Utah had whispered sweetly in his ear.

He liked the idea of becoming something in Utah. He did not know what nor did he worry. Experience and wisdom would encounter circumstances, and he'd adjust as necessary. He took a master's in geological engineering from the Colorado School of Mines. He thought that would be the way.

He liked to cook, and she hadn't complained about the food. In the evening she'd begun doing dishes. She rose early now before he did to run. So he made breakfast, timed for her return. After she'd showered, she'd do those dishes, too. Neither noticed patterns developing.

Noah slid his mug back and forth across the table after breakfast one morning. He hated Kara's questions. She was always asking things. About him. About what he does. About what he did. He wasn't used to that. The locals allowed Noah to simply be, unexplained but accepted, hermetic in lifestyle but communal in times of others' needs.

"Wilderness inventory? What's that?" she asked.

The questions locked on. No evasive maneuvers here. "I count things."

"Hey, I know what an inventory is, you know. What do you count?"

"Land," he said.

"Noah, do you make a profession of being obtuse?"

"Huh?"

"Never mind." She shook her head. "So what do you count?"

He drank more tea. "Roads. I count roads," he said.

"Why?"

"To see where they aren't."

"Noah, do you want to see sunrise tomorrow?"

"It's perfectly clear."

"Like hell it is."

"Now, now, Kara. This is a God-fearing state. No profanity."

"Oh, fuck you."

"I'm shocked. Yes, shocked am I at such language."

She shot *the look* at him. She'd finished her bagel with that god-awful marmalade she liked. A napkin flitted through her hands, cleaning them.

"Why do you look for where roads aren't?" she asked.

"That's what defines wilderness. No roads."

"No roads?"

"Yes. No roads. At least, that's how the feds define wilderness areas for the sake of protecting federal lands as wilderness. No roads."

"I thought wilderness was, you know, wild," she said.

"What makes something wild?" Noah asked.

"No people? Of course. No people, no impacts. Wilderness," she said.

Noah nodded. "That's more or less it. Wilderness Act of 1964. Actually, it began in 1866. Congress wrote what amounts to a homesteading act for miners. A section of that law referred to as RS2477 created rights-of-way to allow miners to build the roads needed to develop the West. Any talk about wilderness begins and ends in the concept of impacts caused by people. Mining. Logging. Ranching. Even recreation. Roads let people into places, and that leads to impacts. Those who mine or log or ranch count on that to keep land out of wilderness designations. Those RS2477 roads are legitimate property rights and allow the holders to maintain and upgrade them."

"So what?" she asked.

"So what defines a road? If a wilderness area is defined as roadless, and you want to develop a mine or otherwise take from the land, then it's in your interest to argue that roads exist. If someone says an RS2477 road exists, I examine it. Fly over it. Photograph it. Hike it and map it. But the argument usually comes down to whether the road in question is a constructed road — or an old trail, or a jeep track. That's not a constructed road, so I fight such RS2477 claims to deny them designation as formal roads. That's the fight. Separating old trails or cattle paths from claims of constructed roads. If it's not a road, the area can be included in a wilderness study area."

"So it's all about what's an impact and what isn't?"

"Yes. I fight claims of roads that really aren't. Wilderness is a lack of disturbance to what is."

"What is?"

"Yep. To what is."

Kara smiled. "Is. From the verb 'to be.' To be. To exist. To live. So I see why Nash and company don't particularly like you."

"Oh, there are others. Loggers. Ranchers."

"So why did you take this on?" she asked.

"Kara."

"Yes?"

"You're annoying."

"Yes. I am."

"Why are you always asking questions?" he asked.

"It's what I do. I ask questions for a living. Sorry if it annoys you."

"You need conversation lessons," he said. "All you do is interrogate."

She flinched. He kept talking, hoping to diminish his insult.

"I help volunteers for the Utah Wilderness Project look for roads. To examine whether they qualify as RS2477 claims."

"You help? What's that mean? Are you a member?"

"Jesus, Kara. Give it a rest."

Kara shrugged. "Sorry. Just trying to understand."

"Understand what?"

Kara, more than a little pissed off, put on a sweater, walked to the door, and turned. "You, dummy."

She left, but her irritation lay thick and palpable inside the trailer. He rummaged through a drawer for what would help him explain. Noah unrolled a map of the Swell on the table. His hands smoothed the curled paper, stroking it as he would a lover.

Kara sat under the tree, levying accusations of being an asshole against herself. She folded her arms in a way that shrinks would notice, nod subtly, and say, "I seeeeeee." Defensive. Self-flagellating. Smack y'self all around with guilt. She watched the trailer, hoping he would come out. She assumed he was pissed and convicted herself of being a pushy bitch.

She crossed the hard dirt runway to the tied-down Drifter. She walked around the ultralight that had ferried her to a medical haven, her fingers trailing over the propeller. She wrapped her fingers around the stick, imagining its remote control of elevators, ailerons, and rudder that created reign over pitch, yaw, and roll. She brushed her hands over the smooth Mylar skin of the wings. She stood at the tail, holding the rudder between her hands. Kara wanted to learn to fly. She could dance up there. Her hands caressed the aircraft for some time.

She was back under the tree when Noah emerged from the trailer. Sitting by her, he unrolled a map and placed stones at the corners to keep it unfurled.

"This is a topo of the San Rafael Swell," he said without preamble or apology. "I mean, part of it. I've got other maps inside. Three rivers cut through it. You can see them here, here, and here."

He pointed to thin blue lines, the cartographer's representations of water, that depicted the Price and San Rafael rivers and Muddy Creek.

"I love this place. I don't know why. You know how it is. You just meet someone, see something, and you love it. You don't know why. I guess you figure it out later. Anyhow, I decided to live here because I fell in love. It's that simple and that complicated.

"It's called a swell because it's a geologic bulge. Lots of Navajo sandstone here. That's the white sandstone you always see in pictures of Utah, with those foreset beds and topset beds of old dunes now lithified. Seen pictures of Checkerboard Mesa in Zion? Well, that's the Navajo sandstone."

His finger traced a wandering line across the map. "That's the Little Grand Canyon. I'll fly you there some day. It's magical. I can't describe it any better than that. If I don't fly through it at least once a week, I feel deprived."

"Your mistress?" she said, defensiveness undermining comprehension.

His glance was sad. "Poor comparison," he said.

"Sorry," she said.

He pointed out roads-that-weren't-roads-but-miners-and-ORVers-wanted-them-to-be roads. Noah clasped his hands in his lap, closing his eyes. He sat still as a boulder, solid, immovable, imperturbable. He raised his head and opened his eyes, clear, bright, and intent with long-held purpose.

"Anyhow, that's what I do."

Kara nodded. They sat opposite each other for several minutes, eye to eye. Kara squared her shoulders and spoke. "Give me your hands, Noah."

"What?"

She reached across the shadowed brown earth and lifted his right hand off his lap. Wriggling closer to him, she grasped the left as well. His head tilted slightly back and to the side. "Close your eyes, Noah."

He did as he was told. Kara closed her eyes, too. She wanted him to feel her, to feel her touch, to feel her trying to flow into him, through him, with him. She didn't play with his fingers, she didn't stroke his palm, she didn't trace her fingers across the back of his hand and wrist. She just held his hands. She wanted to reach him, but this was new ground for her. Love affairs had been contests, competitions, conquests. She didn't want to win, she didn't want to lose, she didn't want a draw. She wanted to understand and be understood. She opened her eyes. "Why did you tell me this?" she asked.

"You wanted to know, didn't you?"

"Yes."

"So I told you."

"Didn't have to, you know."

"Yeah, I know."

"So why did you?" she asked, releasing his hands, frustrated by her ignorance of the means of attaining intimacy, and leaning back against the trunk.

Noah stood. "Because I wanted you to know."

"Why?"

"You'll never make it as Socrates, Kara."

She stood, too, dusting Utah off her Quick-Drys.

"What?" she asked.

He walked toward the trailer. She hastened to his side.

"Never mind," he said.

When they reached the trailer, he pulled the keys to his

Land Cruiser out of his pocket. "Listen, I've got to go into town for a while. You mind?"

Kara, head down, scuffed Utah with her foot. "Why should I mind?"

He glanced at her, trying to discern meaning in the murmuring of the miffed.

"Can I bring you back anything?" he asked.

"No. ... Wait. Yes. Can you get me a copy of that map you showed me?"

"A map of the Swell? Why?"

She stepped inside. "Because I'm going to help you save it."

Noah stared at the door, realizing he was happier today than yesterday.

Chapter 35:

May 27, dawn, a small bluff near Jackass Benches

Noah sat cross-legged on the bedrock, his face lifted to the morning sun. He'd flown Kara to this private, natural altar to introduce her to wild Utah. Noah glanced at her as she slept in her down cocoon. He turned back to the sun and remembered innocence long past. He was sixteen and holding a girl in his arms for the first time. He kissed her. He rolled atop her. His nose touched hers and he entered her and they both moaned as they came. He remembered a shining clarity, an innocence neither feigned nor imagined, bursting from her eyes into his. Sex with emotional honesty for the first time. And probably his last, he thought. He was no longer innocent.

Kara woke. Tendrils of sunlight peeked through the sandstone fins arranged like sentinels around their small aerie. The Buckeye sat nearby. It had been exhilarating for her, experiencing Noah landing it in such a small place.

She liked waking outside at dawn, that crisp air resting on her cheeks as the first stroke of sunshine warmed her nose. She heard breathing and saw Noah. Wisps of condensation oozed from him with each quiet exhalation.

Noah was nude, part of his ritual. Propping herself up on

her elbow, she watched him, not because of his nudity, but because of his breathing — slow, patient, restful, deep. Kara rose and slipped into Quick-Drys and partly buttoned her chamois shirt. She lit the small Optimus stove and set water to boil. She faced the sun, the top of chamois hanging open, her bare legs spread shoulder width apart. Her hamstrings felt cold, her thighs warm. She searched the shared pack, a consequence of weight limitations in the Buckeye, for tea fixings. She carried two mugs to the edge of the bluff where Noah sat. She set his tea in front of him and sat. She sipped hers, cupping her hands around the mug for warmth.

"You make a helluva lot of noise in the morning," Noah said abruptly.

Kara was momentarily flustered. "What do you mean?"

"You've been futzing around here, thinking you've been quiet. Well, you haven't. Damn good thing no one's tracking us."

"Hey, I was quiet. I was just trying to—"

"Yeah, I know. You were trying to, what's the phrase, give me my space."

"Well, I was," she said archly.

He turned and looked at her, grinning. "You're so easy."

She poked him. "I thought you were meditating."

"Well, I wasn't," Noah said and turned his face back to the sun.

"Well, what the hell were you doing?"

"I gather here," he said presently.

Kara's eyebrows lifted. "You what?"

"You heard me."

"I don't understand."

"Neither do I, sometimes," Noah said. "But every few days, I need to sit in the sun. Maybe it's just because I like to feel that warmth on my face. It's different from a fire or a heater. It — hell, I don't know — it sustains me. So I have places where I sit and gather it."

"It?" she asked.

"Strength, I guess. That's as good a word as any."

"Or peace?"

"Maybe," he said. "I think peace comes from some kind of inner strength, so I suppose I gather that, too."

"That why you work out so much? For that kind of strength?"

He waited, then deadpanned, "Naw. I do it to attract da wimmin."

She poked him again. "Jerk."

"Reactionary feminist."

"Asshole."

"Cultural leftist."

"Prick."

"Pomo revisionist."

"Hey!" Kara said. "What's with the labeling?"

"Just showing off my broad knowledge of human affairs."

"Now you are being an asshole."

"Yes, but I'm a well-read asshole. Give me that much."

She paused, then said, "And, it seems, a naked well-read asshole."

He glanced down. "So it seems."

She looked away. "I thought you'd be modest."

"Well, I've seen you naked."

"Did you like what you saw?" she asked.

"Oh, sure. All those tubes in you, bandages everywhere—"

"Not in the hospital, you idiot."

"I'm not going to answer that question," he said softly.

"Well, why the hell not?"

"Because you already know the answer."

He went to his sleeping bag and dressed in the shorts he'd used as a pillow, then set about making breakfast. They sat and ate in silence.

"I love this," Noah said.

"What?"

He spread his arms. "This. I live in magnificent isolation."

"Stop lying to yourself, Noah."

He looked at her sharply. "Excuse me?"

"You don't live in this 'magnificent isolation,' as you call it," she said. "You hide in it."

"What the hell does that mean?"

"You retreat to this isolation whenever you want to escape ... or avoid something ... or whenever you feel threatened."

"What would threaten me?"

"I don't know. Something inside you that you don't want to face."

"Christ, Kara, just when did you become a goddamned shrink?" he said abruptly, shaking his head.

In awkward silence they broke camp and flew back to Greasewood Draw.

Chapter 36:

May 28, early morning, Noah's trailer, Greasewood Draw

"I need to go to the post office."

Kara lay in bed, stretching. Noah sat at the table, sipping tea and reading some sort of green literature. She'd taken to calling it "green crud." He'd glare in mock menace when she did. But he knew that Kara had been reading some of it when he wasn't around. Respect takes odd forms.

"You want to go to the post office," he said. His eyes shifted from the legislative history of a bill he'd been studying to the woman in his bed.

Kara rolled onto her side. "Yes, I need to go to the post office."

"I presume I can't ask why."

"No, this time you can."

"So why do you need to go to the post office?"

"Money," she said.

Noah sipped at his tea. "Um, most folks go to banks for money."

She sat up, oblivious to her overnight cowlick. "I had some mail forwarded to general delivery. I'm hoping there's a check or two there."

"You can use my address, you know."

Kara didn't look up. "I didn't want to impose. Besides, I'd had these forwarded before, you know, I fell."

Noah nodded and returned to his reading. Kara stood. All creatures, great and small, scratched in the morning. Kara scratched in places great and small, shedding overnight static in the damp nooks of her body.

"You might shower first."

"You saying I stink?"

"It's a small trailer."

He ducked, but the pillow glanced off the top of his head. He laughed. Kara disappeared into the shower. Noah listened to the rustling of the removal of tank top and panties. He listened to the creaking of faucets twisted on, the stuttering of the meager water pressure, the cascade of warm water over her soft skin. He listened to the swooshing of soap, Kara's hand curled around it, sweeping it over her abdomen, under her armpits, over her breasts, between her legs. He listened. Or, he would admit, he imagined the sounds of Kara in his shower. He walked outside, breathing heavily. Good lord, has she ever *imposed*, he thought.

Kara bounded from the Land Cruiser before Noah braked in front of the post office. Ever informal in dress, perhaps even immodest by Green River social standards, she jogged to the door, her black Quick-Drys flapping about her thighs. A few twenty something desert cowboys eyed her taut, flexing calf muscles. Guys. We're all just guys, he thought. He waited patiently, rearranging the clutter on his dashboard. Minutes passed. Ten. Then fifteen. He checked his watch and got out of the Cruiser. She sat near the doorway to the post office, forearms draped over drawn-up knees. A torn envelope fluttered in one hand, and some pieces of paper hung loosely from the other. She was crying, private pain presented publicly.

He sat next to her, his shoulder touching hers. She handed the papers to him. One was a receipt paid in full for two months' board at the Olympic Kennels in Queen Anne,

Washington. The other receipt, with subsequent payment due by August 15, was for storage of personal items at U-Do-It Safe & Secure of Federal Way. A key dangled from a chain around her wrist.

"He put Petey in a pound."

"Who did?"

"TD."

He didn't ask. He could guess the story. That slimeball she'd been living with had put her dog in a sixteen-square-foot cage. Any dog of Kara's would not do well in a cage. And TD, whoever the fuck he was, took all her stuff and crammed it into a storage locker. It angered half of him. The other half felt ashamed because he happily realized that Kara had become unbound from another.

"I'm sorry," he said.

He drove her home. She sat alone under the tree until past sundown. Later, she entered the trailer, picked up her Mac, and returned to the tree. Setting it beside her, she leaned against the rough bark and passed through anger and sadness and melancholy and hate and memory and longing and, eventually, arrived at acceptance. He sat in the trailer at the table, unable to read, unable to focus, and unable to help her. She booted the laptop and with careful deliberation ended a life.

To: TopDog@WebWideWorks.com
From: kara@WebWideWorks.com
Subject: Re: holiday
Cc:
Bcc:
Attachments:

---

i should hate you. but i merely pity you. petey loved you. how could you?

if i was not before, i am truly gone from you now.

She sent the e-mail and composed a second.

>
> To: butlerha@ap.com
> From: kara@WebWideWorks.com
> Subject: pls help petey
> Cc:
> Bcc:
> Attachments:
>
> _____
>
> hannah,
>
> td put petey in the pound ... the one in
> queen anne ... pls rescue him ... i'll come
> back for him when i'm better ... and i'm
> getting better ... I promise I am ...
>
> love, kara

She composed a third, wanting to cut all ties to the corporation she helped build. She sent a notice to the ISP to terminate her account. She had to leave that ISP. TD owned it. *Divorce complete.* She created a Gmail account, sent the email addy to her contacts list, then shut down the laptop, lifted it to her lips and kissed it. She walked around the tree, her fingers skittering across the rough, tawny bark. Kara didn't miss the rain anymore.

Kara set her Mac on the kitchen table. Noah looked at her, concern — and questions he knew enough not to ask — brewing in his eyes.

"I'm going to take a shower," she said. "A long, hot, shower."

He nodded.

"Then I'm taking you to dinner. And you're going to wear a shirt and tie. They do have a decent restaurant in Green River, don't they?"

Noah was speechless. She opened the curtain to the shower. She pushed down her Quick-Drys and shed her tank top. She was naked, her back to him, and at the moment, she could give a rat's ass what he thought about it.

"Um, okay. Are you sure—"

"Let it rest, Noah."

He nodded, though her back was to him.

She stepped into the shower and closed the curtain. "Noah?"

"Yes?"

"You're going to earn your dinner."

"I am?"

"Yes. You're going to teach me to fly."

Rushing water drowned out his surprise and mumbled assent. Kara leaned against the stall, her hands beside the showerhead, her face upturned in the lukewarm water. She wept, hoping it would be for the last time, then washed the tears and the past away with Noah's Dr. Bronner's.

Chapter 37:

June 7, late morning, en route to Moab, Utah

At 3,000 feet above the ghost town of Cisco, Noah directed Kara to turn south and descend to 500 feet AGL over Route 128, a thin, black strip of road that hugged the east bank of the Colorado. The Drifter flew over the rolling ground south of Cisco before the tertiary volcanics of the La Sal Mountains rose to the east and the thousand-foot-high cliff of Wingate sandstone hemmed in the river to the west. The bright sun warmed her thighs. Even wearing her Bollés, she squinted as her eyes dwelled on the landscape below.

She checked the positions of the indicator needles in the instruments. Utah's atmosphere was quiet, otherwise Noah would not have let her make her first long cross-country flight down the chute — the narrow Professor Valley carved by the Colorado. She had a post-op appointment in Moab. Her surgeon at Allen Memorial would pronounce her healthy; an FAA flight surgeon would examine her as well and give her a medical certificate so she could fly solo as a student pilot. That excited her. Noah held an instructor's rating; he'd begun putting her through ground school and coaching her through flying the Cessna 206. She was less interested in flying the big birds than flying the Drifter and Noah's elderly but airworthy Airbike. But the FAA considered both light sport planes, weighing more than the FAR 103 limit of 254 pounds, so a sport pilot's license was required. Noah had persuaded her to seek the full private pilot's license — so she could fly the big birds when need arose.

Her quick grasp of the essentials of ultralight flight had impressed Noah. She understood the necessity of gradual, graceful, subtle movements of stick and rudder. Perhaps the hardest part of flight — judging the flare prior to landing — had come easily and naturally in the repeated touch-and-goes they'd flown at Green River Muni. Over Dewey, at the head of the valley, he issued instructions using the mike and earphones in their helmets.

"Kara, climb and maintain angels six. Angels six. Stay over the east bank."

She keyed her mike twice to acknowledge. *Click. Click.* He hadn't taught her that; she'd picked it up from watching him. The Drifter sank in a downdraft. He placed his hands on the controls, poised to take over. But Kara added power, eased the stick back, and regained her altitude. Behind her, he nodded, pleased.

Kara's eyes fell into the scan. Instruments, then ahead, instruments, then to the left, instruments, then to the right, instruments, then above and below. On the eastern horizon, she could see the morning seeds of afternoon cumulonimbus clouds bulking up over the La Sals. She smiled, looking at the flat bottoms of the billowing clouds strung like pearls on the lee side of the snow-kissed mountains. She had never really appreciated the structure of clouds before, pregnant and plump but flat on the bottom where minute, ice-cloaked particles of dust gathered and fell toward earth as rain.

The Rotax 912 droned reassuringly. She sat calmly, right hand lightly holding the stick as Noah had taught her. She felt life through the stick and rudder pedals. The stick became her totem, connecting her to something that made Noah who he was. Now she understood. She knew what he meant by falling in love with Utah. She was learning how to touch Utah, how to allow Utah to touch her. She squirmed in her harness, skittish with a newfound sensuality. She became a soaring vulture, a diving Swainson's, a hovering harrier. She frolicked with eagles off the prow of a ferry chugging through the Inland Passage. She became every creature of flight, living with them, knowing them, sharing with them. She flew on, past Richardson Amphitheater, past the Fisher Towers. She rose above what she had been.

"I have the aircraft. Hands off. Maneuvering ahead," Noah said.

Click. Click.

"Take in the view, Kara." Ahead, volcanic mounds squatted on the floor of Castle Valley next to the La Sals. Noah took the Drifter through a standard two-minute turn, showing Kara the heart of Utah. To the west and south stretched the Canyonlands. Directly west lay Dead Horse Point. To the north rose the Window Arches and Delicate Arch above the Wingate.

"Kara, you okay up there?"

She reached behind her for his calf and squeezed it hard. "Yes. Yes."

Chapter 38:

**June 9, past midnight, Noah's trailer,
Greasewood Draw**

Noah sat at the kitchen table, re-examining and reinterpreting personal history. His hands were clasped around a mug of coffee. He liked coffee. More than tea. But he'd never tell Kara that. He endured tea. Tolerated it. But he drank coffee when alone. In his bedroom slept a beautiful, healed woman. Outside, Utah slept windless and calm. The rhythmic rasp of her breathing — he'd never tell her she snored — floated through the trailer.

He walked to his bookcase, its eclectic contents largely piled in stacks rather than aligned upright. He pulled out his Jeppesen airport directory, IFR and terminal approach charts, a stack of NOTAMs, and a few chart wallets. He knew the aerial highways of much of the Southwest by heart. But the Northwest? He plotted an IFR route from Green River to Seattle, calculating flight time, fuel stops, and emergency airfields. He tucked the charts into the plastic chart wallets and stuffed them into his flight case. He called the FAA's Salt Lake office and was told the weather would be fair and stable for a few days. He called the Associated Press bureau in Seattle. He weighed pros and cons, then tossed out the cons as irrelevant. He'd do it. Tomorrow, check out and prep the Skymaster for a long flight. He'd make the flight the day after.

After turning out the lights, he lay down on the couch, listening to Kara breathing rhythmically in sleep, in his bed. He wondered about the ephemeral nature of proper timing, then fell asleep.

"I need to go away for a few days, Kara."

They sat in the kitchen nook, eating a late supper. Kara had broiled some haddock she'd found at the Melon-Vine market. He'd vanished early in the morning without disclosing his intended whereabouts. When he'd returned, they'd spent much of the afternoon in the hangar, re-covering the wings on a two-seater Flightstar II he had intended to refurbish and sell. Fully loaded with flaps, avionics, brakes, and the hotter Rotax 582, it was worth thirty thousand dollars. But he had begun teaching Kara to fly it and had decided to keep it. She'd made noises about wanting to buy one for herself. The aircraft seemed suited to her while she learned. He had an Airbike he'd built that he really liked — light, agile, docile. That'd be a good aircraft for Kara. They'd postponed discussing details of a sale, both uncomfortable with conversations involving the future.

"Where are you going?" she asked, fork en route to her mouth.

"I've got some business to attend to."

"That's guy-speak for you're not going to tell me, isn't it?"

Noah sipped at his glass of Redhook. Only thing bred in the Northwest worth a damn. He looked at Kara. Make that two things, he told himself.

"You're so astute, little girl."

"You're really askin' for it, kiddo," she barked.

"Yeah, I suppose. Want to take me out back and beat the shit out of me?"

She chuckled. "No, not this time. I'll just add it to the list."

"List? What list?"

"Your growing list of transgressions against women," she said, smirking. "I believe I'm on volume two."

He rolled his eyes at her. "And to think I was just getting to like you."

"Liar."

"Obsequious twit."

"Schmuck."

She toyed with her fish. "When are you leaving?"

"In the morning. Dawn."

She finished her fish, then busied herself with picking up the dishes. As she washed them, Noah called the FAA's flight service to recheck the weather. But he carried the phone into the bedroom and made a second call privately. As she put away dishes, Kara wondered what he was up to. Curiosity — well, sheer nosiness — lay at the heart of her nature. No, she decided. She was a guest. She had no business butting into his life uninvited.

They rose before dawn. As Noah packed, Kara announced her intention to take a road trip, a week touring Capitol Reef, through the Escalante, and on to Kanab. "I'm not sure it's a good idea," Noah said.

"Well, I'll have company in Kanab," she said.

"Say what?"

Kara, sitting in the breakfast nook sipping her morning tea, cloaked herself in a devious smile. "Oh, I made a call last night while you were futzing in the hangar. I've got a date."

Noah's chin dropped. "A date?"

"Yep. I can get my own baby-sitter, you know."

"May I ask who?"

"If you must."

Noah's face reddened. Kara was enjoying this.

"So who is it?" he asked.

"Bill McCorrigan. Actually, Bill and his wife. They're going to meet me in Hanksville this afternoon."

Noah shook his head. "What on earth are you—"

"Field trip. He said they were going to Capitol Reef and

Escalante for a few days to do a little fieldwork. So I invited myself along."

"But—"

"But nothing. I know you'd have a fit if I said I was going by myself. You and Doc, I mean. But the McCorrigans will look after me. So there. Satisfied?"

Noah shrugged his shoulders. "Like I have any choice?"

Kara kissed him on the cheek. "So you go off and do your business, and I'll be back in four or five days. I assume you can get along without me."

Noah rolled his eyes. "Kara, you're ... you're ..."

"Just the sweetest, smartest thing you know, that's what I am. Right?"

Noah nodded vigorously and went into the bedroom to pack. A half hour later, she walked him to his Cruiser as he prepared to leave.

He stopped next to it. "Kara, you can take my Cruiser if you want."

"And have that fuel pump fail while I'm on the road? No thanks."

"There's not a goddamned thing wrong with my fuel pump."

"So you say," she said. "I'll be just fine in my Subaru."

He threw his pack into the back of the Cruiser. He told her to please be careful and climbed into the driver's seat. Kara watched him drive down the long, dirt driveway to the highway and out of sight.

Chapter 39:

June 17, late afternoon, Noah's hangar, Greasewood Draw

The Subaru skidded on the gravel as it turned off Highway 24. Kara was eager to tell Noah what she had seen, what she had learned, what she had felt, what she had loved, what she had observed, and what she had recorded. About flowers common and rare. About plants that grew only in specific geologic formations, addicted to the minerals specific to geological bookmarks like the limestones of the Moenkopi and Kaibab or the sandstones of the Wingate and Navajo. About life zones in Utah, as explained by McCorrigan, five of 'em. About the silvery leaves of aspen brilliant in morning sun. She experienced all this in a day's journey through Capitol Reef and up Highway 12 on Boulder Mountain to the Aquarius Plateau, the highest timbered plateau in America.

She'd met people both common and simultaneously rare, like the young Park Service and BLM seasonal rangers fresh from college forestry and botany programs. They were true believers imbued with a naïve but firm commitment to the notion that nature could withstand commerce. She met rangers who gladly accompanied them on a walk into the Paria River canyon, up the narrows of the Virgin River in Zion Canyon, and along the crest of the Kaibab Plateau. She'd loved the wonderful, small shop in Kanab where a mélange of people, Seattle-like lattés in hand, lingered among fine books and good camping and climbing gear. She engaged in exotic conversations across a small metal table populated by locals tolerant of tourists. She'd bounced over backcountry roads like Cottonwood Canyon Road running straight down the throat of the Cockscomb Ridge. The Paria River ate large chunks of the road during floods, making McCorrigan's jeep-driving skill all the more admirable. She had so much to tell Noah.

The Subaru slewed to a stop. Kara bounded out. Noah stood in the doorway, a beer in his hand. His face was expressionless.

"Noah, I—" she started.

"You're late," he said quietly. "You should have been back days ago."

"Oh, I know, I know. I should have called but where the hell do you find a phone on Skutumpah Creek Road?" She bit her tongue. Damn satellite phone. He knew she'd taken it. But she'd been so busy and so happy and the McCorrigans had been a delight. She didn't know McCorrigan had called Noah daily to keep him posted. Noah sat on the steps and nursed his beer. She stood in front of him, hands on her hips, approaching full Kara fury.

"Oh, it's no big deal," he said. "That neck of the woods can divert your attention, I guess. Yeah. I can see how it happened. Forgot all about us."

Kara cocked her head. "Us?"

"Yep. Us," he said. "New houseguest. Really wants to see you, too. Been waiting a week. Been kinda miserable, too."

"Noah, what the hell are you talking about?"

He idly brushed dust off his shorts. He looked around, at the sky, at the tams by the stream, anywhere but Kara. He knew something she didn't know, and it infuriated her. He rather liked this.

"Ask him. He's in the hangar."

Kara walked to the hangar and opened the door. Leaning in, she called, "Hello?"

When she heard the bark, she screamed, "Petey!" She ran in to sweep up the black mongrel who joyfully leaped over the four-foot fence of his Noah-designed pen and into her arms and she kissed him and let him lick her face and she rocked him in her arms and told him how much she missed him and how she loved him and how sorry she was she'd been away.

Noah sat on the steps of the trailer, sipping his beer, listening. So Petey had barfed twice in his Skymaster. Big deal. Kara was happy. It'd been worth it. And he'd discovered that he liked Petey, too.

Chapter 40:

July 1, evening, Noah's hangar, Greasewood Draw

Patterns emerged. Communal habits were born. Routines were established, the products of unnoticed compromises, adjustments, and common courtesies. For the next few weeks, Noah and Kara spent every waking hour together. Some were in the air; some over tea, maps, and laptop; some in the hangar, maintaining and repairing aircraft. Only night separated them, Kara retiring to the bedroom, Noah to the couch. Petey slept in the bedroom doorway, apparently undecided with whom to sleep.

Osmosis became Kara's primary flight instructor. She watched Noah. What he did. When he did it. How subtly he moved the stick and rudder pedals. She saw where he kept the pre- and post-flight checklists. Training flights expanded from dawn. She learned the flight regime required when the sun heated the earth, creating thermals that made holding altitude and course difficult.

One night, Kara was changing the oil in the Drifter with Petey dogging her heels. Noah poked in cabinets, reorganized manuals, sorted aircraft parts, and rearranged tools. He was

avoiding something. Kara recognized that: Her brothers used
to clean and preen the shop when they'd encountered a
mechanical problem for which they had yet to find a solution.
Noah's futzing avoided the problem — the tandem Airbike.
He loved that bird. She chalked it up to men's love of big
engines — it had a Rotax 582.

Noah knelt and skritched Petey behind his ears. She walked
to the tip of one wing and rested her hand on the new fabric
with its brilliant, white Poly-Tone paint. This was a well-
equipped plane. The 14-inch wheels with tundra tires were
good for landings on rough ground. The brakes made taxiing a
controlled enterprise instead of a hopeful guess. The Airbike
had an electric starter, flaps, trim controls, stroke, dual
EGT/CHT gauges that monitored engine temperature, an
intercom for the helmets, and comfortable, custom bucket
seats. She wondered why they didn't use it more often.

"No balls," Noah said, pronouncing judgment.

"'Scuse me?" she said.

"No balls. This thing is underpowered."

Kara walked to the tip of the other wing. "Maybe."

Noah looked at her. "Beg pardon?"

"Why do you think it's underpowered?"

Noah picked up a 3/8-inch ratchet and clicked a deep
socket onto it. He loosened the bolts that attached the
carburetor to the engine block.

"I don't mean to butt in, Noah, but isn't that a little
premature?"

He kept ratcheting. "Ran rough last time out. Ought to
clean the carb."

"Maybe." She walked over to him. "It didn't seem rough to
me."

"Well, you're not used to this bird. You don't know its feel
like I do."

"I know."

He popped out one bolt and cranked on another. "Still,"
she ventured.

Noah took the ratchet from the bolt. "Out with it,

woman."

"Oooh, woman. I think he's mad."

"I'm not mad. Just irritated."

She frowned, and he saw that. He quickly clarified what he said.

"Sorry. Not at you. I like this plane, and I'd like to use it a little more. But with you on board, it's sluggish."

"So now you're calling me fat?"

"No, you twit. But I'm not small. You put us pretty near gross."

"How close?"

Noah thought for a minute. "Maybe within 50 pounds." He looked at her and asked, "How much do you weigh, Kara?"

"About 120."

He grinned. "About?"

"Wiseass. Last time I checked, I weighed 123."

He picked up a calculator, punched in numbers and hmmm'd.

"It's 42 pounds under gross. Too close. So it's sluggish. So more power."

She snickered. "Typical guy response. More power solves everything. You must be the Tim Taylor of the air."

"And your diagnosis is?" he asked. Kara sat on an overturned bucket.

"My brother used to have this Pontiac," she said. "A '65 GTO. Black Beauty, he called it. Hurst shifter, the works. He coaxed almost 500 horsepower out of it. But when he'd go dragging, he kept losing to this guy with a Charger."

"Ah," said Noah. "The Hemi rules."

"It sure did. He tried everything. Webers, two barrels, four barrels, and he still kept losing. Drove him nuts. One day, Dad was listening as he talked about putting in a nitrous system. Dad just shook his head."

"What'd he say?"

"All Dad said was, 'Stop driving on the street.'"

"Say again, please?"

"He had plenty of power, Noah. But the GTO was too

heavy. So Donny put in a barebones racing seat. He yanked the headlights and tail lights. He fabricated a fiberglass hood. Lessee, things like the spare tire got tossed. He got a few hundred pounds out with lots of minor changes. He never lost again. But he couldn't drive his women around, either."

She smiled wistfully. "Kind of a Pyrrhic victory, I suppose. But he liked winning. And women came easily to him for, um, other reasons."

Noah straightened. "Overweight. Not underpowered." Kara nodded.

"Are you saying—"

"I am," she said.

Noah's eyes flicked over the plane, mentally weighing accessories.

"There's a scale over by the Buckeye. Would you bring it over, please?"

Kara brought over the scale as Noah pondered the electric starter.

"One rule," he said. "No compromising safety."

She nodded. Noah walked around the Airbike, looking at different parts, pondering the possibilities. "I know I've got a pull starter here somewhere."

He removed the starter. Kara noted its weight on a scrap piece of paper. Next he removed one of the custom seats. She weighed it, awkwardly holding it onto the small scale. "Heavy," she said.

"But comfortable."

"Yeah," she said.

"Necessary for your tender ass."

She shot him a look. "My ass isn't tender."

"I'd have to inspect it to be sure."

"Over my dead body."

"Well, to be honest, I did inspect it over your unconscious body."

"Why, you—"

"I'd have to say it's not tender. Firm, rounded—"

"You'll never see sunrise, Noah."

He chuckled as he put the seat back. "Idle threats, woman. Idle threats."

Kara turned so he wouldn't see her smile.

Noah stood back from the plane. "I don't know what else can go."

"Instruments?"

"Never. I won't sacrifice information."

"Now you sound like me. You can remove some without killing data."

"How?" he asked, interested. She picked up a copy of "Ultralight Flying" magazine, leafed through the ads, and pointed to one. He nodded, understanding.

"Ah. Wearables." A wrist computer, worn like a watch, had several functions — altimeter, barometer, airspeed indicator, altitude alarms, vertical speed indicator and a few others.

"Interesting idea," he said. "Hate to give up gauges, though. Too hard to read a watch during turbulence, too."

She pointed to other ads. "Some of these instrument panels are smaller and lighter. And what about HUD displays? In goggles? I'm just saying consider alternatives to what you've got."

Noah rubbed his beard. Alternatives. He looked at the plane, thinking.

"Well, what the hell else is there?" he asked.

"Bare, sealed fabric?"

"Hey, do you know how long it took me to get that paint job just right?"

"Sorry, sorry," she said, waving her hands in front of her, backing away.

She walked around the Airbike, inspecting it. "Gasoline. Heavy stuff."

"Yeah, I guess I could fit a five-gallon tank instead of that ten," he said. Running out of gasoline didn't worry him. Kara didn't yet know he had gas, spare parts, freeze-dried food, and water cached throughout western Utah. He'd have to brief her on their locations some day. All were logged in a notebook he carried in his flight bag. Kara noted the weight of five gallons

— close to 45 pounds. She showed him the total.

"Not bad," he said. "But I'd feel better with a dual carb. More power."

"More maintenance. More parts," she countered.

He sat on the wooden box, deep in mathematical thought.

Kara returned to the bucket. "There's a lighter way to add power."

He looked up, the question in his eyes.

"Tuned pipes," she said.

Noah nodded. "Tuned pipes. I'm not sure I could make some."

"I don't know about these engines, but I would guess that where there's an engine, there's a tuned pipe for it." She walked to a bench and picked up her iPad. "Care to look for some?"

Noah walked to the Airbike, running his hand over the stock exhaust.

"Have to match the pitch of the prop. Yeah. I'll need to use a higher rpm to get onto the pipe. Yeah. This could work. More power, less weight."

He nodded to her, but with little expression, as guys do when girls are their equal in the guys' games. He removed the instruments while Kara took off the exhaust system. They argued over the best way to get the tuned pipes. He wanted to make them; she argued for buying them new. He finally agreed.

Midnight approached. Kara, putting tools away, yawned.

"Let me finish that," he said. "You'd best get some sleep."

Her eyes flashed with anger. Noah turned, surprised. It'd been a wonderful evening. But some demon still lurked in her, he guessed.

"I don't need you to be a goddamned doctor anymore," she snapped.

He nodded patiently. "That's not why I'm suggesting you get to bed."

"Oh?"

"I'm suggesting you get a good night's sleep for another reason."

"Do you always drag out these mysterious moments?" she said, slapping a wrench down on a bench. "Jesus, you do have trouble getting to the point."

"You solo at dawn, kid."

She stared at him. He grinned.

"That direct enough for you?"

Walking away, he chuckled at her lack — for once — of a snappy retort.

Chapter 4i:

July 2, dawn, Green River Municipal Airport

Kara soloed at sunrise in the Drifter. She made five takeoffs and landings to a full stop. Then Noah buckled himself into the rear seat, asked for her logbook, and stuck it in one of his pockets.

"You passed, pilot," he said over the intercom. "Check traffic, climb to and maintain angels seven-five, set course zero four zero." Kara brimmed with joy.

The flat riverside land surrounding Green River gave way to an increasingly chaotic landscape as she eased the throttle to max and the Drifter climbed effortlessly to assigned altitude. Its big Rotax 912 never missed a beat. Like her brother's old GTO. Power in reserve. Power for safety's sake. Understanding of Noah's, of all guys' love for power, more power, grew in Kara. The debate over the Airbike became clearer, his compromise more meaningful. She wriggled against the seatback, seeking the sweet spot. Despite turbulence from westerly winds rising over the Beckwith Plateau, she held the stick easily, circling it with thumb and forefinger, the rest of her hand held in cautious reserve.

The Drifter droned straight and level past Blue Castle, a

small knoll to the north. To the northwest, over Middle
Mountain, and the west-southwest, over Little Elliot Mesa,
small cumulus clouds had puffed up, like tiny bursts of
popcorn. *My pendant of clouds*, she thought. The Drifter bucked
as it crossed a ridge east of Blue Castle Butte. The intercom
crackled.

"Descend. Two zero zero feet per minute. Maintain course
two seven zero. Prepare for rougher air."

Click. Click.

The Drifter sank between the butte to the south and
canyon wall of Beckwith Plateau. A valley loomed ahead.

"Skirt that butte carefully."

Click. Click.

She held the wings level despite buffeting from winds
curling through the canyon. The brown plain rose toward the
Drifter.

"Land dead ahead."

Click. Click.

She sat upright, alert, running her checklist. Ease the
throttle back. Feed in flaps. Check for obstructions, rocks,
brush, anything. Nothing threatened a safe landing. At one
hundred feet, she focused on a spot ahead. Touch down there.
Reduce power. Hold it, hold it. Hard earth rushed under the
Drifter. Chop power. Flare. Feel for the earth. Ease the wheels
down. Hold the nose up. Ease the stick forward. Let her run
out. Touch the brakes. Raise the flaps. Brake to a stop.

The radio crackled. "Kill the engine."

She switched the ignition off, and the Rotax 912 sputtered
into silence. She stepped out and ran the post-flight checklist.
She glanced at the fuel tanks. Plenty there. She pulled out the
wheel chocks and tapped them under the main wheels.
Finished, she looked for Noah. He had walked away from the
ultralight, helmet in one hand and a leather-covered notebook
in the other. His head was craned back, eyes intent on the
canyon wall.

"What are you looking at?" she asked quietly.

Presently, he looked at her. "The Mesaverde."

"Pardon?"

Noah pointed north to the Beckwith Plateau.

"A rock formation. It's Cretaceous. And higher on, slices of the Wasatch and Green River formations. Paleocene and Eocene. Mostly marine deposits. That's a few hundred million years up there. See how they're tilted some? Laramide Uplift about, oh, maybe 75 million years ago."

She said nothing. She was focused on the placid look on his face.

He pointed toward the base of the cliff.

"See those large slabs? Erosion cuts into weaker rock. Gravity breaks off the overhanging slabs. Rock 'round here weathers from the side, not the top."

He walked away, but not far. He stopped, closing his eyes.

"Listen," he said. "Just listen. What do you hear?"

Shrugging her shoulders, she closed her eyes. "I don't hear anything."

"Not exactly. Listen," he said, emphasizing the last word.

She concentrated. "I hear the wind," she said.

"No, you hear the sound the wind carries," he said.

She listened and then looked up.

"Why did you look up?" he asked.

She pointed. High above a bird soared. He shaded his eyes from the sun.

"Prairie falcon," he said. "You can tell it from a peregrine. Peregrine's larger but more slender. And it's hard to miss the facial markings on the peregrine. Bold. And the peregrine's kinda bluish in light like this."

She nodded.

"So why'd you look up?" he asked again.

"I heard a sound."

"What kind?"

"Like a ticking."

"Like this?" Noah made a *kik-kik-kik* sound.

"Yes," Kara said. "Yes. That's it."

"What else do you hear in the wind?"

She tried hard. But wind offered only cacophony, not

symphony.

Shaking her head, she said, "Just noise, Noah. Just noise."

He stood quietly, eyes closed again.

"You'll learn," he said, "to hear signal in the noise."

He glanced down. Something scurried behind a small rock.

"You can hear a lizard's tail knocking a pebble aside. When it runs, its tail waggles from side to side. It hits things."

Noah sighed and walked back to her. "Noah, are you sad?" she asked.

He sat down, arms around drawn-up knees.

"Yes," he said. "Damn. No. I'm not sad. It's something else. Shit, I don't know. I just feel something out here I can't describe."

He put his hands behind him and leaned back. "I know every damn rock out here." He pointed upward. "See? That odd line? A fault. I know all the faults. I know the birds. I know most of the animals, some of the insects, most of the flowers. I just *know* this place. And so many others."

She sat down beside him. "Then what is it that you—"

"Christ, I don't know. I look at a landscape, and I can't describe what I feel."

"Try. Please," she said. He leaned forward and thought for a while.

"You can know something. But that doesn't mean you understand it."

"You lost me, Noah."

"I know all the parts of this place. I know all the parts of the Swell. But something eludes me. Something leaves me lonely out here. As if I can be in the landscape, but I can't possess it. The more I study it, the more I'm frustrated by it. No, frustrated isn't the right word."

He was silent for a while. "Damn, Kara. I want to know it all, possess it all, have it all. And I can't. I don't know why."

His eyes were moist. She turned away to give his tears privacy.

"Whatever that feeling is, I can't capture it."

"What do you mean?" she asked.

"I used to paint. Oils and watercolors. I'd fly out to places like this and study the lines and the shadows and try to capture what it is that's here."

"Sounds like the wrong goal."

He looked at her sharply. She shrugged in apology.

"I mean, why try to capture it?" she said. "Why not try to capture what *you* feel, not whatever it is that produces the feeling?"

He inhaled deeply, then got to his feet. He walked toward the Drifter.

"Noah, wait," she called. He stopped and turned.

"My first big job was making an intranet site for a dam," she said. "A training manual for its operators. I had to figure out how the dam worked. They're incredibly complicated." She looked at the cliff.

"I was talking with a guy who'd worked there all his life. I told him that trying to figure out the dam was driving me nuts. Know what he told me?"

He shook his head.

"He said that a dam is more than the sum of its parts."

"What?" Noah said.

"Exactly what I said. The guy told me that until I came to know the dam as a living organism, until I knew its parts as something beyond their sum, I'd never understand the dam. Or be able to relate to it. Or articulate it."

"Shit," he said. "She likes dams."

She poked him in the arm. "The mechanics, yes. But I'm not sure I like the function anymore."

Noah cocked his head, looking up at the cliff. "Are you saying that—"

"Yes. A wilderness is more than the sum of its parts. And whatever that greater sum is, you're reacting to it."

She turned away. "God, I'm not making any sense. Sorry. It's just that—"

"You make perfect sense, Kara. Somehow, I have to understand the wilderness in terms of me as well in terms of itself."

He shook his head again. "And I thought I did understand that." He sighed. "Guess I have some thinking to do."

"Or some feeling to do. That's what you'd tell me, you know. Me, the thinker? Not the feeler?"

"You're a natural, Kara. You really are."

She said nothing. A few tears glistened. She wiped her eyes.

She grasped his sleeve with her left hand and spun him toward her. Her right hand snaked around his neck and pulled him toward her. Kara kissed Noah hard, her tongue snaking into his mouth. Then she smiled.

"Thank you, Noah."

She turned away, but not before she saw his cheeks flush. He did not look at her. He lowered his gaze, and his helmet, placing it on the ground. He opened her leather-bound logbook and wrote in it.

"What's that?" she asked.

"Your logbook."

He noted the date and her five touch 'n' goes, marked the page "solo," and signed his name and CFI number. "Nice job," he said quietly, handing her the logbook.

"Nice job? That's all I get?" she said.

"Okay, okay. Well done."

"That's better."

She tried to read his eyes. "Noah, did I do something wrong?"

"No. Not at all. It's just that—" He picked up his helmet. "Let's mount up and get the hell outta here."

Kara walked away, confused. Noah watched her walk toward the Drifter and cursed being old enough to understand more than he wanted to.

She had not kissed him. She had kissed a symbol.

He shrugged. Still, it's a kiss. That's progress.

Kara guided the Drifter to six thousand feet before banking it south. The big Rotax engine ferried them toward Greasewood Draw, each absorbed in silent assessment of the other. Neither saw men in a draw hundreds of feet below hurriedly drape camouflage cloth over three large vehicles and two tripod-mounted video cameras.

A tall, thin man dressed in black watched the Drifter disappear. He pulled out a cell phone and keyed in a number. After waiting a few seconds for an answer, he swore loudly at the person who answered the phone.

Chapter 42:

July 9, morning, Manti-La Sal National Forest, near Castle Valley

The Drifter carried them fifty miles into the high country of the Manti-La Sal National Forest west of Castle Valley. Kara sat behind Noah, her head swiveling incessantly. So much to see, so much to observe, so much to record.

Hard work in Noah's makeshift gym each morning had begun to resurrect the woman who raced mountain bikes. She wasn't all the way back yet. The ribs still ached. Headaches sometimes followed her workouts. All was duly reported to Doc, who examined her each week over breakfast at Noah's and pronounced her progress on schedule. The Mac got workouts, too. Kara sat at the kitchen table in the evenings, sorting her growing collection of digitized flora.

He took her on longer flights, some in the Drifter, some in the Buckeye, north and south along the eastern edge of the Swell. He limited her solo work to local traffic and touch 'n' goes at the airport. She appreciated his caution, although she badgered him constantly about getting in some cross-country time. Noah's ground school kept her busy and interested. She learned the intricacies of navigation through the middle of nowhere. In the air, Noah coached her toward mastery of the basics, such as flying straight and level at a designated altitude and achieving precision in ascent, descent, and turns. He insisted on perfection. He was pleased when she asked to repeat a maneuver again and again.

He needed to replenish one of his caches on the Wasatch Plateau west of Joe's Valley. They could make a day of it, take a picnic lunch, enjoy the cool, mountain air. That had excited her, even though he said he'd take the front seat. He didn't tell her he wanted to get her away from that goddamned computer and out into *life*.

The Wasatch greeted them gently — little wind, no turbulence. Noah landed below a ridgeline and taxied to a grove of aspen tinged with silvery leaves. Kara sprang from her seat, her Canon in hand, and jogged toward the horizon, pointing excitedly toward a small herd of mule deer.

"Noah! Deer! Look at them!" she cried as he slowly unwound himself from his seat. "Looks like about two dozen."

He smiled, nodded, and unpacked the gas for the cache. He carried the five-gallon can to a large cairn hidden in the grove. He sat and watched her watch the deer, her camera's shutter clicking furiously. The excitement of the first-time tourist, he thought. She jogged into the grove, smiling, and sat beside him. She shaded the camera with her body, and showed him the frames on the LCD. The deer were tiny spots, and she said something about getting a longer lens soon so she could get better photos. He thought of asking what she meant by *better*, but decided not to. Besides, he had work to do.

"Kara, would you please get lunch? I've got to uncover the cache."

Standing, she reached for a rock. "I'll help."

He chuckled. "Oh, I don't think you want to do that."

"Why not?"

"Snakes."

Kara jumped back with a disgusted shudder.

"Um, I'll get lunch."

The landscape receded to the east, toward Castle Valley. Beyond, haze cloaked the distant peaks in the Swell. She methodically swept her camera from north to south, recording the geometry of the land.

She turned to Noah. "God, that's beautiful."

He grunted, leaning against an aspen, his legs splayed comfortably on the meadow. He sipped from a water bottle, his eyes closed but still seeing.

"How would you know? You never look at it," he said. "You haven't really looked at anything since I've met you."

Die cast, he thought. *Come what will.*

Kara turned around, her lips pressed together. "What the hell do you mean? I've been looking at the damned landscape ever since I left Portland."

"You're still too angry and hurt about something — I don't know what — to look at anything. To really *look* at something."

"That's bullshit."

Noah paused, considering the emotional land mines he could trip.

"No, it's not," he said softly.

"Listen, I've got notes and I've got pictures and I've walked and biked and hiked through all kinds of places. I could describe exactly what I've seen."

"I'm sure you could."

"Then what the hell do you mean, I never look at anything?"

He looked at her. "You never look. You only record."

She walked away and looked down through Olsen Canyon at Joe's Valley Dam. The turquoise water imprisoned by the dam glistened in the noon sun. Shaking her head, she walked back and sat down.

"That's what I do. I observe. I record. It's how I make my living."

"You're just using your father's words," he said. Noah had learned of her father from Hannah when he flew to Seattle to pick up Petey. "Where are yours?"

She jumped to her feet. "You prick!"

She stalked off. He ran after her, caught her arm, and spun her around.

"When are you going to speak for yourself, Kara?" he said.

"Goddammit, don't you realize that—"

"That you're living in a shadow you've got to escape?"

She wrenched her arm away. "Damn it, he taught me values, what to live by. What's wrong with that?"

"Nothing. Just live them your own way," he said softly.

"And who are you to decide how anyone should live?" she shouted.

Noah sat and closed his eyes. "I'm not trying to tell you how to live, Kara. I'm just telling you I know how you live now."

Kara stalked away, arms crossed across her chest. She sat on a rock about a hundred yards away. After a few minutes, she walked toward the deer, still grazing and ignorant of human conflict. She watched for a while, then walked back to Noah, kicking a stone.

"You're still a bastard, Hartshorn," she said, standing over him.

"Yep. Honest one, though," he said. She sat and poked his thigh, hard enough to show irritation, soft enough to sue for peace.

"Hey. Let's have a little more non-violence, girl."

"Don't call me girl."

"What should I call you?"

"Good question. I don't know. Call me whatever you want. You seem to think you know everything." She gave him her *you dumb fuck* look.

They sat quietly, separated by a foot of high mountain meadow. Kara traced her fingers over a rock left behind by a glacier thousands of years ago. Noah sat still, but the seeingness in his eyes fled through the landscape, imagining, remembering, planning, loving, soothing.

"How do I live, Noah?"

He walked away, then turned and spoke. "You work very hard."

"You're damned right I do. And I make a very good living, thank you," she said, snapping at him.

"But you don't sleep well. You haven't slept more than three hours in a stretch for a long time. At least, before you got here. And when you do sleep, you never get rest."

Kara glared at him. "How do you know that?"

"It's in your face. It's tired, Kara. So are your eyes."

"You're talking nonsense."

"Maybe. But I'll bet you used to set your alarm clock for, oh, say six o'clock every morning. And maybe four years ago, you'd wake up when the alarm went off. But perhaps two years ago, you started waking up at quarter to six. And you'd lie there, your mind racing. About what you were going to do at work that day, about whether you'd have another fight with what's-his-name."

"You can say his name."

"I'd rather not."

"Whatever."

"Then you started waking up about half past five," Noah said quietly. "Then about quarter after. Then about five. And maybe even four o'clock. And you'd lie there, restless, unable to sleep, work invading you, that relationship troubling you, everything roaring around in your mind and stealing your rest. And you'd be angry, because he'd be sleeping soundly next to you. He'd be rested. You wouldn't. And it'd piss you off. You'd always be tired when he woke up, because you'd already put in part of a hard day.

"Then you'd get up at six, pretend you'd got your full beauty sleep, and go to work. You'd work hard, really hard. You'd come home, and work would still be there. He'd be there. You'd be on edge much of the time, and you'd go into your study and work some more 'til you couldn't keep your eyes open.

"You'd go to bed," he said. "And you wouldn't really fall sleep. You haven't had a good night's sleep in a long, long time, Kara. I'll bet the coma you were in is the best rest you've had in years."

She sat motionless, her legs crossed and her face cradled in her hands. Noah sat beside her again. This time, only half a foot of the meadow's soft, green-and-yellow lichen carpet separated them.

"How do you see the world, Kara?" he asked.

A few minutes passed. She raised her head, placed her hands behind her, and leaned back, legs stretched out in front of her.

"In full detail. I see everything there is to see. I don't miss anything. I make sure I see and record all there is. I have to. I just have to."

Noah rested his hand lightly on her shoulder. "Why do you have to?"

"I just have to."

Noah waited, turning his head away from her while she dabbed at her eyes with the hem of a sweatshirt she'd put on to ward off the chill of altitude.

"Go on, say it," she said.

"Say what?"

"Whatever else you're going to say. I just know you haven't finished."

"Kara, I'm not trying to make you angry."

She smiled at him briefly. "No, I guess you're not. But you're doing a damn good job of it."

"You don't like hearing this, do you?"

"No."

"Then I'll shut up." Noah lay down, eyes closed. They watched the deer for a while.

"Noah?"

"Yes?"

"I work too much."

"And?"

"I have to work all the time."

"Why? You don't need the money all that much right now."

"I have to keep my mind working. I have to keep taking in

stuff."

"Why?"

"Because if I don't, the thoughts will creep in."

He looked at her knowingly. In a whisper, he asked, "Thoughts of what?"

She stood and walked back and forth. Noah liked watching her pace and talk with her hands. He liked watching her work, liked watching her do her kind of work, even though he believed it had nearly destroyed her.

"I can fix things, you know. I know how things work. I take things apart and I put them back together," she said. "I can watch things and see how they work and then I write a good, clear explanation of how they work. I'm really, really, really good at it. It's what I do. I describe things. I see everything, and I can find the patterns that count in everything I see."

"That's good. You should be proud of that."

"I am."

"So?"

Kara sighed. "Noah, I can't fix me. I hate when thoughts about me sneak into my mind. They make me sad. They make me, um, they make me melancholic. I can fix the external. I just can't deal with what's inside me."

Noah waited. She walked behind him, her hands still conversing.

"I'm inept. I'm incompetent. I'm an idiot. I'm no good at being me."

Noah stood and turned, hands in his pockets, eyes intent on hers.

"Why?"

"I'm scared."

"Of what?"

"Of being."

"I don't know what you mean," he said.

"I can't explain it. I don't know how. And I'm scared of trying to tell you what I'm scared of."

"Please try."

Noah rested his hand on her shoulder. Kara touched his

forearms.

"You're strong."

"And you're stalling."

"Yeah, I know."

He waited a discreet moment. "How do you want to be, Kara?"

Kara turned, and his hand fell from her shoulder. "God, I can't even accept the comfort of your hand. I can't be! I can't feel! I can't let myself feel!"

Noah walked after her. "You were in love with him, weren't you?"

Kara turned away. "I thought it was love," she said.

"What was it?"

"Protection."

"From what?"

"From feeling. From being me."

"What do you mean?"

She walked from the grove and sat on a large boulder, cradling legs in her arms, her head resting on her knees. He sat beside her. She whispered, and he could barely hear her, so he leaned closer.

"I lived through him. I lived with him. I lived for him. I lived for the work. I lived to avoid letting me be me. I never let myself feel anything about me. If I wasn't working, I felt doubt and fear and I couldn't face that."

She fell silent for a while. "I don't know who I am inside, Noah. I mean, I have these feelings streak through me suddenly and they frighten me."

"What kind of feelings?"

"Jesus, you're nosy."

"Yep."

"You always pry like this?"

"I'm not prying."

"Then what the hell are you doing?"

"I'm listening, Kara. You record. I *listen*. There's a difference. I listen. That's what I do."

En route home, flying low through one of the winding slot canyons in the Swell, Noah saw several ORVs. Circling about five hundred feet over them, he could see a black Hummer with an XOX on its roof. A film crew had set up next to an arroyo. A blue Jeep with big, fat, backcountry tires was chewing its way toward the high end of the slit in the earth.

Through the intercom, Kara asked, "That them?"

"Yep."

"We got ammo?"

"No," he said.

"Let's buzz 'em," she said.

"Look closer, Kara." In the shadow of the western wall of the canyon were three men toting rifles. One raised his weapon. Noah banked away, lowered the Drifter's nose to increase airspeed, and sped them out of range.

"Would they shoot?" she asked.

"Not would. They have."

"You're kidding, Noah."

"Nope. So I always check now."

"You're sure your eyes are that good?" she asked.

"I don't check from the air. I check from the ground. I've developed a little inside knowledge. I know who his shooters are. So I find out where they are before I go on a run."

Kara said nothing.

"I don't have a death wish, Kara. Really."

She clicked the mike twice. But she said nothing.

Chapter 43:

July 13, late morning, the hangar, Greasewood Draw

"Noah?"

He groaned. *Incoming.* Another point-blank question en route. But, he thought, turnabout is fair play. He'd asked pointed questions of her.

Noah put down the torque wrench. Checking the tightness of the head bolts on the Rotax 912 was part of its monthly maintenance. Kara lay in the sun outside the hangar on a cheap aluminum chaise lounge. She was tummy-side down, chasing bronze. An unfastened halter top sprawled beneath her.

She peered into the hangar, resting her chin on her hands. She noticed he glanced at her when he thought she wasn't looking. She liked that.

"How come you never got married?" she asked.

He loosened a spark plug, then twirled it out with his fingers. His forearms shook a bit, and he dropped the plug. He stooped to pick it up. Compression test, he told himself. *Focus.* Always do a compression test. He set up the testing gear.

"Noah?"

"I heard you, Kara."

"Well?"

He recalled the women. The junior psychology major when he was in college. The seismologist he'd worked with in his first job out of school with the U.S. Geological Survey. The park ranger at the Needles station in the Canyonlands. That short fling with Annie a few years back. Passion, parting, pain. He'd always excused them as cycle-of-life shit but hell now was he was drifting toward 40 and—

"Noah?"

He spun around and barked at her. "Because no one said yes. Satisfied?"

She said nothing, then, "Oh."

He finished the compression test and moved on to the oil change.

"What happened?"

"I asked. They said no. I went away. Case closed," he said quietly.

Kara sat up, tied her halter top and rolled onto her back. Noah glanced at her again as she did. He liked her breasts — not too small, not too large, tiny nipples and aureoles. When he imagined her on her back, sleeping, or reaching for a lover — for *him* — he pictured her chest as almost boylike, her breasts barely rising over a smooth, pale plain of soft skin, her nipples taut. That excited him, and he felt guilty — as if he were invading her somehow.

"Well, what do you want, anyway?" she asked.

Noah slammed a pair of pliers onto a table. The sharp sound echoed through the hangar. He stalked to the chaise lounge and faced her.

"I want you — I mean, I want a woman to grab the front of my shirt, push her tongue into my mouth as far as it will go, and pull me onto the bed on top of her. I want a woman to tell me she wants me. I want her to show me she wants me. And what the hell's wrong with that?"

Kara rose from the chaise and stood in front of him, face to face. "Nothing at all," she said quietly. "There's nothing wrong with that at all. I think it's sweet, and beautiful. But why was it so hard for you to tell me that?"

Noah shook visibly for several moments.

"I don't know," he said almost inaudibly. "No one to say it to, I guess."

Then he sighed, his broad chest deflating, and he strode away. He got into the Cruiser. Its tires churned against the hard-packed brown earth as it slewed into a 180-degree turn and disappeared down the rutted road leading to Highway 24.

Kara walked into the trailer and showered. Dressed in Levis and a tank top, she wandered barefoot in the shadow of the cliff, thinking about wanting and what it means to want and what it means to be wanted.

Chapter 44:

July 14, morning, the trailer, Greasewood Draw

The lure of bacon woke Noah. Kara, her back to him, stood watch over the stove, spatula in hand. Petey slithered in and out between her legs, looking for food as much as attention. Propping his head up, Noah watched her. He liked Kara's body and how she used it. The way her legs carried her during their walks from one spot on Utah's dusty ground to another. The way her head tilted slightly to the left when she talked. Her shoulders, firm and sculpted from hard hours in the outdoor gym. The musculature in her forearms and upper arms and thighs and calves, finely detailed architecture born of hard rides and dedicated weight training. But his inspections embarrassed him as so much cheap voyeurism. He imagined not watching her. He did not like that idea. But he did not want to deal with that issue, either. Not today. He cursed Doc. This, this was his fault.

She stayed up late now, often spending an hour a night on the phone with McCorrigan. Doing what, he had no idea, because she had been secretive. She had trouble sleeping again. She had started roaming outside in the moonlight, thinking him asleep, then coming inside and breaking out her Mac to do those unrevealed things on the kitchen table, her face lit by the ghostly screen. Doc had told him that her behavior was normal. A reflex. A return to routines of her former life. Kara would retreat to those routines that comforted her before she could abandon them for new ones. Give her time, Doc had said. So he, too, stayed up late. He'd given up pretending to sleep, gone to his hangar, and left her by herself while she worked, seemingly oblivious to his absence.

Like mothers with proverbial eyes in the backs of their heads, she'd known when he awoke. She turned and winked at him. Noah smiled sheepishly. Busted. "Food in ten minutes," she said.

Kara fed Petey as a distraction for Noah's benefit. The weather had turned warm, and he slept in underwear under a sheet. Noah hurried into the shower. When he returned, barefoot in jeans and a T-shirt, scrambled eggs, toast, bacon and home fries were ready. The coffee pot stood in the center, and he knew it contained tea instead of coffee. Noah was beginning to like tea.

She stood by the table, waiting, her hands clasped in front of her waist. He sat, then she did. Kara was not smiling, but she was not frowning, either. He could not decipher this morning's mask. Picking up the platter of eggs, she spooned some onto his plate, setting the platter down slowly and precisely from whence it came. She did likewise with bacon and the home fries. Picking up the coffee pot, she pulled his mug to the center of the table, poured tea into it, moved his mug back to the side of his plate, and turned its handle toward him. She put her hands in her lap, waiting. He'd seen tea ceremonies. This reminded him of such rituals. He took a bite of the eggs.

He nodded to her. "Good."

Kara nodded, served herself, and ate in silence. She usually attacked food with gusto, leaning on the table with the elbow of the arm not involved in food-to-mouth transport. She always talked while she ate. But not now. When she finished, she set her plate to the side. She leaned back against the bench seat, both hands cradling her mug. She closed her eyes until he had finished.

She opened her eyes and looked at him. "We need groceries."

He nodded. "I'll go into town and get some," he said.

Kara sighed. She set her mug down on the table a tad forcefully.

"You do that," she said curtly, slipping out from the table.

She vanished into the shower. Noah shook his head and got the keys to his Land Cruiser. *Wimmin. Shee-it.*

Noah returned from the Melon-Vine with groceries. He called out for Kara to open the door. She did not appear. He nudged it open with his foot and set the two paper bags on the sink counter. Kara sat at the table, not moving, her hands resting on the keyboard of her laptop, her MiFi parked beside it. He sat across from her. Petey sat in the corner, sated and content to watch the humans confuse each other.

"Kara?"

She continued to stare at the screen. "I know it's your home," she said without looking up. "I know I'm a guest. But please, say nothing. Please."

He rose from the nook, uneasy. He collected tea makings, his usual reaction to Kara's moods, good or bad. Fuck it, he thought. Instead, he took a Redhook from the fridge and leaned against the sink. He sipped. And waited.

Kara typed deliberately. He had seen her write before and usually her fingers danced in a frenzied blur. Not now. He watched her backspace occasionally, stop, reconsider wording, and type again. He'd drained the Redhook when she folded her hands in her lap. Her eyes scanned the screen, checking her text. She looked up at him. "Noah, are you attracted to me?"

"Physically?"

She shrugged. "If that's the level you want to answer on."

He sat across the table from her. He didn't need to search for the words; they had been gathering since he had first seen her lying unconscious, blood flowing from a cut cruelly administered by Navajo sandstone.

"Kara, you're like the warm spot in the pond," he said, whispering. "Very hard to find. Once you get into it, you don't want to leave it."

She closed her eyes, revealing nothing. But Noah's anxiety vanished. He'd cast his lot, and it felt good.

"I saw Doc yesterday," she said. "I guess you could say he discharged me from his care. No more checkups. Said I'm no longer a patient."

"He lied. Once his patient, always his patient. That's how he is."

"You know what I mean."

"Yeah, I know," he said.

She paused. He looked into her eyes and saw the deer in the headlights. Sometimes they freeze. Sometimes they run away. Sometimes they merely go back to brunching on a shrub.

"I don't need to stay here anymore."

He nodded. Let the deer decide.

Reaching for the Mac, she touched a key. Faint chirping sounds said an e-mail had been transmitted. She closed the laptop and rested her hands on it, but they were jumpy. She lowered them to her lap.

"But I don't live in Seattle anymore."

He nodded again.

"Am I living here, Noah?"

"I'll never evict you," he said presently.

He got her don't-be-a-wiseass-at-times-like-this look.

"Do you want me to stay?" she asked, incandescent eyes fixed on his. The deer had wrested the spotlight from him.

"Yes."

"Why?" she asked.

Noah scratched at his beard briefly. Then: "I think we can become something."

"Something? Like what?"

"I don't know," he said. "But I know I can't figure it out alone."

She folded her arms across her chest. Eyes closed, she

rocked almost imperceptibly. Then she got to her knees, hands on the table. She leaned over her Mac and touched her lips to his. Noah's eyes widened in surprise. He framed her face with his hands and held her lips to his. She slipped away, sitting on the bench. He took her hands. She smiled at him.

"I want to stay," she said.

He nodded. "I'm glad," he said. "Why?"

"I think it's the same reason."

"You think?"

"I'm not sure yet."

Noah didn't know what to say.

"I can't sleep with you yet," she said.

"Yet?"

The don't-be-a-wiseass look shot across the table again. Noah flinched.

"You saved my life. I need to get over that feeling of indebtedness."

Noah grinned. "A few months isn't enough for my charm to, um, help you overcome that indebtedness thing?"

She sighed. "Are you pressing the issue, Noah?"

"Ah, no," he said, flustered. "Just trying to lighten the mood."

She stood. "I need to take a shower. Would you excuse me?"

He nodded. As she walked away, she said, "I like that warm spot, too."

Her words flowed slowly over Noah, sedating him.

"Kara, what was that e-mail?"

She was inside the shower. She called out over the hissing water, tone matter-of-fact.

"Job offer in Portland. I turned it down."

Chapter 45:

July 18, morning, airborne over Sids Mountain

The phone rang. Kara, drying her hair with a towel, answered it.

"Hello? ... Oh, sure. Just a minute." She motioned to Noah. "For you."

Noah rolled off the couch, a touch foggy. Kara sat at the kitchen table, nursing her tea.

"Hartshorn. ... Oh, hi. ... That asshole! Where?" He was alert now. He turned to Kara, holding the phone to his chest. "Please get that map, would you?" Fetching the map of the Swell from the shelf, she handed it to him. He put the map on the floor and knelt beside it. He drew his finger along a latitude line, then a longitude line, and marked the intersection with a pen.

"And it's today? ... Oh, they're out there already? ... Yes. ... No, don't ask what I'm going to do. ... Right. Just call that guy at the High Country News. ... Yes, suggest that he call Nash and ask him point blank. I'll get pictures to him as soon as I can. ... See if the fucker lies again. ... Yes, thanks. Bye."

Noah sat on the floor with his legs crossed, oblivious to his nudity. Kara sat across from him. "What's up?" she asked.

"Nash. Making another one of his goddamned four-wheeler videos. South of Sids Mountain. Been out there for two days. That asshole knows we want it designated as a WSA."

"What are you going to do?"

He looked across the topo map at her. "I was hoping it would be what are *we* going to do," he said quietly.

She handed the phone back to him. "Call your secret admirer. Check for the guns."

Noah punched in the number. He waited, then asked only one question: "Where are they right now?"

He listened, then ended the call.

"Two are at work, one's in the drunk tank at the jail."

She grinned. "Then I'm in."

Thus began Kara's secret life as a co-conspirator, filling balloons with black acrylic paint, storing them in the Drifter, and serving as bombardier. The peak of the ORV season had arrived, and Xperience Offroad Xtreme was crawling with clients who wanted a good time and a your-eyes-only video shot in spectacular landscapes. Noah and Kara ignored XOX's routine operations; they were conducted in legal, if not environmentally sound, fashion. Three times in the next week a tiny speck in the sky dropped like a peregrine intent on food. They struck the rock-crawling Blazers and Jeeps and Hummers doing things they shouldn't be doing in places they shouldn't be doing them. It didn't seem altogether right to her somehow, but damn, it was fun. And she was good at it. The balloons never missed their targets.

Chapter 46:

July 21, early morning, Noah's trailer, Greasewood Draw

Kara sat in Quick-Drys and tank top on the trailer's step, leaning against the doorway, hands embracing a mug of tea. Noah, drying himself after a shower, watched her as he slipped into his shorts. She'd lost five pounds, working out and running with him each morning or by herself when he'd had business in town. Noah could no longer outrun her. Kara was fit, healthy, and looking damn good now, what with that tanned skin, those legs, and Jesus Christ, those eyes, those blinding, baffling, look-straight-through-you eyes.

He walked past her and ruffled her hair. It had grown, lapping over her ears, and he liked its softness, even still tousled with sleep. As his hand left her head, Kara reached up, held it, kissed it softly, then let it go.

After he'd made breakfast and set it on the nook, he called for her.

"Hey. You. Occupant of my bedroom. Food."

She didn't turn around. "Damn," she said.

"Excuse me?"

She sighed as she got up. "I was thinking. Gee, what a nice, polite guy Hartshorn is. Gracious to a fault. A prince among princes. Now I discover you're living with a woman. Christ, Noah, people will talk."

He chuckled as she sat at the table. He ladled scrambled eggs and turkey sausage onto their plates.

She took a bite of her eggs. "Cheese?"

"Special treat today," he said.

"Why?"

"Because I like you."

More egg vanished into her mouth. "Are you glad I'm living here?"

"Yes, Kara, I'm glad you're living here."

"You're mocking me, Noah."

"No, I'm not."

"Are, too."

He took a bite of his eggs. "See any bacon on this table?"

"No," she said.

"Seen any bacon in the last week or so?"

She shook her head.

"So what do you think that means?"

A small smile crept onto her lips. "You like me."

"Damn straight. I gave up bacon for you."

She leaned across the table and kissed him. He started to slip his arm around her shoulders, but she eased away.

"Noah, we have to talk."

He grimaced. "There isn't a man in the world who's heard those words and not felt like his world's gonna cave in."

She laughed. "No, silly. Not about *that*."

He ate more eggs. "Then what?"

She set down her fork. "Noah, I've got to rebuild my work life."

"I'm all for that."

"I'm serious. I want to live in your life, but I need to live my life, too."

He leaned back, one hand stroking his beard. He didn't speak for several moments. Kara waited, fidgeting with a fork.

"How can I help?" Her bright smile rewarded him.

"I need an office," she said. "I need a place to work." She waved her hand toward the rest of the trailer. "This just isn't an office."

He nodded, understanding. "You need a place to work. I agree. This isn't an office, and it's cramped."

"Yes," she said. "I need to find an office."

Chapter 47:

July 23, after midnight, Noah's trailer, Greasewood Draw

Kara awoke with a start to see a dark form standing over her, shaking her. Nearby, Petey growled in the darkness.

"Kara, wake up," said Noah, his hand over her mouth. "No noise."

She nodded under his hand, and he removed it so she could sit up.

"Petey says we have visitors. Get dressed." She threw the sheet aside and fumbled for her jeans and sweatshirt. She joined Noah in the kitchen. He unzipped two long, leather bags and pulled a rifle out of each.

"Your brothers teach you to shoot?" he asked.

"Yeah, but—"

He gave her a rifle. She felt for the safety. It was on. "Noah, who is it?"

"Who do you think?"

Noah folded back the carpet and opened a small hidden hatch in the floor. He slipped through it, headfirst. Kara followed. They crawled underneath the trailer toward the cliff side. Noah stuck his head out and swore. Full moon. Cradling the rifles in their arms, they crawled to the corner of the trailer. He raised his head, listening. Noah pointed to the edge of the clearing, where tamarisks and cottonwood held court. The stream lay beyond. He crawled to the trees. Kara followed, heart beating faster. Noah took her arm, helping her up. He held a whistle in front of him.

"Cross the stream. Go parallel to the road, but stay away from it. They're smoking. You'll be able to smell them before you see them. Look for the glow of the cigarettes. Find a tree about two dozen yards from that fucking Blazer, okay? I'm going to the other side—"

"Noah, I can't shoot anyone, for God's sake."

Moonlight glinted off his teeth. "Look at the rifle again, Kara."

She fiddled with it, and understood. She grinned at him.

"When I blow the whistle, start shooting."

She nodded. She was going to like this.

Noah vanished into the trees. Kara crossed the stream and sneaked through the greasewood alongside the road. Noah was right. She could smell the cigarette first. She saw the Blazer. Moonlight shone through the windshield, and she could make out two shapes in the front seat. Was there a third in back? Slurred words drifted from the Blazer. They're drunk, she thought. Friday night. Filled with courage consumed at Ray's Tavern.

She braced the rifle against a tall, sturdy cottonwood and flicked off the safety. She listened, but could not hear Noah. A light night wind bore more sound from the Blazer. The unholy trio were scheming.

"... he's got propane... one good shot and the whole damn trailer will blow ..."

"... burn his fucking planes ... 'specially that yellow one ... got my truck with that ..."

She sighted the rifle on the windshield. Her trigger finger was sweaty. She didn't worry about ammo. She knew Noah would keep his weapons loaded.

A whistle shrieked. She fired. A soft, puffing sound popped

from the rifle. The paint-ball rounds splattered against the glass, then against the windows as she swiveled the rifle from right to left. She couldn't tell if Noah was firing. She kept pulling the trigger as fast as she could.

Shouts of surprise and fear erupted in the Blazer. One voice swore loudly. She knew that voice. B-t-h. The Blazer's V-8 roared into life. The big, knobby tires spun, throwing dirt as B-t-h tried to turn the Chevy around. What an asshole, Kara thought. Didn't park facing out. B-t-h had to do a Y turn. She fired until the rifle just clicked. Empty. She threw herself onto the ground. Dad didn't raise a dummy. *Get down when you're out of ammo.*

A loud noise and a bright flash ripped from the Blazer. Something smashed into the cottonwoods. Bits of bark and branches and pieces of leaves showered on her. *Shotgun.* She pressed her face into the ground until the Blazer was gone. She stood, shaking. *Holyshitholyshitholyshit.*

She moved toward the road. Noah jogged out of the brush. She dropped the rifle and ran to him, throwing her arms around him.

"Oh, god, Noah, oh god, oh god, oh god."

He held her tightly with one arm. She pushed away and saw a Ruger .357 Magnum in his other hand. He pulled her back against him.

"I'm so sorry, Kara. ... I had no idea ... I didn't know they'd go this far, attacking me at home."

He held her closely, rocking her back and forth.

"Noah," she whispered in his ear, "did you—"

"No. No clear shot. And I don't think I could have if I did. Unless they threatened you." He took her hand and they walked toward the trailer.

"But the Ruger—"

"Insurance," he said.

She faced him. "Noah, this is getting too weird."

He nodded, eyes downcast. "I know."

"You've got to find another way."

"I know," he said somberly. "But if they had hurt you, I'd

kill them. I'm never going to let anyone or anything hurt you again."

She said nothing and resumed walking. She didn't take his hand.

Near the trailer, he stopped. "I'm sorry, Kara."

She said nothing for a while, then kissed him on the cheek.

"I don't want to be visiting you on alternate Wednesdays," she said. "Or in a cemetery, either."

He chuckled. "I suppose not."

"No more air raids, okay? We'll find another way."

Noah exhaled deeply. "Shit," he said.

"What?"

"You really take the fun out of life, you know?"

She punched him. "You'll never know," she said, smirking.

In the trailer she went to the bedroom, took off her clothes, and lay down. He went to the couch, took off his clothes, and lay down. The moon crept over the trailer. Each could hear the other breathing. Noah slept fitfully, tossing and turning. Kara remained awake, listening to Noah.

In the dark after midnight, thunder shouted and lightning crackled. Noah woke, eyes wide open. He sat up. No rain pummeled the aluminum roof of the trailer. No flashes shot through the windows. Did he dream it? he wondered. The thunder, the lightning, the last few months? He rubbed his eyes. He lowered his hands, and movement in the bedroom caught his eyes.

"Kara?"

She did not answer. She stood in the doorway, starlight shining through a window on bare skin, bathing her in quiet light and soft shadow. He reached for the lamp. "Don't," she said softly. "Please don't."

Noah pushed aside the top sheet and swung his legs to the floor.

"Are you okay, Kara?" he asked.

She leaned against the door jam. Her hair hid her face. "Yes, I'm okay."

He saw the subtle curves of her pale breasts in the faint light. He stood and walked across the room. He leaned against the other side of the doorway.

"My ribs don't hurt anymore," she said softly.

He lifted his hand to her cheek and caressed it. She smiled as he did. He lingered there before tracing his finger across her lips to her throat and downward. As it neared her nipples, it detoured into slow, soft circles around each breast. Kara sighed, closing her eyes and raising her chin.

"You're beautiful, Kara," he said.

"So are you, Noah."

He chuckled low in his throat.

She held his hand over her breast. Her nipple caressed his palm as she moved it around. Her eyelids closed until just a slit of iris gleamed at him.

"You're beautiful. Like Utah's beautiful," she said.

Noah blushed. Even in the dark, she could see his flushing face. She smiled and lowered his hand. Inching forward, she took his other hand and held them low and intimately between them. Their fingers played quietly, dancing lightly over each other's hips, across their stomachs, and down onto the places that mattered. Kara leaned against him, brushing back and forth, her nipples hardening as they traced back and forth against taut muscles in his broad chest. Noah slowly slid his hands from between her legs up the sides of her lithe, firm body, then slipped them around her back. He drew her against him.

Kara held his face with her hands. She kissed him softly, then lay her head against his shoulder.

"God, I like how you feel against me," she whispered. "It's time you slept in your own bed, Noah."

She led him by the hand into the bedroom and kissed him deeply, stroking him until he was hard. Laying on her back, she pulled him atop her and guided him into her, gasping as he entered. Eager moments later, they shuddered in orgasm. Laying in each other's arms, they drifted toward sleep.

"Noah?" Kara said, her voice fading into sleep.

"Yes?" he whispered.

"You can call me 'Sweetie' now."

At dawn, illuminated by the soft, warm, morning light, they discovered they liked looking at each other, liking touching each other even more, and proceeded to reinvent foreplay. They really liked that, discovering neither knew restraints on pleasing the other. A hungry Petey watched the laughter-strewn lovemaking from the doorway, wondering when he would be fed. He was forced to wait until noon.

In the afternoon, neither wanted to jog or lift. Something about over-exertion in the middle of the night, they kidded each other. They packed snacks and water and walked along the base of the cliff until they could hike higher into Greasewood Draw. Kara's rubber-necking kept their pace slow. Sometimes hand in hand, sometimes arms around each other's waist, they walked. They sat in the shadow of a small overhang to eat.

"Should we have called the police last night?" Kara mumbled, her mouth filled with gorp.

"No. We've got no evidence."

"But they shot at me," she said.

"Even if they'd hit you, tough to trace shotgun pellets. And from the sound of the round, it was probably bird shot. No harm, no foul."

"No foul, my ass. I don't like being shot at."

"You get used to it," he said, grinning.

"Oh, you're so macho, Noah. You're walking a fine line, you know."

"You mean, *we're* walking a fine line."

"I suppose," she said hesitantly. "There's got to be a better way than dive-bombing those assholes with black paint."

"Gets the point across."

She took a swig of water. "Noah, you're missing the point."

He cocked his head, curious. "What do you mean?"

"Who knows you do what you do?"

"They do."

"Who else?" she asked.

"A few appropriately connected friends."

"Can those friends make Nash stop intruding on those potential WSAs?"

"In time, I think they can. But it's not easy," he said. "There's only about 50 or so Park Service or Forest Service or BLM enforcement cops for the entire state. Nash has always managed to be where they aren't."

He had been wondering how Nash managed to accomplish that.

"Exactly," Kara said. "The nature cops can't catch 'em. You can't broadcast your paint bombings, 'cause that's not exactly legal, either. Assault is assault, you know. So the right people really don't know what Nash is doing."

Noah didn't like having his save-the-world strategy questioned.

"So what's your point? Who are the 'right' people?"

"All the people, Noah. We the people. Wouldn't it be better to broadcast what they do and where they do it so all the people knew?"

"Excuse me?"

"PR, Noah. PR. Turn the spotlight of publicity on them. Right now, they can attack us. But they can't fight all the people all the time."

A thoughtful look creased his forehead. "You've got an idea?"

"A glimmer. Give me time to think about it."

"This have something to do with this office fetish of yours?"

She grinned and didn't reply.

"Sweetie, have you been doing sneaky things behind my back?"

She took his hand. "Let's just say I have a vested interest in you being a law-abiding citizen instead of a goddamned environmental terrorist."

They packed up their water bottles and picked up a few pieces of Snickers bar wrappings that the wind had scattered.

They headed back, holding hands.

As they reached the base of the cliff, Kara spoke. "I got a traffic ticket the other day. In the Cruiser. Just in case you get something in the mail."

"Why, you scofflaw, you."

She made a face at him. "Curious thing, though," she said.

"How so?"

"This guy pulls up behind me on that old state highway, you know, the one that runs past the airport. Lights flashing, siren, the works."

The stern look on his face alarmed her. She thought he was angry at her.

"Who was it? I mean, can you describe him?"

She shrugged her shoulders. "Yeah. A short, fat guy. Even had those Cool Hand Luke sunglasses, you know, the kind you can't see through."

Noah exhaled sharply. "The sheriff."

"Yeah, yeah. I guess so."

"What'd he write the ticket for?"

"Said I had a tail light out. I couldn't check it right there, so I just took it. But that's not the weird thing. He asked me why I was driving your Cruiser. I told him it was none of his business."

Noah chuckled.

"When I said that, he asked, 'Living with him?' I told him again it was none of his goddamned business. He told me I ought to be more respectful of law and order. I could get into serious trouble."

"That's the sheriff, all right."

"Then he asked me about you."

Noah nodded, urging her to continue.

"He asked where you'd been flying lately, and I asked him what the hell that had to do with a tail light being out."

Noah chuckled. "I'm sure he didn't appreciate that."

"I don't get it," she said. "Why was he giving me the third degree? When I got back, I checked out the tail light, and it's working fine. What gives?"

Noah took her hand, and they resumed walking toward the hangar.

"The sheriff went to high school with Nash. They're tight."

"Oh? Oh!" she said.

"Yeah. Now do you know why I didn't call the cops last night?"

Chapter 48:

July 26, evening, Tamarisk Restaurant, Green River

Noah woke late. A blanket lay neatly folded at the foot of the bed. Noah slept warm, but Kara slept cool, so she used the blanket. He looked around. No Kara. He wondered what the hell she was up to now. A Thermos sat on the stove with a Post-It stuck to it: "I wanted to let you sleep, darling Noah. Otherwise I'd have left breakfast. Enjoy the tea. Please meet me at the Tamarisk around 6. XOXOX, K.

"P.S.: I'm buying. P.P.S.: You're a horny, rutting bastard. P.P.P.S.: I love horny, rutting bastards."

He shook his head. She liked the fiat accompli, the broad sweep of the magician's cape revealing the finished trick. She liked to have all her ducks in a row before unveiling her Machiavellian designs. He was no different. He, too, liked to keep the crowd guessing until the end.

After breakfast, he spread his briefing materials on the kitchen table next to a legal pad. He sketched out the testimony he planned to give before the state Senate's standing committee on natural resources, agriculture, and environment. A bill that would weaken protections for state-listed endangered and threatened species during certain mining activities had been quietly making its way through the Legislature. He wanted to raise the bill's profile and had told environmentally astute reporters he would testify. He had testified several times on RS2477 issues, particularly before county legislatures. He knew the drill. He knew what to say. He knew the buttons to push. Late in the afternoon, he cleaned up his books and himself and put on clean Levis, his boots, and a denim shirt. After putting Petey in the hangar — he had free rein there now; no pen prison for him — he drove into Green River to meet Kara, wondering what sleight-of-hand she would produce.

Kara waited in front of the Tamarisk, wearing a form-fitting, ankle-length, black cotton dress and holding a slim leather briefcase. Kara? In a dress? He smiled as he approached her. Slipping a hand around the back of his neck, she kissed him eagerly. He'd never suspected her capable of public displays of affection.

"You look beautiful, Kara."

She beamed. Something had excited her, and he guessed it was not the compliment. "Thank you. Oh, you trimmed your beard. I like it."

He pshaw'd as they found a booth in the rear. They ordered and sipped at coffee while they waited. Apparently her tea habit was confined to the privacy of the home, he thought. He was still learning about her.

"So what's in the briefcase?" he asked. It lay on the side of the table, near the sugar packets, salt and pepper shakers, and ketchup.

"An alternative," she said.

"Not *the* alternative?" he asked, chuckling.

"No, you twit. Just a *possible* alternative. You'll have to help decide if it's a reasonable alternative."

"You sound like a lawyer," he said wryly.

That, for the umpteenth time, earned him the *don't-be-an-asshole* look. He was getting used to it.

"So what's this alternative? An alternative to what?"

"It's not that simple."

"So explain it," he said.

"After supper."

"Okay," he said.

They ate. Kara did most of the talking, fueled by the excitement she had found with the McCorrigans in southwest Utah. So he just listened.

"—and it was just like you said. Remember how you told me once knowing geology was important to a botanist? I couldn't understand that. But Bill and Sarah and I were hiking through the Grand Wash Valley in Capitol Reef when he found some Harrison's milk vetch. He said it was kind of rare. Apparently, the only known populations exist in the park. He said it only grows on Navajo sandstone. Some plants acclimate themselves to certain minerals. Evolution, I guess. For example, he said that Barneby reed-mustard only grows in certain formations, too, in this case, Moenkopi and Kaibab. Maguire's daisy only grows in Navajo, too. And fishhook cactus, well, Wright's, anyhow, only grows in Morrison and Entrada."

"I know," Noah interrupted. "You know those badlands north of I-70? Those hills that are kind of tan or grayish brown? You've flown over it."

Kara nodded. "I think so. What about it?"

"See any green there? Vegetation?"

Kara closed her eyes, trying to picture it. "No, I guess I haven't."

"It's Mancos shale. You won't find many plants there."

"Why not?" she asked.

"Selenium. Toxic to plants. And there's clay that swells when it rains, and shrinks when it dries. Plants can't get established. Knowing the geology helps you identify plants. Some grow on one formation, but not others."

Kara smiled. "Don't you see? Those are patterns," she said. "I love patterns. I've always liked flowers. But there's so much more to them for me now. And it's all about patterns. Data can be mapped, analyzed, and interpreted as patterns rather than individual plots."

"So what's your point?"

"I'm not sure. Bill taught me plants are like mine canaries. They indicate the health of an ecosystem. Certain species are food for deer. If they're gone, no deer. Some are better pollinators. If those are gone, the bees have nothing to do. Others are location specific, or, in this case, geologic formation specific."

"Mining is formation specific, too," said Noah.

"What do you mean?"

"Well, you said you found patterns. Some flowers only grow in certain places, in certain formations, right?"

"Yes. So?"

"Same with minerals. That's what I did for a living for a long time. I looked for patterns in the geology." He unfolded a paper napkin from the black metal canister standing watch over the salt and pepper shakers. He drew a rough map of Utah.

"Want copper? Look for igneous Tertiary intrusions into limestones, probably Pennsylvanian or Permian. The limestones act as a catalyst with metallics in magma — hell, it's mostly a kind of enriched water, anyhow — and you get concentrations of copper."

He drew an X on the napkin. "Just south of the Oquirrh Mountains you have exactly that. And presto, you have one of the world's largest open pit copper mines. And you'll find zinc, lead, molybdenum, and probably some gold as well for your troubles."

He drew another X. "Need potassium carbonate?"

"What?" she asked.

"Potash. It's mined from the Paradox formation and concentrated in huge ponds outside Moab. Uranium? Check the Morrison formation."

He drew more X's. "Need coal? Find Cretaceous sediments. Deposits in an ancient sea. Lots of organic material. So mine Cretaceous rocks, like Mancos shale near Price. Zinc. Silver. Iron. Formation specific. Patterns. Like the flowers."

She nodded. "And?" she asked.

"Kiss those flowers good-bye."

"What do you mean?"

"After I'd leave, the mining engineers would come in and attack the landscape. They'd blast it, strip it, leach it, drill it, courtesy of the General Mining Act of 1872. God bless the Homestead Act for the mining industry. And it bred most of the Superfund sites in the West."

"What?"

He crumpled the napkin. "Long story. Mind if we save it for another time?"

She nodded. "Anyhow, I've got something to tell you," she said.

She took a sheet of paper from the briefcase. At the top it read, "Graduate School Application, University of Utah."

He stared at it. "You're ... You're ..."

"Thinking about grad school. Bill's idea. I really like him, you know. He's a wonderful teacher. He told me I'd already earned his respect over the clay phacelia thing." Her grin suggested she didn't take that too seriously.

Noah was flustered. Too much information, too fast. Too much change, or, at least, change in an arena he hadn't expected. He slumped in his seat, hands around the coffee cup in front of him. "So you're going to school."

"I said I'm thinking about it."

"Where?"

"In Salt Lake. At the university. Bill's program, maybe."

"When?" he asked. When, the telling question.

She smiled. "No, not this fall. Next fall. I need time."

He cocked his head, confused. "Time? For what?"

She smiled, such a beautiful smile, fully comprehending, fully revealing, fully dispelling fear.

"For us, silly."

They walked out of the Tamarisk hand in hand. In the parking lot, Noah suddenly shoved Kara behind him and pinned her against Cruiser, his back against her. She could feel his muscles tense. A black Humvee with a large white XOX on its side rumbled slowly east along the street. A thin, ascetic-looking man sat at the wheel, a black Stetson perched low over his forehead.

"Nash," Noah said, as the Hummer idled past. Noah got into the driver's side of the Cruiser. Kara got in and touched his arm.

"Noah, I need to say something to you. You won't like it."

He turned toward her. "I think I know what," he said.

"What?" she asked.

"That Nash has me spooked."

"Something like that," she said.

He held her face in his hands.

"I haven't been completely truthful with you. I'm sorry about that. But those guys have done nothing in the past month that they haven't done before. I've found them on my land and chased them off. They've provoked fights. I've patched holes in the fabric of the Drifter. Yes, that's right. They've shot at me. Hit a propeller once, and I had to do a dead-stick landing in a canyon. They've threatened me with baseball bats. But I've always been able to deal with that. But I can't now."

He stopped, drawing a deep breath. "The difference is you."

Her eyes widened, not comprehending. "Me? What about me?"

He dropped his hands from her face.

"I'm in love with you, Kara," he said quietly. "You're the difference. If I'm spooked, it's because they can attack me now through someone I love."

She looked ahead, her hands folded over the briefcase in her lap.

"You love me?"

"Yes," he said, starting the Cruiser. The Buick V-8 erupted into life and drowned out her whispered reply.

Noah parked near a three-story brick building on the

western edge of the business strip. They walked down an alley on the side of the building to the rear and up two flights of wooden stairs. She produced a key, proudly waved it in front of him, opened the door, and stood aside.

"You first," she said, bowing. He stepped into a small office containing a desk in the corner and a folding table. To the rear was a bathroom. On the desk sat her laptop, a Canon photo printer and a cheap monochrome laser printer, and a flatbed scanner. All but the laptop were new.

He looked around, puzzled. "What is this?"

"My office," she said, sitting in a rather spiffy office chair behind the desk. "Courtesy of Staples of Moab."

"You went to Moab today?" he said.

"Yeppers. I did indeed. I needed stuff."

Sitting on a corner of the desk, Noah remained baffled. "Stuff for what?"

"Among other things, an alternative."

Noah noticed other things. Chargers for her cell and sat phones. An Ethernet line from the Mac to a jack in the wall. A filing cabinet. A bookshelf holding paper, binders, other office supplies, and books. A poster of Arches.

The map was taped to the wall behind her desk. *That* map. He started to say something, but she shook her head. *Let it be.* They'd deal with it some other time. He nodded. He scratched at his beard, thinking about the possibilities residing secretly in her office.

"Kara."

"Yes, Noah?"

"You're as devious as I am. And I'm bloody devious and secretive."

"You're right."

He slipped off the desk, slid one arm under her thighs and the other around her shoulders, and lifted her out of the chair. He sat, Kara on his lap.

"Hey! That's sexist."

"So call the PC police."

"I just might, you dummy."

They kissed. He slid his hand under her dress, but she pushed him away.

"Oh, no, no, no. No time for that."

He reached for her, and she danced away. "And why not?"

"Work to do," she said. "Get up. I need to sit."

He rose, and she sat, opened the laptop, and booted it.

"Do you have any clue what I've been doing these past nights?"

"I know about last night," he said mischievously.

That earned him *the look*. "Sorry, sorry," he said, backing away.

She called up a few programs and was quiet for a minute.

"Noah, I've made about six dozen phone calls in the last few weeks."

He blinked. "Excuse me? To who?"

She grinned. "Mostly to McCorrigan."

He threw his hands up and looked for a place to sit. Finding none, he sat on the floor, his back against a wall, griping that someone ought to get another chair. "I give up," he said. "I suppose you're going to tell me?"

She smiled. "McCorrigan gave me ideas."

"I'm going to have to talk with that man," he said. "Putting ideas in that pretty little head. Terrible thing."

"More sexism. Strike two. You expect to get laid again soon?"

Silence fell. The relationship was too new, too fragile, for kidding thoughts like that. Kara regretted it the instant the words passed her lips.

"I'm sorry," she said.

"We're new at this, sweetie. Forget it. Just remember to forget my goofs, too."

She smiled, relieved. "Deal."

"Now give," he insisted.

She asked him to remove a few books from the bookcase. One was McCorrigan's "Guide to the Flowers of Southwest Utah."

"How's that book organized, Noah?"

MAPPING UTAH *297*

He leafed through it. "Color of the blossoms."

"Right. The principal data is color. The organizing key is color," she said.

He got it quickly. "And you're going to put it online?"

"Yep."

"Well, I'll be damned."

"Pretty neat, huh?"

Noah nodded. "Damn straight. But what about his royalties?"

Kara explained that McCorrigan didn't think an online guide would affect sales. And, if they did, he didn't much care.

"Not too many people carry computers into the field, Kara."

"Noah, this is the tablet age. I'll carry a mini iPad in the field."

"I see. And the phone calls?"

"Data calls, mostly. I've been downloading pictures from his files. And we've been talking about organization and so on."

She looked at him shyly. "Want to see it so far?"

He moved to her desk, standing behind her, his hands on her shoulders. She liked the warm, firm pressure as he squeezed her shoulders lightly. Smiling, she ran the links on the website she'd begun.

"I've only got white and yellow so far. See the symbols? Those stylized flower petals? You click on the color you want, and it takes you to this."

She clicked, and a page of thumbnails loaded. "Then you can click on individual flowers." She clicked on one. A new page had an enlarged view of a dwarf evening-primrose. Below was a description, range, and comments.

"Problem," he said.

"How so?"

He leaned over her to touch the track pad. He smelled dusky, earthy, basic. It made her feel like she was outside, naked under a warm rain.

"—so your viewer has no further decision cues," he said.

"I'm sorry, Noah, my mind drifted. What'd you say?"

He scrolled down the page, and thumbnails of white-colored flowers rose from the bottom and passed out of sight through the top of the window.

"Well, I don't want to be critical, but the only decision the viewer can make is color. Then she finds this mass of — how many?"

"About three dozen so far."

"That's a lot of photographs, small on screen, for the reader to check. The inexperienced person might get frustrated. Maybe there's more decisions she can make that cuts down on the number of thumbnails she has to examine."

She rested her hand on his. "Ideas?"

He knelt beside her. "Well, you're trying to build a yes-no key, right?"

She nodded. "Yeah. On-off. Binary."

"That's what traditional key guides do. They're called dichotomous keys. The viewer is usually presented with an initial choice — in this case, color — or sometimes more and gradually works through ever finer key decisions to reach a conclusion, or an identification."

"I get it," she said. "Like those answering machines that run you through menus of choices to connect you with the department or person you want."

He slipped his arm around her shoulders. "Right. You just have to figure out what the additional decisions are that the viewer needs to make."

"Oooh, oooh," she exclaimed. "And the website explains these decision points in a sort of how-to-use-this-guide page."

"Yes," he said. "Yes."

She leaned back, her neck resting comfortably on his forearm. "Damn. I guess I need to know more about botany. I'm clueless beyond color."

"Not that hard, Kara. Leaves can be definitive. Flowers don't bloom year-round, you know. So you've got identification features like simple or compound leaves. Or number of leaflets. Up to five, five to eleven, and so on. Or the arrangement of leaves on the stalk. Just the shape of the leaf can be definitive when combined with the shape of the apex and the contour of the margin. Even the base, whether it's rounded or cordate or truncate can be—"

"Hang on a minute, Noah." She typed swiftly, taking notes.

"Okay. What else?"

"Number of petals, for example. Or inflorescence."

"What's that?"

"The arrangement of the flowers around an axis. And there's whether you're dealing with a raceme or a panicle."

She continued to type. "Damn. This is getting complicated."

She put her hands to her cheeks, closed her eyes, and rocked from side to side. Noah had seen this before. It was her thinking mode, not to be disturbed.

"I wonder if I could build a search engine, or a form, so you could check off these characteristics, and the site would bring up the candidates that fit the description," she said presently. "Damn. That'd be stretching my skills at the moment."

"At the moment," he said quietly.

"I could ask Bill if he's got a computer geek who could figure this out."

"Or who could teach you," he said.

"I suppose."

Noah walked to the bookcase. "This could really be something, Kara. But it would take a helluva long time to do."

She grinned. "Ah, that's the beauty of it. Bill told me all I have to do is to figure out how to organize the site, and then he can use grad students as trained chimps to plug in the data and the pics."

She smiled. "That's what I do, Noah. I create things that others can take and build on. We're called consultants, you know."

He laughed.

"That's what Bill likes about this," she said. "It can be constantly updated. You don't have to wait for a new edition.

He's cleared it with his publisher, although they weren't overjoyed. But he's got the rep to have it his way."

Noah walked to the desk, bent over, and kissed the top of her head.

"Kara, that's terrific. Great idea."

She touched his hand, resting on his shoulder.

"I've got another one," she said, her voice small, quiet, unsure. "I don't know if you'll like it. It's my keep-Noah-alive-and-out-of-jail plan."

"You're on a roll, Kara. Don't stop now."

She turned off the Mac and slithered past him to the bookcase. She slipped the rubber band off a rolled-up map of Utah and taped it to the wall. The map featured WSAs proposed by the UWP. She handed him a pen.

"Can you mark the spots where you've found the XOX boys playing where the UWP says they shouldn't?"

He cocked his head, curiosity aroused. "Sure."

She pushed him toward the map. "Show me some."

Noah touched the pen to his lips, thinking. He made X's on the map. San Rafael Swell. Lost Spring Wash. Sids Mountain. Mexican Mountain. Eagle Canyon. Desolation Canyon. Book Cliffs.

"Those are pretty close to home," she said.

"It's where I concentrate what I do. Other people work other parts of the state." He made more marks on the map in southwest and southeast Utah.

He turned when he'd finished. "Now what?"

"And I suppose you've got evidence of this?"

"Well, I saw them."

"So you say."

"Hey," he said, a bit miffed. "I was there."

"How can you prove it? How can you prove *they* were there?"

"I see your point," he said.

"Think, Noah," she said. "You've got a video cam mount on the wing of the Drifter, don't you? It's not there just for show, is it? And we can get a GoPro video cam for your helmet, too."

Noah grinned. "I got you now, Nash."

"Exactly," she said. "I can put those videos and stills online. Picture it, Noah. Someone goes to, say, *www.XOX-badguys.org*. It's that map of Utah, with outlines of the proposed WSAs, and dots scattered through them. She clicks on a dot and another page loads — with links to stills and videos. The page has dates, descriptions, GPS coordinates, everything. You don't have to say they're doing anything illegal. *Just present the data*. That's all you have to do."

She thought for a moment. "And, we can stash the video on YouTube. We can drive Web traffic to these videos in so many ways. You know people who can blog? Do Twitter alerts? We'll start a Facebook group. You *are* on Facebook, aren't you?"

"That social network thing? Isn't it just for kids?"

"Noah, you're such a Luddite. The point of using Twitter and Facebook is that so many other people can send us tips and retweet the posts that we write. And you, being an expert in wilderness issues, can write a blog for the site, too. Not only that, but–"

"I can't write," he said.

"Bullshit. I've read your testimonies to the legislature and some of the op-eds you've had in the *Salt Lake Trib*."

He shook his head to clear it. "How did you—"

She smiled. "I'm a researcher, remember? Can you say, 'Google'?"

"But how do we—"

"We'll deal with the details of production later," she said. "Right now, we need prime content — video of Nash's operation."

He shook his head. "But Nash could deny it. Say we made up the GPS coordinates, that kind of thing."

"Pictures don't lie, Noah."

"What do you mean?"

"Didn't you tell me," she said, "that he likes to make those videos and run those trips in really spectacular areas?"

"So?"

"Anyone who knows Utah will recognize those places. He can't deny that, so he—"

"So the reason he uses those places results in his undoing, eh?"

"You're smart, Noah. For a Luddite."

He slipped his arm around her waist quickly and drew her to him.

"Yeah," he said. "But I'm good in bed."

She pushed him away and laughed. "Too little data."

He kissed her. "I'll give you data, sweetie. Any time you want."

He returned to the map. "I'm not sure my video from the raids is good enough. When the Drifter hits turbulence, the camera gets jostled quite a bit."

"So we'll get more. Start over."

"Dangerous. We'd have to be low to get photos that aren't blurred," he said. "Vibration. Shooting from a safe altitude isn't going to work."

She chuckled. "Noah, you've got to get out more. Think high tech."

"Pardon?"

"Gyroscopically stabilized lenses," she said. "I know at guy at *The Seattle Times* who shoots sports. Autofocus, stabilized telephoto lenses, two-hundred millimeter, four-hundred millimeter. He gets tack-sharp shots. And we're going digital."

"I'll be damned," he said. "Hellishly expensive, I bet."

"Not that much. And I can afford it."

Noah said nothing for a bit. Then:

"No, I can afford it. My problem, my project, my bankroll."

"How about, *we* can afford it?"

He idly ran his hands across the bookshelf. He asked, "Can we?"

Spreading her hands out on the desk, she looked at him directly.

"Noah, I've worked damn hard for the past ten years or so. I get paid sinfully well for what I do. And I plan to do more of what I used to do in Seattle. I can do it here. I'm portable. And I've lived like a pauper. My dad taught me to be frugal. So I saved. I saved a shitload of money."

He leaned over the desk. "How much is a shitload?"

She leaned back in the reclining chair.

"Almost a half million dollars. I'm a pretty sharp online investor, too."

He whistled. "Holy shitload."

She folded her hands across her lap.

"And since we're comparing financial penises, sweetie, what about you?" she asked.

"What do you mean, what about me?"

She shrugged. "Well, since I've been here, you've told me you do this and that, but I haven't seen you do much of this and that. You've been around me all the time. Barely any lessons, no charters, and just a few shuttles we went on. Which I really liked, by the way."

"You been talking with Annie?"

"She does your books, Noah. She let enough slip to let me figure out the income from the Hartshorn Flying Service is, well, less than reliable."

"No, I suppose I've been preoccupied lately," he said, a smile on his face.

"I don't like being a preoccupation, you know."

"Sorry. Guess you could say I've been obsessed."

She laughed. "That's better. I've never been an obsession before."

"Hey, don't flatter yourself, kid."

"Don't call me a kid," she said.

"Don't call me a Luddite," he said.

"You're a technophobe."

"Six million dollars."

She stared at him. "What?"

"Six million dollars. I'm worth six million, not counting the planes."

"Wha— how—"

"Gold."

She shook her head. "Gold?"

Noah sighed and sat on the desk. "Gold. Enough to get married, have a half dozen kids, put 'em through college and retire and do some—"

"What, no Lexus?" Kara said. "How on earth did you do this?"

"It's not a pretty story."

"Six million dollars? That's a helluva story, Noah."

"You don't make much as an engineering geologist working for the mining industry, Kara."

"Then how—"

"The West is loaded with deserted mining claims — gold, silver, and so on — that are as much as a hundred and fifty years old. Over the years, when I found one, I marked it on a map I kept in a safety deposit box."

"You mined them?"

"In a way. Miners back then took the gold they could see. They left the gold they couldn't see."

"I don't get it."

"When the price of gold climbs, it's profitable to rework the tailings."

Understanding dawned on her face.

"I'd fly sodium cyanide and plastic membrane to an old mine site and make a small leach pond to work the old tailings. Pretty simple to extract the gold. Do enough old forgotten mines on weekends and it adds up."

"The hell you say," she said, marveling. "Why'd you stop?"

He walked around the room as he spoke.

"I was working this old mine in Nevada. The membrane liner I used leaked while I was away. The acid flowed downhill to a nearby stream. Dead fish. Dead birds. A few dead deer next to the stream. I assume they were poisoned by the yellow boy flowing into the stream."

"Yellow boy?" Kara asked.

"Just a label for overly acidic water that flows out from old mines that once used this technique. I soon learned that thousands of old mines like that one I'd worked have polluted thousands of miles of waterways."

"So you stopped," she said.

"Yeah. I stopped."

"Six million dollars later."

"Yeah," he said quietly. "Six million dollars later."

Kara heard the sadness in his voice. She didn't push it.

"Let's go home, sweetie," she said.

The Cruiser bounced down the dirt road. Kara complained about the shocks. He said the shocks were just as good as the fuel pump, that she read too much into the cacophony of noises that aging created in things mechanical. The debate continued as they walked hand in hand toward the trailer in the moonlight. "Face it, Kara, I know more about cars than you do."

"Bull," she said. "I'm a damn good mechanic."

"Yeah, but I'm better."

"Are not."

"Am too."

He turned toward her, letting go of her hand. "C'mere, please."

She stood in front of him. "Closer, please," he said.

She shuffled nearer. "Closer."

She leaned against him, her hands at her sides, too.

Her breasts pressed against his chest. Her right thigh slid, naturally, easily, intuitively, between his legs. Her face rested in the crook of his neck. She raised her arms to encircle him, but he gently pushed them down.

"Just like this, Kara. Just like this."

He rocked from side to side. She did, too, her breasts brushing back and forth against his chest. Her nipples hardened. He could feel them through her dress, tracing against him. "I like this," she whispered. "I like this."

"So do I," he said.

The Utah night cloaked them. She remembered the lightning — and shivered. He felt it, but didn't ask. Whatever it was, he assumed it was part of healing.

"I need to tell you something, Kara."

She tensed, so he turned his head and kissed her lightly on the ear.

"Easy, now. Nothing overly dramatic."

She relaxed. He could feel her resting against him, chest to chest, hip firmly to hip, thighs caressing thighs. She fit perfectly against him. Perfectly.

"What is it?" she asked.

"You're smarter than I am."

She stepped back, surprised. "What do you mean?"

"Exactly that. You're smarter than I am."

Hands on her hips, she cocked her head. "Why are you telling me this?"

"Because I want you to know it."

"Why?"

"Because I needed to admit it to myself."

"I don't get it."

"Long story. I won't bore you with it."

"Well, if it's true, and I'm not saying it is, does it bother you?"

Taking her hand, he led her toward the trailer. "It did. Now it doesn't."

"Why not?"

"I was looking after you for a long time. And I thought I was smart enough to do it. I never saw when you started to look after me, and when I noticed it, I resented it. That you were smarter than I was, that you knew what I needed before I knew I needed it."

"Noah, I'm sorry, oh, god, I'm sorry. I didn't mean to—"

She couldn't see it, but she sensed his smile, hearing it in his words.

"You were smart enough to realize that I needed looking after, that I've longed for someone to look after me. When you got your office, I was furious. I was mad that you'd left the trailer. I was telling myself at first, why can't she work here? At home? I know the answer. Too small. We'd eventually get in each other's way. Become irritants to each other instead of partners."

She leaned against him again. "Partners," she said. "Nice word."

"Yeah. It is." He dropped her hand and walked away, then turned to her.

"I realized that you needed to work, in your own space, in your own way, and you knew that I needed to work in my space in my own way. I realized that you'd made taking care of me part of your work, part of your life."

Moonlight reflected off the tears trickling down his cheeks.

"I was so ashamed, Kara."

She hugged him fiercely, and he wrapped his arms around her.

"Never be ashamed, Noah. Never, never, never."

He stepped back, his hands on her shoulders.

"I've got to check the hangar. I'll be back in a bit." He hurried off.

She knew enough to let him go.

Noah snapped off the lights, locked the hangar, and walked to the trailer. Opening the door, he stepped inside to find it dark. Kara stood in the doorway of the bedroom, holding a candle that illuminated her bare, slender body.

"Noah?" Her whisper floated through the trailer.

"Yes?"

"I love you."

Chapter 49:

July 28, late morning, Kara's office, Green River

The *XOX-badguys.org* site should have priority, they decided. Botany could wait. The site should focus on all transgressions against proposed or actual WSAs and not be limited to Xperience Offroad Xtreme to avoid accusations of bias. Noah argued that the site should not be called *XOX-badguys.org*. Kara asked why.

"If you put up a site, you're acting as a publisher," he said. "A good litigator could argue, under Utah law, that any and all depictions of activities contained in the site are prejudicial against those individuals depicted, and thus defamatory. The site might be what the law would call a fair and accurate summation, but a good lawyer might be able to get us on injury to reputation. Our only defense would be if it's provably true that the activities depicted are illegal. The prejudicial name 'bad guys' could be that lawyer's loophole."

Kara made a face. "Okay, who are you? What have you done with Noah? God, where did that gibberish come from?"

Noah reddened. "I used to hang around with lawyers."

"Well, it's advice for wimps, 'scuse me, and I'm no wimp,"

she said. "After all, wouldn't you like to get Nash into a courtroom?"

"Good point," he said. "Keep the name."

They went to Kara's office each morning. Noah flew in the afternoons, hunting, scouting, running down tips on environmentally destructive ORV activity fed to them via email, Twitter, Facebook, even Pinterest. On one of his first flights, acting on a tip from a friend in the Forest Service, he found ORVers had constructed two miles of illicit trails in the Shay Mountain roadless area that lacks state or federal protection near the Manti-La Sal National Forest. He flew over Indian Creek, an area the BLM had once considered for inclusion in Canyonlands National Park, and where he'd once rock-climbed "Scarface," a legendary vertical crack in perfect Wingate sandstone. Using the new high-tech photo gear, he captured uncontrolled erosion caused by ORV use. A Moab friend emailed him digital images depicting ORV damage in the Behind the Rocks area. He spent three days away from Kara — neither much liked that — overflying the Canaan Mountain WSA near Zion. ORV use had been forbidden there for nearly two decades. Yet ORVers, through excavation and blasting, had decimated hiking trails and other natural features. Flying over the Swell left him in tears. Once-natural hillsides had fallen prey to the destructive churning of big tires and bigger, Hemi-powered egos. He flew over ORV defilements that had forced the UWP to drop areas from consideration as a WSA, places like Poison Spider Mesa. Using schedules and locations downloaded from Experience Offroad Extreme's own secure website that a computer-savvy bank teller friend had hacked, Noah photographed video operations in other WSAs proposed by the UWP. Flying over Wild Horse Mesa, he saw XOX vehicles — and a dark green vehicle he was not surprised to see. But it made sense, he thought, collating recent observations into cohesive patterns. He shook his head. He was starting to think like her. He checked ridgelines for hostiles with guns, made a low pass and photographed the green vehicle. He made sure Kara never saw that photograph.

Kara worked the phone, email, Twitter, and Facebook. Noah had given her a list of UWP honchos and acolytes. These were people who had scoured the state, examining and recording the faint tracks through the wilderness that the ORV hordes claimed met RS2477 standards. The mention of Noah's name unlocked their records, unfolded their maps, revealed their photographs and videos, and unsheathed their notes from hiking trips through despoiled areas. The wealth of information collected by volunteers astonished her. Hundreds of volunteers, contributing tens of thousands of hours of their time and tens of thousands of dollars of their own money, had roamed most of the UWP's proposed WSAs, documenting known and potential RS2477 claims. Reams of information flowed into her office, via email, via snail mail, via social media, via people stopping by with shopping bags full of data. Kara scanned everything onto her Mac and backed it up on two more external hard drives Noah bought her.

She heard stories and saw evidence. One visitor brought in pictures of an RS2477 claim in the Paria-Hackberry area.

"Where's the road?" she asked.

"There's no road," the man said. "It's a river bottom."

The spurious nature of most RS2477 claims infuriated her. She'd never considered herself a true believer, a green-blooded enviro. But she detested deceit. Righteous anger allowed her to focus with a purpose she had never known doing commercial work. The daylights hours she worked stretched into evening hours as she methodically organized the data, scanned photos, stripped documents out of emails, and formatted Web pages. One wall became a multi-colored forest of Post-Its, her favorite organizational tool. The simple navigational concept of a map with dots as hyperlinks to YouTube videos, Twitpics, Instagram images, and Facebook photos grew into a sophisticated but easy-to-use site. It depicted the chicanery of false claims that a road is a road is a road — when in fact the road was an old jeep trail long gone to brush, or a path through desert grasses set down by deer, or a dry wash with no hint of vehicular history.

Noah brought in fresh photos and videos. Noah saw little of Kara, but noticed that she had abandoned routines that had rebuilt her health. He loved what she was doing; he feared the consequences on her well-being.

One morning, Kara rushed from the shower, dressed quickly, grabbed a mug of tea, and fled out the door with a quick "Love you." He ran after her.

"Stop," he said. She looked at him, askance.

"Please go back inside." His face bore the serious look of the lifeguard that she hadn't seen in some time. Obediently, she slunk back into the trailer.

"Take off your clothes," he said inside. "Please," he added hastily.

She grinned. "Why, Noah, I didn't know you were into quickies." She slipped out of her blouse, pushed her Levis down, and stepped out of them. She advanced toward him. He pointed to the bedroom.

"Shorts and tank top. Running shoes. Now." She stopped, confused.

"Kara, you haven't worked out in weeks. You haven't jogged, you haven't lifted, you haven't done a goddamned thing that you know you ought to be doing. You're working too long, you're not eating well, and I'll be damned if I'm going to let this go on any longer."

She stood in front of him, shaking in anger.

"And just who the hell do you think you are to decide that, goddamn it?"

"The man who loves you. That enough?"

Her anger vanished. She walked into the bedroom and changed.

They worked out for an hour and showered together. Under the warm water, confined in the tiny bathroom, they made love. The website could wait. Work could wait. Work had descended to second place in her life.

Kara sent Hannah a press release announcing the debut

date of the *XOX-badguys.org* site and asked her to get it to the
right people in the Salt Lake City bureau of the AP. The *Salt
Lake Trib* and the *Deseret News* buried the story inside. But the
High Country News picked it up, and one of its reporters called
Kara. That resulted in a favorable story on the HCN's web
home page. Within a week, the bad-guys site had recorded
more than forty thousand hits. The Facebook group attained
thousands of likes. The Twitter account drew thousands of
followers. Kara worked with friends of Noah's to get a
community blog under way. Email feedback and blog
comments poured in. But much of the traffic consisted of
denials from PR reps of mining, logging, and ranching
organizations. The ORVers sent thinly veiled venom. A few
emails promised mayhem on Kara. She admitted to Noah that
those frightened her.

One night, she admitted something else. Noah arrived
around supper time to chase her out of the office and found
her face down on the desk, smacking the top of the desk with
her fists. He walked quietly around the desk, knelt beside her,
and rested his hand on her back. He'd learned. She'd talk. All
in good time.

She turned her head to look at him. "Hi," she said weakly.

"Hi, yourself."

She leaned back in the chair, rubbing her hands over her
face.

"I think I have a problem."

He kissed her on the cheek, then sat down on the floor.
The *map* looked down on them. They didn't notice. The map,
the fucking map, had receded in their minds.

"And what might that be?"

She reached for the track pad and moved the cursor.
Clicking on an icon, she opened the window holding unread
email. She scrolled through it.

"That's two hundred emails since this morning."

"That a lot?"

"Well, we've been averaging more than a hundred a day.
I've been trying to answer them. Even wrote several stock

letters, you know, choose the one that fits as a reply, copy and paste. You know the drill."

"And?"

"I can't keep up. And most of the emails have more stuff. A lot of photos, more descriptions of ORV activity. As if we don't have enough already. I could do this twenty-four hours a day, just dealing with the email. And then there's helping address some of misleading blog comments and dealing with the threadfuckers and trolls."

"So we get a computer geek to handle the bulk of this."

"It's not just that," she said.

"Oh?"

"Damn it, I want my life back. I want to hike. I want to ride my bike. I want to go into nowhere to see what's there. I want to work on my flower site. I don't have time for any of that."

He pulled her out of the chair. "Let's go home, have supper, and fuck our brains out," he said.

She giggled. He'd never heard her giggle before.

"Much as I'd like that, Noah, it doesn't solve the problem."

He pulled her against him. "Fortunately for you," he said, "you're sleeping with a guy who can manufacture time."

He took out his cell, pulled up a number from his contacts list, and hit send. Kara waited, arm loosely wrapped around his waist, leaning tiredly against him.

"Hello, Hal? Noah. ... Yeah. ... You've seen it? What do you think?"

He listened, and Kara grew curious.

"Hang on, Hal. She's here, and I want to put you on the speaker."

He pushed the speaker button. They stood arm in arm, listening.

"Kara? Hal Thompson. Helluva site. The blog's great. And I can't believe how that Facebook group is taking off. We're getting calls here about it, mostly positive. A lot of our members have phoned or emailed about it."

Noah whispered in Kara's ear. "Hal's the UWP's executive director."

"... and it's giving us a lot of visibility. I'm not sure if that's good or bad, but donations have picked up. We've got you to thank for it. People think the site's ours. So thanks. Kudos on a really nice job. Wish we'd done it."

Noah broke in. "Hal, we've got a problem. And an opportunity for you."

"Talk to me, Noah."

He looked at Kara. She guessed what was coming, and she nodded.

"We'd like to hand over the site, the blog, the Facebook group, everything to the UWP."

"What?" said Hal.

"Kara's been doing it herself. One-woman show, and it's grown beyond what one person can do. Some of your people have Web experience. Kara could transfer the files, and they could upload them to the UWP site. I've got to fly up for that hearing, and I could bring up the other stuff we've got."

"Geez, that'd be wonderful. And we've got folks itching to research and write about this stuff. Lemme talk to our webmaster. I'm clueless about this stuff. I'll ask her to call Kara later this week and do the deed. That okay with you, Kara? We'll credit you, of course."

Kara's relief was palpable. "Yes, and to be honest, I don't really need or want the credit. Just consider it an in-kind donation. Wouldn't mind a tax deduction out of it, though."

"I'm sure our finance guys can work that out. Noah, this is great. And are you sure you still don't want to take a more formal role with our legal and lobbying people? Shame to have that law degree gather so much dust."

Kara stared at Noah. She stage-whispered, "You son of a bitch. You're a goddamn lawyer?" Her voice carried to the phone.

"You didn't know, Kara? We went through law school together. Then he ran off to Green River. I've been trying to get him involved for a long time."

"Hal, we've got to go. We'll talk about it when I fly up. Promise."

Good-byes were exchanged, and Noah clicked the cell phone off.

Kara just stood there. "You're a lawyer. I'll be damned."

"Just something to do while I was looking for diversions," he said.

They walked down the stairs and through the alley to the Cruiser. Neither noticed the black Hummer parked a block down the street to the west. Neither noticed a blue Blazer parked a block up the street to the east. Neither noticed that the two vehicles had been there for the past three nights.

At the trailer, Kara sat quietly in the Cruiser as Noah started to get out.

"Kara?"

She said nothing.

"Kara, is something wrong?"

She shook her head. "Thank you," she said quietly. "Thank you."

"For what?"

"Being smarter than I am."

Chapter 50:

August 16, after midnight, Kara's office, Green River

The phone chirped, waking Noah. He untangled himself from Kara's leg, happily sleeping between his thighs. He padded into the kitchen, stumbling over Petey. He fumbled with the phone, and put it to his ear.

"Hello?" He listened for a minute, anger slowly flushing his face.

"Be there in fifteen minutes." He dressed before waking Kara.

"Noah, wha—"

"Get up. Get dressed."

She sat up, brushing the sleep from her eyes. "What's wrong?"

"Somebody trashed the office."

He drove the Cruiser down the alley behind the building. Parked out front was a dark green Jeep Cherokee, the sheriff's patrol car. Its candy bar — the rotating blue and red lights atop the roof — lit the building stroboscopically. The sheriff, a short, fat man, stepped from the shadows.

"What happened?" Noah asked tersely.

The sheriff pointed the beam of his club-like flashlight toward the door to Kara's office. The lights were on. Someone was inside. The sheriff's idiot deputy, Noah saw. He loved crime scenes and photographed everything with the cheap digital Casio point-and-shoot the sheriff had bought to keep him occupied.

"Someone complained about noises out back here, so Sam stopped by to check it out. Found the door open and smelled gasoline."

Kara sprinted up the stairs.

"Ma'am, don't go—" the sheriff called out. Noah nudged the sheriff's arm and shook his head.

"They must've heard Sam's patrol car and took off," the sheriff said. "He didn't see anybody. Damn good thing he got here when he did 'cause—"

Kara appeared on the landing and called down to Noah.

"They took most of the files, Noah. Cabinets and all."

Noah glared at the sheriff. "You know goddamn well who did this."

"Got no witnesses, Noah." The sheriff shrugged. "For Christ's sake, you started all this. If you'd left him alone—"

"Someday, sheriff, you're going to have to decide whether you're the law or a goddamned accomplice."

"Now, see here, you—"

Noah put his bearded face inches from the sheriff's.

"You know fucking well you can stop this. But do it soon. Nash has lost it, sheriff. He's gone from crimes against nature to crimes against people. I can handle myself. But if that asshole ever hurts Kara, I'll come for you first."

Noah brushed angrily past him and ran up the stairs, two at a time. He could smell the gasoline. Inside, the deputy snapped away, the flash winking.

"Get out," Noah said. The idiot deputy started to say something, but Kara interrupted. "You heard him," she screamed. "*Get the fuck out of here.*"

The deputy defiantly took one more photograph and left.

Noah and Kara surveyed the damage. The desk had been shattered with a sledgehammer. So had the flatbed scanner. One external hard drive had been smashed; the other was missing. Her laptop had been thrown against a wall and smashed. Papers had been piled on the floor and soaked with gasoline.

Kara walked through the chaos of vandalism, her face reddened with rage. Noah shook, barely able to control his anger.

"Kara, you got your cell?"

She shook her head. He walked to the landing and yelled at the sheriff, who was talking into a handheld radio.

"Call the fire department, damn it!"

The sheriff shrugged. Noah screamed at him again.

"You should have called them first, you fucking fool!"

The sheriff angrily put down his handheld and reached into his car for its radio. Noah went back to the office. Kara stood behind the carnage of the desk, carefully removing *the map* from the wall and folding it. She tucked it inside her blouse. The map with Noah's markings on it had been shredded.

"How bad is it?" he asked her.

She shrugged, still angry. "Recoverable."

"Really?" he said, surprised.

"I've got that other external drive. It's in my briefcase. I've always believed in physical separation of backup devices. And I have digital photographs of everything tacked to the wall."

"That's something, anyhow. Kara, I'm really sor—"

She touched a finger to his lips. "I'm mad as hell," she said. "That asshole is doomed. I don't know how, I don't know when, but he's fucking *doomed*."

Noah sat at the kitchen table, drinking coffee and thinking. Kara showered. Afterward, she sat opposite him, wrapped in one of Noah's denim shirts. Neither spoke. Noah had his thinking habits; so did she.

Noah pushed his mug away.

"Kara, you got your phones handy? Both of 'em?"

She shrugged. "Sure. Why?"

"Just get them, please."

She got her satellite phone and her iPhone and set them on the table.

"There a speed dial number you don't use?"

"Take anything above five," she said. He programmed a number into each phone. That surprised her. Her lovable Luddite knew more than he'd let on.

"This will get worse, Kara, much worse, and I think soon."

She nodded.

"We try to stick together as much as possible. It we can't, we make sure we're with friends in safe places. Agreed?"

"Yes."

He pushed the phones across the table toward her.

"If shit happens, and I'm not around, hit speed dial seven. A friend will answer."

"A friend?"

He chose not to answer. "It's late. Bedtime, dear one."

Chapter 51:

August 24, late night, Noah's hangar, Greasewood Draw

Kara declared war against Xperience Offroad Xtreme. But she set the rules of engagement: "It's got to be legal. Or close to it, at least." Noah gave her a directive, too: "No more office in town. You'd be a sitting duck." They walled off a corner of the hangar for her office. Electrical outlets were installed, a new Mac laptop purchased, scanner and printer replaced, furniture bought at a yard sale and trailered home in a U-Haul. Noah surprised her with an air conditioner for her makeshift office, a luxury he would not allow himself in the trailer.

Kara gave her files to the UWP, but kept copies of the XOX files. She urged Hal not to let XOX transgressions dominate his organization's site. She would keep *XOX-badguys.org* attacking only XOX, independent of UWP. Noah and Hal appreciated that. It would deflect heat from the UWP.

She sat on her desk. The warm night and the privacy of Noah's hangar let her dress Greasewood Draw casual, her black Quick-Drys and a bright red sports bra. Noah lounged in the chair behind the desk, wearing only shorts. They had jogged in the twilight before sitting in war council.

"Trouble is," she said, "I'm not sure how best to go about this."

"What do you mean?" Noah asked.

"Where's his weak spot? I'm a pretty good hacker. I could check his credit, bank balances, and so on. A guy that interested in breaking the law probably doesn't declare the really big money he makes from these private video shoots. If Nash doesn't give the IRS tax on that money, then he has to be hiding it somewhere. I doubt he could he explain what he earned if he's breaking the law to do it. I could ask my friend Hannah back in Seattle if she knows any IRS people."

"I disagree," Noah said. "IRS stuff is way over our heads. Do what you do best. PR him to death. Put up the website. You've got ammunition. Organize data, remember? And put it into public view. He sells videos. Keep telling — no, keep *showing* — people who visit the site where his videos were shot, when, and, if we can confirm the names, especially who was there. I'm sure that will piss off his high-rolling clients. Won't do their images any good. Attack his client base. That'll get to him. And he'll make a mistake."

She nodded. "I guess you're right. What are you going to do?"

"Find his weak spot. I think I know what it could be."

"What?"

"I don't want to tell you yet. Forgive me. Borrow your phone?"

"Sure." She slid the cell across the desk. Picking it up, he walked out of the hangar. She shook her head, puzzled, and stood in the doorway as Noah walked across the dirt runway to the tree. He sat comfortably against it, talking on the phone. He did not return for an hour.

When he re-entered the office, he smiled at Kara and handed her the phone.

"And I shouldn't ask?" she said.

"Nope," he answered.

Kara rolled her head around slowly, trying to loosen tired, tense muscles.

"I've got another idea," she said.

"And that would be?" he asked.

"You haven't told me how, but you seem to find out when he's going on a shoot. Right?"

"I've got a few sources that have worked."

She smiled. It was not a warm, friendly smile. He prayed that cunning, sneaky, devious smile would never be directed at him.

"Can you gather a crowd on short notice? Green people?"

"Yeah, I suppose so. Yeah. I could."

She explained her idea. He looked for flaws. He found none.

"I like it," he said. "Damn, I *love* it."

He yawned. "I need sleep. Flying to Moab, then Kanab tomorrow."

Her eyes widened. "You are?"

"Yeah. I'll take the Skymaster. Be back in time for supper. Would you stay with Annie while I'm gone?"

She nodded. He walked to the door but turned when Kara didn't follow. "Kara?"

"Turn out the light, please, Noah."

He flicked the light switch. In the darkness he could hear her slipping off her clothes. From the blackness by the desk came her voice.

"You know what I never did in Seattle?" she whispered.

"What?"

"Make love on a desk surrounded by weird planes."

Later, Noah slept well. But not for as long as he'd hoped. Kara woke him twice.

Kara and Annie sat at the kitchen table in the trailer, nursing mugs of tea.

"So you're at war?" Annie asked.

Kara nodded. "I can't really get my life back until this is over," she said.

Annie smiled. "You mean *your lives* back."

"That, too," said Kara. "We haven't talked much about the

future, but we can't until Nash is out of our hair."

Annie reached across the table and touched Kara's hand.

"I'm happy for you, Kara. He's a wonderful man."

"I know. And I'm sure I can train him out of all his bad habits."

Both laughed. Kara finished her tea and left for the hangar. Annie stayed to do paperwork for Noah's charter service. That did not take long.

Noah called at noon and told her he'd be staying in Kanab. He wanted to see a BLM bigwig about her idea, but he was in the field until morning.

"And Kara, there's something I'd appreciate you doing."

"Sure. What?" she said, walking around the office with her cell phone.

"Go into the main hangar."

She walked out of her office. The Buckeye and a rebuilt Rans Coyote sat in the hangar. She smiled at the Buckeye. She had become damn good at flying it.

"Okay, I'm in the hangar."

Noah directed her to a shelf lined with aircraft tech manuals.

"There's a wooden box behind the manuals. Take it down, please."

Pulling down manuals, she found the box, and set it on a workbench.

"Open it, please."

Under the lid, his Ruger .357 rested on maroon velvet. She gasped.

"It's loaded, Kara. You know how to use it?"

"Yes, but—"

"Kara, I love you. There are dangerous guys out there. I'm asking you to take that gun and your phones wherever you go whenever I'm not around. Even when you're in the trailer. Even when you jog. You understand?"

"I do. But it makes me nervous."

"Consider the alternatives. You fell on your head and nearly qualified for one funeral a few months ago. I'd rather not see you qualify for another."

"I love you, Noah."

"I love you, too. Watch your back."

Chapter 52:

September 5, late afternoon, Book Cliffs WSA

For three days, Nash and his video crew captured the rock-crawling heroics of a Denver banker, a Tahoe developer, and the owner of a Salt Lake auto parts chain in a proposed Wilderness Study Area in the Book Cliffs. Environmentalists said they shouldn't be there. No matter. Nash's source had told him that BLM and Forest Service rangers were tending to wilderness elsewhere. So the snorting, supercharged machines crawled through narrow gullies, over tall rocks, and across native grasses. Their huge tires crunched through the thin botanical safeguard against erosion, a soil cap that wouldn't recover for a hundred years. At night the high-paying clients would chow down on huge cuts of beef and drink bottles of scotch they thought were many years old, served by the kitchen crew of B-t-h, Little Man, and Furtive Eyes. Nash oversaw every detail but kept in the background. He let the clients think they'd picked the most photogenic routes and spectacular backdrops for the videos they alone would own.

For those three days, Nash cursed as Noah's yellow Drifter overflew the area, filming. By day, the kitchen crew became sentries, standing on bluffs and ridges with carbines, out of sight of the clients. Nash didn't want them reminded of their

unethical intrusion into the WSA. The ultralight kept far
enough away to avoid rifle fire. Nash thought it was also far
enough away to prevent clear photographs of the miscreants.
But each time he looked up and saw the Drifter, he swore. His
patience, already wafer-thin, eroded.

In the mid-afternoon of the third day, the ultralight
approached closer. That annoyed Nash. The shoot ended in a
few hours, but he worried about the goddamned pictures. He'd
seen the website, the YouTube videos, the increasingly popular
Facebook group. He'd gotten calls from environmentalists,
annoyed at his transgressions. He, of course, had denied it, told
'em to fuck off, and hung up. But now he was getting calls
from politicians normally blind to his activities, thanks to
discreet, unreported cash campaign contributions. He didn't
need that asshole taking more pictures, so he ordered the
clients to pack it in. They threaded their way down toward the
road where they'd parked the trailers for their mechanical
stallions.

He sat on the hood of his Hummer and radioed his sentries
to fire if that fucker flew any closer. Soon, the deep Utah
silence swallowed the rumble of the rock crawlers. All Nash
could hear was the annoying whine of a Rotax engine, the
ultralight darting in and out, frustrating the rifle-toting clowns.
The fat man was supposed to keep tabs on Hartshorn.
Goddamned if he's going to get his cut, Nash thought. Where
the fuck was he, anyhow?

The drivers of the big machines neared their trailers, many
miles away from the site of the shoot. They were tired; they
had long drives ahead to return home.

The Denver banker, the scion of a wealthy family
prominent in Colorado Republican politics, rounded a turn,
goosing the throttle of his high-powered, much-modified Jeep.
Two green Forest Service pickups blocked the road. Several
dozen protesters waved signs and screamed epithets. Two
Forest Service rangers, one carrying a shotgun, ordered the
man to stop and leave the vehicle. One ranger spun the banker
onto the hood of his Jeep, told him to assume the position,

and frisked him. He was given a summons to appear in federal court in Salt Lake. His Jeep was confiscated. A writer from *High Country News* stood to one side, scribbling furiously in his notebook, taking names. Three TV journalists with ENG cameras mounted on Steadicams recorded the banker screaming at the rangers, "Don't you assholes know who the fuck I am?"

The rangers forced the Tahoe developer and the Salt Lake auto parts dealer to stop, too. They would receive court summonses as well. The developer tried to evade arrest and drove his machine at a poor angle up an arroyo wall. It overturned. Rangers dragged him unceremoniously out of his machine. The ENG cameras recorded the arrests, surrounding by the noisy, raucous green army Noah had summoned. As Kara predicted, Noah's gyroscopically stabilized, digitally enhanced, high-powered lens and digital camera would convict them. Newspapers and TV stations in Salt Lake, Denver, and Reno would carry stories that would piss off Nash's clients. He would escape prosecution, because he and his armed punks would leave the proposed WSA by a lesser-known route. The three clients, angered at Nash's abandonment of them, would make phone calls. Nash's pool of clients would shrink.

Kara's plan had hurt Nash. He boiled with fury.

Chapter 53:

September 9, evening, Ray's Tavern, Green River

Kara and Noah drove into Green River to celebrate with dinner and a few beers at Ray's Tavern. She wore an ankle-length black maxi dress, recently purchased. She liked dressing up. She'd bought a few fashionable dresses online because she was tired of her constant uniform of Quick-Drys and tank tops. She'd also bought a few things from Victoria's Secret, but Noah didn't know about those yet.

The Land Cruiser bounced along old State Route 24, approaching the turnoff to Green River Muni. Noah drove as Kara chatted idly about botany.

"I found a Tahoka daisy this morning on my run. And you haven't run lately, y'know," she said.

"No on one and yes on two," he said.

"Say again?"

"I said, yes, I haven't run lately. And no, you didn't see a Tahoka daisy."

"The hell you say. I got a picture, and I keyed it out in McCorrigan's guide."

"Wanna bet?" he said. "Sure," she said.

"How confident are you?" he said, slyness creeping into his voice.

"I'm right. You're wrong. That's confident."

"What are you willing to wager?" he asked

"Name it."

"If I'm right, you're on top for a week."

"Say what?" she said.

"You heard me."

"An attitude like that," she said, "might result in no sex for a week."

"Hey, you wanted to bet. You in or out?"

"Okay, okay," she said. "And if I'm right?"

"Then I'm on top for a week."

She slid over next to him. "We should have more bets like this," she said, resting her fingers on his groin. He pushed her hand away reluctantly.

"Lemme drive, for cryin' out loud."

"So why didn't I see a Tahoka daisy?"

"You didn't check the range. The Tahoka doesn't grow around here."

"Then what did I see?"

"False Tahoka. Smaller head, leaves not so elaborately divided."

She moved back to the other side of the seat, frowning.

"Hey. Didn't mean to burst your bubble. It's a beautiful flower."

"I've got a lot to learn about botany, Noah," she said quietly.

Noah glanced in the rearview mirror. He tensed.

"Kara, get out your cell." His tone of his voice said *do it, do it now, do it fast*.

"Punch in 345-555-1402. Hit 'send' if I say so."

"What's wrong?"

"We're being followed."

She looked into the passenger's side mirror. Behind the Cruiser a black Hummer and a dark blue Blazer followed, matching the Cruiser's speed.

"What's the number to? The sheriff?"

"No. State police. I don't trust him."

They rode past the airport turnoff, down a side street, and parked near the tavern. The Hummer and the Blazer rumbled past and out of sight.

The night out went well. Noah introduced Kara to two men dressed in park-ranger clothing, one from the BLM's Kanab office, the other from the Forest Service office in Moab. In town on business, they said. They told Kara they'd seen her website, and, unofficially, liked it. Appreciated her work toward a better environment, they'd said in politically correct language. And, unofficially, they told her they hoped the site "would put a few bad asses in deep shit." Kara liked them and protested when Noah and the BLM guy went off to talk privately.

Noah and Kara walked to the trailer, stopping to grope at each other like teen-agers. Near the trailer, she walked away from him, arms stretching toward the sky. Thin tendrils of cirrus drew icy rings about the moon. Standing in the moonlight, she called out to him.

"Noah?"

"Yes?"

"I never felt so free."

Chapter 54:

September 11, after midnight, Noah's trailer, Greasewood Draw

Caution prevailed. Each night, usually around midnight, Noah and Petey walked down the dirt road. Petey needed to flush his innards; Noah needed to flush bad guys. They saw a slow-moving, big-tired, dark-colored SUV rumble past Greasewood Draw a few times. Petey would bark. Noah would pepper the miscreant with paint pellets as it roared off. They would wait, ten minutes, fifteen minutes, half an hour, to make sure the vehicles didn't return. One night, Noah saw a dark Cherokee with a barely visible decal on its side, parked on the highway. Petey barked. The Jeep fled, tires screeching. Noah didn't have to guess who it was. And he began to assemble the pieces of other things he knew.

Kara would be asleep when the nightwalkers returned. Petey would curl up in the bedroom doorway. Noah would shower — a habit started when he began sharing his bed with Kara. He stepped out of the bathroom, toweling himself. A shaft of light startled him. A nude Kara was opening the fridge.

"Kara?"

"Sorry, Noah. I was thirsty." She opened the carton of

orange juice, drank from it, and started to put it back into the fridge.

"Wait," said Noah. "I'll have some." He drank and returned the carton to the fridge. Kara's soft laugh echoed through the trailer.

"What's so funny?" Noah asked.

"Your thing."

"My thing? Oh—"

He looked down.

"My god," he said. "Good OJ, I guess."

Kara sat on the floor, and he could faintly see her hand, beckoning him.

"Let's not waste it, lover."

Kara and Noah lay silent save for labored breathing, entangled on the floor, uncertain whose arm was whose and whose leg was where. Petey awakened to discover he'd seen it all before and knew it did not lead to food.

Rolling onto her back, pulling her leg from its warm, moist home between Noah's legs, Kara sighed.

"So that's what it's like to be screwed by a lawyer."

"Cheap shot," Noah muttered, gently cradling her breast. She folded her hand over his and held it there. "Sorry," she said.

"No worries."

"I love you, Noah Hartshorn, Esquire," she said.

"I love you," he said.

Hands moved, stroking here, caressing there. Later, she sat up and crossed her legs, looking at him. "Noah?"

He rested a hand on her knee. Go ahead, it said.

"Can I tell you something?"

"Like I could stop you?"

"Noah, I'm trying to be serious," she said. "And I'm not very good at it."

He sat across from her, legs crossed too. "Sorry. You're not the only one."

"When you say you love me, what does it mean to you?"

she asked.

"Ouch," he said. "Could I tackle the meaning of life? That's easier."

"You're dodging."

"Yeah, I suppose so," he said.

"What does it mean?" she asked again.

"Give me your hand, please," he said.

She shuffled closer and lay her hand on his leg. He held it.

"Helps me think," he whispered. She squeezed his hand.

"Noah, please don't take this wrong, but isn't that a problem? One that you've said I have? Thinking, not feeling?"

"I don't understand," he said.

"You said holding my hand helps you think."

"Well, it does. I like the feeling. I like the sensation. It says you're here, you're connected to me."

"So it helps you feel, not helps you think."

He nodded. "I guess you're right."

"So what do you feel?"

He exhaled heavily. "Look," he said. "I'm not trying to duck this. But would you like tea? I think this is something we need to talk out in the light."

"Okay."

As he made tea, she leaned against his back, arms around his waist, chin resting on his shoulder, breasts pressed against his shoulder blades. Rocking back and forth, they waited quietly for the water to boil.

"I like this," she whispered.

"So do I," he said.

He kissed her. The water boiled. Tea was infused. He poured two mugs, handed her one, and sat on the floor, his back against the refrigerator. She sat between his legs, facing him.

"Your thing's kind of wrinkled," she said, giggling.

"It's a penis, not a thing, and you wrinkled it," he said.

She laughed. The sound of sipping and slurping relaxed them.

"Loyalty," Noah said presently.

"Loyalty? To what?" she asked.

He closed his eyes, looking for the words. "To you. To what you feel. To what I feel. And if that sounds trite, well, I'm sorry."

"I think it sounds beautiful," she said, smiling. "But suppose you don't exactly believe in what I believe in?"

"Not a problem," he said.

"Why not?"

"Well, sweetie, as we've seen, you're wrong most of the time and I'm right."

She laughed. It woke Petey. Yawning and stretching, he looked around. Seeing his friends, he relaxed, rearranged himself, and went back to sleep.

"Like hell," she said.

"Okay, so I exaggerate. But the point is I'm loyal to your expressions of belief, because I love the heart behind the beliefs."

She stroked his hand, then kissed it.

"And you?" he asked.

"Me?"

"Yes, you. You started this."

"Damn," she said.

"Excuse me?"

"I just flashed on TD, that's all."

"Why?"

"I don't know. It just came to me, something that's always annoyed me. I didn't understand it until just now."

"Well?"

"Do I have to?"

"No. But I'm listening."

She fidgeted. "I told him I loved him. And he told me he loved me."

"And the problem?"

"I never sensed that he respected love. I mean, he respected my work — hell, I helped make him a millionaire. In a sense, he respected me. But I don't think he respected my feelings. Or his, for that matter. I was — well, we were — a convenience. Sex, work, money, one-stop shopping. Kara-Mart."

She shook her head. "I guess he really fucked me."

Noah sipped at his tea.

"You're not fucking me," she said. "At least, not that way."

"What am I doing?"

"No, Noah, it's *we're* doing."

"And that is?"

"Do I really have to tell you?"

"Yep."

"God, Noah, I love you. You call it loyalty. I call it respect. We're building. What, I don't know. But you respect the building. I love you for it."

Setting down the mug, he whispered, "C'mere, dear one."

They woke up Petey again.

Later, with Petey sleeping and Noah's thing re-wrinkled, they sat cross-legged on the floor across from each other, fresh mugs of tea between them. She asked why he went to law school.

"I was duped," he said. "Hal talked me into it. I was seeing this girl—"

"Really."

"It's ancient history, Kara. I was seeing this girl, well, professor, actually, who taught there. They ganged up on me, so I did it. Just call me juris doctor."

"So, did you open a practice?"

"No, that never really interested me. And my motive kind of vanished."

"You mean she broke up with you," she said, teasing.

"I prefer to think that we followed diverging interests."

"Yeah, right."

"Turned out she was sleeping with the dean."

"So, what'd you do? With the law degree, I mean," she asked.

"Well, I spent some time in the law school's environmental practice clinic. Got tired of it. Well, tired's not the right word.

Felt like I was fighting small battles and missing the overall war."

"So you became a terrorist. An eco-terrorist in the air."

"Oh, for Christ's sake, Kara," he snapped. "I'm not the bad guy here."

"A terrorist is a freedom fighter is a terrorist is a freedom fighter. Depends on your POV," she retorted. Noah tensed briefly, then sighed, his anger easing.

"Okay, okay. Truth is, I love to fly, and the idea of flying and fighting turns me on, damn it."

"And getting shot at?"

"It's a kick, too. Besides, I know what I'm doing. I felt I could do more in the air than I could in a courtroom."

"So you became the airborne avenger."

"Jesus, Kara, what's with you? You've been up there with me. You liked it, too, you know."

"Yes, I do. Well, did. But it didn't work, did it?"

He sighed. "Working, maybe. But slowly. I wanted action now. I wanted those guys out of the wilderness. So I flew into the hornet's nest, so to speak."

"You sound like the kind of guy who'd run with the bulls at Pamplona."

"Naw. I did something more dangerous."

"What's that?"

He grinned. "I ran with the politicians."

"Pardon?"

"I got hooked up with the UWP through Hal. I knew the law, I knew the issues, I knew the politicians. So I volunteered, testifying at hearings, lobbying the politicos. Hell, that was more frustrating than the clinic. But at least I got, well, get, to pitch a different morality at the people who make the laws."

Lifting her mug, she drank the last of her tea and set the mug down. The action was deliberate and precise. Kara acted almost ritualistically before she made pronouncements.

"Do we plan to be together for the foreseeable future?"

"That a proposal?" he asked.

"No. A statement of loyalty," she said quietly, looking

straight into his eyes.

He leaned over and kissed her. "I don't see us being apart."

She smiled. "Neither do I."

They were silent for a while.

"So what's all this noise about me being a lawyer?" he asked.

She thought for a moment. "I'm loyal to you. To what you believe. I think you need to believe that the rule of law, of order, will eventually bring you what you seek."

"And what's that?"

"An end to the guilt you feel."

"Over?"

"Over how you made six million dollars."

Noah sighed, his shoulders sagging. Kara rose to her knees and embraced him.

"You're right, you're right, you're right, damn it," he said.

Chapter 55:

September 14, midday, Greasewood Draw

Noah and Kara, returning from a cross-country training flight, saw the ruinous result of evil at the same time. Noah lowered the nose of the Drifter and pushed the throttle forward. The ultralight swept over the cliff-side field a mere wingspan off the ground. Kara stared in horror at the furiously burning trailer as it flashed by under the wings. The Drifter banked and Noah barked over the intercom.

"There. Two o'clock."

A dust plume rose over the dirt road to Highway 24. He redlined the big Rotax. But the ultralight protested, loaded with more than three hundred fifty pounds of Noah, Kara, emergency supplies, water, and cameras. The Drifter could not keep up with the dark spot that raced north on the highway.

"Noah, look!"

"What?"

"That car."

Noah stared at the distant vehicle. He saw a flash of blue. The SUV was big and boxy. "I think we know who that asshole is," he said.

He eased back the throttle, setting up his approach to the

field. Even under duress, Noah attended closely to the details of landing an aircraft.

Noah walked a dozen feet from the Drifter, helmet in hand. Kara sat in the plane, her four-point harness still fastened, staring at the charred, twisted aluminum trailer and softly crying. Noah heard her and dropped the helmet. He released her harness and plucked her from the seat. She buried her face against his chest. He set her down at the tree, embraced her, and kissed her.

"Thank God you're with me," he said quietly.

She hugged him. "Why?"

"Because I can't deal with this alone."

Noah jogged back to the plane. He ran his post-flight checklist to insure that he and Kara would be safe when next they flew. Only then did he turn and stare blankly at the ruins.

Kara jumped to her feet, screaming. "Petey! Where's Petey?"

She called for her dog. Petey loped out of the hangar, barking.

"Petey!" Kara shouted, running toward him. She swept him up into her arms, hugging him, whispering to him. Kara set Petey down, relieved.

She stared at the smoldering evidence of cowardice. Arms folded across her chest, she walked aimlessly around it, shaking her head.

"I'm sorry about your computer," Noah said. The new Mac, a replacement for the one smashed in her Green River office, was in the trailer, he thought. She'd never left it in the hangar.

"It's in my car. With the back-up drives. Sixth sense, I guess," she said.

"That's a relief," he said, his voice flat.

Kara looked at him. His face held no sign of anger, no sign of regret. And he'd thought of her first. No one else had before. She leaned against him.

"This was your home," she said faintly.

He kissed her forehead. "And yours, too. It will be again, Kara."

She held his hand, not squeezing it, not clutching it. Just connecting, just being human. They stood in the bright sun on the hard brown earth.

"Noah, why aren't you upset?"

"Insurance," he said.

She nodded. "Still ..."

"Insurance. And I have money. I can replace everything."

"But they—"

Anger edged into his voice. "They had motive, and like a idiot, I gave it to them."

"What do you mean?"

Noah sighed. "Never turn your back on a wounded animal," he said.

"Beg pardon?"

"Remember when he hit me?"

"Yes, but—"

"I hurt him worse. Twice. He lost face in the diner, and that little charade in court — he had to do, what, 400 hours of community service? Where all those XOX morons could see him? I hit him harder than he ever hit me."

Kara let go of his hand and poked through the debris. She touched a piece of burnt, crumpled aluminum. It was the door. She picked up a mug. It was the only mug she'd seen him use of those in his cabinet. His favorite. She kicked at the charred ruins. His life in shambles. Her new life in shambles.

"I'm going to check the hangar," he said, calling to her as he ran down the runway. Kara nodded, holding his mug, guarding it against destruction.

Moments later he screamed. She ran into the hangar. Noah sat on the dirt floor, head in his hands, shoulders shaking, surrounded by mayhem. Malevolence had cut the strut wires of his Flightstar. Destruction had broken engine parts off the Airbike with a sledgehammer. Pestilence had slashed the Buckeye's parachute with a knife. Anger had cracked the fairing of a single-seat Drifter with a rock. Noah quivered with rage. He'd bought the second Drifter and a Rotax 503 with Kara in mind. Something for her to rebuild, to salvage. A gift. Now it was carnage.

She led him to her car. Noah leaned against it, shaking. She made tea with her camp stove, poured some into a mug, and offered it to him with both hands. He sat on the hood, sipping the tea. She put away the stove and closed the hatchback. She walked to the front of the car and sat on the hood, her shoulder brushing against him. He did not move. He just sipped at the tea, holding the mug in both hands. Then he shifted the mug to one hand and put his other arm around her shoulder. She smiled.

"Kara?" His eyes stared into a distance she could not yet fathom.

"Yes?"

"Thank you."

"For what?"

He lifted the mug in salute. "For the tea."

"The tea."

"Yes. The tea. Nicest thing anyone's done for me in a long, long time."

They walked out of the office of his insurance agent later in the day, hand in hand. Destruction had been surprised and fled, as cowards do, into the camouflage of distance before the Land Cruiser had been targeted. Nestled into its bucket seats, they drove in silence west on I-70, then several miles north up Cottonwood Draw, and stopped near Sids Reservoir. They sat on a rock overlooking the Swell to the north. Noah stared at the insurance check. Kara leaned against him, her arm over his shoulder, humming softly.

The agent had inspected the damage with the sheriff. Statements had been taken; suspects had been suggested. Evidence, such as it was, had been found. Fingerprints had been collected. Witnesses? the sheriff had asked. None, Kara had said. Noah had fumed, watching the sheriff poke and probe through the ruins. Kara did the talking. Noah had refused to go near him. The sheriff and Noah didn't get along, she knew, but the look on Noah's face was murderous.

He handed her the check. She looked at it, three lowly digits followed by three zeroes. She said nothing. She just hugged him.

Noah sighed. "Long day."

Kara nodded. Noah fidgeted, shifting around on the rock. He slapped his hand hard against the rock, startling her.

"Those bastards didn't cost me money. They cost me time," said Noah. "It took me more than 2,000 hours to build and rebuild those planes. That's a year of 40-hour weeks. This goddamned check won't buy back those hours."

He stamped his foot hard on the ground. "Damn. *Godfuckingdamn.*"

Kara said nothing. She was still angry about what they did to him. To *them.* It had shocked her to see Noah uncharacteristically range through such extreme emotions — when they landed, to be so apparently calm, then descend into pain, then emerge in wrath.

Noah was walking in circles, muttering schemes of retribution and times of visiting it on the assholes *he knew* did this. She brushed her fingers on his hip as he passed by. "Come. Sit down," she said.

He sat. He was not calm. "Noah, can I ask you some questions?" He nodded. At least he was listening. "Where did you get the planes?"

"The Rans was a kit. I bought it and built it. That alone was 400 hours."

"That other Drifter?"

He sighed. "Bought it as salvage. I was going to give it to you. It didn't need a lot of work. I thought you might like to work on it yourself."

She'd suspected as much. "Okay. And the others?" she asked.

"Lessee, the Buckeye was a wreck. I bought it as salvage, too."

"Take long to fix?"

"Well, yeah. More than if I built it from a new kit."

Kara had wriggled across the rock until her hip and leg touched his. She spoke quietly, and he had to lean closer to hear. "Why?" she asked.

"Well, I had to build some new parts. And made new frame bends. The engine was trashed, so I found a used Rotax 503, a single carb. God, I hate those dual carb 503s. Too much maintenance. Another carb to have something go wrong. Then again, the 503 is a pretty reliable engine. It—"

"Noah. You're rambling."

"Sorry."

"Don't be," Kara said, laying her hand on his thigh. "I don't mind."

"What about the Airbike?"

"That was a salvage job, too."

"Why didn't you just buy new parts for them?"

"Didn't want to."

"Why not?"

"Even machines have life. I like to restore life. Just plugging in new parts isn't the same."

"Jesus. A Boy Scout for the new millennium," she said, snickering.

He elbowed her sharply but said nothing.

"Sure, they cost you time, but you're the one who decided to pay that high a price," she whispered.

He turned abruptly, an angry remark forming but arriving stillborn.

"Yeah, I guess if you look at it like that, I suppose so."

"You've got that check. You can buy more mechanical souls to save."

Noah sighed. "Yeah. But—"

"But what?"

"I hated losing."

"Losing the planes?" she asked.

He said nothing. "Or losing to those assholes?" she said.

"Christ, you're full of questions," he snapped.

"Sorry." He slipped his arm around her shoulders briefly,

then retrieved it. He rested his elbows on his knees and leaned forward, resting his chin on hands curled into fists. "Don't be. I'm just ... I'm ..."

"You're what?"

He stalked off, then turned. "I'm rattled. I'm fucking rattled. All right? Is that what you wanted to hear? You happy?"

"No, that's not what I wanted to hear."

"Well, what the hell did you want to hear?"

Kara stood, arms at her side. "I just wanted to hear whatever was inside you. That's all I will ever want to hear from you."

Noah lowered his head into his hands and wept. Kara turned and cradled his face in her hands. She kissed him softly, then rested his head against her neck. Noah calmed down. He sat, cross-legged, on the earth. Kara sat in front of him.

"You're a fox," he said.

She smiled, looking down at her clothes, smudged with ashes.

"You mean because I'm so damn gorgeous?"

Smiling, he reached for her hand. "No. You're cunning."

"Why, whatever do you mean?"

He stood and pulled her up. "You know goddamned well what I mean."

They walked back to Cruiser. He opened the door for her. She climbed in and fastened the seat belt. He started to close the door and stopped.

"You did it again, damn it," he said.

"You're welcome," she said, smiling as he reconsidered the consequences of the devastation of his toys.

Chapter 56:

September 14, after midnight, Noah's hangar, Greasewood Draw

They slept in the hangar on worktables they'd shoved together. Noah had hung a candle lantern. Kara had furnished foam pads and a sleeping bag she'd opened to cover them both. Gear bags with clothes hung from pegs that normally held tools. Mosquito netting hung over the worktables.

Through the evening they worked on the planes. It had been hard, sweaty work, and the evening had been warm. Noah had stripped to his shorts; Kara had discarded her T-shirt. She'd hauled bent and busted frame parts and shredded Mylar wing covering. Noah had assessed damage and removed parts; Kara had sorted the debris into salvageable and unsalvageable piles. Every now than, fury would overtook her, and she'd throw a smaller part against a wall. Later, Noah hauled a jug of water out of the Cruiser, and they washed each other with sponges before slipping into the makeshift bed. Fatigue and anger covered them like a blanket. Sleep came, but they woke often at the smallest of sounds. Wind rustled trees. A screech owl hooted. Mice poked around for food. Those sounds Noah and Kara knew. They listened for another sound:

Would the assholes who did this return?

Noah woke and turned his head. No Kara. He rolled off the worktables and groaned. Sore muscles. Throbbing temples. A Thermos sat on a workbench. Beside it was his mug. A spoon peeked over its rim. Kara had made tea. He wondered where she was. After slipping into his cargo shorts, he poured tea and shuffled outside.

Kara sat by the blackened trailer. He walked to her. Her mug was cradled in her hands. She wore only the T-shirt and underwear she'd slept in. She was weeping. He said nothing. They sipped at their tea, warmed by the morning sun, chilled by the remnants of calculated terror.

"I fell in love with you in that trailer," she said presently.

He nodded. He loved the sound of her voice, a low, soft contralto that resonated within him.

"Where did you fall in love with me?" she asked.

He pointed west over the Swell. She nodded.

"Somehow I knew that," she said softly.

She looked at him. "Noah, I've often wondered ..."

"What?"

"How did you find me?"

"I heard you crying," he said.

She turned her head toward him. "You did?"

"I dreamed it for a week. I felt it. I heard you crying."

She leaned against his shoulder. "That's a delusion, you know."

He chuckled. "So's your map, then."

She nodded. "Are we both crazy?"

"If we were," he said, "how could we tell?"

"Where will we live?" she asked, her voice small.

He shrugged. She rested her hand on his forearm, gripping it firmly.

"Where will we live?"

He shook his head. "I don't know. Motel, I guess, for a few days."

"Then where?" she asked.

"I don't know."

She sighed, letting go of him. She padded barefoot around the trailer, holding her mug. Suddenly she heaved the mug at the ruins. "Fuck!"

She ran to her car. He set down his mug and ran into the brush alongside the road. Kara started the car and punched the accelerator. The Subaru slewed into a hard turn and fled around a curve in the driveway. Noah emerged from his shortcut through the brush and stood in the road, arms folded across his chest. Kara braked hard, and the Subaru stopped inches from him. Noah walked to the driver's side, reached in, and switched off the engine. Kara wept uncontrollably. The map lay across her bare legs. Noah helped her out and folded her into his arms.

"I want a home, Noah," she whispered. "I want a home."

He kissed her softly. "I know. I do, too. We can rent another trailer for a while. Just for a while. We've work to finish."

She clutched at him. "I don't want to live in a trailer any more, Noah."

He kissed her. "Then we've decisions to make," he said.

"Yes," she said. "Decisions."

"I love you, Kara."

She dropped the map and kissed him deeply.

Chapter 57:

September 16, Noah's hangar, Greasewood Draw

Circumstances delayed decisions. Noah needed to fly to Salt Lake to keep dates with legislators, lobbyists, and the UWP leadership. Noah suggested she stay with Annie again until he returned. But he worried about leaving the hangar unprotected.

The morning before he left, he and Kara had just risen from their makeshift beds when they heard a loud, sputtering noise. Kara lunged for the Ruger, but Noah caught her and shook his head.

"Doc's truck," he said. Kara, relieved, chuckled. "Oh," she said. "Don't want to shoot him, I guess."

They stepped outside to greet him. The noisy engine of Doc's old Chevy C10 had masked four vehicles trailing it. Doc stepped out, shading his eyes. He saw the ruins of the trailer and frowned.

"Love what you've done with the place," he said, shaking Noah's hand and getting a warm hug from Kara. "Nash the decorator," Noah said grimly.

"Heard he's saying he was in Castle Valley when it happened," said Doc.

"Nothing happens without his say-so, Doc. You know

that."

"Yep, I suppose." Doc turned. "By the way, I brought company."

Six men stood behind Doc. Noah recognized a few. "Well, Jim, hi, over there, yeah. Car accident, wasn't it?"

Jim nodded. "Yeah. My Jeep overturned near Neversweat Wash. Broke my leg. You flew in and took care of me until the chopper got there."

Doc identified the others. Two were sons of a couple lost on Mexican Mountain when spring had suddenly become winter. Noah had found them.

"This is the first shift, Noah," Doc said. "There's plenty of folks who owe you. Get about your business. We'll look after here."

"How'd you know?" he asked.

"Annie," the doc said.

"Annie," Noah said.

"Knows all, tells all." Doc chuckled.

Noah shook hands with each man, nodding his thanks. Kara followed, thanking them, too. Noah and Kara walked behind the hangar and showered. While dressing, Kara noticed Petey, sleeping as usual.

"Noah?" Kara was looking at Petey.

"What about him?" he asked.

"He's vulnerable, too."

Noah rubbed the dog's tummy. "Petey, how could I have forgotten about you?"

Noah stood and kissed Kara. "Sorry I didn't think of him sooner."

"I'll take him to Annie's, too," she said. "We'll make sure he stays out of harm's way."

They lingered over breakfast at the Tamarisk. Noah used Kara's cell phone to talk with UWP people about last-minute details of the hearings. Kara busied herself with hard-drive housekeeping. She wouldn't let the laptop out of her sight. Noah put the cell phone down and looked across the table at

Kara. She didn't notice. After sipping at his coffee, he touched the top of the computer's screen.

"Hello?" he said.

She looked up. "Oh, sorry. What?"

"Do you want to live in Green River?" he asked.

Her eyes widened, then narrowed. "This some kind of trick question?"

"Do you want to live in Green River?"

"Under what circumstances?"

"Any circumstances."

Closing her eyes, she folded her arms across her chest. She sighed. "No."

He leaned back, silent.

"I'm sorry, Noah," she said quietly.

He reached for her hand and squeezed it firmly, almost forcefully.

"There's no need to apologize," he said.

"Why not?" she asked.

"Because you told the truth. You think I've been under the impression that Green River would be the be-all and end-all of your dreams? Hey, I'm not as much of an idiot as you think I am."

"Hey," she protested. "I don't think you're an idiot."

They fell silent for a while.

"I thought you wanted to stay in Green River," she said.

"So did I. But someone smarter than me — um, that would be you, Kara — told me a while back that I've been hiding."

"So where do you want to live?" she asked.

"With you," he said.

She smiled, lifted his hand, and kissed it. "And where might that be?"

"Don't know."

"Well, I don't know, either."

"Well, then add it to our to-do list. Find a place to live."

Our. Such a magic word, Kara thought, as they left the restaurant. *Our.* Pronoun. First person. *Plural.*

Chapter 58:

September 23, afternoon, Green River Muni

Kara drove Noah to Green River Muni. He told her he loved her, that they'd sort out where to live when he got back. With the Skymaster's engines at full military power, he climbed to pattern altitude and circled the field, watching her drive toward old State Route 24 in the Cruiser. On impulse he lowered the nose, dropped full flaps and flew close to the ground, whipping alongside the Cruiser. Kara waved. Then the Skymaster climbed to en route altitude and shrank to a dark, distant dot in the bright blue Utah sky.

Noah returned a week later. Kara climbed all over him after the Cessna had stopped on the parking apron. He was excited but wouldn't tell her why. She pleaded with him to tell her and got only his Cheshire cat smile of refusal, his chuckling, laughing silence.

"Tomorrow. I'll tell you everything tomorrow. We'll go on a picnic. Okay?"

She said sex would be a distant memory if he didn't goddamn tell her right now. They never made it down the dirt road to Greasewood Draw. She pulled the Cruiser into the trees and yanked off her T-shirt and Quick-Drys and ordered

him to ravish her and "I mean right now, you pompous idiot."
But he didn't tell her. His mouth was otherwise occupied.

Chapter 59:

September 24, late morning, southeast of Temple Mountain

Despite being strapped down, the picnic basket bounced aimlessly about the seat. "So where are we going?" Kara asked. "Into the Swell," he said.

"Gee. Could you be a little less vague, Noah?"

The Cruiser rolled west on Goblin Valley Road. It lagged behind a long line of rental RVs and campers driven by tourists milking the late-season hot weather. Trailing behind the Cruiser were more vans, RVs, and ever-present Jeeps driven by California college kids procrastinating on the first few weeks of classes. Nearly all would turn south for Goblin Valley State Park. None was interested in the geology, Noah told Kara. Or that violet-green swallows nested there. They only wanted to see the place where the movie Galaxy Quest was filmed. They wanted to brush against something famous. Hollywood's attention meant harm to a fragile landscape. Everyone wants a piece of the rare, the innocent, the precious, he told her. Like Nash. Like Nash's clients.

"Temple Mountain Loop," he said presently. "I know a few isolated—"

"You mean you want to get laid."

"I didn't say that."

"Wasn't last night enough?" she asked, poking him in the shoulder.

He rubbed his face in mock contemplation. "Well, you owed me those."

"Those? Aren't we the grand lover. And how, pray tell, did I owe you those?"

"Hey. You saying I, um, don't satisfy?"

"I have high standards."

"Oh, right. That why you laid down in the runway and said fuck me?"

"Don't close your mind to new experiences, Noah."

He chuckled. "Yes, dear," he said. "Anyhow, you owed me those for all the nights I was up in Salt Lake."

"How do you figure that? You're the one who decided to go."

"Well, would we have made love had I stayed?"

"If you'd behaved."

He shot her a look. "Hey. I've been a good boy lately."

"True, true," she said, brushing her fingers through his hair. The RVs and campers in front of the Cruiser turned south as Noah had predicted. The Cruiser passed a slot in an upthrust of Navajo sandstone that presaged the Swell beyond. A glance in the mirror showed vehicles behind the Cruiser turning south. He turned back to Kara.

"So I would have deserved sex each night, right?"

"Hypothetically," she said.

Neither saw the blue Blazer and the dark green Cherokee emerge from the train of tourists turning off for Hollywood glory and follow at a distance.

"Well, then, I wasn't there for a week that I would have had sex. So you owed it to me."

Kara laughed.

"Do that again," he said.

"What?"

"Laugh."

"Why?"

"Because I like to listen to it. That's all. I just like to listen to it."

She undid her seat belt and scooted across the seat. Draping her arm over his shoulder, she kissed his cheek and leaned her head on his shoulder.

"No one else ever did, Noah," she said quietly. "No one else ever did."

The dirt trail became rougher; the Cruiser's old parts became noisier as it bounced over ruts despite Noah's careful driving. Its fat tires struck rocks and Kara, still sans seat belt, would become briefly weightless. She didn't mind. She liked landing against Noah, her hips striking his, her breasts glancing against his upper arm, her arm around his shoulder clutching his neck, her other hand braced against the roof.

"Noah," she said. Her voice had that tone, a gathering of clouds before a torrential downpour of questions. Noah took his eyes off the corrugated road to steal a sideways glance at her. Uh-oh. *Incoming.* Again.

"Yes?" He spoke loudly. The Cruiser was whining in second gear. He shifted into third. High gears and low revs best mastered rough terrain.

"Am I home?" she asked.

"Say again?"

"Am I home?"

"I don't understand."

She bounced a bit as the Cruiser heaved her.

"Where is home for you?" she asked.

"I guess back in Greasewood Draw."

"Where was it before then?"

His forehead scrunched a little as he thought.

"I guess that apartment I had outside Salt Lake, you know, when I was doing that lawyer thing."

"That was a home?"

"What are you getting at?" He twisted the wheel to avoid a nasty rut.

"Where is home now?"

"I don't have a home. Trailer's torched," he said.

She took her hand from his shoulder and folded her arms across her chest. "So where is home?"

The Cruiser found a level stretch. He stopped and turned off the engine. He turned, his arm on the seat back behind her. He did not notice sunlight glinting off metal or a windshield, somewhere downhill behind the Cruiser.

"Why do I have the feeling I'm taking a test?" he said.

"If that's your interpretation, so be it," she said, staring straight ahead. The road curled through a canyon hemmed in by walls of pinkish-white sandstone. She loved the geometry of Utah's landscape, its geomorphology a world of rectangles and polygonal solids. So unlike the Northwest.

"Home is here," he ventured.

"What do you mean, here?" she asked

He leaned forward, his hand on her chin turning her face toward him.

"Right here," he said. She started to speak, but he shhh'd her. "Wait." He started the engine, drove the Cruiser a hundred yards, and stopped.

"Now home is here. And if I drive another hundred yards, home will be there. And if I drive to, hell, I don't know, Timbuktu, home will be there."

She looked at him. "Noah, what the hell do you mean?"

"I have no intention of driving the next hundred yards without you. If I drive to Timbuktu, I have no intention of driving there without you. I will not drive anywhere without you. Or anywhere we don't agree to go."

He started the engine, shifted into first, and let out the clutch. The Cruiser lurched forward. Behind them rose a cacophony of growling sounds, but it was submerged by the rumble of the Cruiser's engine, hard at work.

They rode in silence as the Cruiser bucked her against him. Slipping her arm around his shoulders again, she buried her face against his neck. He could feel the warm, wet tears on his neck. "Noah?" she asked.

"Yes?"
"You passed."

Noah, glancing in the rear view mirror, noticed dust rising behind them.

"Company's coming," he said quietly.

Kara twisted in the seat. A blue Blazer bounced into view, airborne as its powerful engine drove it over a hummock in the road. Behind it, a dark green Cherokee was weaving in the dust.

"Shit," she said. "It's them."

"No doubt. Buckle up, please. Tightly."

She fastened her seat belt tightly. Noah floored the accelerator, and the Cruiser surged forward. Noah looked at Kara. "Don't worry," he said.

"Like hell," she said. "That Blazer is faster than this bucket."

"Yeah. But I know the road. No one knows this place as well as I do."

Kara placed her hands against the roof of the Land Cruiser to brace herself against its wild bucking and bouncing. Noah eased the Cruiser ahead of the Blazer and Cherokee. The Jeep, its wimpy six-cylinder underpowered for this kind of pursuit, fell back. The road worsened as the Cruiser raced up a series of difficult switchbacks onto level road in a narrow arroyo.

Then the Cruiser's Buick V-8 sputtered and died.

"What the fuck?" Noah shouted.

"God damn it, Noah, it's the fuel pump. I warned you to change the damn thing! Why didn't you fi—" she screamed.

Ripping off his seat belt, he turned, grasped her arm, and shouted.

"Move! We have to go. Now! Move! They're closing!" He jerked his thumb toward the rear.

She could hear the rumble of the Blazer's engine and the whine of the Jeep as they labored up the switchbacks. Kara reached behind the front seat and grabbed her go-bag. Inside were her laptop, sat terminal, and the phones — both satellite and cell — and basic camera kit. Noah, his pack in place, pushed her toward a narrow side canyon that led to higher ground. The mornings in the gym behind the hangar rewarded them. They ran easily up the slot, emerging on an expanse of slickrock. A few hundred yards across it were narrow fins separating little slot canyons. Good hiding places. Good escape routes. Running across the slickrock, rear guard to Kara's point, Noah glanced back.

B-t-h crested the slickrock, trailed by Furtive Eyes and Little Man. B-t-h carried a tire iron, Furtive Eyes held a baseball bat, and Little Man smacked a headless ax handle against his hand. Noah couldn't see the other two he expected. They would have guns.

"Hurry, Kara. Those fuckers don't look happy."

Noah ran easily behind Kara. Scanning the sandstone fins ahead, he picked a route that would get them out of sight quickly. They'd run hard for nearly 200 yards. The strain of the harsh pace showed on her face. Long morning runs were one thing; lengthy sprints were another. Kara fought to keep up as Noah passed her, taking her go-bag. He slowed until she drew near enough to take his hand. He pulled her along, but she stumbled and lost her footing a few times before they ducked behind a fin.

Noah stopped to scheme. He could see Nash's three henchmen running across the slickrock. The fat sheriff would be panting further back in the arroyo. Nash would somewhere behind the first three, running easily, as if swift pursuit were beneath him. Let the hunters flush the hunted. That'd be his attitude. Three narrow canyons opened nearby. Noah handed Kara the go-bag and pointed to one of the little canyons.

"Go in there," he said. "The left one. Run about 100 yards. It opens up. Take the easier slope when it does, to the right. Use the sat phone there. Emergency speed dial seven, remember? Follow the instructions of the person who answers. Then keep moving. Head northwest. In about a mile, you'll come to a road — tourists use it — and flag down the first car you see. Get the hell outta here. I'll lead them into a maze. Got it? Right and northwest. Okay. Go, Kara. Get your ass moving."

"But Noah, I can't lea—"

"Kara, just go. Now. They're only seconds behind us and I don't want them to see which slot you go into."

He pushed her to the mouth between two fins and hurried to another narrow slot. Kara was gone, and he felt relieved. He looked over the bedrock rise. B-t-h, Furtive Eyes, and Little Man were half way across the slickrock. They were gasping now, especially B-t-h. Good, he thought. He'd run the bastards into the ground. He made sure they saw him and darted into the canyon, barely as wide as the wingspan of the Drifter. He ran easily, dancing from one nubbin of bedrock to the next. He knew the acoustics of narrow canyons. Sounds carried incredible distances. He paused several times, listening. He could hear the huffing and puffing of B-t-h, the clicking of Furtive Eyes' cleats, the why-don't-I-wait-here whine of Little Man who feared Noah but would never admit it.

Dropping his pack, he pulled out a water bottle and took a swig. Slipping on his pack, attention diverted, he missed the movement hidden in the dark shadow cast by the dusky red sandstone wall of the narrow canyon. Nash, too, had a baseball bat. He swung it. Noah ducked but not soon enough. The fat end of the hard ash Louisville slugger crashed into his upper back, cracking a shoulder blade. He howled in pain, staggered, and retreated, facing Nash.

"So, asshole," Nash said, smiling with evil intent. "Thought you knew this place better'n me, huh?" He raised the bat over his head again. Noah dropped his pack and backpedaled, holding his right shoulder and grimacing. As Nash stepped forward, he brought the bat down hard. Noah stepped in under the bat, and kicked Nash in the balls. Nash fell to his knees, screaming. Noah grabbed his pack and staggered away. He rounded a corner of the canyon and froze. It ended in a cliff about fifteen feet high. A box canyon. Noah had known the trail ended here, but he'd counted on having two good arms. He'd climbed out of this before.

Cornered. He turned, back against the wall. Keep Nash in front of him. The pack. It held the Ruger. He hurriedly rummaged for the gun. He pulled it out and raised it just as Nash's bat smashed down on his forearm, breaking it. Nash kicked the Ruger away. That would be too easy. Nash wanted to beat Noah, to pulverize him, to make him suffer, to make him fucking beg.

Noah could still fight. He still had one good arm. Dodging another swing, he moved right, keeping his left side toward Nash. Triumph flooded over Nash's face. He had Noah cornered. The three goons lurched into the canyon, panting heavily, bent over. B-t-h glared at Noah. Nash had Noah pinned against the wall. B-t-h advanced. That prick Noah was right where he wanted him. Outnumbered. Kill the fucker, B-t-h shouted.

B-t-h, Little Man, and Furtive Eyes growled like feral dogs as they circled Noah. Nash watched, poised with the bat ready to inflict more pain. Noah crouched, a basketball player defending Doom playing low post. Furtive Eyes meekly swung his baseball bat at Noah. It missed. Nash leered at Furtive Eyes.

"For chrissakes, hit the fucker, you goddamned wimp," Nash screamed.

Little Man, too far away to connect with his ax handle, threw it at Noah, hitting him in the left shoulder. Noah instinctively grabbed it. He spun to face Little Man, and B-t-h struck from behind. The tire iron cracked across Noah's broken right forearm. B-t-h swung again, and the tire iron crunched two of Noah's ribs. Noah fell to his knees. The tire iron whistled through the air again, striking Noah in the head, fracturing his skull just above the left ear. Noah toppled onto the bedrock, barely conscious and moaning. The three miscreants surrounded him, leering in triumph.

Kara ignored Noah's orders. She ran up the gully, digging her sat phone out of her go-bag, and turned left, not right, and ran along the crest of the sandstone sidewall of the canyon

Noah had taken. Looking down, she saw the unholy trio. Noah had a good lead. She expected Nash but did not see him. Farther down the narrow canyon, where the climb was steep, the sheriff leaned against the rock wall, his face beet-red. Sweat puddled on his chest, staining his tan shirt. In that instant, she understood everything. *Nash and the sheriff.*

Down the canyon, she saw the broad slickrock rise she and Noah had crossed. The Blazer and Cherokee were parked there. She pulled the satellite phone from her pack and punched the speed dial. A man answered. She did what she was trained to do. She reported her observations and, checking her GPS, gave the location in latitude and longitude. The man said a state police helicopter would be overhead in 20 minutes. Stay out of sight, she was told.

The hell she would, she thought. She said no, they'd catch Noah before then, and told the man what she was going to do. He said he'd be waiting and wished her luck. She punched the "off" button and stuck the phone inside the waistline of her shorts. As she jogged back toward the head of the canyon, she pulled their new Canon digital camera out of her go-bag. Thank God they got a zoom lens, she thought, running harder, looking for a good vantage point atop the fin.

The pursuers crowded around the prey. The wheezing of heavy breathing was loud in the narrow canyon. Little Man walked around Noah warily and picked up his bat. He nudged Noah's feet. Noah didn't move. Little Man poked at the foot harder. Nothing. Emboldened by beer they'd consumed while shadowing the Cruiser, Little Man swung at Noah's right leg and broke the tibia. Little Man stepped back, grinning smugly. B-t-h sat down heavily on the sandstone, the tire iron braced across his lap. He looked at his confederates. "That'll teach the bastard," he panted. Furtive Eyes and Little Man nodded. Noah lay almost motionless on the hard, unforgiving sandstone.

Kara ran along the fin, well ahead of the sheriff below, who had been reduced to a stumbling walk, stopping frequently, wheezing, and holding a hand to his chest. Below, Noah fought with Nash as the three miscreants crowded around. She stopped, pulled the laptop and satellite terminal out of the pack, and set them up. She lay down, braced the Canon and its telephoto lens, and clicked the selector dial to hi-def video. She pushed the shutter as B-t-h cracked Noah's arm with the tire iron. She panned the camera as Little Man broke Noah's leg. Again and again, she recorded each blow, each assault, each damning act the foursome committed. She wept as she did, wishing she had the damned Ruger in her hand. But she kept her laser-like focus on using her only weapons — video and a sat phone.

Plugging the camera and sat terminal into the laptop, she downloaded the video. She booted her e-mail program, praying for the processor to hurry. After dragging icons of the videos into the attachments window, she typed in an email address the man had given her and clicked "send."

She hit speed dial seven on the satellite phone again. She took a deep breath and walked along the ridgeline to a vantage point above the carnage. God, she hoped this worked. Let them be stupid — and surprised, she prayed.

B-t-h looked at Nash. He nodded. B-t-h nodded and pointed at Furtive Eyes. "Finish him." Furtive Eyes blinked. "Finish him?"

"You heard me," B-t-h said. "Do it."

Furtive Eyes backed away. "Hey, that wasn't in the—"

B-t-h lurched to his feet. He picked up the tire iron and pointed at Furtive Eyes maliciously. "You chickenshit."

B-t-h walked heavily over to Furtive Eyes and sucker-punched him in the gut. Furtive Eyes dropped the bat as he doubled over, yowling in pain. The remnants of his alcoholic courage spewed green, chunky, and vile, splattering on the sandstone. B-t-h dropped the tire iron and picked up the bat in his right hand and smacked it against his left as he approached Noah.

"You're dead, asshole," he said, kicking Noah in the ribs with his scuffed, heavy workboots. Noah moaned. B-t-h walked around Noah, kicking Noah's hip, then his head. He stepped on Noah's broken leg. Little Man winced as he heard Noah's fibula break. Noah groaned and instinctively tried to roll away.

B-t-h stepped back and gripped the bat with both hands. He took a few practice swings, getting the feel of the 36-ounce menace. He smiled, lacing the air around him with mumbled profanities. Nash backed away, the better to see. He smiled with satisfaction. The fucker was going to pay now.

Standing aside Noah's head, B-t-h placed the bat on Noah's forehead, getting the range down, the same way a ball player taps the plate while scrunching his spikes into the batter's box. He raised the bat over his head.

"Stop!"

An electronic voice crackled through the air. B-t-h whirled around, his head snapping from side to side, looking for the source of the sound.

"Put down the bat and step away from that man," the voice ordered.

B-t-h and Little Man looked up. Furtive Eyes was still huddled on the bedrock, puking. Above, silhouetted against the sun at the top of the fin was a tall, lean figure. Kara held the satellite phone at arm's length in front of her, pointing its speakerphone toward the malevolent quartet surrounding Noah. From the phone's speaker emerged the tinny but distinctly male voice, authoritative, demanding, insistent.

"This is BLM agent Robert Logan. In less than two minutes, a state police helicopter will be overhead. Two sharpshooters will be aboard. Drop your weapons. Return to your vehicles and await arrest."

B-t-h and Little Man did nothing. They stared at Kara, but with the sun at her back, they could not tell who she was. Kara spoke into the phone, but softly, so B-t-h and Little Man could not hear them.

"Bob, they haven't dropped their weapons," she said.

The BLM agent spoke again from the speaker.

"I am looking at video transmitted to me in the past three minutes by satellite. I can see a Blazer. It's blue, and has Utah tags 578H43. I have video of you, Butch Sanderson, swinging a tire iron against Noah Hartshorn. I have another showing you standing over Noah, who appears to be unconscious. The video shows Andrew Miller striking Hartshorn. I say again, drop your weapons. If you are holding anything capable of harming a human being, the sharpshooters will fire. Drop those weapons *now*."

Little Man dropped the tire iron he had picked up and fled over the bedrock. Furtive Eyes, now aware of the voice from the sky, panicked. He struggled to his feet and stumbled across the bedrock. B-t-h swore loudly.

"Sanderson," the BLM agent ordered, "if you don't drop that bat now, the charge will be attempted murder instead of aggravated assault. Now put down that bat!" B-t-h backed away from Noah, then threw the bat at him. It glanced off Noah's chest. B-t-h walked off slowly and insolently.

Nash was furious, his face red with rage. That asshole Hartshorn was going to escape what he deserved. Moving slowly, trying not to be noticed, he picked up the Ruger. Kara, watching B-t-h, didn't notice. Nash backed away, the Ruger in his hand, until he reached the other canyon wall. He slipped into a small shadowed crack. Raising the Ruger, he aimed at Noah's chest, just thirty feet away. He couldn't miss. Then he'd shoot the bitch. That had to be her on the ridge. It was a bluff. Those pictures wouldn't be any good. There was still time before the chopper got here, time to get up there, destroy her camera and computer. No one could ID him. His Hummer was nowhere around. Nothing connected him to this. Who'd take the word of these three jokers against his, anyhow? He'd slip into the maze of canyons and get the hell out. Leave these jerks for the cops. His finger tightened on the trigger.

"Nash, no!" a raspy voice shouted. The sheriff, his face beet red and slick with sweat, braced himself against the canyon wall about twenty feet from Nash. His hand was stretched out toward Nash.

Nash's gun hand wavered as he looked toward the sheriff.

"Stay out of this," Nash shouted.

"Damn it," the sheriff gasped, "I didn't get into this for any killing."

"You fucking asshole, you're in it. Now shut the fuck up."

Nash steadied his aim, both hands on the Ruger. The sheriff fumbled for his holster, pulled out his .38 police special, and pointed it at Nash.

"No, god damn it, Nash, don't do it!" he screamed.

Nash turned and aimed at the sheriff. The sheriff fired. The bullet tore into Nash's chest, spinning him around. He stumbled, hit the canyon wall, and fell. The sheriff dropped his gun, clutched at his chest, and collapsed.

Kara screamed into the sat phone. "Hurry, god damn it, hurry!"

Below her, Nash's three henchmen ran across the bedrock. Little Man tripped, striking his forehead on the rock. He struggled to his feet, falling behind the other two, blood gushing from a jagged cut. Kara ran to the head of the tiny canyon. In the distance, she could hear a faint *whoop-whoop-whoop*. Without thinking, she climbed down the nearly vertical cliff face. When she reached bottom, Noah, somehow, was crawling toward Nash. She fell to her knees beside him. "Get ... my ... pack," he said.

She ran to his pack, grabbed it, and rushed back to Noah.

"Help ... me ... get to ... Nash," Noah whispered.

Kara dragged Noah, wincing with pain, toward Nash. She cringed as Noah grimaced.

"Gauze ... get gauze pads ... out ... front pocket."

Noah somehow got to his knees and ripped open Nash's black shirt with his left hand. Blood streamed from the hole in Nash's chest. He pressed the gauze pads against the wound. "Press ... hard ... lean over him," Noah said.

Kara leaned hard onto Nash, pressing the gauze against the wound. She put all her weight against him, praying she was hurting the bastard. Noah crawled toward the sheriff, lying on the bedrock. He made it half way before he collapsed unconscious.

Seconds later, a Bell Jet Ranger, its whirling blades kicking up clouds of reddish dust, landed at the mouth of the canyon. Four state police officers with guns drawn and three paramedics rushed toward the casualties of the war.

Kara knelt silently several feet from the cluster of people huddled on their knees next to Noah. The sheriff was dead. Nash was gravely wounded, and a state police officer held fresh gauze over his wound. Noah was near death, his cracked ribs puncturing a lung. The paramedic worked feverishly, slipping a tube down into his throat to help his breathing and starting an IV to replenish the fluids he was losing through internal bleeding. More *whoop-whoop-whoop* sounds preceded the Air Life Bell 412 from Grand Junction. Doc jumped from the chopper, followed by two more paramedics. He ran to Noah. The first paramedic nodded and went to tend to Nash. Radios in the choppers crackled but went unanswered. The medics hoisted Nash into the state police chopper. Kara watched numbly as it lifted off, turned, and sped low over the landscape toward Price. Kara could give a shit whether Nash lived or died. She sat listlessly on the slickrock, ashen, shaken, not comprehending.

Doc called to Kara. That jolted her.

"Hold this," he said, handing her an IV bag. "Higher."

One of the medics could have done that. But Doc knew Kara needed to do something, to act, to feel useful. She held the bag with one hand and held Noah's hand in her other. His hand was limp. Her lips trembled as she tried to speak to him, to reassure him.

"Don't leave me, Noah," she sobbed. "Stay with me. Oh, god, Noah ... stay with me."

Her eyelashes fluttered as tears spilled past. A medic put a respirator bag over Noah's mouth and squeezed it. His chest rose almost imperceptibly.

"Color's bad," Doc said. "Let's get him the hell outta here." The medics ducked low under the spinning blades as they carried the litter to the Bell 412 and strapped it inside. Kara leaned over Noah, kissing him, talking to him, begging him not to leave her. Her tears dropped on Noah's ashen face.

"Ma'am, we've got to go," said one of the medics. "We've got to get him to the hospital fast." Doc climbed into the chopper and took Kara's arm. He pulled her to the door and helped her out.

"Sorry, Kara," he shouted. "No room. I'll call as soon as I can."

A state trooper shepherded Kara away as the chopper rose, banked, and sped toward the good hands of waiting surgeons at Allen Memorial Hospital. Kara stood motionless until well after the chopper had vanished. The trooper touched Kara lightly on her shoulder. "Ma'am? You okay?"

She turned her tear-stained face to him. "No ... I'm ...," she said, searching for words.

"Do you need help? Anything at all?" he said, concern on his face.

She sniffled. "No ... I ... Yes ... Noah's Cruiser. Fuel pump's gone."

He nodded. "We've got vehicles coming. We can tow it out."

"No," she said.

"Excuse me?"

"Get me tools and a fuel pump, please. I'm driving it out of here, sir," she said. Salvage it. Save the Cruiser. Save Noah. The trooper drew a radio from his black, weapon-studded belt. He talked into it for a few minutes.

"It'll be at least an hour, maybe more, ma'am."

"I don't care. I'll wait."

He nodded. "Okay. We've got to secure the crime scene anyway. We'll keep you company."

She smiled wanly. "Thank you, sir."

Kara climbed to the ridge and collected her laptop, sat link, and the camera. After packing them into her go-bag, she sat on the ridgeline where she could see the Cruiser, weeping and waiting for a replacement for the faulty fuel pump that might have killed Noah.

Chapter 60:

September 25, before dawn, Allen Memorial Hospital, Moab

Kara sat next to the hospital bed, her hand on Noah's forearm. She couldn't hold his hand. IVs stuck in the backs of his hands carried different medicines and fluids from plastic bags hung on stands on either side of the ICU bed. Electrical leads counted how many times he breathed and how often his heart beat. Doctors had operated on him for nearly eight hours. Incisions ran across his chest, his right hip, shoulder blade, and his lower leg. A hole had been drilled in his skull. Bone had been taken from his hip and grafted onto his splintered lower leg. Screws had been inserted to hold the mess together. He'd limp for a long time, maybe permanently. His broken arm had been reset, screwed, and casted. The hole in his lung had been closed. Bleeding from rib-nicked arteries had been cauterized.

Doc stood with Kara beside Noah's bed. She had asked the surgeon: "Will he be okay?" The surgeon had answered: "Too soon to tell."

So she asked Doc: "Is he going to make it?"

"Yes," he said without hesitation.

"Tell me the truth," she said.

He rested his hand on her shoulder. "He'll live."

Kara stared at Noah. It had all happened so fast.

"Although," Doc said, "a few months ago I would have been less certain."

She looked up at him, questions forming in her eyes. He smiled at her.

"A few months ago he didn't have you. Believe me, Kara, he'll live."

She covered her face and sobbed. "Oh, god, Doc ... if ... what would I ..."

He embraced her. "You gotta believe, Kara. You just gotta believe."

A nurse woke Kara. She'd fallen asleep in the chair. For a moment, she didn't know where she was. She stumbled, hurrying to reach Noah. The nurse caught her arm.

"Easy, Kara. Easy. Nothing's changed. That's good."

Kara nodded, looking at Noah, a bandage wrapped about his head, partially covering his face. Tubes. Wires. Splints. His skin, gray and wrinkled.

"C'mere, Kara. I've fixed the other bed."

She shook her head. "No ... I want to be near him ..."

She pushed the chair close to the bed and sat, leaning her head against Noah's shoulder. The nurse draped a blanket over her and left. Outside, she leaned against the wall of the corridor. She brushed tears from her face with her hand. Doc was reading Noah's chart. He handed her a handkerchief.

"When I got to Noah," he said, "know what I found in his hand?"

The nurse, daubing her eyes, shook her head.

"A bottle of aspirin. Even barely conscious, he knew the sheriff had suffered a heart attack. He was trying to save him."

Doc turned away, his own eyes tearing.

Chapter 61:

September 28, early morning, Allen Memorial Hospital, Moab

Kara rarely left Noah's side. She took little notice of the comings and goings of doctors and nurses. That worried Doc, so he put her to work. On the third morning after Noah's surgery, he walked briskly into the private room Noah now occupied, still chained to medical monitoring technology.

"Come here," he ordered. Doc handed her a bowl of water and a sponge.

"Bathe him. He needs to be touched. He needs to be touched by you. Get to work." He walked out, closing the door. Outside, he crossed his fingers.

She stood beside the bed for a long time, holding the water and the sponge, looking at Noah. Nothing moved but his chest, rising and falling slowly. The special bed rotated to help avoid bed sores, but Noah had not moved, blinked, wiggled a finger, or even moved his head.

"I'm here, Noah," she said softly. Carefully, gently, she opened his hospital gown. Seeing the long bandage over the incision doctors had made from navel to sternum made her gasp. Dipping the sponge into the warm, soapy water, she brushed the sponge tentatively over his skin. Noah made a sound, not a moan, just an exhalation that coursed through his vocal chords. But the sound encouraged her. Moistening the sponge again, she washed his neck, his face, his shoulders, then down his arms, cleaning his fingers one by one. Pulling the blanket down to his feet, she washed everywhere else she could reach that wasn't covered with bandages. The sponging became vigorous. Life, she thought. He needs to *feel*. He's hard, muscular. She'd have to press harder to make him feel again.

She dried him, careful not to brush against tubes and wires and bandages. Finished, she fastened his gown and pulled the blanket over him. The hard lines on his face had softened. The pallid skin seemed warm. Maybe it was an illusion, she thought. But she felt better. He must feel better. She walked to the door and opened it. She knew Doc would be standing outside.

"What else?" she asked, head up, her voice firm. "What else can I do for Noah?"

That afternoon, a tall, lean state police investigator arrived. He politely knocked before entering. He showed his ID, asked about Noah, and apologized that the needs of justice had to interfere with Kara's concern. He spoke gently. He had questions. About the attack. About everything. Kara asked to shower first. The investigator nodded and said he'd talk to Noah.

"Maybe he can't hear me, maybe he can. But I know him," said the investigator. "I've always liked talking with him."

Kara smiled warmly at him and went into the bathroom. When she returned, dressed in clean Levis and a sweater, she sat in the chair, hands folded in her lap. The investigator brought her up to date on what he knew. The sheriff's heart attack had been massive and instantly fatal. Nash had survived surgery and regained consciousness but refused to talk. He faced charges of attempted murder for the attack on Noah and intent to commit murder on a police officer, the sheriff. The three henchmen were singing, indicting Nash and each other, trying to get reduced sentences. B-t-h and Little Man faced attempted murder charges. Furtive Eyes, who had not actually struck Noah, faced accomplice charges. With "proper encouragement," the investigator said, chuckling momentarily, Furtive Eyes had turned state's evidence.

Nash faced tax evasion charges. Investigators armed with a subpoena had drilled a safe deposit box belonging to Nash and found more than two million dollars in cash. Nash had another account, under an alias, in a Salt Lake bank — a bank controlled by one of his private video clients. That man, too, faced charges. Nash's account there held more than three hundred thousand dollars. IRS agents could not find legitimate sources within Nash's books to account for so much free cash.

"That's a lot of videos," the investigator said. "Nash has been at this for some time." All investigators did, he explained, was follow the money. Noah had given the leads to his BLM chum a few days before.

"An insurance policy, he said," he said, looking ruefully at Noah.

They'd been closing in on Nash before the attack. Somehow, the investigator said, Nash had found out. Maybe that explained what happened. The BLM, Forest Service, and Park Service had decided not to press charges regarding the WSA intrusions. Convicting Nash and the unholy trio on attempted murder and accomplice charges would satisfy them and avoid disputes about whether to try them in state or federal courts.

"Your videos, the ones you sent to Bob and others we lifted off your computer's hard drive, just about guarantee them a long, long stretch in prison. And ..." He stopped, realizing what he was about to say.

"If he dies?" Kara said quietly.

"Yeah. If he dies. This is Utah. They should die, too."

Kara nodded. "Noah won't die. He just won't."

The investigator was momentarily flustered. Presently, he asked her to tell him what she saw and did. He produced a digital tape recorder. Over the next two hours, Kara told him everything she knew. He thanked her and prepared to leave.

He turned and held out his hand. Kara took it. The investigator smiled.

"You were brave, Ms. McAllister. He's alive because of you."

She blushed and smiled. After the investigator left, Kara walked to a window and looked out for some time. She phoned Annie. Kara needed some things, one in particular. She told Annie where to find it.

Chapter 62:

September 30, early morning, Allen Memorial Hospital, Moab

Noah lay unconscious in his bed. Kara had bathed him and, with a nurse's help, gotten rid of his hospital gown. With great care, they had lifted Noah and slipped one of his sleeveless black tank tops over him. *He looks like Noah now.*

Kara stared out the window. Behind her, tucked in a corner, stood a card table she'd appropriated from the doctors' locker room. Her laptop sat on it, surrounded by maps, several botany books, and dozens of pieces of paper. Annie had brought her fresh clothes, Noah's antiquated tape player, and work to do, busyness to keep worry at bay. One of Bach's solo cello pieces floated through the room from the music box's speakers. Outside, in the parking lot, Annie played with Petey. *He's life. He's unrestrained joy.* She wished she could take Noah by the hand, help him out of that goddamned maze of tubes and wires, and lead him outside to play with her and Petey. *That's what life should be.*

She sighed, went to the table, and unfolded *the damn map. Why am I doing this? I know where I'm supposed to be. I know where I am. I know where I want to be.* She stared at the map, unable, as ever, to discern indications, directions, however discreet, however subtle. *What should I be thinking about? Is that what this goddamned thing does — focus me?*

The map poked at her. It made her think about *meaning.* She shook her head. *The meaning of what?* She sat in the chair next to Noah, resting her hand on his chest. She wanted to feel his *life,* to feel his burliness, his power, his love, rising and falling under her touch. She wondered if Noah liked Bach. She hadn't played much classical music in the trailer, just some Prokofiev and Brahms during her darker moods, back when she was sick.

God, was I sick. Sick in the head. She realized she'd spoken that out loud. She glanced at Noah. *Had he heard that?* She rested her head on the bed, nuzzling the side of Noah's chest gently with her face.

"You're a prick, Noah, you know that?" she whispered. If Noah heard that, no sign was apparent. The thin white line on the green screen of the EKG monitor did not spike. His respirations did not increase in frequency or amplitude. She shook her head. *I'm trapped in patterns. Looking for patterns. Looking for reasons. Just looking — and never seeing.* She pushed the map away. *I want to rip that damn thing to shreds.* But she couldn't.

"Noah, do you mind if I do some work while you're sleeping?" she asked quietly. No answer. No sign. She leaned over the bed and kissed Noah, longing for his lips to part and his tongue to sneak into her mouth and tease her. She loved sleeping with him, making love with him. Noah had reinvented love for her. Noah demanded that her mind contribute to what their bodies did. She kissed him again.

"I love you, Hartshorn."

She resumed creating Web pages of flowers. Mechanical, thoughtless work. Insert text. Insert jpeg. Add link. Insert text, insert jpeg, add link. She forced her finger to stay on the track pad, inserting text, inserting jpegs, adding links. Dad the Engineer stood sternly over her. Focus, he demanded. Focus resolves external problems. Focus cures distress. But Kara's attention kept drifting to the hospital bed, to Noah. She pushed the laptop away.

"Fuck you, Dad," she said loudly, hunching over the table, banging her fist on the table so hard the laptop bounced. "Fuck you, fuck you, fuck you."

Fifteen minutes later, Noah's nurse entered to check his vitals. Kara was huddled on floor, swaying back and forth, holding a crumpled map to her chest. She was crying hysterically. The nurse called for a doctor. Together, they picked Kara off the floor, lay her on the other bed, and sedated her.

Kara awoke. Her hand felt warm. She liked that. The feeling filtered up her arm, across her face, and down across her chest. Warm, soft, quiet peace. Opening her eyes, she saw a form, still fuzzy around the edges. A woman. Shorter, fuller than her.

"Annie?" she whispered. The warmth became a firm squeeze.

Annie was holding her hand. "Yes."

Kara sat up, but momentary dizziness overcame her. "Noah?" she asked.

Annie shook her head. "No change. I'm sorry, Kara."

Kara rubbed her face with her free hand. They sat in silence for a while.

"Annie, help me up, please," Kara asked.

Annie slipped her arm around Kara's shoulders. "God, Annie, I didn't know you were so strong."

"Hartshorn School of Weight Training, girlfriend."

"Pardon?"

"He built me a weight machine. It's in the hangar at Muni, in a corner."

Kara still held Annie's hand. "Were you two ..."

Annie smiled. "Not really. He helped me through a sad time."

Kara cocked her head.

"Divorce," Annie said.

Kara nodded. "Goddamned Samaritan," she said. Annie

laughed.

Kara smiled. *I like her.* Kara had never had close woman friends. Letting go of Annie's hand, she stood. She wavered for a moment.

"Christ, what'd they give me?" she said after catching her balance.

"What you needed."

"Excuse me?"

"Rest, Kara. You needed rest." Annie hugged her.

"I've got to go. Petey's probably hungry," Annie said.

Kara grinned. "He's always hungry."

Annie walked to the table, took a pen, and scribbled on a piece of paper.

"I'm staying here," she said. "Call if you need anything."

"I will," said Kara. *I will. God, will I ever.*

As she opened the door, Annie said. "Talk to him, Kara. When he wakes up, you may not get in another word."

Kara laughed and hugged her again.

The map sat crumpled on the table where someone had placed it. Kara folded it and walked over to the hospital bed. She placed it on Noah's chest and drew the blanket over it. *Bring him back. Please bring him back.*

Chapter 63:

October 2, mid-afternoon, Allen Memorial Hospital, Moab

Noah, doctors told her, had to decide whether to live. He lay silent and pallid in his mechanical bed. *He'd love this bed. He'd want to bolt a big Rotax to it and see what it could do.* For two days, she had settled into a routine. She did not sleep; rather, she napped frequently, an hour at a time. It left her fresh and *focused, damn it.* But now she didn't mind that feeling as much. She didn't weep anymore. She could care for him, sponge him, talk to him, make sure music was playing, and help the nurses. She focused on the music. *It saved my life when he played it. It roamed around my mind, keeping the lightning at bay. I could follow it out of the darkness.* She wondered what Noah needed to spurn, what demons he had yet to exorcise. What he needed to *live. He's so damn strong.*

She worked on the flower website. When she couldn't figure out a taxonomy or ID a flower from her own file of pictures, she sat in the chair next to Noah with a book or the computer in her lap, and explained to him what the problem was. Sometimes she figured it out, other times she didn't. She remembered something he'd said once. *If there's a problem you can't solve, find some part of it you can. Then go back and look at the whole problem again. Piece by piece.*

Sitting next to him, her hand on his chest, feeling *the damn map* under his tank top, she thought about that. "Noah, is that what you've been teaching me? Solve what you can? When you can?"

She squeezed his arm. *I always had to have the definitive answer. To everything. All at once.*

"Noah, you're still a prick," she said, kissing him. "But I love you anyway."

The setting sun warmed the dark Tertiary volcanics of the La Sals to the east. Kara stood at the window, lost in reverie, a momentary respite from focused thought, accepting what Utah granted her eyes. A soft, low moan startled her. Noah's head moved slightly. She rushed to the side of the bed.

"Noah?" she whispered. Then, louder, "Noah!"

His mouth opened, lips moving. She leaned over the bed, her face inches from his.

"Could ... you ... live in ... Moab?" he croaked, barely audible.

She kissed him. "Yes. Yes. I'd live in hell with you."

His lips moved again. "Moab ... would ... do."

She covered his face with kisses. "Oh, god, Noah, wake up, wake up!"

He lay quiet. Then he spoke, hoarsely but earnestly.

"Find us ... a home."

Kara ran to the door, jerked it open, and screamed for a doctor.

Chapter 64:

October 4, afternoon, Castle Valley, Moab

Doc stood next to the Skymaster. Annie was set to fly him back to Green River. Doc embraced Kara and smiled. "Now what?" he asked.

"I suppose I'll have to marry him now," she said.

"Have to?" Doc grinned.

She blushed. "I love him, Doc."

"He know that?"

"Yes."

"About the marrying?"

"I think so. No, I know so. He knew before me."

"He asked you?"

"No. But I'll tell him when he should," she said, grinning.

Doc kissed Kara on the cheek and climbed into the Skymaster.

Kara walked back to the Subaru and watched happily as Petey jumped in.

Windows down, Delta blues curling around her from the iPhone, *the fucking map* in her lap, Kara drove the Subaru lazily north on Route 191 through downtown Moab. Petey sat on his haunches in the passenger's seat, head out the window, living life on the road as dogs do — wind in their muzzles. Even the cacophonous mélange of Moab's tourist season — overheated cars, overstimulated pedestrians, and overagitated bicyclists contending for traffic lanes downtown — could not shake her mood. *Noah's alive.* He faced months of rehab, but he was already demanding to be *let out of this goddamned hospital right now.* Kara chuckled. *He'll never change. Thank God.* He'd demanded hand weights to start rebuilding himself. He was in pain but he wouldn't let the doctors and nurses see it. When she was alone with him, he told her how much it hurt. *He gives me the good, he gives me the bad. He gives me everything.*

As the Subaru threaded through traffic, she thought about what could be salvaged from Greasewood Draw. About what could be repaired. About what could be rebuilt. About what could be saved. Already, plans were forming in her mind. Locate a large, vacant garage. Get a trailer. Haul the wrecked ultralights there. Fly the working ones down to Canyonlands Field airport just north of town. Ask Annie to ferry the big birds there. Rent hangar space.

Find a home.

Just before a bridge over the Colorado, she turned northeast onto Route 128. The map felt warm under her hand. She smiled. *That's not the sun burning through the windshield.* She could read the map now. *I can feel it.* Picking it up, she brushed it against her cheek.

The narrow, two-lane highway — the river road — snaked through Professor Valley, shadowing the Colorado. Across the river, to the west, rose a cliff nearly a thousand feet high. She glanced at the towering red wall, the morning sun burnishing the black streaks of desert varnish smudging it from top to bottom. *Wingate sandstone. Or is it Chinle topped by Wingate?* Noah had been teaching her the geology of Utah. *I like knowing that. I like knowing what is what and where it is.* But she also liked to just *look at it.* She pulled the car onto the riverside shoulder of the road and stepped out, letting Petey bound across her lap first. She sat on a rock away from the road, looking at the massive sandstone cliff. Above lay the Navajo, the salmon-and-white remains of ancient dunes. And above that, the Entrada, into which the architects of wind, water, ice, and desert heat had eroded — *no, sculpted; a greater hand had to have done this* — the arches that gave the national park its name. *Fire and ice. Creators of landscapes.* She laughed aloud. *Fire and ice. Noah and me. Creators of life.* She shook her head. *I must be in love. Why else would I be so poorly poetic?*

Summoning Petey, she drove on, rounding the buttress of Mat Martin Point. *God, I loved flying through here.* Her mind replayed the magnificent spectacle permanently encoded there — the Green and the Colorado cracking through the White Rim sandstone to craft the intricate carvings of Canyonlands and Dead Horse Point, the volcanics of the La Sals rising above them. *It's magic. Or is it God?* Observing and recording, she knew, would be not be enough to explain the quiet, mournful ache inside her when she saw them, the ache Noah had tried to explain out at Beckwith Plateau. *Wilderness is a feeling, not an explanation.*

Ahead rose Castle Rock. The map warmed her hand. The Subaru turned into Castle Valley, threading through steep S-turns before the road straightened. To the east, cone-like mounds of grayish-black volcanic rock rose from the valley floor. From the air, they had looked like inverted ice cream cones, dimples on the landscape. *We'd flown so high.* The road turned rough, winding up the foothills of the La Sals. Houses were tucked into ravines here and there, hidden away from the palatial estates that had been built in the shadow of Porcupine Rim. She knew the road looped around the La Sals and emerged south of Moab. As it curved under Bald Mesa, she stopped on a wide gravel flat next to the road.

Taking the map, she stepped out of the car. Petey darted ahead before sitting down, facing west. A brisk wind scoured the plain, so she retrieved a windbreaker before joining Petey. Kara looked past him, over Spanish Valley and into the Canyonlands. She sat next to Petey, her arm around him. She nuzzled him, and he licked her face.

I've never felt so calm. It seemed irrational to her, with Noah lying in pain in a hospital bed. But he'd be okay. He'd curse himself into shape. Now she'd be spotting him when he lifted. She'd be watching him, making sure he took it slowly, making sure patience ruled his recovery. Nuzzling Petey again, she rose and walked around. *I like it up here. Noah would, too.* Facing north, she looked through the slot of Castle Valley toward Arches. That quiet inner ache left her eyes moist. *Just the wind. It's just the wind.*

She turned to rejoin Petey. From a distance, she could see him chewing on something. She walked faster.

The map! He's chewing the map!

She ran as fast as she could across the hard-packed ground. Then she slowed as she neared him. He wasn't chewing the map. Petey lay partly on it, his paws holding the map flat. He had taken an edge of the map in his teeth and slowly, methodically pulled on it, tearing off a strip. Then another strip. And another.

She sat next to Petey and helped him tear the map into little pieces. She gathered them in her hands and walked to western end of the gravelly rest area. Smiling brightly, she threw the pieces into the air. The wind carried them toward Jimmy Keen Flat. They floated easily, a collective consciousness intent on a patch of higher ground where a home could be built. She whistled for Petey and ran for the Subaru.

Craig Melvin

ABOUT THE AUTHOR

Denny Wilkins professes journalism at a small, private university in the Northeast. He has climbed, kayaked, photographed, skied, and otherwise meandered aimlessly through the American West for decades. He has degrees in geology, environmental studies, and communication — and has tried to make use of them as a co-founder of the cultural blog ScholarsandRogues.com.

Made in the USA
Lexington, KY
28 February 2014